Praise for *98 Reasons for Being* by Clare Dudman

"Meticulously researched . . . Dudman's historical novel reveals the man responsible for [the Struwwelpeter (Shockheaded Peter)] stories and weaves a new mythology about his time in charge of a mid-nineteenth-century Frankfurt mental asylum."
—*The Washington Post*

"Clare Dudman knows that every reader is a de facto psychiatrist, piecing together a theory of character and coherent narrative from elusive and contradictory information. In her quietly compelling second book, Dudman positions us firmly in the healer's chair. . . . *98 Reasons for Being* has its own stubborn weight and mass. Dudman is self-confident enough to take her time. Page by page, the novel accumulates . . . it is not easily forgotten."
—*Chicago Tribune*

"A beautifully written, emotionally powerful biographical novel . . . While Hoffmann and Hannah are primary, all of the patients and staff at the asylum are exceptionally well drawn, and through them Dudman explores the nature of madness, prejudice, and love."
—*Booklist*

"Again using her keen intelligence and deftly economical writing to illustrate an important moment in the history of science, the British Dudman, whose 2004 *One Day the Ice Will Reveal All Its Dead* presents the birth of plate tectonic theory, creates a life for the pioneering psychiatrist Heinrich Hoffmann. . . . Dudman's artistry matches her historic research, and the combination is very rich."
—*Kirkus Reviews*

"In a pre-Freudian time, when mental illness was little understood and women's problems were attributed to irregularities in their nervous and reproductive systems, it seems nothing short of miraculous that doctors like Hoffmann achieved medical breakthroughs and actually cured some of their patients. Dudman has crafted a compelling tale that skillfully blends fact and fiction, giving her work the ring of verisimilitude." —*Library Journal*

98
REASONS
for BEING

Clare Dudman

PENGUIN BOOKS

PENGUIN BOOKS

Published by the Penguin Group
Penguin Group (USA) Inc., 375 Hudson Street, New York, New York 10014, U.S.A.
Penguin Group (Canada), 90 Eglinton Avenue East, Suite 700, Toronto,
Ontario, Canada M4P 2Y3 (a division of Pearson Penguin Canada Inc.)
Penguin Books Ltd, 80 Strand, London WC2R 0RL, England
Penguin Ireland, 25 St Stephen's Green, Dublin 2, Ireland (a division of Penguin Books Ltd)
Penguin Group (Australia), 250 Camberwell Road, Camberwell,
Victoria 3124, Australia (a division of Pearson Australia Group Pty Ltd)
Penguin Books India Pvt Ltd, 11 Community Centre, Panchsheel Park, New Delhi – 110 017, India
Penguin Group (NZ), cnr Airborne and Rosedale Roads, Albany,
Auckland 1310, New Zealand (a division of Pearson New Zealand Ltd)
Penguin Books (South Africa) (Pty) Ltd, 24 Sturdee Avenue,
Rosebank, Johannesburg 2196, South Africa

Penguin Books Ltd, Registered Offices:
80 Strand, London WC2R 0RL, England

First published in Great Britain by Hodder and Stoughton, a division of Hodder Headline 2004
First published in the United States of America by Viking Penguin,
a member of Penguin Group (USA) Inc. 2005
Published in Penguin Books 2006

1   3   5   7   9   10   8   6   4   2

Copyright © Clare Dudman, 2004
All rights reserved

THE LIBRARY OF CONGRESS HAS CATALOGED THE HARDCOVER EDITION AS FOLLOWS:
Dudman, Clare.
98 reasons for being / Clare Dudman.
p.   cm.
ISBN 0-670-03424-X (hc.)
ISBN 0 14 30.3800 1 (pbk.)
1. Psychiatric hospital patients—Fiction.   2. Mentally ill women—Fiction.
3. Jewish women—Fiction.   4. Germany—Fiction.   I. Title: Ninety-eight reasons for being.   II. Title.
PR6104.U528A614 2005
823'.92—dc22   2004066141

Printed in the United States of America

For my sons

CHAPTER 1

Haus Stein West
Judengasse
Frankfurt-am-Main
6 March 1852

Dear Dr Hoffmann,
Most Esteemed Sir,

I understand from acquaintances of my late husband that you are something of a champion of our race. If this is true, sir, I beseech you then to be so kind as to examine one of our most precious children, my daughter Hannah.

She has always been a good child, sir, obedient and dutiful towards her parents, but lately she seems to have had trials, sir, and they have caused within her a change. Where she used to be lively she is now still. Her eye is dull. She speaks not. We no longer hear the sound of her laughter. She weeps but is without tears. Unless I command her to move she sits as though carved from wood. Nothing I can do seems to affect her. Please, sir, would you see her? I am a humble widow, and even though my trade is always in demand it does not make me rich. But I shall pay what I can. My brother is also willing to contribute a little if necessary. Our community are also considering coming to my aid. My daughter is all I have left, sir, she is my precious jewel.

Your hopeful and most humble servant,
Martha Meyer

It is quiet, just now it is quiet. The windows hang open as if they are sleeping mouths. A few minutes ago a boy ran along calling for his dog, but now there is just a waiting where his voice has been. And from the city end of the street it comes: a single horse with its iron shoes making sparks on the cobbles. Behind the horse a creaking cart with three occupants: a round-faced driver with dark hair and red cheeks, a small middle-aged woman sitting upright, and between them another figure, longer, leaner, wrapped completely in shawls, leaning one way and then the next with every jolt as if something inside her has given way. When the cart stops she subsides on to the woman beside her then eases herself slowly upright again. The older woman rises quickly from her seat, steps on to the pavement and then tugs at the girl, urging her to follow. In the time it takes for the girl to clamber down the woman has removed two bags from the back of the carriage.

'Stay here, will you, I shan't be long.' She waits for the driver to nod and then, after heaving a bundle on to the pavement beside the two bags and the girl, she marches up to the nearest door and knocks loudly. At the sound the windows of the street bristle. Inside each one there is just the slightest impression of movement: a head turning, a curtain dropping, the leaf of a house plant springing back into place. The driver catches the leaf out of the corner of his eye. He stares at it to see whether anything will follow, but nothing does.

'Come on, come on,' the woman says to the door, glances at the girl and then knocks again. 'Come on.'

Now there is another sound. Something is being drawn slowly across the door on the inside, stopping and then being drawn again. The woman steps back one pace as the doors are jolted apart. Before them, his head shimmering in the gloom, is a blond giant.

'Yes?' His voice is too spindly, too weak for his broad shoulders and massive frame. Even though the door is over six feet high the man has to stoop a little to clear its threshold. For a moment the woman is silent, but then she finds her voice.

'We're expected,' she says. 'Dr Hoffmann, he knows we're coming.'

The giant's head moves slowly from side to side, taking in the view.

'That one, eh? What is she, not all there or just a raver?'

'Are you Dr Hoffmann, then?'

The blond man grins at her sneer. He is astoundingly ugly: beneath a wide forehead trimmed with protruding thick eyebrows is a large bulbous nose, and beneath that a long curved chin. 'No.' He draws the word out, keeping her waiting as long as possible. 'Dr Hoffmann's on his rounds. I expect he'll want to see her when he's finished. I suppose you'd better come in.'

The woman nudges the girl forward. When she reaches the blond man he quickly whips away the scarf that is covering her face and whistles.

Why a light? So sudden. Then in the middle of the light the face of the Devil. Not the Devil I thought I knew, but another one with lips so moist and fleshy they are like the insides of his mouth. He draws them together, twists them into an anal ring, but instead of swooping forward to kiss me he stays where he is. And then there is his sound. A whistle. A noise drawing me close. When you whistled I would always come. Kurt. My Kurt. Is this your messenger? But before I can ask he is gone. I am out of the light, into the darkness where no one will find me. Kurt. There is still time enough for you to come.

How still they are: the girl slumped, at the end of her journey to a chair, while her mother is poised and taut. When the door opens the woman rises quickly to her feet.

'Dr Hoffmann?'

But it is a young woman with small insignificant features, her dark blonde hair pulled tightly back into a small cap on the back of her head. Between her two large front teeth there is a gap almost large enough to house a third. 'He's busy,' she says. 'Says I've got to deal with you.' She looks at the woman and then the girl. 'This one here, is it? What's her name?'

For a second the mother stares at the girl, then finally speaks carefully. 'My daughter, Hannah.'

The girl narrows her eyes. 'You're Jews!'

The woman nods.

'I didn't think he . . .' She stops, bites her bottom lip for a few seconds, then continues more loudly, 'Well, I'm Angelika. Her . . . minder.'

'Well, mind her well, if you please. She's . . .'

'Is that all you've got?' Angelika interrupts impatiently, swinging the bags and bundle on to her back, one after the other.

'Yes, that's all. I didn't think she'd be here for long. Our doctor seemed to think . . .' This time the woman's voice fades away.

'What did he think? She's got the miseries? We've got a lot of those in here.'

'He thought she'd soon be cured. That's what he said.'

The girl sniffs, pulls at Hannah until she rises, and begins to lead them from the room. 'No one gets out of here very quickly.'

'Our doctor said . . .' The mother's voice trails away again.

'What?' Angelika stops in the doorway. 'What did your Jews' doctor say?'

'Nothing.'

'He must have said something. They always do.' Angelika turns around, her eyes flitting quickly over the mother and then the girl. 'You may as well tell me, I'll find out soon enough, he'll tell me. I have to know, see, since I'm the attendant.'

The mother looks around her, gulps and then lowers her voice to a whisper. 'Nymphomania, that's what he said. I saw him write it down. Then I looked it up. But it's stupid, not true, not my Hannah. It's just something someone's said.'

'Word gets around.'

'But it's not true.'

'No smoke without fire, that's what they say.'

'It's all lies . . .' the mother insists, but then her voice fades and stops.

In the wood-lined hallway the mother is as silent as the daughter and, as the solitary beam of light from the door illuminates them both, Angelika is struck by how alike they are, how their heads tip at exactly the same angle, how the daughter seems like just a longer-drawn-out version of the mother. She tips her head to the side for a few seconds, examining their faces, then sniffs again and straightens up. 'You can go now,' she tells the mother. 'Tobias here will show you out.' The giant lollops forward from his seat by the door, but the mother turns away and throws herself around her daughter. 'Hannah!'

My name. Cried out. Far away. Somewhere I can't reach. Behind invisible veils that are clinging so tightly to me it is as if they have grown there. Kurt. Oh, my beloved one. Oh, most adored. Once you cried out my name and there was so much pain and happiness in your voice. A searing sound I couldn't touch, something I search for now, but it is hidden in the folds of other things, a colour I think I see but which then fades away. Kurt. Kurt. Kurt. If only I could trap you in my layers, I would clutch you to me, but it would not be like this, not this too-warm hugging, not this squashing, suffocating, pressing together of layers, not this something binding itself to me so there is nothing in between. No space, no room, no way of blocking out words. I shall not listen. Go. Go. Go. I shall not hear them. They are flimsy gauzes, wafting in my face as if they are true then drifting away like smoke. They are not for me, they are for another girl, the girl who isn't there, not any longer, not in this world.

Lies. I know what they are. Another curl of smoke mixing with the air. It shall not touch me. Cold air and a hand holding mine, not your hand, another's, someone smaller, harder, gripping my bones too tight, crunching them together. And then a stinging slap. Fingers that are not mine leap up and I feel them burning. Hot. White. Pain that won't go away. A white cap and hair the colour of old dead leaves swept into it. Honey, you would say, honey-coloured hair, and once, do you remember, you stared at some that was in the street in front of us. But I prefer black, you'd said, touching mine. Not black, I said, dark brown. Dark brown, you'd said, and laughed. All right, dark brown hair I like the most, dark brown, just like this, and you'd caught hold of my hair and tugged it a little, just enough to hurt.

Not like this. Not this white pain. Not small scraps of hair mixed in with cloth and light where there was dark, cold where there was warmth, and I am so naked the air can stab me with its sharpened fingers and draw out cries and tease out screams. And the slap comes again. And another. One each side so the hurt is equal. Then a face near my face. Pimples on her chin. A space where her breath

6

comes, stifling mine with the too-sweet smells of the apple-wine barrel.

But my veils are there. I draw them tight. The world becomes a distant place. And then pain on the arm that used to be mine. The place where you touched twisted and pulled. The skin that you said was yours squeezed until it breaks. Then something at my legs. The gauze is thickening but I know it is there. Down and down. A light flashes through. White, grey, clouds of smoke and the finest silk, floating down, muffling everything.

Behind the bars the window is open. At nine o'clock it was thrown wide to let the night air out and the day air in. At noon it will be closed because today there is a suspicion of rain. At the same time mattresses will be turned, the beds will be made and the pots will be emptied. An hour later the stove outside the room will be cleared out and relaid. Fifty minutes later it will be lit. Everything is dependable and ordered. The fire in the stove will gradually catch light, the flames will leap precisely from paper to wood to coal. At four o'clock the wrought-iron stove inside the room will be just warm and two hours later the whole surface will be too hot to touch. Everything will be ready. At nine o'clock, after the evening recreation, the key in the lock will be turned and the women will enter. They come here just to sleep. The assistant will say a prayer: the choice will depend on her mood. There are four beds, four tables, four chests. There is not much room. On each table there is a Bible and on each chest of drawers a plain white earthenware bowl and a jug. Underneath the high iron-framed beds are four small pots. Bladders are to be emptied frequently and by arrangement. Everything is tidy, bare; only the slumped figure against the bed disrupts the order. Angelika has emptied the contents of Hannah's bag on to the bed by the window and then sorted through the contents. She has kept a brush with a chipped mother-of-pearl handle and a paisley scarf for herself and has bundled some of Hannah's underwear into a bag for the fire. The rest she has partly folded and partly crushed into just one drawer of the chest. The others will soon be filled with the asylum clothes: crude brown woollen articles that are suitable for a girl like Hannah. She is, after all, just a seamstress's daughter. No one with any stature. There are people here who live as genteel a life as they do outside, with their own servants and furniture. Hannah will have just a bed, a table and a chest, which is more than she is used to in any case. She will also have the asylum clothes and a quarter-share in Angelika. She will have all these things whether she would like them or not. At the moment she requires nothing. She lies where Angelika pressed her down and then left her; curled up, her knees close to her chest, as inert and lifeless as a fallen leaf. Except for the slight shift in her uppermost arm as she breathes, she moves not at all. The hours pass. The sun rises over the roof of the asylum but the room chills. Although the sky is clear winter has barely finished and the air is cold.

At eleven o'clock the door rattles and then opens.

'Get up,' Angelika says. 'The doctor wants to see you.'

When Hannah doesn't move she marches over, breathes in deeply and then presses her mouth over Hannah's ear. 'Up!' The shout would dislodge even the soundest sleeper. Hannah's head jerks back against the bedpost. For a few seconds it stays there, and then slowly it is lowered again towards her legs.

'Get up!'

Hannah's body curls up a little more.

'Up!'

Now it breathes out with a sob.

'I'm not having this.' Angelika reaches down and grabs

8

an arm. 'He says he wants to see you now. He won't like waiting. There'll be trouble for both of us if he does.'

She pulls roughly and Hannah follows. Although Angelika is scrawny she is strong. She hauls Hannah to the bed, looks at her and then straightens her clothes.

'Stop crying,' she says. 'It won't do you any good at all to cry.'

Hannah sobs again and then is quiet.

'Look,' Angelika says, her two large teeth glimmering in the late morning twilight of the room, 'if you do what I say, things will be easier for you.' She tries to look into Hannah's face but the girl has inclined her head. 'Look at me!' She crouches and catches Hannah's chin with the fingers of one hand. When their eyes are in line she begins to talk again in a soft wheedling voice. 'If you and I get on, Hannah, things will be so much better for you. I can make life pleasant – or not so pleasant. Remember that.' She stops, narrows her eyes and holds Hannah by the shoulders. 'Are you listening to any of this at all?' Breathing out noisily, she stands and then allows her arms to drop by her side. 'Oh, just get up, will you, and come with me. We can't mess about here any longer.'

Words form pictures in the air. I do not listen. Instead I watch them thicken, spread out, one scene and then the next, like the clouds. Do you remember the clouds, my love? You saw such things within them: a promise of happiness, a threat of some unavoidable sadness, a prediction of what is to come. You spoke as if you believed the wind could show us the future with its turbulent artistry and I laughed. I saw nothing there, except once I thought I saw your face become old. If I shut my eyes I would see it now. It is in the place I own and I am its only visitor. Nothing matters. Nothing happens. Nothing is heard and nothing is seen. Sometimes there are memories as sharp and clear as paintings: you coming into my mother's shop and smiling at me; lifting the red flannel from the shelf and throwing it open so it covered me; feeling for me through the cloth. Your hand catching hold of mine. The sudden burst of light as you lift a corner and come under too. The fire of ginger on your breath.

'Here she is, sir. She was a little reluctant to come.'
  'So I see.'

Whiskers. An otter's head. His mouth opens, and a small red tongue moves within. Clouds and more clouds. I watch them surge briefly from his mouth and disappear.

'What is your name?'
  Angelika nudges her but the girl remains mute.
  'Will you not say? No matter, I can see it in here. Hannah . . . A pretty name.'
  Hoffmann is leaning against his desk, regarding the girl that Angelika has pressed into the chair in front of him.
  Angelika sighs and the doctor glances up at her. 'You may go,' he says. Although he is speaking to the assistant, his eyes have returned to his patient in the chair. 'I shall ring for you when I'm ready.'
  When Angelika has gone he looks at the paper in his hand and then glances again at the girl.
  'Nymphomania,' he says, and his voice rises at the end to make the word a question. He frowns and taps the paper with a pencil. For a few minutes he continues to rest against his desk and look: the girl is quiet, withdrawn, there is no sign of any sort of mania at all. He scribbles on the paper with a pencil. By the word 'nymphomania' he adds a question mark and then the word 'latent' carefully encased in brackets.

The room waits. It will know nothing. I tell no one. No one except the man who holds my heart in his hands. Kurt. I don't have to close my eyes to see you. Wait for me, my beloved. Then warmth under my chin. Blue eyes. Not yours. Distant. I look once and then look away. They are not yours. And whiskers, all sorts of colours, brown, red, grey. The fur of a small animal, licking his teeth.

Hoffmann returns to his notes, tries to write where he stands but then gives up and retreats behind the desk. If there were symptoms of nymphomania they are not apparent now. He flicks through the pages of notes, trying to establish who first suggested the malady, but there are so many notes and crossings-out it is impossible to say. He takes a fresh sheet of paper and begins again. She has the signs of green sickness, that is all, perhaps a little melancholia. Sometimes the doctor who is recommending the admission exaggerates his case just to ensure its proper consideration by the council. Maybe Hannah's physician felt compelled to shout this case more loudly than usual because the town asylum rarely admitted Israelites.

Hoffmann draws the Jewish doctor's letter from the file of papers and smiles. The letter is reverential; Hoffmann, apparently, is the girl's only hope of recovery. He shifts in his chair; this ridiculous faith in his abilities is making him feel uncomfortable. He has been in this post only for a year and already he has discovered that treating the mentally ill is not at all straightforward or predictable. Hoffmann combs his beard with three fingers and remembers a patient he has just discharged; a similar case of simple melancholia that was easily treated and cured within a few months. All that was required was a little granola and iron, as well as taking the precaution of prescribing a diet that excluded anything too spicy or strongly flavoured. He scribbles his notes, referring back to all that has gone before, before talking out loud to the girl sitting in front of him.

'It is good you have come here now.' Even though his clipped, careful words initiate no response, he smiles then goes to stand in front of her. She is pale, bloodless; a quick pull at her bottom lids confirms her anaemia. 'It is just a small imbalance, easy to correct,' he says, then reaches for her wrist, his mouth silently forming numbers.

My heart beating: I feel it through his fingers, my footsteps keeping up, running after you because you're calling me. Kurt. Wait. I am coming too. Behind the thud of my feet there is something else. A humming. A tune that I know; something my father used to sing. Before I knew you. Before you loved me. Before then.

CHAPTER 2

From Dr Hoffmann's case book, 10 March 1852

REPORT ON HANNAH MEYER

Hannah Meyer. Israelite. Twenty-three years of age. Seamstress and resident of Judengasse. Stature above medium, habit meagre and with signs of emaciation. Chestnut-coloured hair, eyes brown and downcast. Physiognomy sad and unchangeable. Phlegmatic temperament. Disposition gloomy. Robust infancy but variola at six years. At fourteen subject to pains in the head and leucorrhoea. Menstruation established at fifteen with difficulty. Since then menses have been irregular and scant and often accompanied by cephalalgia, sadness and insomnia. Dutiful and obedient child. Offspring of a father who committed suicide. Since then domestic trials and difficulties have resulted in melancholia. Aged twenty-two and three months, menses suppressed and patient more gloomy and sedentary. Insomnia and an increased degree of sadness, often accompanied by panic terrors. Accusations of lewd behaviour were pinned to her door, which presumably have resulted in a diagnosis of nymphomania. In the month of November she was bled thrice from the feet, without any improvement in her health. On 26 February she disappeared from the house and returned the next day. Since then she has not spoken, and has maintained an obstinate silence for two weeks; her appetite is capricious, she moves not, nor sleeps. On 9 March she was admitted into the Institute for the Insane and Epileptic. She refuses to speak but will walk and do whatever is directed of her. Pulse 80. Skin dry, cold to touch and brown. Melancholic. Anaemic. Granola with iron prescribed with every meal.

The staircase to the first floor is opposite the doctor's office. The rather grand flight with its bannisters and treads of polished brown stone leads to a more austere one of bare boards and oiled wood above. The corridors in this place are always dark, and even now, in the middle of the day, they are filled with shadows. Even the most cynical and sane are startled here by ghosts, and find themselves catching their breath and listening for footsteps. Just now it is hushed. A few minutes ago a deep-throated wail was snuffed out somewhere far away, and then, closer, a woman's high laugh terminated with the sound of a slap. Angelika is nudging Hannah forward, shoving her in the back to indicate direction, and Hannah is treading softly, without looking, up the stairs and then right, along the corridor, then stopping, waiting. There is a door, heavy looking with an obvious lock, the metal around the keyhole dented and shiny with use. Angelika shoves Hannah to the side and opens it. The room is bright after the darkness of the corridor. Even though a cold wind blows through the open windows at the back the air is stale, for the room is filled with rows of desks, and behind each desk is a woman working at something in front of her. When the door bangs against an adjacent desk the laugh that rang out moments earlier starts up again and again it is slapped quiet. Hannah doesn't look up. She doesn't see the small woman with the old face rub her cheek and then chew at her lip. She doesn't see the large assistant with the ornate white bonnet and large angular jaw blow at her hand and rub it on her apron, then smile across at Angelika.

'The whore?'

Angelika nods.

'Put her over there with the rest.'

Angelika nudges Hannah in the back again so that she will move forward but there is nowhere to go. The room is crammed with desks and chairs. Angelika shoves at chairs until she has forced a way across to the window, with Hannah following her. Here there is a space slightly larger than anywhere else in the room and, tucked under the desk, a stool.

To the left of the space is a young woman with pale hair wound neatly inside a cotton bonnet. Her skin is pale, with large freckles merging to form complicated shapes across her nose and upper cheeks. She works at her sewing with a striking intensity, her head bowed, and accompanies each stab at the cloth with a quietly drawn-in whistle. When Angelika prods at her back the woman darts forward as if stung.

'Make room, make room – Grete, did you not hear me?'

'You want me to move?' The woman turns, the eyelids around her pale green eyes pulled back.

'Yes, yes, that's what I said.'

'But I . . .' The eyelids slide together, and when they separate again they draw with them a film of tears.

'Move, Grete, just move.'

But Grete cannot just move; before her every action she has to carry out essential rituals and checks. She gives the cloth she has been working on several shakes and then places it back on the desk. Then, with her right hand, rubs each finger of her left along its entire length. Each one has to be checked in case it has accidentally picked up something that should not be there. Her fingers are long, the knuckles like knobbly joints of twigs, and as they go about their task they shake.

'Move.'

But Grete's head makes three short, violent shakes. Before she rises she must check her hands, the desk, her work, the lap of her skirt, even the floor. She begins again on her left hand, her mouth silently forming numbers. Each finger must

15

be checked three times, and after that the cloth and then the surface of the desk. It is important that everything is examined thrice.

Angelika waits until Grete has started on her second finger, then reaches forward and pulls. As Grete is yanked from her chair she wails, a sound so sharp and sudden it seems as though the air is seared. Even Angelika pauses for a second before reaching out with a foot and propelling Grete's chair a few centimetres along the floor. When she thrusts the woman back down again in her new place the wailing stops. For a short while Grete is still and quiet, her arms outstretched, the pale twigs twitching in spasm. She looks at her hands with wide eyes, then she draws herself up in her chair and hunches her shoulders together so the cloth of her blouse is caught in their two sharp blades. Now that her hands are close to her face they begin again their methodical movement, one finger and then the next, this time accompanied by some whispered words: 'You can't, you mustn't, you mustn't.'

When Angelika shoves Hannah down in the adjacent chair Grete recoils as if she has touched something that is too hot.

'This girl needs some stuff to sew, Grete. Give her some of yours.'

The woman shakes her head and the hands move faster.

'Give her the black.'

But the woman shakes her head again. 'You . . . mustn't . . .' Her words come between small gasps for breath.

'Grete! The black, now.' Although Angelika's voice is quiet it has a blunt edge which causes Grete to look up quickly over her shoulder, nod, and then look down again, but her checking continues.

Sighing loudly, Angelika grabs some of the stuff in front of Grete and shoves it over so that it sits in front of Hannah.

'Your work. When she has finished her fussing Grete will show you what to do.'

Hannah shows no sign that she has heard; she sits with her head bowed, except for the stillness of her hands, a dark imitation of Grete. Angelika stands back and regards the scene: each woman seems to have something to do. It is all that matters. If anyone came in now everything would look well, under control and productive. Even Lise, the slut who causes Angelika so much entertainment, appears to be hard at work on the other side of Hannah. It is an illusion, of course, but Angelika gives her favourite an affectionate slap on the shoulder, then begins to work her way to the side of the room.

Grete tips her head and watches her go. Still breathing hard, she spreads out her fingers and inspects them, then she picks up the cloth and shakes it and inspects the desk. It is only after Angelika has reached the door and opened it that Grete looks at her new neighbour. The quietness of this girl appeals to her, but if she were to hand her a cloth there would have to be so much examining and inspecting that the thought of it all exhausts her. She looks again at Hannah and gives a quiet sob.

'Do you want this?' From the other side of Hannah, Lise's large hand produces a mass of uncarded wool. 'You can have these too, if you wish, I don't need them any more.' The hand's owner is middle aged, wide and handsome. Around her head is twisted a red cotton scarf, and around her neck she has two more: one of them bright blue and the other purple, twisted around each other like a decorative rope. On top of all this she wears a man's frock coat, the collar turned up to reach almost to her head. Beside the wool she places a pair of wooden carders. Her irises make a strange pulsing movement as she whispers loudly in Hannah's unlistening ear, 'I am . . .' Lise stops, her mouth moving but not making a sound. She shuts it tightly so her lips disappear and then opens it to begin again. 'Rothschild . . .' She stops again, frowns, opens and shuts her mouth, stretching her lips. 'He wants me, he told me . . .' Her frown deepens and now involves the whole of her face. She takes a breath. '. . . for his mistress.' With these words spattered out, Lise's body relaxes. She slumps on her chair, a happy but empty smile on her face.

Wool. Oily in my hand. A mess of fibres, one overlapping the next in a never-ending mesh. It is its own world. If I look I shall see it; the space between the threads, the place I could inhabit if I were small enough. How I would be lost there. How like a forest it is, the sticky fine fibres holding me back like the undergrowth. I go inside, I think about making my own path, cutting through and finding my way, a route no one else will follow.

It tumbles from my hand. I follow it to the floor. My piece of world. From far away the chant of a prayer. Not mine. Theirs. Kurt's.

Tobias is waiting at the doorway while Dagmar, the other big-boned assistant, finishes the prayer. He is carrying a large cauldron. His long blond-haired fingers wrap around the wire handle and the pot sways and slops a little of its contents on the floor. A meaty smell fills the room. Behind him comes Angelika with dishes and spoons, and behind her follows another man, Antoni, the manager, sharp nosed, older, smaller and darker than Tobias, carrying a large covered tray. The food has been delivered from two streets away, and Tobias has brought it slowly up the stairs to the women's work room. Later Angelika will have to supervise one of the more docile and able women as they follow in his footsteps with a cloth. A lot of food is needed to feed the ninety-seven patients in this place and the small kitchen downstairs can cope only with preparing a little food. So it feeds the rich. That is how the manager's wife, Frau Antoni, spends each morning – chopping and frying and stewing so that by noon the smell of a feast drifts up the stairs to the nostrils of the occupants above. They taste the bacon in the air, they chew on the ghosts of freshly roasted steaks, they let their tongues slide into the promise of egg yolks and sausage; but that is all they do. The food for the majority is brought from outside and it is deliberately bland and accidentally cold. Today it is Monday and there will be soup and then carrots and cabbage; tomorrow there will be soup and then a meat-flavoured stew; the day after that soup and more vegetables. Everyone knows exactly what to expect. It is written in the log downstairs, but no one needs to look: only on Sunday is there an expectation of meat in portions large enough to see.

Tobias places the cauldron on a desk and Angelika and Dagmar ladle out the soup and pass it along the rows. The bowls are received with either great interest or none at all. Sometimes the cauldron is not stirred and those served last are luckier than those served first. Today there are fine filaments of pork, and the odd piece of potato and leek. Lise, the stocky woman with the scarves, attends to her meal immediately, her slurps following each other in rapid succession; while Grete, on the other side of Hannah, starts her inspection of her spoon, then her hands and then the spoon again. While one licks and swallows the other turns her piece of cutlery again and again so a reflection of the sun glances off one wall and then the next.

'Don't you want that?' the wide woman asks when Hannah doesn't move.

'You're a greedy woman, Lise. Leave her be.'

'Well, she's not . . .' Again the woman with the scarves has forgotten her lines.

Grete pauses in her cleaning and leans as close to Hannah as she dares. 'Eat your food, child, you'll get nothing else.'

Voices drift through my veils. I let them come. I let them enter. When they tell me to get up and go with them I do. The breath of the wind. The sickly smell of blossom. A trough of water, steaming in the cold air. A bag of clothes. They are not my hands. But I watch them. They take hold of the clothes and plunge them one after the other into water. They are not my hands but I feel their pain. I watch the water scalding the skin and the flesh turning red. They catch hold of the great green bar of soap and I watch it slowly diminish as it passes by the grater. The small shavings are paler than their mother. They turn naked hands into the fur-covered paws of an animal. Then they are scattered over the water. I watch some of them dissolve. I wait for others to drop away under the surface and for their scum to appear in puddles on the top. The washboard fits under her chin. She knows what to do without thinking. The hands that are not mine seize the cloth and begin to rub.

From the window on the first floor Hoffmann looks out. It is an idyllic scene, one that could be happening anywhere, except here it is outlined with bars. The dark bank of cloud that had been threatening rain has disappeared and the day is bright. Behind the asylum there are two small gardens separated by walls. Both of them are set out with grass and shrubs and trees, and a washing line has been strung over part of the grass. Hoffmann pauses and watches as the new girl hangs a selection of shirts and blouses on the line. Even from this distance he can tell that she moves in a dream. Although she is moving slowly she is taking little care with what she does; once each garment is hung and fastened she goes mechanically on to the next. One shirt hangs by the cuffs of both sleeves, a pair of pants is hung by one leg and a waist, a pillowcase is pegged at the corner and billows out in the breeze to form a bulbous outline. For a few seconds Hoffmann watches the shapes, then, when his view is partially obscured by his breath, he draws the pillow on the glass and the girl standing beside it. He regards his sketch for a moment then grins and wipes it away. The girl has gone, returned inside for another load. He hums the first few notes of an anthem and, clicking his fingers in time, starts to walk down the staircase.

I see you. There you are; playing tricks on me, pretending to be somewhere else when you have been here all the while. I see your back, your legs stretched below, your arms waving at something in front of you. Kurt. I run. I open my arms, soon we will be together and no one will break us apart. There is your voice, your whistle. Why do you not turn? Why do you not run to me as I run to you? I throw my arms wider; you are so wide, there is so much to envelop. Kurt? I wait for the warmness of you but it doesn't come. There is just wet cloth and air that escapes from it with a grunt. They are playing tricks. They know how much I hurt and they are hurting me some more. Pinching my bruises. I tear at their joke. I grab at handfuls and pull. They will not trick me. It falls away and I pull again. Tearing. Ripping. The feeling of something resisting and then giving way. My skirt. I feel it collapsing from me. The parts of me it held escaping too. I step from it. I pick it up. Even though it is heavy I can throw it far. The wind catches it and it opens up. A dark bud. A flower without petals. Cold. The wind, touching me too. Surging inwards and upwards, tugging at my blouse, wanting it, shearing it with its invisible fingers. I help him in his task. I loosen, unfasten and at last the wind has its way. I watch it go. It somersaults away from me, its arms that were my arms waving and laughing. Then I stop. More arms, pale above the red raw hands, folding one over the other, clutching at the chemise and the long open legs of the drawers. Will the wind have those too? The arms reach towards the clear cold sky. Her arms. Not mine.

It is inconvenient and slightly improper that Tobias is first on the scene but he is. For a while he watches her, quite happy to observe what lies beneath the cast-off skirt and blouse: her curved narrow shoulders, her swiftly moving rib cage and her right breast changing shape as she reaches up. The sound of footsteps behind him forces him forward. It is essential that he be seen to be covering her up, but not because it is cold. When she fights him off he bats her back. She seems as insignificant as a doll in his arms. He wraps a blanket roughly around her and as the owner of the footsteps, Angelika, remonstrates and scolds behind him he carries her in, through the kitchen and into the doctor's room at the front.

'What are you doing with her?' Herr Antoni is in there, sorting through papers with his quick bird-like movements. 'He won't want to see her now, he's . . .' He stops as Tobias allows Hannah to tumble on to the floor. When she attempts to rise her blankets fall from her and she stands without shame, pulling at the naked skin of her arms.

'Angelika!' Herr Antoni's voice is too loud and he has dropped his papers. As he stoops to pick them up he gives the impression of a heron scooping up a fish. 'Take care of this . . . and Tobias – get the doctor.'

When I move the arms come too. They are not part of me. They are strange lifeless things, twitching and hurting. If I could I would chop them away. But I cannot move. The big one with the bright hair and sly whistle has fastened me down and now the other one who says that she owns me is making sure I cannot work free. Kurt! If only you were here. You could tell them. These are not my hands. These are not my feet. There is nothing of me left. I am not here at all.

'What happened?' Hoffmann asks. 'I just saw her from the window, she seemed quite calm.'

'I think it was the clothes on the line, sir. She seemed to see something, I saw her running.'

'Hannah!' Hoffman speaks into her face. They are level, his eyes reflected in hers. 'What is it?'

But she twists away. He reaches out, holds her chin, twists the face back so it is again looking at his. 'What frightened you?'

She does not answer.

'What, Hannah?'

And they wait.

'She will not speak, sir.'

'She tore off her clothes.'

'She threw them away, sir, and Tobias covered her up with this blanket. Is that the nymphomania coming out in her, sir?'

Hoffmann shakes his head. 'I believe, Angelika, that she simply wanted to be free of her clothes.'

I make the mouth shut. I draw its lips together so much they ache. Nymphomania: I remember the word said another time. As if I could ever love another.

She is panting. When the doctor brings his small brown stethoscope near she strains away so hard he replaces it in his pocket and instead withdraws his watch. He holds her wrist tightly and counts. 'One hundred and twelve,' he says to everyone close, and they nod as if the number means something. It does not. 'High,' he says, and they nod again. Then he touches her forehead. 'And hot now,' he says. 'The douche, I think, Angelika.'

And the girl grins. 'Yes, sir.'

'And with it a little camphor, inhaled with steam.'

'Sir.'

'You get her ready and I shall be along presently.'

'Yes, sir, at once, sir.'

'And after that an ice blister.'

The girl's mouth opens wider.

'Keep it on all evening. Only a little bread at vespers.'

'Yes, sir.'

'Then we'll see.'

CHAPTER 3

Haus Stein East
Judengasse
Frankfurt-am-Main
7 March 1852

Dear Sir,

I have been asked to write a few lines concerning an acquaintance of mine: Fräulein Hannah Meyer. I have known the young woman since her birth as her family and mine have rented adjacent rooms in the same house for many years. I have sometimes been able to help Frau Meyer with her accounts before the Fräulein trained herself to take over this task. They are a fine family, sir, hard working, always paying their taxes on time and making an honest but not over-profitable living. The Fräulein herself is almost as talented a seamstress as her mother, and I can vouch personally for her repairs. Her patching on my trousers is stitched so finely that my wife declares it is quite invisible.

Of course, the death of the father was a severe blow to us all. He was a true gentleman, skilful, polite, always keeping his affairs to himself. He left a void that we all tried to help fill, but there is only so much we can do. Those of us who continue to live on this miserable Frankfurt street are the most unfortunate in our community; so money is always short. But the two women coped well. They were helped a little by our own charitable associations, but mainly they helped themselves: they reduced their circumstances, let one of their rooms go to another family, were generally sensible to their situation, as one might expect. You see, sir, they are clever women, and Frau Meyer has always had an independent character. There were gentlemen callers then, of course, owing partly to the nature of Frau Meyer's business, and partly for more social reasons. The Fräulein, and the Frau too, are considered to have a certain allure. Everyone remarks upon it. But I would just like to say that everything was very proper. Frau Meyer would see to that, and anyway, living as we do, many families to a house, it is impossible to have very intimate relations without a host of people becoming aware of it.

I am hoping that this may go a little way to reassuring you that not all that you might hear about the young woman is true. Some of my fellow citizens have malicious tongues, sir, and a few have too little to do.

Your humble servant,
Jeremiah Cohen

There is a large part of the bath tub which lives. Along the top of one side, where the light from the window catches it, there is a coat of green slime. On the other side, covering it from top to bottom, is a scattering of minute orange nodules, small scraps of a fungus that is slowly weakening the whole structure, swelling and growing with each drenching. The bath is never fully emptied. At one end there is a permanent puddle. It is black on the wood and in shadow, and sometimes, when Angelika looks quickly, it seems that she sees something moving there, something silvery and long like an eel that has grown from nothing overnight. In the middle of the room is a large wooden screen reaching most of the way to the window and halfway up to the ceiling. The tub is the only thing on this side of the screen, and there is a second tub, acting as a reservoir, on the other. The screen is there to give the illusion of privacy, but Tobias ensures that he is the one who is standing on the ledge behind, his massive head and shoulders protruding well above and with an excellent view, while Angelika works below, filling buckets from the reservoir and lining them up on the ground beside her. In the bath the girl is still struggling, straining and tugging with frantic little movements at the wooden lid that covers half the bath and which Angelika has fastened down with a lock. Tobias notes that the chemise Angelika has found to cover her, which was pulled over her with such great difficulty, is the sort that becomes translucent when wet. He touches his lips with the end of his tongue.

Cold. The girl that isn't me is cold. A skin of cold, underneath, adhering to whatever lies below, holding her down. Rise, I tell her, but she cannot. Something stops her. Something holds us both.

For one long minute Tobias rests with the bucket in his arms.

'Go on, then.' Angelika always finds herself whispering in the bath house. For another minute he just looks, relishing the view. 'Aren't we supposed to wait for our precious little doctor?' His words trail away as he sees the shadow of Hoffmann approach the open door.

'Camphor.' Hoffmann has entered with quick small steps. 'I can't smell any camphor.' He marches over to the bath, ignores the occupant and peers through a hole in the lid. 'And tepid water, Angelika, I do not see any of that either.'

Angelika emerges from behind the screen. 'It was a bit of a struggle, sir, I . . .'

Hoffmann doesn't wait for her to finish. 'Well, it's a little late now in any case.' He stands up and glances at his patient. 'I think we had best just proceed with the douche.'

'Yes, sir.' Angelika turns to hide a tight triumphant smile. She had never intended to bother with the business of warming the water; it was far too much effort and anyway she regarded it as an unnecessary indulgence. The mad cannot feel the cold: this is a view widely shared by the assistants of the asylum, and as far as Angelika is concerned it is an undeniable fact.

'Tobias?' Angelika inclines her head slightly in the giant's direction. There may be a ladder of command but Angelika likes to prove to herself now and again that she is not quite on the bottom rung.

Tobias glances down, smiles quickly then begins his slow tipping.

Ice. From nowhere, ice in a long moving mass. Hard, solid, sharp. Her mouth opens. My mouth opens. I let her scream.

The three remaining occupants of the room smile: Hoffmann's smile is intended to be reassuring, conveying a professional satisfaction that a cure is on its way; Angelika's is one that escapes from her, the betrayal of a malicious glee she would prefer to hide; while Tobias's is unguarded, an open leer, dividing his face with a slash. 'That's good, isn't it, sir, just what you wanted?'

Hannah is quieter now that the bucket is empty. Hoffmann allows his eyes to travel slowly to the speaker, glares at him for a moment, then says, 'I would appreciate it if you would just get on with your work, Tobias.'

Tobias snorts to show he is not cowed then begins to carefully tip his second bucket. The girl's blouse is sticking to her skin in a most satisfactory way, and Tobias is enjoying every curve and every patch of darkness. As usual the implication of what he sees causes an immediate stirring in his genitals; but Tobias is hardly conscious of this, all he knows is a sensation of intense clandestine pleasure. He tips the bucket with care so that his view is not obstructed, and in spite of himself Hoffmann admires the way the stream of water is so controlled and even. The water hits Hannah squarely on the head.

Again it comes. The cold. Head into chest. Chest collapsing into spaces within. Mouth opening, the jaw aching with effort. I let her scream until she has no more voice.

While the doctor counts, Angelika and Tobias set up a satisfying rhythm. One bucket follows the next, with little break in between. The girl draws in breath and then screams again, but it is weaker now. Soon it is inaudible above the sound of the water and eventually it stops altogether. Then there is just her open mouth, her chest rising and falling as it fuels silent sobs, her hair lying like river weed over her face and shoulders and her arms outstretched, taut as they push against the side of the bath.

No breath. No space to scream. Nothing to do but shut my eyes and wait. Nothing. Instead of cold, nothing. A nothingness outside joining the nothingness within.

Eight buckets. One more. Hoffmann nods at Angelika. The water in the reservoir is petering out. Angelika tips the almost empty barrel, trying to gather more water in her bucket. Although it is difficult to see in the gloom behind the screen the water is cloudy, and smells of the river. When it falls through the air on the more illuminated side of the screen, Angelika notices that it is slightly orange, as if it is full of rust. She wonders whether it tastes of metal, whether the girl swallows any, whether she knows. Then she wonders whether she will see it on the rags she will use to dry her.

'Last one,' she says to Tobias, passes it up and folds her arms.

From somewhere far away there is a voice. Up. Get up. But there is nothing to move, nothing to say.

When Hoffmann and Angelika go to lift the girl they find her set, her legs apparently fused to what is beneath. Hoffmann feels for her pulse. It is slower but also fainter. He frowns a little, then indicates to Angelika that they must pull again. But Hannah has become a dead weight. After trying a few more times he calls for Tobias. He comes quickly, his eyes flicking over the girl before dwelling on the furred Y at the top of her legs. Angelika tuts and nudges him away, so that she can drape a sheet around Hannah's shoulders.

Hoffmann is also inspecting Hannah. She is paler than before, and although her eyes are open he suspects that she sees nothing. He passes his hand in front of her but the lushly fringed eyelids do not even flicker. He has heard of this happening before; the brain has been cooled too much and the blood has retreated to somewhere in the stomach. Instead of shocking her from her depression he seems to have made her withdraw more fully into a stupor. If Greisinger is right, if all forms of madness are part of a continuum of symptoms, each one representing different stages of the same disease, then it appears that Hoffmann, with his therapy, has forced her into a more intractable phase. The simple melancholia has become something more complex. He stands back. 'Just get her out,' he says flatly to Tobias, then walks up and down the short extent of the room, up to the screen then back to the door, slapping irritably at his thigh. He should have insisted on the warm water and camphor. Next time he will insist that everything is done just the way he says.

Tobias reaches forward, grabs Hannah under her arms and begins to pull. The girl retches once, the large beads of her vertebrae describing an arch through the sheet. Hoffmann pauses by the door and looks back. The girl looks even paler now than when he saw her this morning. But perhaps that is good. Quite often it is necessary for a patient to become more ill in order to reach the crisis and the cure; Esquirol would know. He decides to consult the work of the great master in his office. 'Take her to the kitchen for some camphor in steam and I shall come to see her shortly.'

As soon as he is gone Angelika sits on a bench at the side. Hannah is out of the bath now but her legs dangle limp. When Tobias lowers her to the ground they fold away beneath her, so he stands with her, his big hands stealing out from her armpits, smiling at Angelika while his fingers creep slowly forward.

'What shall we do with her?'

'You heard him.'

Tobias allows his fingers to stretch farther forward and dig slowly into the soft flesh in front of the girl's arms.

'Stop that!'

'Why, do you want some?' The hands shift position, reach out again. Between the fingers the small soft ridges of goose-pimpled flesh whiten.

'Leave her, Tobias, damn you.'

Tobias lowers his head so his mouth is next to Hannah's ear. 'Oh, I do believe you have a rival, my little whore . . .'

Sometimes I can make everything go. The world goes on outside but I am buried so deep that no one can reach me.

*I see but take no part. A bowl of steam. A hand sprinkling
white powder and then the tiny crystals skittering around
on the surface of the water as if possessed by some evil
spirit. Then vapours making the air transparent. Then a
head, not mine, forced forward with a shove. The clear air
changing into liquid in another's nose, another's mouth, and
then trickling down into each passageway, each burning
tube. A cough opens the way for more. A hand at the back
forces downward. The neck strains, hurts, longs to
straighten. At the edges of the bowl the water still bubbles.
Little streams escape upward as if they are weeds.*

*Down. A face staring back. A faint shadow. And then
another face. Yours. And at once I am here. Looking, examining. Searching for the mole by the corner of your lips.
Waiting for you to smile back.*

She is so still now, hardly the same creature that raged and
struck out in the laundry. Angelika has a bruise on her arm,
which she will repay with interest later. But for now Angelika
takes Hannah's arms and crosses them over her chest.
'Recently departed,' Angelika mutters; she smiles and checks
the bladder on Hannah's forehead. Indeed, it seems to
Angelika that part of Hannah has departed. Her face lies
slack and vacant. Behind her eyes there is no indication of
spirit. There is still some ice but it will need to be renewed;
rivulets of water are running from the bladder on Hannah's
forehead on to the rags placed beside her for this purpose.
Angelika inspects her again. Then, confident that she will
remain exactly where she is, departs for the kitchen two
flights below.

*You weren't there. My nose touched the surface and it broke
into pieces. Another trick. My voice escaped. I heard it, a
sound shattering air, breaking it up, splinters of air and*

splinters of face. On and on. My mouth outstretched. Kurt,
Kurt, Kurt. As if yelling your name would bring you back.
Be quiet. Too late, too late to stop. Quiet. A hand in the
middle of my back pushing down. So much heat after so
much cold and nothing I could do to stop it. The hot sticky
water then no breath. No breath at all.

Tobias has no business here on the women's floor. He has
been dismissed by Angelika, but after wandering downstairs
and seeing the assistant Hugo confortably in his place by
the door, he has returned up the stairs with a little bread
and beer stolen from the empty kitchen. Frau Antoni sees
him climb the stairs as she leaves her living quarters. Like
her husband she is small, round, dark of hair and florid of
cheek. The two are like the matching pairs of old figures
that emerge from clocks to indicate the weather: Frau Antoni
bringing tidings of wind and rain, while her husband promises sunshine with a sparsely toothed smile. As Tobias thuds
up the stairs she notices the bread and beer and says nothing:
the man's size always causes her some apprehension and she
is glad to see him go on his way.

Tobias was always a freak. No one in his family could
explain his existence. While his siblings reached a normal
size and stopped, Tobias kept on growing. His mother was
glad to be rid of him. When she discovered that he would
be required to live in if he took up the offer of a position
at the aslyum, she demanded that he take it at once: Tobias
was expensive to feed.

But Tobias enjoys his build. Never does he feel the urge
to stoop to make himself seem smaller. He likes the way he
can look down on most things and see what people thought
they had hidden away: keys shoved on the top of dressers
and small mysterious packages tucked out of sight – Tobias
can inspect them all. He also likes his feeling of power. His

strength has always kept pace with his growth and it has given him a visible confidence. He can solve a tavern brawl simply by approaching it, and it is this arrogant, bulky presence which makes him a useful addition to the asylum staff. He is given more liberty than the rest of his colleagues; his petty transgressions are ignored by Herr Antoni as well as by his wife, and he is used to being allowed to wander around the building at whim.

Now, still tearing off corners of the black bread and shoving them in his mouth, he enters Hannah's room. He looks around. Everything is pretty much the same as he left it half an hour ago, but Angelika has gone. He is a little disappointed. It is Angelika he has come to annoy. He annoys her as much as he can because he likes to have her attention. One day he aims to have her attention entirely. It is something he thinks about in his specially built bed in the epileptics' wing. She would be a little small for him, of course, most women are, but Angelika is strong and aggressive and these are two qualities he admires in any gender, but so far she has shown him no sign that she is interested. He stops by the bed and looks.

Hannah's open eyes startle him for a second, but after inspecting them for a few minutes he decides that it is as if they are shut. With one finger he touches her cheek, then, as there is no response, carefully moves the finger down over her chin and on to her neck. Angelika has succeeded in dressing her, but it is just a nightgown, a single layer of cloth between her flesh and the world. The neck of the gown is open and Tobias's finger wanders inside. The flesh here is more moist than the dry skin of the neck and his finger runs more quickly. The boniness of the collar bone gives way to something less resistant, something warm. He remembers catching hold of her earlier, feeling the weight of her in his arms and the softness at the end of his fingertips. Her strange living deadness is oddly attractive. He could do anything, he decides, anything at all, and no one would ever know. He reaches out, allows his fingers to extend over the small fullness of her breast and make a cage.

'Tobias! What are you doing in here?'

He turns around, wonders whether his hands have been masked by his body and decides that they have.

'Seeing if the young lady is all right, sir. After all that trouble in the laundry I thought . . . well, I was just passing and . . .' The slow workings of Tobias's brain uncover an idea: an opportunity has arisen to land Angelika in trouble, and a sly smile twists his mouth. 'I saw she was all on her own, sir, so I thought maybe I'd just watch her until her assistant returns.'

'Well, you can go now. The boy by the door, he is waiting to be relieved.'

Once you brushed my face with your fingertips. Just one cheek. Then there was your word, murmured, hardly a word at all. Beautiful. Even though my eyes are too small and my chin too big. Beautiful . . . You brushed my cheek. You said that word. Beautiful. But only to you, I said, and you shook your head. No. You are.

Hoffmann stands where Tobias stood and watches. He does not see Hannah's face, not altogether. He sees the open eyes, just the eyes on their own, and waits for them to blink. Then he sees just the mouth, slightly open, forming silent words. He stoops forward to hear them but he cannot. Then he sees the neck and the vein throbbing there. He feels for it and counts. 'Still too fast,' he says, but there is no one here now to nod. He makes notes on the board of paper he has with him. 'A little calmer,' he writes, 'pulse reduced. One hundred. Maintain ice pack.' Then, humming a tune to himself, he walks in circles around the small room, from bed to bed, waiting for Angelika to return with a new ice pack.

CHAPTER 4

From the Report of the Clerk to the Town Council of Frankfurt, 1853

OBSERVATIONS ON THE RUNNING OF THE CITY'S INSTITUTE FOR THE INSANE AND EPILEPTIC

Lunch is at noon. After lunch there is another prayer, and then the patients are allowed an hour for recreation and exercise before starting work again at two. Everything is calm and ordered. If the weather is fine the patients are allowed to walk sedately around the garden. They must walk slowly. They must take care not to become excited and late for work. At four o'clock there is a half-hour break for a tea of bread and fruit and then work continues until six. The patients who would normally have paid employment outside the Institute are expected to work here too if they are calm and well enough. They stuff mattresses with horsehair, they spin, weave, and knit, they launder, they make straw hats, and articles for the Institute itself: chemises used for restraint, sheets, and articles of coarse clothing. The superintendent, Dr Hoffmann, ensures that the services of the patients are advertised around the town so that everyone in Frankfurt knows of their labour, and its excellent reputation for quality and uniformity; the sewing is always neat, the stitches usually even and the weaving always tight and well finished. The proceeds from the sale go partly to the asylum and partly to the patient in the form of a small present or treat. But the real reason for work, the doctor tells me, is therapy. Meaningful work is considered to be of great benefit to the health and well-being of the mind and body. After six there is a controlled amount of leisure: a quiet game of billiards is thought to be of benefit, and a careful game of draughts is considered not to inflame the minds of the players. At regular intervals there is a concert with gentle music as this too has been observed to be of some temporary benefit. At seven o'clock the prayers are said for a supper of buttered bread and either beer or salad depending on the day. At nine o'clock the residents retire to bed.

Wolfgang Harting, May 1853

The door unlocks. Angelika inspects the room with a sniff. Hannah is, as she expected, exactly where she left her. She stands aside with her candle to allow three women to enter: the dark, squat Lise, who stumbles and has to be caught; the frail and fairer Grete, who pauses briefly at the entrance so that she can inspect the inside of her shoes and then the hem of her dress; then Ingrid, a woman with the stature of a well-fed child but whose face is fringed with shorn grey hair. She holds a mottled piece of cloth to her face which she constantly kneads with two fingers.

While Grete enters the room, checking the floor and then under her bed, Lise, with Ingrid in tow, walks over to Hannah's bed by the window. Lise's scarves have become unravelled during the day, and the one on her head has slipped to reveal a portion of shaved hair. She walks with a strange tottering gait. It is a characteristic that Hoffmann has only before noticed in men, but he makes the same prognosis in this woman: general paralysis of the insane. Already she has an embarrassment over certain words, and this together with the walk and delusions of grandeur are a sure sign. Hoffmann has a test. If he suspects a creeping paralysis he asks his patient to walk away from him in one direction then suddenly asks them to turn. The patient in the early stages of paralysis will invariably stumble. He will then ask them to read certain words from a card, words rich with consonants: 'sixty-six', 'substantiated', 'Solomon's songs'; words that require the tongue and lips to perform turns and twists of their own. And the patient will invariably stumble over these too. They will stop. Their top lips will tremble and Hoffmann will smile and pat them on the back. You've done very well, he'll say, and the patient will smile back. For the patient with creeping paralysis has one overwhelming blessing: contentment. All cares can be dismissed with a wave of a hand and a promise of tomorrow, even though the tomorrows are limited in number. Hoffmann has estimated that Lise has less than a year.

Angelika watches with her arms folded as Lise and Ingrid investigate the motionless form on the bed. Ingrid is most interested in Hannah's chemise: she takes a loose fold and pulls it gently towards her, silently rubbing the cloth between her fingers. Lise is interested in the girl herself. 'I know you, I think.' She sounds a little uncertain. She turns to Angelika. 'Oi, you' – she pauses, her lips working on a word – 'servant-girl. Do I know her, eh?'

Angelika tolerates a certain amount of rudeness from Lise. In fact the woman's arrogance amuses her. The doctor has explained that she is not long for this world, and this has tempered Angelika's instinctive indignation.

'Maybe you do, maybe you don't – how would I know?'

'I think I've seen her. Maybe she's one of Rothschild's children. She looks like she could be one of Rothschild's children.'

Lise leans over her and talks into her face. 'Wake up, child. I want to . . . s-speak to you.'

Angelika watches as Ingrid, standing close to Lise and still holding her piece of cloth to her face, tucks the end of Hannah's chemise in her mouth and begins to chew. There is a thoughtful aspect to her face, but Angelika reminds herself that this is an illusion. There is absolutely nothing inside that head. Her mother's dog has more intelligence. When Ingrid dies, which she expects she will before too long because the little woman's face already has the crumpled look of the old, she is hoping that the doctor will tell her what he finds inside her skull. She imagines there will be nothing. Perhaps just a little brain the size of a walnut, but apart from that an empty space.

Lise has lost patience with the silent figure on the bed now and has begun to prod her with a finger. 'Wake up, won't you, I need to . . . s . . . talk to you about your father.'

'Leave her, she will not wake.'

'Why, what have you done to her?' Lise walks her strange half-walk, half-dance over to Angelika and whispers to her loudly, 'You can tell me, I won't let on. Is it a . . . p . . . p . . . poison?' And lowering her voice further, 'Or a little witchcraft?'

'She's just ill, Lise, like the rest of you.'

'I'm not ill.'

'You are. Remember the pains you had yesterday?'

'Ah, that was just the c . . . c . . . curse of Eve.'

'No, Lise, remember the sickness? Remember you said you didn't want to even see food ever again?'

Lise shakes her head.

'Well, maybe you'll believe Grete. Ask her.' Grete looks up from her checking. She has inspected the sheets, the blankets and the floor beneath. If she is interrupted she will feel impelled to begin again. 'You were ill,' she says shortly, and continues her counting. Angelika knows precisely how ill: twelve grains of tartrate of antimony mixed with a little hellebore and gamboge sprinkled on her evening bread. A powerful purgative, used specifically on patients such as Lise to persuade them that they are indeed unwell and not fit for the world outside.

After the women have been persuaded into their night-clothes, emptied what they can into their pots and knelt by their beds to pray, Angelika blows out the candle. Their prayers are finished in darkness. Lise's is short, a few mumbled words, and she climbs awkwardly into bed. At forty-two she is the second-oldest woman in the room after Ingrid, but until recently used to be the most agile. A short woman, she has spent the first part of her life working hard on a smallholding just outside the city walls. The constant bending, stooping and stretching kept her tendons taut, and her calf muscles were so well developed they were like two miniature hearts giving her blood an extra little shove back up to her chest every time she squatted. Now these muscles are becoming atrophied, the nerves controlling them no longer the efficient messengers they used to be. When Hoffmann eventually performs his autopsy he will find her brain atrophied too, the grey matter softened and distorted with small voids and adhesions to the cortical substance.

But for the moment all that anyone can see of Lise is a face worn by the weather, a round, wide nose covered in small red veins, and a throat with skin as well cured as the finest harness. In her infrequent moments of sanity it is the smell of the earth that Lise misses most in this place. That, and her husband, whom she had become used to, like an old pair of slippers. He'd be waiting for her, he told her, when he brought her here, but his eyes slipped away. He would wait in his own way. He would stray again but he would have to find his own way back this time. There would be no pleading, no promises of never again, no sleeping on the floor for months until Lise allowed him back into her bed. A long time ago he acquired an unwanted little memento of his adventures and passed it on to Lise: a small, sore chancre that appeared where he had touched her. He laughed when she showed him, then showed her his back: a mottled rash of red. 'It's the pox, my darling. The great pox of kings and noblemen.'

The doctor had prescribed mercury. It had given her strange dreams in which she found herself eating the choicest fruit, and she had woken each morning dribbling. She had inspected her pillow for hair, twisted in front of the old tarnished mirror in the church to look for spots, but had found nothing. 'Maybe we're cured,' he had said, spreading the glistening ointment of mercury on to his chest. 'It happens.' But Lise knew that somewhere inside her the pox was waiting. One day it would appear when she wasn't expecting it and strike her down: a lump under the arm, a throat she couldn't make swallow or a livid scattering of pink smudges on her chest. She became afraid to look, afraid to extend her arm and reveal her skin, and eventually, afraid to go out. The smallholding sprouted dandelions and then thistles. The cabbages grew flowers. Her husband reminded her that the only part of her that had ever proved fertile was now withering away too. He had taken her hands and stroked them. 'Our treasure, Lise,' he had said, and her fingertips had quivered. 'Think of what they can do.'

But after that they had done very little. They had become poor, the odd windfall coming from whatever deal her husband managed to make with his big words; for he was never one for soiling his hands or exercising his head. She had tried to go back to her smallholding but the outside was too big, too full of people with their spiteful eyes and malicious tongues. Some days they had had nothing to eat at all. Life became something she endured, waking each morning to long again for the night and the chance for oblivion to return. There was no cause for joy and plenty of reason for sorrow.

But then one day she had woken with her idea. In spite of her age she still perceived herself to be an attractive woman; after all, God had seen to it that her body had never been strained with the trauma of childbirth. He must have been saving her for some other purpose. She looked herself up and down in the piece of mirror that still remained in their cottage. She pursed her lips, drew her stomach in and thrust her inadequate bosom out. She was desirable – no, more than desirable, irresistible. If her husband could stray, then so could she, but her straying would be a profitable one. She would not be a prostitute, she told him, how could someone like her be a prostitute? She was too clever, too witty and too attractive. No, she, Lise Schmidt, would be a well-paid mistress. She would probably be given her own apartment in the new part of town on the Bleichstrasse if she found the right man. She would send for him when she was ready. Of course, her husband had just laughed. He had never had faith in her, she told him, and he had laughed again. It was only when he saw that she had traded her wedding ring for a few scarves that he had stopped his laughing. She had wrapped herself in all of them to show him: silks in every colour that she could find. She had to have them, she told him, for her dance, and he had sat open mouthed as she had performed it for him: with every turn a scarf was removed and underneath the scarves she wore little except her long white chemise. She had lifted it suggestively but he had refused to be seduced. Instead he had walked silently away. She had expected him to be gone for days but this time he had returned the same night with a couple of men she had never seen before. He had asked her to perform her dance again and she had done so joyfully, glad of the practice. But they too had not been seduced. She consoled herself that they were not rich enough anyway; she expected that only the wealthy would prove themselves discerning. Instead they had huddled together all night, one of them writing things down on paper, then a few days later, just after she had started walking in her scarves up and down the Rossmarkt, one of them had bundled her into a cart and brought her home. Then later that night her husband had persuaded her into the cart again and taken her to this place that was supposed to be a home for the wealthy, but clearly wasn't. Her gratitude at being fed, clothed and rested was short lived. When, she demanded, would she meet the wealthy owner of this establishment? One of them tried to convince her that the small bearded man was the man in charge, but his trousers were worn and his waistcoat was drab. When she had protested to the wench called Angelika, the girl had told her that she was ill, and before she could meet the wealthy owner she would have to become healthy.

Now she finds all this difficult to remember. Her past life in the open air is only the vaguest of memories. When her husband visits she often fails to recognise him unless he is wearing the red scarf she gave him once when she lusted after him. These days she lusts after every man. She will proposition each one that she comes across in the most unsubtle way by lifting up her skirt above her waist. Some days this causes Angelika to laugh, other days she slaps her and calls her a slut.

As soon as Angelika has closed the door and the women are left in darkness Lise starts on her secret vice. Not even Angelika has discovered this one yet. Lise plunges her hands into the place where she had once found the chancre, inspecting and feeling for lumps or places sore to the touch. When they find nothing she allows them to stay there, her fingers moving like the restless legs of spiders. She groans once. It is a soft sound, barely above a murmur, but Grete snorts and turns over in her bed. Lise holds her breath, counts to five and then lets it out carefully; a long and low sigh into her pillow. She waits for a few moments and then allows the spiders to begin their work again. This time her groan is loud enough for the door to open. It is just five short steps from the door to Lise's bed. Angelika grips a corner of Lise's blanket and pulls it sharply upwards.

In the nothingness a sudden sound. A cry. Flesh against flesh. Then footsteps: one, two and the bed creaking again. And then a quiet; a quiet filled with hurting. On and on. Someone breathing in with short quick gasps and not breathing out. And then another hurting. One that will not go. It creeps up with careful feet. A forest. The birds made silent with screaming. I open her mouth and she drowns the sobs with a noise of her own.

Since it is not yet April the patients of this place are allowed to sleep in until eight o'clock. In a few weeks they will have to heave their complaining bodies from bed an hour and a half earlier. According to the principles of dietetics, which guide current practice in all the asylums for the insane, it is important that everything is disciplined and regular. Only if the mad can rely on a predictable regime will they be soothed from their illness. It is important to maintain a balance between work and sleep, and important to follow the seasons; light and dark, warmth and cold.

Angelika opens the door so ferociously that it bangs against Ingrid's bed. The idiot cries out hoarsely then opens her eyes. Her stare is unfocused, blank. She draws in breath and begins a repetitive deep-throated cry. It takes some time for Angelika to wash her, but by the time she has finished Grete has still not managed to emerge fully from her bed. She has found it difficult to concentrate this morning. The disturbances during the night have exhausted her, and twice she has forgotten which hand she has checked and which fingers, and has had to start on the frustrating process all over again.

Angelika inspects the room. Lise is still asleep. She lies on her back, her mouth closed, small exhalations forcing her lips to part in a quiet explosion of sound. Hannah lies still, her body too rigid for her to be sleeping. Angelika's short command causes her to rise immediately, drop her feet over the side then sit at the edge of the bed, motionless again, her head bowed.

Lise has to be woken by a handclap close to her ear. 'Is it late?' she says as soon as her eyes are open. 'Why didn't you wake me? He'll think I'm a . . .' She looks around her. 'My scarves . . .' Her voice rises in pitch. 'I must have them.'

When Angelika holds the bright patches of colour out to her she grabs them from her, then, when they are carefully smoothed out on the bed, grabs hold of the hem of her nightgown and pulls it over her head.

'Cover yourself.'

But Lise is taking no notice. She throws the nightgown on her bed and takes up one of the scarves. Then, appearing to concentrate deeply, she begins to wrap it around herself: around her chest, crossing over and then going back around again.

Angelika looks about the room and sighs. Grete is standing by her bed, looking at the small area of floor in front of her as if it is a pit full of snakes; Ingrid is partly dressed, standing still with her mouth open, a string of dribble gathering strength at the corner; Lise is standing in the middle of the room, naked apart from a single red scarf; and Hannah is sitting motionless on her bed, looking at her hands.

'These are not my hands,' Hannah shouts into the sudden quiet. 'Who has taken them?' She turns them over and inspects their upper surfaces, then lifts them to touch her face. 'This head is wrong also. Please tell the woman who brought me here to give them back to me.' When Hannah stands Angelika's eyes widen and she takes a small step backwards. Hannah wrings her hands, then frantically pats her face and her hair. 'You must go and find her quickly. She has taken the wrong girl back with her.' Hannah runs at Angelika, grips her by the shoulders and shakes her once, vigorously, and then again more weakly. Then she clutches her hands to her own head and pulls. Angelika watches as she removes clumps of hair, crying out as she does so. Then her legs buckle, and her arms flail. She forms fists with her hands and strikes out, but as she does so she sinks lower and lower until she is on her knees at Angelika's feet, still hitting out with her fists but now groaning and sobbing.

In the house where I live there is another girl. I see what she sees: my mother bringing in water from the pump, the water slopping over, making dark patches on the floor, the light of the open door and footsteps on the stairs, then the room darkening again as someone enters behind her. It is someone big, his brown hair curling over his eyes and over the collar of his shirt at the back. Kurt. I hold my breath. You are holding out your arms, smiling, but I cannot move. Mother, I cry, but she doesn't hear. She allows the bucket to fall gently to the floor, smiles as the other girl skips forward instead of me; nods happily as this usurper is drawn close and smells the sweet odour of his sweat. Mother. I scream into her face. What have you done? But she just smiles and raises her hand. Why are you pretending that this strange girl is me? But she doesn't hear. Listen, I say, and shut my eyes so I cannot see the soft parts where my fists are striking again and again. Behave yourself, she says in a voice that belongs to someone else. She takes my hands.

She holds them down. I can hear my voice screaming so loud it hurts my throat. Be quiet, she says. A hard hand on my face, but my mother's hand is soft. I can't remember opening my eyes but all at once I can see. The door is still open. The floor is lit in a pale triangle. Through it I smell the Judengasse: the stench of the gutter, the smell of bread baking without yeast, honey, milk, cinnamon and ginger. In the distance someone is practising a passage from the Bible. The Hebrew tells of another world; there I would be safe. Kurt, I say, but you are silent. Mother, I say, but she is gone.

CHAPTER 5

From Dr Hoffmann's case book, 12 March 1852

REPORT ON HANNAH MEYER

Douche resulted in stupor. After assistants allowed to administer steam bath with camphor patient exhibited symptoms of mania. Obscene language and raving. Patient restrained for a short time in a chemise and ice pack administered. Patient returned rapidly again to stupor. Ice pack maintained until evening. Pulse 80. Skin dry and cool. Disturbed sleep. In the morning delusions and mania returned. Pulse 120. Patient restrained and for a short time isolated. This resulted in a lower pulse but delusions persisted. Purgatives and emetics administered and then, following Dr Jacobi's recommendation, Mr Galvani's voltaic pile.

Hoffmann looks at the parcel recently arrived from Dr Jacobi at the Siegburg asylum and wonders where to place its contents. Almost as soon as it was built the Frankfurt asylum became overcrowded. There is not a single room in the entire establishment that is not already taken. The place is over-stuffed with the insane and their assistants. It is a phenomenon seen throughout the whole of western Europe and the civilised parts of America; it is as though the presence of an asylum entices people into madness. As new wings are built so the insane crawl out of their hovels and mansions to fill them. The new building for the epileptics was almost immediately inundated with the more generally insane, the house bought for the women melancholics extended to take more as soon it was acquired. It is something Hoffmann and his colleagues discuss with each other at length through the misleading intimacy of their new journals on psychiatry. The number of mad is growing, they say, and tease each other to provide reasons. Urbanisation causes anxiety, say the town doctors, looking up from their town council statistics; people are forced to live unnaturally in crowded conditions and in unhealthy, polluted air. They become tense and withdrawn, their nerves crackle and then disintegrate. But the conditions in the countryside are no better, retort their rural companions. There is as much poverty here as there is in the town and it is getting worse. The strain doesn't take long to show. Madness is everywhere, and always has been. It used to be hidden away in the backs of houses. It used to be chained down in stables and sheds. It used to be caged in baskets hired out from the town council and placed in the living spaces of their slightly saner relatives. It used to be confused with poverty and criminality and dwelt in filth and terror in prisons and poorhouses. On rare occasions it has been revered as holiness, its victims deified or vilified as possessed. The mad were either visionaries or the familiars of Satan, supremely blessed or adamantly damned.

Some of the old ideas hold sway. Hoffmann knows that some of his respected colleagues in Prussia still confuse insanity with immorality. Not Jacobi, of course, he is a somaticist, a man of science, but there are others whose ideas still belong to the romance of the last century. Hoffmann snorts, experimentally lifts the parcel, testing its weight, and drops it quickly back on his desk. Heinroth in Leipzig, for instance, believes it is just a matter of control. All that is needed is a little moral training and those with sickness of the soul will be forever cured. It is just a question of enabling the higher human mind to gain control of its baser animal instincts. Psychists! Hoffmann snorts again. How can the soul be ill? If it is part of the Divine Healer, how can part of Him be corrupt? They do not consider the importance of physical illness. Hoffmann eyes his case book on the shelf in front of him. In every case it is quite clear to him that the disturbance of the mind has been brought on by a disturbance of the body. Cure that and recovery quickly follows, but the psychists do not agree. No doubt they would either dismiss Jacobi's gift as an example of quackery, or utilise it as a form of punishment when the patient allows his animal side to take control; whereas Hoffmann, although not convinced by his esteemed colleague's latest idea, is curious. Underneath the hefty wrappings of paper is a wooden box. The lid is sealed with wax and a couple of tacks. Hoffmann works at it until he can prise it away. The box is partitioned unequally and stuffed with straw. Clearing away the stalks, Hoffmann can see and feel the glint and coldness of glass. It is a tube, the walls curving together at the end to form a lip, and inside the tube, a grey metal. Galvani's pile. Hoffmann has waited a long time to see one so close. He plunges his hands in, carefully curving them around the glass, and pulls. It is heavier than he expected. He grips tightly, his hands sticky on the glass, and pulls again. It comes out cleanly this time, the straw rustling as it moves. Standing now, he lifts it clear of the box and places it slowly on the desk, then steps back. At the bottom a wire has been fused into the glass and pokes out a thumbnail's length from the tube. Inside, this wire is joined to the first of a series of metal plates. Hoffmann examines it for a few minutes, tipping his head and stepping from one foot to the other to see right around it, but it is the same in all aspects. Then he looks again in the box.

He finds the lid wrapped up in a cotton handkerchief – glass again with another wire fused through, a hook at both ends, one for attaching to the top metal plate inside, the other outside the tube. Beside the lid there are wires and instructions. Hoffmann inspects the writing. The script is old fashioned and looped: Jacobi's instructions on how to assemble the pile. A quantity of sulphuric acid is also needed, some absorbent material cut to size, as well as, of course, a suitable patient.

Hoffmann sits down on his chair, stroking his beard. A recalcitrant patient, Jacobi suggests, obviously curable but the recovery proving to be slow. Hoffmann's slight frown disappears. His hands vanish into the box again and, humming a tune that is half hymn, half anthem, he withdraws rubber-cased wires, copper electrodes, and a small brown glass vial. Hoffmann consults Jacobi's notes again: nitric acid. The patient must be prepared in advance. Jacobi recommends blistering behind the ears. This dilution he has found to be ideal. Of course, it takes a few days for sufficient exfoliation to take place. Just the upper epidermis needs to be removed.

Hoffmann picks up the bell on his desk. He had been hoping to make a start today. If there must be a delay he had better start immediately.

'Ah, Frau Antoni, the very person. Would you find Angelika, please, and tell her to bring her new charge to see me as soon as possible?'

'You want her immediately, sir?'

Hoffmann smiles and nods his head.

'It can't wait a few minutes?'

'No, Frau Antoni, I need her now.'

Hoffmann sits back, noting with amusement the two floury streaks outlining each buttock on the back of the woman's black dress as she moves reluctantly towards the door. No doubt he has interrupted her baking again. When the door closes he stands again at his desk and repacks everything apart from the vial into the box. He will have to conduct his experiment in here. It is not a very satisfactory solution but it will have to do.

She moves, this girl that is pretending to be me: moves between forest and street without effort. Sometimes she is even here beside me. I see her out of the corner of my eye: an image, a shadow, a face. She looks like me. When she smiles it is not a kind smile, but a sad, taunting one. With the face come lies. I will not take him, she says, or this will not hurt.

She sews like I sew. Her stitches point the same way and her needle catches the light in time with mine. When my customers talk to her they think they are talking to me. Wonderful work, they say, and she simpers. Maybe I simpered too.

My mother brings her my books and when she has finished my work she receives the kisses that should be mine. They are light things, resting like some brilliantly coloured insect on my head. It will not hurt, she says, and strokes the skin behind my ears. This does not hurt, she says in a voice that I know. But the insects sting. They bite tiny holes and inject their poison. And she holds down my arms.

Hoffmann inspects Angelika's work: the blister she applied a few days ago has worked well. The skin behind Hannah's ears is red, raw, the top layers coming away like bark from a felled tree. He pats her shoulder then turns to his desk to where Jacobi's equipment is unpacked and waiting. He pulls a cloth band from a box. It is supported by a collar of wire so that it makes the shape of a shallow coronet. A length of wire is swept over the top, and where it joins with the cloth a series of metal junctions leads eventually to two rod-shaped electrodes.

Come, she says, pulling me so I cannot refuse. This will not hurt. Around me, so many leaves, so many branches. She pulls me forward, pushes me down, and I become entangled. From the twigs come crawling insects seeking out their friends. She holds me there. She makes a crown from thorns and presses it over where the insects lie. They sting again. This will not hurt. A man's voice now. If I could peer through the leaves I would see him. Not Kurt. You would not do this. You would kiss my hurt away. The leaves are turning into soil. I can smell them: brown and blond like her hair.

'This will not hurt.' Wearing gloves, Hoffmann accidentally touches one electrode with another. There is a spark and a short, sharp whiff of burning rubber. Hannah's scream jerks her head away so violently that the complicated headdress is dislodged. She shuts her eyes, screws them up, so her eyelashes are almost hidden in the folds of her lids. She clenches her fists and thrusts them down hard on her lap.

'*Shema Yisrael, Adonai Elohainu, Adonai Echad* . . .'

'What is she saying, sir?'

Hoffmann finishes readjusting the headdress and listens to her whispers. 'Hebrew. Some sort of prayer.' He looks at the girl. She seems paler than ever. His hands hover uncertainly over the electrode near her ear. But Jacobi has claimed some success with this method. He shifts position slightly, so he is standing directly in front of her, squatting so he can hold her eyes level in his.

'Hannah, look at me.'

Her eyes do not open. Instead her voice becomes louder. '*V'ahavta et Adonai Elohecha.*' Her voice rests a while on each syllable.

'Hannah!' The doctor's voice is louder.

Her eyes open. For a few seconds he knows that she sees him.

'You know that I am trying to help you?'

She nods, her face white and rigid.

'Good. Now listen to me, this treatment will make you feel better. It is a little frightening maybe, but if you will just sit still, this will all be over very quickly.'

'But the Devil was laughing in my ear! It must be the Devil. Only He would do such things.'

'Nonsense.' Hoffmann tuts, turning to examine the connections to the pile.

'He sent insects to sting me, and then He . . .'

'Just sit still.' Then, holding the girl's shoulder steady with one hand, with the other he reaches for the electrode and draws it closer to her head. 'This will not hurt you.'

I see his face. When I close my eyes I see his face. It is not like the face I have seen the Catholics draw, but something paler. This demon is not from a hot place but from somewhere cold. He parts the leaves with long-nailed fingers. He breathes the scent of burning hair and from his eyes come sparking needles. I hear my father chanting. His voice becomes mine. My God, the soul You have placed within me is pure. You created it, fashioned it and breathed it into me. You constantly safeguard it for me . . .

But this demon will not be chased away with words. He clutches me to him. He covers me in layers of his own, fine and sticky like spiders' webs. He wraps me in them again and again, turning me over. I shall love the Lord my God with all my heart, all my soul . . . The words come louder and faster until they stop. There is nothing there. Just an emptiness that sucks me in like the heated glass of the physician's cup once drew in my flesh and then blood. I call for

Jehovah and then I call for you. No one answers. The emptiness pulls everything away. As the small lacerations of the physician's scarifier once yielded their precious fluid, so this cap draws me away now. There is nothing of me left.

As the electrode is finally hooked into position, her lips stop, the jowls of her cheeks twitch and the skin that covers them stretches like cotton drying over a frame.

Angelika finds herself holding her breath. 'Is she all right, sir?'

'Of course she is.' Hoffmann's hand hovers over the electrode. Jacobi has not recommended a precise time in his notes. He squats down to inspect her face. Her eyes are closed again, stretched up into her forehead as if someone is pulling them there, and her mouth is open, the teeth clenched in a cadaver-like grimace. He wills himself not to reach out, not to touch. It is too early to stop the experiment just yet. Hannah's mouth gives a sudden little gurgle.

'Sir!'

The doctor tuts. This assistant's fussing is irritating him. 'Angelika, if you cannot be quiet, you will have to wait outside. The patient is quite comfortable. There is no need for alarm.'

'Yes, sir.'

How did I fall here? I do not know. It is the place where leaves turn to soil, where nothing lives except the small white fungus that grows from dead things. There is no need to move. No need to search for a way out. If I lie still enough the fungus will consume me too. The leaves fall and make no sound.

For a few seconds after the gurgling stops he doesn't move. He pretends he doesn't see Angelika's eyes flick from his face to his patient. He is almost certain that Jacobi recommended at least five minutes in his last communication. He passes his hand in front of the girl's mouth but there is no movement of air, no sensation of warmth. His hands leap quickly then to his gloves. He hurriedly pulls just one on to his right hand and then fumbles with the electrode at the hook at the top of the pile.

'I think it's worked, sir. Look.'

But when Hoffmann looks at the girl it seems to him that she looks back at him with the face of an idiot. All her anger, fear and spirit have been replaced by a void. She has slipped farther down Griesinger's slope of symptoms: from melancholia to stupor. When Angelika offers her her hand she takes it meekly and rises to her feet. Her pulse is weak, slow, a distant flutter, and when Hoffmann tips her face back and examines her eyes he feels that he is falling into such a bottomless place that his hands reach out to feel the solidity of her chair.

CHAPTER 6

Extract from the German Journal of Psychiatry,
1843

OBITUARY: PROFESSOR JOHANN CHRISTIAN HEINROTH (1773–1843)

It is with sadness that we note the passing of our revered teacher Johann Christian Heinroth, Professor of Psychiatry at the University of Leipzig. His major work, *Treatise on the Disturbances of Mental Life* (1818), described how the mind consists of three layers: a layer of base instinct, above that a layer of consciousness and intelligence and, at the top, a layer of conscience. This upper layer of conscience, he said, is constantly in conflict with the two lower layers, which, probably as a reflection of his strict Lutheran upbringing, he referred to as sin. According to our most learned professor it is these sins which drive the soul down to lower levels. It is then that the mind, and therefore the body (both are parts of the same entity), becomes ill. Therefore, in order to treat the insane it is necessary to show, by example, a healthy and religious life.

We continue our master's work in the treatment of our patients here at Leipzig, and it is a credit to him that many of our patients make considerable progress and often recover to lead exemplary lives in the world outside. Following Professor Heinroth's recommendations we assess each patient most carefully; we provide a diagnosis and prescription; and then we guide them back to health with the gentlest of therapies. We have found it of greatest benefit to talk to our patients on a regular basis. We discuss with them the conduct of their lives and show how, in the future, their conscience might best gain precedence in the face of all temptations. For some patients this type of moral therapy is all that is needed. For others, of course, more severe methods are required: shock baths, restraint in chairs or on beds, or sometimes punishment in the form of revolving chairs or wheels have all been found to be of benefit. It is remarkable how quickly some patients see the profit in allowing their conscience to hold sway after these therapies. If they can talk, they declare most vehemently that they will no longer go astray; if they cannot, they often lead a life of calm and increased tranquillity.

There is nothing else left to do. Hoffmann slumps back in his chair and goes through the list in his head, then opens his case book and goes through the list again. He has tried everything: the douche, ice packs, restraint, emetics, purgatives, blisters and plasters on the head and chest, bloodletting and even a little galvanism. But nothing has caused the girl to come anywhere near a crisis and therefore a cure. In fact she seems to have retreated; her movements have become slow and her eyes dull and vacant. It is as though she is a puppet, compliant, made from wood or papier mâché, hollowed out and completely empty inside. Now that he is alone he allows his face to show defeat. There is so little room in this place: how he would love to be able to offer warm baths, hours of edifying labour in the open air, bracing walks or even just pleasant spirit-enhancing views. He thumps the book shut again. Yet he is sure that this girl is curable. Even though the melancholia has now become more entrenched he is sure that the right therapy will lift her stupor and that she could be returned to her mother smiling and talking. He had been quite certain that her stay in the asylum would be just a matter of months, three months at the most; so confident in fact that he had made a little bet with Antoni. Now, whenever they pass the girl together, Antoni gives him a knowing little wink. 'And how are you today, my little flower?' he says to the girl, knowing he will initiate no response. 'Not much improvement I would say, Herr Doctor?' Then he walks ahead, jangling whatever change he has in his trouser pocket.

Hoffmann shoves the papers on his desk away from him so violently that some of them fall to the floor. A whole guilder. How could he have been so foolish as to have wagered a whole guilder? If Therese finds out she won't speak to him for a week. His wife made her disapproval of his last little bet abundantly clear and gave her confident opinion at the time that it would never happen again.

He rings his bell angrily and summons Frau Antoni. She obviously knows about her husband's wager because when he asks her to summon Angelika and the new girl she allows a pleased little grin to appear on her lips.

'You mean you want me to go now, sir?'

When Hoffmann nods, she sighs and bustles away.

Hannah is still the new girl. There has been an unusual lull in admissions. Except for the strange case brought in last week – a man who insists he is a woman – the composition of the place is exactly as it was when the girl entered a month ago. No one else has been admitted but no one has been cured either. He flicks through to the case notes of the newest patient: Josef Neumann. Hoffmann had stripped the young man down to his bare essentials, and thus exposed, the gentleman had had to admit that there could be no doubt that he was indeed a man.

'But I don't feel a man,' he had wailed at last, trying to cover up the offending evidence with a long bony hand. 'In spite of this, this aspect of me, I am much happier dressed as a woman.'

Then he had asked for his clothes back, but Hoffmann

had ensured that the grinning Tobias had tied them all in a sack and taken them away: they were far too fine to be destroyed. The man was of a delicate build, and had persuaded some poor dressmaker to fashion him a set of beautifully fitted clothes; even Therese would not have turned her nose up at them. There was a blue brocade dress, the bodice boned to give it shape, a pair of blue silk slippers, a series of lace-trimmed petticoats, a delicate chemise, a corset with the laces left loose, even, Hoffmann noticed silently, Tobias less so, a pair of woman's pantaloons, joined at the waist, but with the crotch, front and back, left open.

In return Josef had been offered a pair of plain brown woollen trousers, a white cotton shirt and a black knitted waistcoat.

'I can't wear these!'

But Hoffmann had made it clear that he had no other option. They had left him alone with the clothes, Tobias standing guard just outside the door, and when they had returned the man had been fully dressed. For a while Hoffmann had regarded him. There was something wrong. The man was wearing the clothes as if they were hurting him, but there was something else too. It was then that he noticed the hair. Somehow Josef had fashioned it into a woman's style: pinned up in a lump at the back, segments at the front allowed to dangle down either side of his face. When he had noticed Hoffmann's stare the young man had backed away. 'Not my hair, please not my hair. It's all I have left. Please, I beg you, allow me to leave it for now. I couldn't bear for this to go too.'

So Hoffmann had relented. After Josef had been taken away Hoffmann had drawn a sketch of him on a piece of paper and added it to his notes. He looks at it now. He is quite pleased at the way he has captured the expression on the man's face. Josef had no chin to speak of, and above it his lips seemed permanently drawn into a Cupid's bow. Above this the well-rounded cheeks led to most unusually shaped eyes: elongated almond shapes surrounding irises of the most stunningly intense blue Hoffmann had ever seen. Too pretty for a man, Frau Antoni had whispered to him later as she had served him coffee. No wonder the patient was confused. Anyone would be. Sometimes, it seemed to her, God wasn't always concentrating when it came to crafting people.

Hoffmann grins. On occasion Frau Antoni is so full of an idea she has to share some of it with anyone she meets. He is rather fond of the little woman and her bustling ways. Almost everything is too much trouble, it seems; she murmurs little protests at most things, especially those to do with her husband, and yet she always completes her tasks with efficiency.

A loud knock at the door is followed immediately by Frau Antoni's noisy entry. 'Angelika is busy with Ingrid, sir, a little mishap on the way to the closet, so I told her that I was sure you wouldn't mind if I brought, um . . . Hannah, that's right, isn't it? . . . myself. That is all right, sir, isn't it?'

Hoffmann nods. 'Of course. I shall ring for you when I need you.'

'Sir?'

'Yes?'

'Well, it's just that I may not come very quickly, sir. I'm baking, you see. My apple slices . . .'

'Apple slices?' Even Hoffmann can hear the saliva wetting his voice.

Frau Antoni grins. 'I'll make sure I keep you one, sir.'

The girl is still standing at the door. When Hoffmann motions her forward she doesn't move, so he gently directs her towards the chair with his hand on her back. There is little resistance. When he presses on her shoulder she sits. It is the easy chair, well padded and with high wings either side.

It is the one Hoffmann uses if he has to read one of the long and tedious reports from one of the councillors in town.

'Are you comfortable, Hannah?'

She makes no response.

For a minute he inspects her, then walks behind the chair and pulls out a footstool. He helps her to sit farther back in the chair and places her feet on the stool.

'Now you are comfortable,' he says, then, humming quietly to himself, sits behind his desk.

Since nothing has worked he will do this. Even though he is a somaticist and believes that insanity is a physical illness of the brain, he will try this. He will try Heinroth's moral therapy and prove to himself that it does not work. After all, it can do little harm. All he has to do is to get the girl to talk.

But she will not talk. He tries every question he can think of but the girl makes no reply. She sits exactly where he has placed her and says nothing. He looks at his watch. He has allowed himself an hour, and half of this has gone already. It is a little extravagant when there are so many other patients who require his attention, but he has decided that he will give Hannah an hour of his time every day for a week and see whether there is any improvement. It is not just a question of Antoni's guilder, he tells himself, it is a question of pride. He has promised so many people that the girl will soon be well – her mother, her rabbi, her Jewish doctor and Antoni – that it must be so. Also he has told himself, one person he hates to disappoint.

'It seems to me, Hannah,' he says at last, 'you are a little sad.' Not even a question, but there seems to be little point in asking any more just now.

'I was sad once. A long time ago now, when I was about your age.' He stops. Her eyelid flickered. He is sure her eyelid flickered just then. Perhaps she is interested.

'I studied medicine in Heidelberg, you see. You know Heidelberg? A pretty little place, isn't it? But perhaps you've never been there.' Of course she hasn't, he chides himself, she is just a poor Jewish girl; it is highly unlikely that she has ever been out of Frankfurt at all.

'Well, Heidelberg is a very fine place to study medicine, but it has one major disadvantage: there are no patients. That is not entirely true, I suppose. There was a clinic where we could watch more experienced doctors at work sometimes, for a fee, but it was very small . . . the trouble with Heidelberg was that there was nowhere for us to practise being real doctors.'

He pauses again. There is no reason at all why she should be interested in this, and that promising flicker of the eyelid has not been followed by another. He decides to continue anyway. 'So I persuaded my father that I should complete my studies elsewhere. Eventually I ended up in Paris, watching operations. I had this idea I'd be a surgeon then, you see. So I went to the big Paris hospitals. There is not much to see really, you know. There were so many of us jammed in, looking down. Such a little table and so many heads, all of them in the way. We used to get so frustrated. What were they doing? "Heads," someone would shout, and there would be a parting, like Moses, Hannah, dividing the seas, and we would have a glimpse of someone and their insides . . .'

He stops again. He shouldn't be telling her all this. He is sure this is not the calming talk Heinroth had in mind. For a few seconds he allows the memories of screams to pass. 'But before I went to Paris I went to the famous medical school at Halle. It's there that I became so melancholy. You see, it can happen to anyone, Hannah, even a doctor. Any one of us can become ill with too much sadness. At Halle there is a clinic for students. It is quite well known, everyone wants to study there. Even though you are a student you can still take charge of patients. You take down their details.

You make a prognosis and suggest a treatment. Of course, everything is checked. But the only way to become a doctor is to *be* a doctor.'

Still nothing. Perhaps nothing he can say will make any difference at all. He looks at his watch. There are only fifteen minutes left. He decides to talk a little louder.

'It is only the people who cannot afford a doctor who come to the clinic. The rest are too rich to be practised on by students. I saw such poverty there, Hannah, much worse than in Frankfurt. Here we look after our own. Quite often we were asked to come to where the people lived, and I saw such dreadful things. And one day I was asked to visit a woman. She had recently had a baby but the baby had died.'

There was definitely a flicker then, a stronger one than before. He sucks in some breath and speaks a little louder still.

'And when I got there, to this woman's cottage . . . well, it wasn't a cottage, more like a shelter, somewhere you'd put an animal, maybe, one that was used to living outside. It didn't even have a door, I remember that, and part of the wall next to where the door should have been was falling down, and inside it was black, completely black, soot over everything. They'd had their fire in the middle of the room, you see. No chimney, just the fire. But the fire had gone out. So it was cold, and there was the woman, lying there, not moving at all, but her eyes were open, staring at nothing. I looked around for the baby. At first I couldn't see it, I thought someone had taken it, but then I noticed some rags in the crook of her arms, and there it was.'

She is listening now. He is quite certain. He continues quickly. 'I'd brought a box for the baby, but I didn't know what else to do with it, so I wrapped it up and decided to take it with me to the church in the hope that they could help. You see, I had no money at all. I had very little to feed even myself. Being a medical student is so very hard.

Almost no one has enough money. All of it goes on books and private lectures and the granting of favours and loans. You know, I even had to pay for my seat reservation in the lecture theatre! Isn't that ridiculous?'

He is losing her. He shouldn't be grumbling over such trivialities. He needs something to stir her soul. But he can't help providing a little more detail.

'My father had managed to acquire some help for me from his masonic lodge. Oh, I was so grateful, but I had spent all that and I had nothing spare left at all. I thought maybe the church might be able to help. I had passed a rather grand building belonging to some congregation on the way and I felt sure that they might be able to do something. So I filled an old cup that I had found with water from the well, made her take a few sips, promised that I would find someone to help her, then lifted the box and made my way to the door. It was then that I saw him. Well, I heard him really. I trod on something soft and it gave a little cry. It was impossible to see in the darkness. I knelt down and his eyes opened. The whites of them was all I could see. It was a small boy. Such a thin, dirty boy. He couldn't speak. He couldn't walk. He was lighter than the baby's box in my arms. When I gave him some of the water too he took one sip and coughed so much that he couldn't drink any more. What could I do? I couldn't leave the boy in this place with no one to take care of him. So I carried him in the box with the baby. The church said they would take the baby but not the child. When I told them about the mother they said they would see what they could do. She wasn't ill, you see, Hannah, she was just hungry.'

Was that a nod? It was such a small movement it was impossible to be certain, but he continues more enthusiastically. 'So the boy came with me. They said they would allow him to share a bed with another child at the clinic –

after all, he didn't really need a whole bed to himself. But before he could go near a bed he would have to be washed. They said that I should do it. So I lit a fire in my room and took him in there. He could sit for a few minutes but he couldn't stand. His skin was stretched tight over a swollen stomach filled with air. When I washed away the dirt the skin seemed so translucent I fancied I could see his every blood vessel. Above his stomach his ribs throbbed as quickly as an insect's thorax. When I held my stethoscope to his chest there was just the quietest sound: a faint fast wind passing through a tree with few leaves. Then, when I tapped, I could hear a cavity ringing like an empty jar. I gave him the milk from my evening meal. He sucked it carefully from the spoon. He looked so serious and so sad. But I thought he might last, Hannah. I thought that if he were fed and looked after he might grow strong enough to withstand the lesion I'd heard inside him.'

The girl's mouth is a little open now. Hoffmann notices that it has a determined shape, slightly downswept, the bottom lip full though rather pale.

'I put him to bed in the evening, and after he had watched me in silence for a few minutes he closed his small dry hand around my thumb and held it tight. I stroked the long hair that I had spent so long brushing clean and promised that I would be back to see him in the morning. I think he understood. He gave a little nod, as I think you did a small while ago.'

Her mouth closes.

'But the next day I was delayed. There had been an interesting case in the pathology laboratory and the lecturer had allowed us to investigate it ourselves. So I was late. And when I reached the boy's bed there was just the other child there. No one could tell me what had happened to him. It was as if he hadn't been there at all. I kept asking people, had they seen a very small boy? Maybe they'd seen him crawling past them. He was barely bigger than a baby. But no one had. At last I found him. The sister who helped in the night came on duty again and said that she had been with him. He had gone peacefully, without a murmur. She had not had time to do much about him, just simply placed him in a baby's box because he fitted it quite well. I found him on a shelf on his own. Just before I left him at the church I lifted the lid. He was smiling. His hair was spread out around his head and he was smiling. Even though I was sad that he was dead, I couldn't help but feel a little comfort too. He was smiling. As if he had seen something joyful, Hannah, and he wanted to tell me about it.'

Hoffmann looks at Hannah and then at his watch. He is late. Almost ten minutes late. He rings the bell violently. Hannah seems to have retreated again anyway. He is not sure he has made any difference at all, but he is willing to try again tomorrow.

Shock-Headed Peter

Just look at him! There he stands,
With his nasty hair and hands.
See! his nails are never cut;

They are grim'd as black as soot;
And the sloven, I declare,
Not once this year has comb'd his hair;
Any thing to me is sweeter
Than to see Shock-Headed Peter.

CHAPTER 7

Frankfurt-am-Main
3 April 1852

Dear Sir,

I understand from acquaintances of mine that you have in your care one Hannah Meyer. I would just like to say be wary of her. She is not what she seems. Some would have her all sweetness and innocence, but I know a different side. She can be vindictive and spiteful and a menace to all good Christian women. She is also flighty and is quite unable to relinquish that which she has set her mind on but which is not rightfully hers. I should like to warn you to be particularly vigilant when she is around men. She uses her wiles to entice them to herself. I feel I have to warn you about all these things as it is my duty as an upstanding citizen of this free city of ours, and I would not be able to live with myself if something happened that I had opportunity to prevent by giving you this, what I hope to be a timely warning.

A well-wisher

It is Hannah's turn to empty the pots and turn the mattresses. She enters the room with Angelika. They say nothing; they know what each of them will do. It is always the same, an easy sequence, well established. Hannah will see to the pots on the left-hand side of the room, Angelika to those on the right. Then Angelika will take the bucket outside and empty it while Hannah sweeps the floor. It is quite safe to leave her; Dagmar, Angelika's sharp-faced colleague, is in the room next door. Besides, these days Hannah is no trouble at all. She does everything she is told, nothing more, nothing less. Angelika pauses at the door with the bucket and watches the new girl with her brush. She is as she always is, her face averted from her task, her eyes resting on a point somewhere far away. For a second Angelika wonders what she sees and then decides that maybe she is seeing nothing at all.

'Make sure you do well into the corners. I shall be checking when I come back.'

The girl gives no sign that she has heard.

Sometimes there is a window. Through the window I see such things. A baby curled up in rags. A child smiling in a box. I come close and the window is gone.

Dagmar pokes her large head around the door to check. The girl is so quiet, her broom makes the softest voice on the floor. Hush, hush. Dagmar closes her eyes for a few seconds and dreams of trees she once knew. When she was young she used to think herself a boy and led her brothers up to the highest branches. Even though they were larger and older they could never climb as high. These were her moments of triumph: looking down at her brothers clinging to where the branches were thick and safe, while she climbed higher to where the branches were almost twigs and they had to cry out and take notice of her. She opens her eyes, smiles at the memory and, with her usual heavy-footed stride, returns to her task.

Now I see a man. I blink and the man remains. I creep forward and the image stays. A man walking in a garden. A man with a piece of newspaper wrapped around his head like a bonnet, long hair falling out either side, a coat wrapped around his waist so it drops like a skirt. He is picking the first spring blossoms from the trees, piling them on the brim of his paper hat then threading them through his clothes. When all the blossoms are gone from the tree he turns. He looks up at my window as though he knows I am watching him, and when he sees me he waves. I cannot move. My hands are holding something I must keep on holding with both my hands. Is it you? Has someone caught hold of you and changed you as someone has changed me?

'Get down from that bed!'

The girl does not move. Angelika rushes forward and goes to pull her from where she has climbed to see through the window, but then stops. The girl is smiling. In fact her face is lit up with such a beatific radiance that Angelika feels stunned by its glare. She peers through the window, trying to see what Hannah sees. But there are only a few of the male patients, the calmer ones, taking some exercise in the small space below.

'One of them taken your fancy, has he?'

But the girl's smile has disappeared. In its place is the set placid face with its eyes staring far ahead, seeing, Angelika decides firmly, absolutely nothing at all.

Hoffmann regards the girl sitting in his chair. Just at the moment he is finding it difficult to believe that this face could ever smile. It is as inert as it has ever been. But he has no reason to doubt Angelika. 'Just some of the men, that's all she could see,' she had said, 'nothing special at all, just the men walking around.' He opens his case book full of notes and papers. He leafs through until he comes to the anonymous letter, the one slipped through the door early one morning from 'a well-wisher'. He reads it again and glances at the girl. Could it be true? He once overheard Tobias call the girl a whore to that other male assistant, Hugo. At the time he ignored it, but now he wishes he had taken up the matter and asked Tobias to explain himself. He makes a note in his book, removes the letter and rereads it. Then, looking at Hannah again, he slowly tears the letter into small pieces. It was all probably just gossip, he decides; a town like Frankfurt has gossip running through it more efficiently than sewage down gutters.

Through my window I see just enough. The leather arm of a padded chair. A bearded face. The man who spoke before. The one who says he is helping me but then turns into Satan. Then I leave him behind. I enter my place. At its edge are leaves and the twisting of branches, in its depths there is just me and the smell of the earth. It is where I must go and be with all the other things that have perished. My head sinks among the soft domes of a fungus. They shower their dust into the air and I breathe it in.

Hoffmann clears his throat. The start was difficult last time too. 'So, Hannah, last time you heard a little of my life. I would very much like now to hear a little of yours.'

He waits. Nothing happens. Deep within his waistcoat his watch ticks. Maybe he should ask her something more specific, something innocent, something she can remember easily, from the recent past.

'The others in your room, Hannah, what do you think of them? Have you made a friend among them yet?' But he knows the answer. It is quite safe to ask. She has made neither friends nor enemies; she walks among them like a

73

ghost. Again the girl makes no sign that she has heard. Hoffmann swallows a tut and leans back. It is going to be exactly the same as the last session. Heinroth's disciples make no mention of this happening. In everything he has read of their work their patients talk at length.

'Are you going to say anything at all, I wonder?' he says, mostly to himself. He rocks forward, leans his head on his hands and looks at her.

Outside the office, in the corridor, there is a loud thud of wood against wood, incorporating the twang of many musical notes. Hoffmann grins. It is the sound of someone very clumsy trying to be quiet.

'Damn it, I always hit that confounded door jamb.'

'Hush, hush, Herr Müller, Dr Hoffmann is in there talking to a patient.'

'Sorry, sorry, I'm always in trouble here, aren't I? Is that door jamb dented now, do you think? Oh, my poor Marianna, do you think she minded being hit like that? What will she think of me? Would you mind if I opened her to take a look?'

'Perhaps if we go upstairs, first, Herr Müller?'

'Yes, yes, of course . . . hardly the place for opening cases here, I suppose . . . Ah, Tobias, would you mind opening the door again, there's a good fellow. I think actually I left something in my carriage. Oh, you'll get it for me? Thank you, thank you so much . . . Ah yes, of course, Frau Antoni, please lead the way . . .'

The voices fade.

'I forgot – it is our night for a little musical entertainment.' Hoffmann feels he is talking to an empty room. It is so awkward talking when there is such little response. Maybe he is expecting too much too soon. Maybe if he talks about someone they both know.

'Ingrid, of course, will be most enthralled.'

A blink, no sign of interest. Hoffmann shifts in his chair. 'Ingrid, you know, I believe actually not to be an idiot at all.' He waits, as if he is talking to someone else, someone who will express a little surprise, even a little outrage. But Ingrid, they'd say, is like a very young child, quite clean and docile, but still a child.

'All that is wrong with Ingrid is that she cannot understand her fellow humans in the slightest regard: not just speech, but also the things we say with our hands and faces. It makes no sense to her at all. To Ingrid, I believe we are just like all the other objects in her world: except that we rather irritatingly move, and are inconveniently noisy.'

Hoffmann drums his fingers on the desk. He wonders whether he is saying too much; maybe he should not be talking about another patient like this, but he really can't see the harm. The girl is probably not listening anyway, and Ingrid herself is unlikely to mind.

'She used to be a beggar, you know, that's how I found her. She's one of the few patients in this place that I have asked myself to admit.' He gives a short laugh, pleased with himself. 'Of course, I deliberated over it for days. And why do you believe she should enter the asylum, I asked myself, how do you think she'd benefit? I wrote my replies down, of course. In the end I had to petition myself three times, all of it recorded on paper for the council. I thought someone would read it and find it amusing, but no one did. You know, Hannah, I don't think anyone reads all these reports they require me to write. They just like to know I am wasting my time; it makes them feel happy to know that I am filling out forms just as quickly as they are thinking them up. It gives them a purpose, it makes them feel useful.' He grins; one of his favourite topics is the inadequacies of the town council.

'In fact it was because of all their bureaucracy that I first came across Ingrid. She was sitting under their very noses, begging on the steps of the Romer . . . a long time ago now, when I was first starting up in this city. I'd had to come home quickly from Paris, I'd been summoned, in fact. It was obvious to everyone that my father was dying, and my mother, who is really my stepmother and also my aunt, and my two sisters needed me. I think they expected me to cure him, but of course I couldn't. Doctors can't really cure anyone, you know, they just help nature take its course as quickly as possible. Nature cures with a crisis, have you noticed that? A fever, a boil erupting, a haemorrhage . . . any of these things can cause a crisis and then the illness will end: either with a cure or else with death.'

He looks at Hannah. This is not a suitable subject for a doctor to be discussing with his patient. But his mouth is often uncontrollable; an endless torrent of nonsense, his father always used to say. Hoffmann smiles. His father used to accuse him of driving away his customers by sitting on the top step of their house, waiting for an audience to regale with his ridiculous stories of flying carrots and chickens that flew to the moon. Sometimes he'd take him out to see clients, but only on condition of complete silence; you're giving an old man a headache, he'd say. But those last few months his father hadn't complained at all. Hoffmann had sat by his bed and talked endlessly about all the things he had done and all he wanted to do and the old man had listened and smiled without a word. Perhaps he wasn't really listening at all . . . just as this girl isn't now.

'Anyway, the reason I was in the Romerberg that day was that I had had to take another examination in order to practise medicine in Frankfurt. Bureaucracy again, you see, Hannah. Just because I was fully qualified in Prussia it didn't mean that I was entitled to practise in Frankfurt. There were more expenses, more fees to be paid, and more forms to fill in, as well as the little business of a dissertation. Oh, all I wanted to do was to get out into the city and practise what I'd been training to do for the last five years, but instead I was messing around with bits of paper and becoming steadily poorer every day.'

A yawn, the girl yawns. Hoffmann stops at the movement, watches while her hand automatically rises to her lips and her eyelids fall, flicker and then open again. He is boring her! He is boring someone in a stupor. Even his wife would be amused at that.

'But I was telling you about Ingrid.' He is determined to continue; even a yawn is some encouragement. 'She was quite a mature woman even then, but at first, when I saw her, I thought she was a child. She is so very small, isn't she? And someone had dressed her to look even younger, or tried to . . . but it hadn't worked. When I went closer I realised that this was just a tiny woman dressed in the long pantaloons and dresses of a child. She looked ridiculous – all those frilly layers and then this slightly grizzled head protruding from it . . . and she was just sitting there, holding a bowl between her legs, all white layers and ribbons, her dress drawn up around her thighs. She wasn't looking at the bowl at all, there was very little money in it, a couple of hellers, and she looked as though she wasn't aware of the coins and wouldn't have noticed if anyone took them out. She was playing with some material. It was a bit of brightly striped cotton and she had it up to her face and was trying, it seemed, to unravel it thread by thread. When I asked her name she just batted me away, as if I were some irritating fly, and continued with her pursuit. She looked well fed, I thought, and her clothes, although not quite clean, at least did not much smell either.'

The girl shifts her legs; her eyes move, swivel slightly towards his. 'I kept seeing her, of course. She seemed to spend her whole life either sitting on those steps or, if shooed away, sitting by the fountain. Always she had a piece of cloth with her which she was endeavouring in some way to undo. Well, I passed my examinations and became a doctor, started my practice and work at the charity hospital. My father died, I married, started societies, wrote poems and songs, I moved from house to house . . . but the little woman in the Romerberg didn't change at all. Once I tried following her at the end of the day to see where she went but she just took the road down to the Mainkai and disappeared between two houses. After that I used to invent stories about her in my head; you see, she was so oddly clean and so obviously well cared for, and yet she spent her days begging, it seemed so mysterious to me. Eventually it became a habit of mine always to give her something when I passed. I discovered by accident that she was very fond of fruit, so whenever I had a spare heller I used to buy her an apple or a plum and put it in her bowl with whatever coins were there already. She always noticed the fruit immediately. In fact she would fall on it as if she had not been fed all day, but from the look of her I knew this couldn't be true. After several months of this she began to watch for me, whimpering and holding out her hand when I approached, and if I didn't immediately produce something to eat, she would hold on to my coat, rubbing it between her fingers until I gave her something.'

Hannah's eyes are evidently watching him now, and her mouth is slightly open. Listening, he thinks, definitely listening. He carries on, careful not to change the timbre of his voice and to keep everything the same.

'But then, one day, she wasn't there. I went back every day to the Romerberg for a month but she failed to re-appear. I asked people in the Romer about her but no one seemed to know her. I realised then how little I knew about her, and I wished then that I had made greater efforts to find out more. In the end I gave up. There seemed to be nothing I could do to find her, but each time I went to the Romerberg I used to look out for her. Years passed, I became a father, one child following another. I wrote my little plays and books, and *Struwwelpeter*, of course, I wrote that too, and a friend was kind enough to publish it for me . . . so many people have bought it, everyone assumes I am a rich man . . .' He sighs then laughs. 'You know, it has even been translated into English? Ah, so much fuss, Hannah, over such silly little rhymes and funny pictures, sometimes I . . .' He pauses again, glances at his bookcase and passes his hand over his beard. 'Sometimes I . . .' His voice trails away. For a full two seconds he stares in silence at the slim, long white spine lying horizontally on his bookcase, then he shakes his head and looks again at Hannah. He mustn't lose her. It is so easy to drift off into his own reverie. He takes a quick breath and continues. 'Then I took up teaching anatomy at the Senckenburg Institute, the revolution, such as it was, came and went . . . The Romerberg, of course, didn't change. Every time I passed it still seemed a little empty. I still looked, no longer expecting to see her, but then, suddenly, she was there again.'

So many words outside me, on and on, a dangerous charm. He draws me out, his words singing in my ears like a flute. Am I his rat or his forfeited child? Look, he says, and spreads his colourless arm, here is a woman who is also a child. Watch, he says, as the years pass and I change but she stays for ever what she is: without voice, without reason. And the man who doesn't need a pied costume to play his tricks makes me look. He holds my head in his hands and prises my eyelids open with his spiky fingers. And when I see I so much want to be Ingrid: thinking of nothing, longing for no one, my head entirely occupied by how much I can unravel.

'But something had changed, Hannah. The piece of cloth she held was ragged and full of holes, her dress was torn and her legs were bare. And she smelt, Hannah, she smelt of human misery. When I approached her, she batted me away again, she had forgotten me entirely, so I paid a small boy to watch her, and to follow her if she moved, and went to buy some fruit and came here to do my work in the asylum. She didn't move. All day, he said, she didn't move. She went once to squat over a drain in an alleyway, but the rest of the time she stayed where she was by the fountain. When I returned in the evening she was still there. She fell on the fruit, all nails and teeth, and also devoured some bread and cheese. But then, when I tried to touch her, she cowered from me, shrieking loudly when I raised my hand. So I moved away, out of the small circle of space around her, and so, as far as Ingrid was concerned, ceased to be. When the lamps were lit, she moved. She walked a little as she walks now, her head held aloft, her fingers still working at her cloth. Age had slowed her. This time when she entered the alleyway I was able to see exactly where she went. There was a small door, just large enough for her to enter, and beyond that a tunnel. I peered in, it was scarcely big enough for my head, and listened to her footsteps fading away in the blackness. They were steady, unhurried, of course; she knew exactly where she was going.'

Tunnels and dirt, is that all there is? I move from my world to the next and it is all the same. The girl-woman has changed. She has become no older or wiser, merely poorer. I watch her. Only I can see. She is an innocent thief; she takes whatever she finds and then moves on: an amber

necklace, a shawl with an open weave, a small bottle. I
know this air: it is damp and rolls up from the river, it
collides in the warm cellars and causes rolls of fog, but the
girl-woman and I walk through it all as if we can see in the
dark. We walk without stumbling, every step trustingly
placed until we come at last to an empty house by the river.
How does he find us? I just know that he does.

Hannah is listening intently now. He knows that he has her.
He tells her how Ingrid fought and kicked like a savage cat,
how she howled and scratched so that Antoni walked with
a limp for several days afterwards. He tells her how he
searched around the place she lived for clues but there was
very little to tell him who Ingrid was and who had once
looked after her. There were old plates on the table, a couple
of blackened saucepans on a range where some mice were
nesting and a wardrobe full of musty clothing. It was the
wardrobe that interested him, and he had spent some time
looking through the pockets of dresses far too large for
Ingrid, and shaking out shawls and bonnets. Whoever had
worn them had gone long ago and left no indication of her
identity. Some of the clothes were well made from expensive material, and the house itself had been no hovel. But
whether the woman who had lived here had been a relative
of Ingrid's it was impossible to tell. All that was certain was
that Ingrid was now alone and in need of care.

Ingrid. It is a name Frau Antoni decided on for her. He
likes to think that Ingrid was the daughter of someone who
loved her; someone who gave up her position in life just to
look after her. He hopes that whoever it was would approve
of her new name and life. With the help of fruit they calmed
her, washed her and dressed her. At the sight of a pretty
new frock she whooped and her fingers worked excitedly
at the lace-trimmed hem. She became used to her life at the

asylum quite quickly. She proved to be completely continent and so was entrusted with a mattress instead of straw. She slept well; she became quiet and docile, attaching herself literally to one patient then another, hanging on to the cotton of their skirts.

He stops. He has said enough; from now on the tale of Ingrid would become enmeshed with the tale of Lise and the tale of Grete.

'I should like to be for ever a child.'

Hoffmann leans forward. It is her first coherent sentence for some weeks, said without tears or screams. She has a pleasant voice, he notices, low for her age, and with the trace of an accent which he finds exotic.

'But surely not like Ingrid?'

The girl shrugs and sits back, silent again. For a whole minute Hoffmann waits for more words to come but there is nothing.

'You know,' he says at last, 'Ingrid has a secret.'

The girl's mouth opens wider: the single sign of interest.

'Soon I shall show you what it is.'

CHAPTER 8

Flescherfeld 19
Frankfurt-am-Main
10 April 1852

Dear Sir,

I would like to make a plea on behalf of my niece, Hannah Meyer, since I understand that she is still unable to ask for anything herself. It is most important to our family, sir, that she continue to observe our religious laws. In particular, we are concerned that she observes the Shabbat. If you can reassure us, sir, that she is to be excused all work from Friday night until Sunday, we would be grateful. Also, in the matter of food, I have arranged for kosher food to be supplied to her by the same kitchens that provide for the rest of the asylum. There is a member of our community who works there, sir, and she has agreed to pack some of her own food for Hannah.

We are not a particularly liberal family, sir. Our religious laws continue to be of great importance to us. It is a matter of some concern that most members of our community seem to be straying from the old ways in an effort to become integrated more fully in German society. It is not a path my family approves of in any way. We believe that equality does not have to be earned but is the natural right of all people.

I trust that I shall have your full cooperation in this matter and look forward to hearing from you.

May the God that we share bless you, sir,

Leopold Levi

'But how can we do that?' Frau Antoni rests her floury hands on her hips. 'It's special treatment. Who does she think she is?'

'A Jew, I suppose,' her husband says. 'It's important to them, what they eat.'

'No pigs!' says Tobias, and smirks. 'My mother says there used to be a funny picture on the bridge, all these Jews sucking from some great fat sow.'

'It was worse than that, Tobias, much worse. And not funny at all.'

'Quite shameful in fact.' Frau Antoni takes one small step closer to her husband.

'Ah yes, my dear, there's thugs and barbarians in every race.' Antoni finds himself looking up at Tobias. He quickly lowers his eyes.

Frau Antoni sighs. 'Ah well, I suppose if that's his orders, I'll just have to make sure it happens.'

'It's not too tiresome, is it? Just a dish on the tray with the rest?'

'It'll cause trouble, these things always do.'

'But those two old women with the fits and that new patient, Herr Neumann, they all have their own food.'

'They pay for it, Tobias, that's different.'

'I don't see how.'

'Well, it is, that's all.' She shuffles away down the corridor and Antoni smiles fondly after her. How much she loves to grumble! It is one of the reliable things in his life: his wife's

84

ever-lengthening list of gripes. He is sure that it mak[es her] happy, in spite of what she says. It gives her somethi[ng to] say at the butcher's, something to discuss with the middle-aged man she still calls the bread boy when he calls at the door, and it is her small moment of triumph at the dress-maker's: no one's life is quite as bad as hers, no one else has quite as many petty irritations. He is sure that without them she would become quite miserable.

'I'll have to redesign the rota completely, of course.'

'Yes, yes, I know, it's a terrible burden. I don't know how you endure.'

Angelika looks up at Antoni suspiciously. 'Well, it takes time, sir, you know.'

'I know, I know, it's terrible, terrible. Such an unbear-able nuisance.'

Angelika grins, showing the gap between her teeth. She can't hold it in any longer. Herr Antoni has this ability to make her laugh, whatever her mood. It is most irritating.

'So it can be done, then, if you show extreme fortitude and endurance?'

She gives him a small kick on the shin. 'But she will be able to work on a Sunday while the rest of us are in the chapel?'

He nods sorrowfully.

'Well, I suppose that will be all right, then.'

'Good girl.'

As she rises from her seat he helps her up with a small slap across her rump.

Hoffmann opens the door to the women's day room. The room has been cleared of the desks, which have been stacked at the side, leaving a space with just chairs in the middle. In front of the desk Herr Müller is sitting; a large man with short, restless fingers. He is holding a violin across his lap, gently stroking one of its strings.

'Ah, Heinrich, my friend, the rest of them say they will be along presently.'

'I was wondering, if you had time . . .'

'Of course, of course, Ingrid's little treat. It will be a pleasure, as always.'

'And here is someone else I would like you to meet.'

Hoffmann stands aside and then gently shoves Hannah into the room. She stumbles forward a few paces and then stops. Herr Müller stands and walks across the room to meet her.

'Ah, Heinrich, where do you find them?' Herr Müller reaches out and raises Hannah's chin with his finger. 'Such an exotic little pearl, such eyes, such a mouth . . . ah, if only I were younger.'

Another face. Red, flushed, large, stupid. Would I do this to him? Would I reach out and raise his chin and tell him what I think he is? Yet I let him be. It is easy to make him go. I do not have to shut my eyes. He is gone. There. Vanished. Out of my mind.

'Gustav!' Hoffmann's voice is gently reproachful. He tuts and draws Hannah away to sit in a chair. 'You'll never change, will you?'

'I very much hope not! How would life be then, if I could not lust after every woman I meet? Dull, boring, full of woe. Just like yours, in fact, old man!' He slaps Hoffmann on the back. 'Speaking of which, how is that Therese of yours these days?'

'Quite well, thank you!'

Müller laughs at the injured tone. 'Oh, she keeps you on a tight leash, my man. What has happened to you? You

86

never go out. You never have fun. The Tutti Fruttis have forgotten what you look like. Just the other day, Professor Hess, I mean Herr Strawberry, was asking what had become of you. Do you know what I said?'

Hoffmann smiles sadly and shakes his head. 'What did you say, you old idiot?'

'I said the Herr Onion had been chopped up into small pieces and made into a stew by his mistress, that's what I said.'

'Very good.'

'Yes, we thought so. But seriously, man, we are missing you. Will you be coming this Tuesday? It is going to be quite interesting, I feel. A lecture from Herr Chestnut on his recent travels to Egypt. He has made some fascinating finds, I hear.'

Hoffmann shakes his head. 'I'm sorry.'

'Oh, come on, sir, a man has to have a little pleasure in life.'

'No, it is out of the question.'

'Therese?'

'No, no, it's not that at all.'

'What is it, then?'

'This place.' Hoffmann spreads out his arms. 'It requires all my attention and then more besides. There are ninety-eight souls here, all pleading for attention.'

Herr Müller drops his smile and his face sags either side of his chin. 'But what about your practice? You still have that too?'

Hoffmann sits beside Hannah and sighs. 'It goes on, somehow. How I would love not to have it, not to have to do it, it is just a distraction. This is my real work, my purpose in life, my calling, I suppose.' He sighs again. 'But it just doesn't pay enough.'

'Then you should ask them for more, my friend. The stingy lot. Tell them.'

'I have, I have. If I could do only this, Gustav, I could do so much.' His voice has become louder. He is conscious of it bouncing around the painted walls of the room. He stands up, walks closer to Müller and lowers his voice. 'This girl here, Hannah, she is perfectly curable, I am quite certain, but this place has so much lacking. There is too little space, too few distractions. It's difficult, Gustav . . . there is so little else I can do . . .' His face brightens. 'But it makes what you do for us so much more important.'

'You really think we help?'

'Yes, yes, I am quite certain.'

'Well, that is good, is it not?'

'Yes, that is something wonderful. Now, I wonder, would it be all right with you if I were to leave this young lady in your care for a few minutes while I call for Ingrid?'

'That would be completely satisfactory,' Müller says meaningfully.

'Gustav! If I didn't know you so well I'd have to make you leave.'

'But you do know me, don't you, Herr Onion?'

'Most regretfully, sir, yes, very well indeed.'

The buzzing of voices is replaced with quiet. Now I am able to listen to the sounds of my place: the soil settling, the insects crawling, their legs shifting minute stones and grains, a worm swallowing the earth, heaving the rest aside. Here no one will find me. I can lie hidden and no one knows that I hide.

Hannah! I do not need to move. I do not need to see. Hannah! But his voice charms me forward. Look, here is Ingrid.

The woman-child. Her eyes look at me but they do not see. I stare back. Young and old. Knowing and unknowing. Another dark place, hers, quite beyond my reach.

With one hand gripping Hannah's dress, Ingrid reaches with the other for Hannah's scarf and pulls. When it does not come she cries out and reaches again.

'Leave it!'

The small woman doesn't hear.

'Now, I think, Herr Müller.'

A single note, clear, long, loud, and then another.

Ingrid stops as if bewitched. She turns and walks towards the sound as if something is pulling her.

'Look,' Hoffmann whispers to Hannah, 'look.'

I think I see a thread held taut, so fine it is invisible. As it pulls the woman-child it pulls me also. That sound. The red-wooded violin in its yellow-flocked case. Your long, clever fingers coaxing the right note from its string. The sound warbling, moving up and then down until it settled in its place in your ear. But it isn't you.

Hannah is watching, her mouth open, her arms bracing herself upright.

'You see,' Hoffmann says, 'Ingrid's secret: she is a musician. Notes of music stir her like nothing else. The sound of a flute, a violin, a singing voice can divert her from whatever she is doing.'

Ingrid and Herr Müller collide gently in the middle of the room. Ingrid watches intently the fingers of his left hand making patterns on the fingerboard and then hers move too. She holds them up, turns her wrist, the palm of her hand supporting an imaginary violin in the air, and then her other hand leaps up to join it, scraping at the air in time with his. She shuts her eyes, she sways in time, and when the music ends she stays there, swaying a little longer, and then she starts to hum a rough imitation of what she has just heard.

'Not a perfect parrot perhaps, Hannah, but an adequate one. We found out by accident. If she hears singing she will listen. If she hears an instrument she will play it too. Her memory for notes and rhythms is quite remarkable, do you not think?'

Hannah's head drops slightly. Hoffmann decides it is a nod.

'It is what she loves best in the world. I tried for so long to find some way to communicate with her, but found nothing except this. There are never any words, just the notes, and sometimes she claps and dances in rhythm. It seems to give her such pleasure. I try and make sure that before every concert she has this . . . chance of joy.'

The woman-child hums the same tune again and again, her eyes shut, her mouth smiling with such serene pleasure. The man who says he is helping me touches my hand. I look at his fingers: short where yours are long; squatly straight and stiff where yours arch upwards; nails stripped to the quick where yours are trimmed neatly into curves; his still, yours always twitching to be elsewhere. Once I held your hands still in order to inspect them. I turned each over and examined your fingers one by one: on the left hand the grey grooves where the strings had been, and on the right the impression of the heel of your bow on your thumb. Then we had held our hands against each other and compared their outlines: mine a smaller version of yours. You had smiled, and, holding my eyes with yours, forced my fingers into the roof of a single cathedral: my knuckles interlocked with yours, our forefingers held erect, a church, not a synagogue, my joints aching with the strain.

The man's short fingers lift and then come down again. And my eyes travel from fingers to hands, arms, shoulders,

his face. His eyes hold mine, but they are not your eyes.
They are tired, the skin below them sags into bluish pits.
And while he holds me in his stillness it seems to me that
all things are possible. Hannah? The blunt ends of his fingers
press into mine. His eyes are a faded cobalt, dull even
through their film of tears. I want so much to make them
smile. I make my head nod. It is the slightest movement but
his hands grip mine, squeeze once; he sees it.

The Story of Johnny Head-In-Air

As he trudg'd along to school,
It was always Johnny's rule
To be looking at the sky
And the clouds that floated by;
But what just before him lay,
In his way,
Johnny never thought about;
So that every one cried out –
'Look at little Johnny there,
Little Johnny Head-In-Air!'

Running just in Johnny's way,
Came a little dog one day;

Johnny's eyes were still astray
Up on high,
In the sky;
And he never heard them cry –
'Johnny, mind, the dog is nigh!'
Bump!
Dump!
Down they fell, with such a thump,
Dog and Johnny in a lump!

Once, with head as high as ever,
Johnny walked beside the river.
Johnny watch'd the swallows trying
Which was cleverest at flying.
Oh! what fun!
Johnny watch'd the bright round sun
Going in and coming out;
This was all he thought about.
So he strode on, only think!
To the river's very brink,
Where the bank was high and steep,
And the water very deep;

And the fishes, in a row,
Stared to see him coming so.

One step more! Oh! sad to tell!
Headlong in poor Johnny fell.

The three little fishes, in dismay,
Wagged their tails and swam away.

There lay Johnny on his face;
With his nice red writing-case;

But, as they were passing by,
Two strong men had heard him cry;
And, with sticks, these two strong men
Hook'd poor Johnny out again.
Oh! you should have seen him shiver
When they pull'd him from the river
He was in a sorry plight,
Dripping wet, and such a fright!
Wet all over, everywhere,
Clothes, and arms, and face, and hair.
Johnny never will forget
What it is to be so wet.

And the fishes, one, two, three,
Are come back again, you see;
Up they came the moment after,
To enjoy the fun and laughter.
Each popp'd out his little head,
And, to tease poor Johnny, said,
'Silly little Johnny, look,
You have lost your writing-book!'

CHAPTER 9

The Causes and Cures of Epilepsy: A summary of
the findings of the eminent alienist Esquirol,
Institute of French Psychiatrists, 1798

Epilepsy is most often caused by onanism. Other precipitating factors
are syphilis, violent passions, chagrin, anger, fear caused by dogs,
visions or dreams, cessation of menses or healing of haemorrhoids,
labour or orgasm.

Patients are often sensible to the approach of an attack: they have
various sensory hallucinations including that of smell, when a fetid
odour is often detected. They also hear drums or thunder. A most
useful indication of an approaching attack is the sensation of a cold
vapour running from their extremities and proceeding to their arms,
legs, chest, stomach and finally their heads. In this case attacks may
be prevented by applying a tourniquet to an arm, amputating a toe
and generally anticipating the track of the aura with a ligature. It has
also been found to be of some benefit to amputate small tumours, to
fire a gun near by, to violently pull back an arm or head. It is important always to ensure the evacuation of any worms or foreign bodies
lodged in the stomach. Patients may also, of course, be bled and
purged of mucus. A mixture of valerian, musk and opium has also
been found to be occasionally useful. As has the administration of
calomel.

We have not found the following to be of any palliative value at
all: earthworms, the dried afterbirth of a first-born, ground-up human
skull, or dried brain thereof, backbone of a lizard stripped of its flesh
by ants, the heart and liver of a mole or a frog. We have also found

that inserting an amethyst under the skin has no observable curative effect whatsoever.

During an attack the only recourse is to ensure that the patient is not injured, and that the tongue is protected from the teeth with a roll of linen. It is recommended that where possible epileptics should be kept together and away from other patients because it has been found that an epileptic attack in one patient may induce an attack in another. It is recommended that epileptics are put to sleep in low beds.

The night had brought another patient. Even though he had been left in the basement he could still be heard. His yells and screams had kept everyone except Lise, Ingrid and a couple of the deaf epileptics awake until the early hours. At eight o'clock Tobias has still not arrived at his post by the door so Antoni has to let the doctor in himself. Even though Hoffmann lives a couple of streets away in his own house and cannot possibly hear the sounds of the asylum, Antoni sees that he too seems exhausted. He leans against the wall until Antoni has opened the door fully, then treads heavily and slowly down the short length of corridor to the office. Giving a quiet sigh, Hoffmann opens his files to admit the man.

'Do we have a name, Herr Antoni?'

'Someone said Dieter, sir.'

'Nothing else?'

Antoni shakes his head.

'I gather he is secure?'

'The restraining chair, and a locked door.'

It is all they can do.

In the women's room the chairs and desks have been moved back into rows. Lise, Hannah, Grete and Ingrid enter in that order, one behind the other, and take their places at their desks. Their progress into the room is slow and this morning Angelika has less patience than ever. She frowns and helps Lise roughly back to her feet as she falls against the desk; she shoves Hannah hard in the back when she stops suddenly for no apparent reason; she stares at Grete and gives a long sigh as she waits for her to check the soles of her shoes, a recently added feature of her routine; and Ingrid she presses down into her chair, muttering threats that the woman accepts as blankly as she accepts the plate that is eventually placed in her hands.

Gradually the room fills. The breakfast and the medications are administered with equal apathy. Everyone is subdued. At the slightest threat of disorder Angelika and Dagmar bite at the air with sharpened voices. 'No talking.' 'Eat.' 'Sit up.' 'Shut up.' 'Swallow.' 'Now.'

The women acquiesce. Only Lise smiles, but she does not laugh or talk, just looks from time to time towards the door and whispers to Hannah, 'Today, she said. He's coming for you . . . Today. For s-s-sure.' She stops when Angelika looks at her, then holds a finger to her lip, nudges Hannah and winks at her as if they are sharing a secret.

Something is holding me down. It doesn't hurt, it is just there. It holds me down and makes me see: a baby in rags; a hollow lined with leaves; a child with a blackened face, so light he floats in the air; a child-woman, a blue ribbon in her grey frazzled hair; a small idiot dancing; a violin being played without a sound; a screech; the smell of the earth; leaves shaking and shaking above me, not with the wind but with a scream that comes again and again; and then blood rushing from me, filling cups and bowls; and the Devil, all the time the Devil, looking on and smiling.

Today the women are making mattresses. Some of them stuff while some of them sew. It requires concentration, but not too much. Lise staggers to the window, instructed by Grete to fetch more horsehair from the sack there, because even though she limps she is quicker. She peers through the window and whoops: outside on the pavement there are gentlemen with top hats and tails. She reaches through the bars and rattles the window, then shouts wordlessly. Then she stops. The hand that has touched the window has become cold, and the chill is passing up her arm like the icy fog that used to flow sometimes over her smallholding in the autumn. She stiffens, looks down into the street, and one of the men looks up. His alarmed face is transformed by Lise's mind into one that gives a welcoming smile of recognition. Around him the street seems to glow. Lise blinks but it is still there; surrounding the man's face is an aura, as though he is a saint or an angel. Then, before Angelika can reach her, Lise is climbing up, lifting her skirt, hooting and calling, beating her arms and legs to chase away the chill that is creeping slowly up past her shoulders.

Have I lost you? Sometimes I think that I have. I have to try so hard just to remember: your brown curls, the mole by your lips, your eyes, half shut, staring at something past my shoulder, your fingers making high bridges over the strings. Some of these things I can see so clearly, but then they fade and become something else. I am afraid without them. Sometimes I try to draw them on paper but I am not skilled enough to bring you back. One eye, I remember, had a fatter lid than the other. If I looked into this eye I could see it dreaming. The other eye was wider, looked more

*intensely. Did you know I called this your seeing eye? A
seeing eye and a dreaming eye. Sometimes I wondered with
which one you regarded me.*

At precisely eleven o'clock Lise drops on to her desk with
a muffled thud. For a fraction of a second she is still, and
then her head arches up, her jaws lock in a grimace, her
eyes roll back, and her body begins to rock up and down
with convulsions.

*The Devil is watching us. Sometimes he takes one of us and
rocks her in His hellish place. I should not be here. I do
not belong. Something must have happened, a mistake,
someone thinking I was someone else. Someone must be
taking my place, creeping into my life so I am not missed.
What have I done? Why do you not come?*

While Dagmar holds her down, Angelika takes a linen roll
and rams it between her teeth. Then these teeth grind and
work upon each other until through them comes the sound
of a voice that is being strangled. At the back of the room
someone begins to sob.

*The door opens. But it is not you. How I long for your
face, your voice, your footstep on the floor beside me. It is
not you. It is the man with the faded eyes. The one who
says he will cure me. How does he know? He steps lightly
around the desks. How does he know what to do? He
touches the one possessed and she is still. Is he some angel?
Does he dare to fight even Satan? Around him the world
becomes still and calm and for an instant I see you. As you
were. At that moment. That moment. The shadows of leaves
on your face. Your hands gripping my arms so tight that
afterwards there were eight small blue fingerprints I watched*

change colour and wished would never go. I love you. I hear your voice, it is clear and loud in the stillness. It's all that matters, you say. It's all you need to remember. I love you and it makes everything all right. Everything we do, everything we've done, everything we will do. I shake my head. I want to believe you. All's well, Hannah, believe me, all's well.

Lise collapses in Dagmar's arms. Her head lolls forward, her nose bloody, and at the corner of her mouth a short trickle of vomit. Her eyes open and then immediately close again.

'The infirmary, I think. Is there a bed free?'

Dagmar nods. Hoffmann goes to the door and calls for Tobias, then looks around the room. Shifting chairs and tables, he approaches the woman who is sobbing. 'All is well,' he says, touching her briefly on the shoulder. 'Don't worry, all's well.'

All's well. He draws near. I shut my eyes, make one face disappear to replace it with another. One lazy eyelid hiding your dreams. All's well. Your voice coming close, whispering in my ear. All's well. We fall together into the nest of branches. I feel them catching my skirt, scraping my arms. All's well. It is a bell pealing, marking out time. Your fingers moving from their purple prints. Your voice warm in my ear. You know I love you, Hannah. All's . . . The peal is cut short as your lips find mine.

Hannah?

I open my eyes. All's well, he says again. But there is a weariness in his voice. The cloth of his waistcoat hangs loose as if it were made for a larger man. Hannah? He rests his hand on my shoulder and squeezes it. I look up. I will talk to you later he says.

I wait and wait but he doesn't come.

CHAPTER 10

Report on the academic progress of Carl Philipp Hoffmann

DATE OF BIRTH: 8 MAY 1841

Latin: Carl Philipp shows little aptitude for this subject. His understanding of the basic grammar is poor. No doubt his performance would improve if he were to listen more in class.

Greek: The young gentleman seems to be experiencing great difficulty acquiring even a very basic vocabulary. Needs to pay attention and stop interrupting others.

Music: Progress poor. Lacks a musical ear. Will not sit still.

German: Unable to concentrate for more that a few minutes at a time. Verbal and debating skills, however, are good.

French: The young man is easily distracted. Indicates no interest in either learning or practising a foreign tongue. Seems to find the greatest difficulty in remaining seated at a desk.

English: Slow. Tiresome interruptions in virtually every lesson.

Algebra and geometry: Displays no logical ability whatever. Work untidy and of a generally unsatisfactory standard.

Religious study: Incapable of quiet contemplative study.

Natural science: Carl Philipp shows more interest in killing species than in studying them.

Physics and chemistry: Poor memory and understanding in both subjects.

General physical ability: The boy is poorly coordinated and undisciplined. He is rash and will not wait his turn.

Angelika looks around the room. In spite of the doctor's reassurances the women are disturbed. She sighs; one outburst so often leads to another. Madness, Herr Antoni told her once, is infectious. It is why the epileptics are kept separate. It is best that their fits have no witness. She marches up and down the room, encouraging the women to sew. Some of them are weeping and the woman who sobbed continues to do so, rather theatrically, and Angelika gives her a sly little dig in the shin with the toe of her shoe as she passes. It has no effect. The rest of them are motionless, as if shocked into a stupor, staring, without moving, at the walls, each other, or the work in front of them. Only the new girl sews. It is a little disturbing to find her carrying on so diligently, as if nothing has happened. Angelika pauses by her desk and watches her. Her face is placid, pale, shows nothing; attractive, Angelika supposes, in a mysterious way, which must be why the doctor is so interested. Even though Angelika stands there for some time the girl does not look up, but continues to sew, a mechanical stabbing and pulling at the cloth. Angelika begins to fancy she can see a slight smile softening her lips. Hannah's madness is a comfortable one, then, and Angelika feels a brief pang of jealousy. The new girl has commanded such attention from the doctor and Herr Antoni, and now she appears to have access to some happy inner world where no one can touch her. Angelika is tempted to nudge her back into the real miserable one that everyone else must endure.

Something hard on my arm. My needle breaks its rhythm. You are gone. I look for you with every blink of my eye but there is nothing left. There is just the ticking. Just my needle, knocked from my hand, plunged into my leg. There is the thread, grey and dirty-looking like the cloth. And a hand on my arm, holding tight, fingers pinching. Her face pinched too. When the door opens she stands back, quickly. We both look. It is not him. She sinks beside me, her hand pulling the needle free. A stinging pain where the needle was. A small dark stain spreading on my dress. There is no need to wipe the needle clean. The cloth does it for me. In and out. Sewing this ticking is much like sewing the stiff cloth of a man's coat. The needle makes its pattern in the cloth again and again and I do not need to think. I am back with you.

The day passes. Dagmar returns without Lise and the two assistants exchange glances and whispers. Still unconscious. Lucky woman. Looks dead already. Probably soon will be.

Gradually the women are returning to their work and becoming quiet. Angelika paces the room, glad that nothing is happening and yet wishing also that something would. The door opens. The women look up. But it is just Tobias, then Frau Antoni, then the new assistant no one really knows yet, then Hugo, and then Tobias again with his black cauldron of food.

How will you enter this place, my love? Maybe you will show me a secret sign that you are on your way. Maybe you will pretend to be one of them, dressed in blue trousers and jacket, one of their caps upon your head. Oh, you would look so strange, my love. Not like you at all. Maybe at first

I would not know you. Then I would see your eyes – too alive for this place. Maybe I would betray you by my gasp.

I inspect each face, each object that comes before me for signs: the way my spoon lies upon its dish; the way the plate covers my bowl of kosher meat; the way a hand holds it out towards me. I do not look up. There is no need. The fingers are too large. I know it's not you. The plate is resting on the table. Another hand lifts the lid. An O hangs in the air and around it there is silence. This is not your sign. It is not what you would do. It is the work of someone cruel, someone who wants to remind me who I am: a yellow ring crudely painted on a thick piece of paper, the edges made transparent with grease. Jew. A sign from long ago. A ring sewn on cloaks and coats so everyone knows.

I trace the circle with my finger and someone laughs. I pick up the spoon because it is important not to let it show. I ease the meat on to the spoon and move it to my mouth. I am careful to keep everything the same. Nothing hurts. The meat slides into my mouth and it tastes of home. I swallow and swallow again. I will give them nothing. I will let them see no part of me. The spice lingers in my mouth, burning and then changing to something sweeter. I smell it in the air before me. I see its brown dust and my mother grinding it slowly in her mortar. She sings one of the old songs: a place where the sand is so hot it scorches the feet and the bleating of sheep lulls the shepherds asleep. And there you are. Walking through the door of our kitchen unannounced. Just walking in and taking my hand. Putting a finger to your lip and tipping your head towards the door. Follow me, you say, and I do. Into the street then out into the city. It is a long way but I am there already.

Angelika considers forcing the girl to finish her meal but her eyes are in too distant a place. Maybe tomorrow. The sun disappears behind clouds and then buildings. The lamps are lit. No one can see to sew, so the mattresses are abandoned. Angelika and Dagmar clear away the horse hair, pack it carefully away into sacks, and roll up the cloth. The door remains shut.

It is night. He is not coming. That man who fights demons. I thought he was an angel. I will see you later, he said, and as I remember his words something drops away inside me. He has forgotten me. I fall after it. First I waited for you, Kurt, and now I wait for him. So many broken promises. The fall is unending, bottomless; it is a dread that fills me and will not go away.

The supper is prepared: bread and jam that anyone can eat. Angelika and Dagmar serve it out with gloomy faces. From far below the raving man begins his nightly wailing. How much louder voices are at night, they think. Angelika wonders whether she can stand it without crying into her pillow. Dagmar thinks of nothing just to see whether she can. Nothing, nothing, nothing, but there is always something there.

Maybe he will never return. Tomorrow someone will come to me and tell me he is gone. That is what happens. All the things I want, that's what they do, they go and I see them no more.

At three o'clock, when the morning is still quite dark, the man in the basement begins his maniacal greeting of the dawn. Antoni turns over in his bed and finds his wife staring at him.

'Do you not know where the doctor keeps his opium?' she says.

Her husband says nothing but creeps from his bed.

There is nothing to see, so I retreat. I know where I will go: into that comfortable place where you are. I wake, I wash, I dress: none of these require my presence. Your face is a shadow in front of me. I walk along corridors and down the stairs to the place where I sit. I eat. I watch my needle. Into the cloth and out again: stabbing and withdrawing. But this is something seen from a distance. I am here. With you, no one can touch me.

Hannah! he says.

I look at the needle. It keeps on going. In, out, it is reliable, even, does what I say.

Hannah! I couldn't help it. Please come.

Above the needle: his eyes. Tired, a line where the sagging stops.

Come! Please.

So the needle stops. I rise and I feel his hand heavy on my shoulder. The warmth of it coming through. He pushes me before him. We step together. Out of my place, into his. He pauses at the door and looks at me. Good, he says, most pleasing. Something in my life is working.

It would be enough for now if she just listened. Hoffmann inspects her again when she sits in his chair. For a time she is with him, here, in this room, it is obvious in the way her eyes flit around, noting the desk, the bookshelf behind and to the side, the cabinet where he keeps his files, and the charts and ornaments on the shelves above the bookcases and behind his desk. He follows her eyes, and regrets what she sees: the clean white bones of an aborted child threaded on a wire, a prehistoric skull showing an example of early trepanning, a couple of relics from a friend's trip to Egypt and a model of the winged horse Pegasus. He shifts so that the skull and the skeleton are hidden. How macabre they must look. They seem inappropriate decorations to him now, but when he first placed them there they appeared to be so much at home, merely a reminder of his latter days as teacher of anatomy in the Senckenburg Institute.

'I am sorry,' he says again, and her eyes become still, settle on him like a hungry insect. 'There were problems at home.'

She says nothing, but her eyes are still with him. It is important to keep them there. 'Shall I tell you? Would you like to know? If I tell you, would you try to tell me a little about you this time?'

For a few moments her face is still. He thinks he sees her eyes retreating. 'Hannah?'

It is not enough to bring her back. He makes a quick stride towards her and grabs her hand.

Her eyes shift. Lock on to his.

'Will you try to speak?'

A nod. It is slight, but it is there.

'Very well.' He pauses, allows his words to have space and importance. 'Children, I believe, Hannah, are a blessing, and we have three: my youngest, Eduard, a sweet blond little man of four; my daughter, Line, a sensible child, although only eight a little mother to Eduard already; and then there is Carl Philipp, my eldest, my heir, I suppose, almost eleven years old, and, I'm afraid, at the moment a burden to anyone who has the misfortune to care for him.' He stops. He sounds so harsh. 'But I love him, of course, everyone has fond recollections of small things that he has done or said, but it is so difficult when he will not listen and will not sit still.' His voice has become louder. He can hear it; louder and higher. He brings his hand down on to the desk. He notices it is curled up into a fist.

'On Tuesday he brought home his school report, which was dreadful as usual, all his teachers telling me once again what I know already: the same things, how he interrupts, won't wait his turn, will not learn and seems to be intent on preventing everyone else learning too. What can I do? I talk to him, I try to reason with him, but of course he won't listen. Sometimes he does make promises that he will improve but of course that never happens. Then at lunchtime yesterday he upset the cook and then the maid. As well as the usual fidgeting at the table he said something about his food which was not to his liking, something about it not being fit for a dog, and when the maid said that that was an unkind thing to say when the cook had spent so long in the kitchen preparing it, he marched straight into the kitchen without asking to be excused from the table and told the cook that she was wasting her time, that she might as well just let the carrots be instead of cooking them into pulp, that in his opinion they would taste much better raw anyway.'

Hoffmann sighs, looks at Hannah and smiles tightly. 'He says he thought he was just being helpful, he can't seem to accept that what he did was so very rude. The maid told him, and I told him, but he just wouldn't have it. Then I informed him that he was about the age when he might be expected to be invited to dine occasionally with his mamma and myself at the big table, but of course this would be out of the question if he continued to be so discourteous and could not even be relied upon to sit still at the table.'

Hoffmann is pleased at the response. Hannah is listening quite intently, her eyes widening and narrowing as he speaks.

'So when I came in after my morning visits, the house was in uproar, doors being slammed, the maid shouting at the nanny and the nanny shouting at Carl Philipp and the cook shouting at everyone . . . my wife was out, you see, at her salon with her friends. Anyway, it took some time to calm everyone down, and I was just on my way out again to come here when the nanny came to see me. She is a good woman, does more than a nanny should really, and Eduard and Line adore her, but when she came to me in her smartest clothes I knew there was something wrong, and then, when I looked at her face, I could see that the woman was almost in tears. So I made her sit down, and asked her what was the matter. It took her a long time to form the words but in the end she said she would have to leave, she was very sorry, but she couldn't stand it any more.'

He says so much. I cannot help but listen. He unwraps everything and holds up the raw insides for my inspection. Kurt would never say such things. Sometimes I would look into his dreaming eye and wish that it could speak. What are you thinking? I would ask, but he would never say. Some men, my little willow, he'd tell me, have few words.

Hoffmann rotates one thumb around the other. 'Ah, Hannah, Hannah, do you really want to hear about all this?' He waits for her to nod.

'Carl Philipp hasn't always been such a difficult child. Of course, he has always had rather too much to say for himself, but until now he always seemed to me to have a kindly streak. Sometimes, we have such entertaining conversations: ways to arrive at the moon, what might be in the middle of the earth, whether it would be possible to train his brother Eduard to answer in barks if that was all he heard. He has such strange and wonderful ideas. If only people would take the trouble to listen, but no one does. And he is bright, in spite of all that his teachers say about him at school, I am sure he has a good brain. When he was two, Hannah, I made him his book, the one I told you about, the one with a picture of a naughty little boy called Struwwelpeter on the front. You see, I knew that even at that young age he wouldn't care for any of the books I could find in the shops: they were such ridiculous things, nothing to interest a child, full of long moralising stories and a few small black-and-white pictures. Carl Philipp, I knew, would like something with more colour, so I just bought some paper and paints and drew some for myself. I knew the stories very well, I had told them to my young patients so many times. Children dread the visit of the doctor, and who can blame them? We prod them, make them bleed or itch, even give them potions to make them sick. A story or two, I often found, helped them relax, sometimes even made them smile. So thinking up stories for Carl Philipp was easy. He loved it at once. In less than a month he could read the words below the pictures fluently. I swear it, every word, clear and correct. It gave me such pleasure to have him sitting on my lap, his warm little body curled up against mine, saying my words and pointing to my pictures . . .'

He stops, looks at Hannah with wide eyes. 'Recently something changed. He has become wilful and disobedient. Yesterday he took a knife from the cook's drawer and proceeded to throw it at the table. When the cook asked him to stop he took no notice so she called the nanny. When the nanny said there would be no supper if he didn't cease immediately he just plunged the knife into the wood in front of him and told her she was an ugly old woman, and that was doubtless why no one had asked her to marry her. Her nose, he said, was like a witch's, her voice was like a nail being passed over slate and his mother had said that she had the worst complexion she had ever seen in her life. I think it was the last thing he said that really hurt the woman. As soon as she finished reporting all that he had said she burst into tears.'

He drops his head and then shakes it slowly. 'It's terrible, terrible,' he says, 'such an insolent tongue in the child. My wife, she says that he takes after me, of course . . .' He stops himself. He leans forward at his desk and rests his head on his hand. His face is twisted as though he has something sour in his mouth and he wants to spit it out.

He keeps me from my other place. It is as though he is holding my hand, and even though I twist and pull he holds me fast with his secrets and the things he should not be telling: a wicked child he cannot own; a wife who lashes him with her clever tongue; a household that has him by the neck and is squeezing tight. I listen. I need to hear the end. He relaxes his grip. He takes another breath.

'But although I've always talked, Hannah, I don't think I've ever said such rude and hurtful things, even as a child ...' Why does his wife always make this comparison? But Carl Philipp is her son too. He remembers his entrance into the world, and his own tender feelings towards Therese; she had suffered for so long and there had been little he could do. When will it end, she had asked again and again as the pains went on into the night and then into the next morning, and as usual he had had no answer. What is the use of having a husband for a doctor, she had gasped between spasms, if he can do nothing to help me when I suffer? He had not replied, simply smoothed away her hair from her brow and, when she could not talk, reassured her that soon it would end. And at last it had: Carl Philipp had fallen mewling into his hands, spraying him with his water, his first action in the world, baptising his father with the contents of his infant kidneys. A warning, Therese says, when she talks of it now, of how he was to afflict us later. But at the time Hoffmann hadn't noticed. Although he had helped many children into the world this was his first son. He had cut the umbilicus and held him aloft. A boy, a fine boy, well done, my dear, and Carl Philipp had given his first cry: lusty, strong, a promise of happiness.

He shuts his eyes briefly. They were happy then. Three

years after Carl Philipp, little Line arrived, and four years after that, Eduard: three fine strong children, well spaced with plenty of time for Therese to recover her strength. He remembers the house noisy with laughter and voices, Therese running to him with Carl Philipp's first picture, his first written word, then one day indicating for him to be quiet so they could both spy upon the boy sitting with his father's book, mouthing the words. But that was long ago now, before the revolution, before politics, before this mental asylum had caught and entangled him with its problems and fascinations. Now he comes home to criticisms, almost every time Therese sees him she greets him with a complaint: the house is too small and its location too noisy; his children are idle and rude; his mother too interfering and demanding; he himself has become boring with no interest beside his work . . . the list, it seems, is endless. The only thing that seems to bring her any sort of happiness is her time at the salon with her friends. They at least, apparently, have something interesting to say. He sighs and Hannah looks at him with a little curiosity and, he thinks, understanding. It is so comforting to tell her, to tell anyone at all without any interruption.

I wait for him to continue but nothing comes. There are words he does not speak. Hold me here, I want to tell him, hold me here with your secrets and I will stay.

'But I must get back to my story. The only way I could persuade the nanny to stay, after an hour spent trying to placate her, was to give her a substantial pay rise, and then of course she told the maid and the maid told the cook and now they all want a pay rise too. The cook calls it 'the Carl Philipp guilder' because it is such a trial to everyone to have to live in the same house as him!'

He smiles down at the table and traces its grain with a

finger. He needs to say more to make the story complete. 'Then when Therese came back and added everything up she discovered that my promises had made us quite significantly poorer, so poor in fact that she would have to cancel a trip to a health spa she had promised herself some time ago with her friends from the salon.'

It is not enough to keep me. I hear other secrets; whispers drawing me away. My father in the room behind the shop counting his money. The clink, clink, clink of too-small coins hitting the plate. Is that all they paid? My mother showing her disapproval of them and him with a snort. You are too soft with them, Mosche, if this goes on we will not be able to afford to eat. Then my father's eyes on mine. Shh, the child will hear. She needs to know, Mosche, needs to know how useless her father is, how he is too frightened to take what is his.

'My wife, Hannah, is a very determined woman. She thinks there has to be another solution to all this, and if I can't think of anything then she will.' He glances across at her, wondering what she makes of all this. As usual he has probably said too much. He looks uneasily around the room, reassuring himself. Hannah is very unlikely to repeat what he has said to anyone and at least she is still listening. But Heinroth, he is sure, would never have talked about his domestic problems to anyone. Heinroth – Hoffmann grins as he thinks of it – probably denied he had problems of any kind at all.

'Well,' he says at last, 'it's your turn.'

He looks at me but his words have let me go. There are too many other voices calling me away: talking quietly, wheedling, promising. I want to be rid of them all, back in the place where nothing hurts. He shifts in his chair, rests

his head again on his hand, looks at me. He speaks but his
words are indistinct, hopeless, devoid of power.

'Hannah? Will you not talk?'

I should speak. There was a promise. I try to remember.

'Hannah?'

A hand separating weeds, reaching out, pulling me down,
covering my mouth.

'Not yet?'

Words come and go in my head. They are disconnected,
unreal, cannot be spoken. I shake my head. He smiles, a
dim glimmer of white. Never mind, he says, maybe
tomorrow.

The Story of Fidgety Philip

Let me see if Philip can
Be a little gentleman;
Let me see if he is able

To sit still for once at table:
Thus Papa bade Phil behave;
And Mamma look'd very grave.
But fidgety Phil,
He won't sit still;
He wriggles
And giggles,
And then, I declare,
Swings backwards and forwards
And tilts up his chair,
Just like any rocking horse; –
'Philip! I am getting cross!'

See the naughty, restless child,
Growing still more rude and wild,
Till his chair falls over quite.
Philip screams with all his might,
Catches at the cloth, but then
That makes matters worse again.
Down upon the ground they fall,
Glasses, plates, knives, forks and all.
How Mamma did fret and frown,
When she saw them tumbling down!
And Papa made such a face!
Philip is in sad disgrace.

Where is Philip? Where is he?
Fairly cover'd up, you see!
Cloth and all are lying on him;
He has pull'd down all upon him!
What a terrible to-do!
Dishes, glasses, snapt in two!
Here a knife, and there a fork!
Philip, this is cruel work.

Table all so bare, and ah!
Poor Papa and poor Mamma
Look quite cross, and wonder how
They shall make their dinner now.

CHAPTER 11

From the Prussian newspaper The Freethinker, *11 January 1845*

THE MCNAGHTEN TRIAL — FURTHER DEVELOPMENTS

Further to the findings of this most influential trial we have to report that the courts of England have now established a set of rules which are to be called the MCNAGHTEN RULES.

Readers will probably not need to be reminded that in this trial a Scottish wood turner, McNaghten, was found to be not guilty on the grounds of insanity of the murder of Private Sect, officer and protector of the English Prime Minister Robert Peel. This decision was reached by Judge Tindall and based on the evidence of nine experts, including the physician Dr E. Monro, who all agreed the defendant was insane and therefore could not be held to be criminally responsible for his actions.

This, of course, has set an important precedent. The conclusions of the English courts can be summarised in a set of rules as follows:

(i) A man is presumed sane and responsible until the contrary be proved.

(ii) The verdict of not guilty on the grounds of insanity can only be reached if it can be proved that (a) the defendant had a defect of reason from disease of the mind and did not know what he was doing; or (b) the defendant did know what he was doing but did not know that what he was doing was wrong.

It is expected that these rules will become the established law throughout the kingdoms of Europe and the newly independent colonies in the new world.

It confirms the importance of the mad doctors in courts of law and we anticipate serious consequences for all mad houses and prisons throughout Europe. We predict that the asylums will be filled with the criminally insane while the jails in turn will be emptied. Felons will claim to be mad in order to escape the hangman's noose or the guillotine.

'Dieter Zimmermann!' Hoffmann lifts the flap over the cell door.

'You know him, sir?'

'Yes, Antoni, I know him: as a child of ten, as a young man of fifteen . . . he was a patient. His parents were worried.'

'Looks like they were quite right to be, sir.'

The isolation cells are semi-subterranean places situated in the wings of the main building. Each small room sees little light – just a few weak beams of a wintry sun in the very early morning – and consequently each cell has the atmosphere of a cave. Everything is damp; objects, if they stay there long enough, acquire a fine green patina. The raving quickly become ill in body as well as in mind. Lung disease is rife, and as Hoffmann passed the rest of the doors a moment ago it seemed to him that each occupant wheezed as he ranted, and each scream was accompanied by a cough.

Dieter appears to be more peaceful now. Last night, Antoni said, he had disturbed everyone yet again, with loud moans and then whimpering until his attendant had soothed him into sleeping. It had been a twitchy sleep, full of cries and little starts.

When Hoffmann enters, Dieter is sitting perfectly still on his mattress, staring ahead. Hoffmann notices the darkened semicircle of sawdust beneath the man's legs.

.'Hello, Dieter.'

The man slowly raises his head, the grin of an idiot stretching his lips as he does so. For a few seconds his eyes rest on Hoffmann's face. 'My Lord!' he says at last, then grins again, as if in anticipation of a promised pleasure.

Hoffmann frowns. This is not the child he remembers. The boy he knew was mischievous, spirited, a little callous perhaps, but certainly not this almost empty vessel of humanity. 'Are you hungry? Would you like something to eat?'

'My Lord, forgive your humble servant!'

Hoffmann turns to Antoni, who is hovering at the entrance.

'Did he eat?'

Antoni nods. 'Quite well, as if he hadn't seen food for some time, in fact. Hugo said it was a little embarrassing to watch. Quite desperate, he said.'

Dieter is still grinning at Hoffmann, with the demeanour of an adoring dog. Without thinking, Hoffmann reaches out and pats the man on the head.

'My Lord,' Dieter says again, and his mouth remains agape, his tongue hanging loose.

He obviously has some sort of creeping dementia. Hoffmann lost contact with the family some years ago when they moved to Sachsenhausen on the south side of the river. Dieter had been found the previous week near by, in an old dilapidated shed on the city side of the bridge, shouting and kicking out at whoever came close. After the guards had ruled out drunkenness they decided that the best thing would be to request that he be admitted to the asylum. It was quite plain to everyone that that is where he would land eventually, anyway.

It was only after they had removed him from the shed that the body of an elderly woman had been found next to him under a heap of old rags. She had died from a broken neck.

'Do you recognise me, Dieter?' Hoffmann asks, but the man looks back blankly. Hoffmann strongly suspects that he is incurable. Perhaps, with time, he might be entrusted with simple chores. Perhaps, if he were closely supervised, he could help the men who work with some simple fetching and carrying.

Hoffmann gives Dieter a final pat and a long string of dribble gathers at the end of his tongue in appreciation.

'Good man,' Hoffmann says, and follows Antoni to the door.

'That which seems to us blind accident actually stems from the deepest source of all.'

The sound comes from behind him, a high voice, a man imitating a child. Hoffmann swings around. 'Mr Antoni, did you hear . . . ?'

'Yes, sir.'

They both regard Dieter, whose mouth is just as gaping and saliva-ridden as before. Of course he knows Schiller, his father would have seen to that. Hoffmann remembers him as an intelligent man, university educated but otherwise self-made; very much like Hoffmann himself.

'You remember Schiller?'

Dieter gives an inarticulate gurgle.

Hoffmann examines the eyes but they seem to be just empty holes. Yet the man seems so unaccountably happy just to be spoken to that Hoffmann feels a smile spread to his own lips; it seems more like the result of an infection than an indication of his mood.

Experimentally he pats the man's head again and walks towards the door.

'Good man,' he says over his shoulder, just as before.

'He that is over-cautious accomplishes little.'

Twice now Hoffmann has failed to witness this miracle.

'Perhaps he is like a parrot, sir, picking up what he's heard and singing it back.'

Hoffmann nods. 'A previous life,' he says, 'when he was a rational and happy being. A lesson at school, I think, driven home rather well.' Then, looking hard at Dieter, he repeats the words that seem to nudge him into another consciousness: 'Good man.'

Dieter leers back.

'Good man,' says Hoffmann again, louder.

Dieter gurgles and the string of saliva stretches then falls from his mouth on to his knee.

'Oh, come, Herr Antoni, we have others to see.'

'It is the mind itself which shapes the body,' the childish voice calls out as soon as Hoffmann turns away, and giggles as he shuts the door.

'It is the mind itself which shapes the body,' calls out Dieter again as they reach the stairs to the ground floor.

'It is the mind itself which shapes the body,' Antoni repeats slowly to himself. He looks at Hoffmann. 'Do you think that is true, sir?'

Antoni is a short, solid man with a nose so sharp that Hoffmann is always reminded of a bird when he sees it, an impression intensified by the quick small movements Antoni makes when he talks. Now he allows his head to tip slightly so he can regard Hoffmann with one narrow eye as he waits for his answer.

Hoffmann repeats the words silently to himself. The mind shaping the body. The mind making the body ill or well. It sounds like Heinroth's philosophy: the conscience taking control, and the rest of the mind and body reacting according-ly. It is something he does not believe and yet it seems to be working in Hannah.

'Perhaps, Herr Antoni,' he says at last.

Sometimes now I leave my world. Nothing happens. I look out and then retreat again before anything can touch me. Small glimpses tell me all I know: a barred window and a garden below. In the garden a man with his coat wrapped around his waist. A small man with a small head, cheeks round and soft looking like a baby's. When he walks his hips wobble from side to side and when he sees me watching him he pretends he doesn't but he wiggles his hips a little more. A bee in a hive. Their dance. Something I saw once. When you took me by the hand and showed me. It is so easy to retreat, so easy to remember. We meet outside my mother's shop. It is our second meeting and you tell me that today you'll show me something sweet and so we walk to where there is a garden with a hive. Mine, you say, spreading out your arms, or it will be one day. You ask a man standing close by to open up the hive and he does so at once. Even though the bees grow angry and flow thickly around the hive with an irritable buzz, they do not seem to sting. After a while they settle and start their dance. All wiggles and twitching tails and walking one way and then the next. You laugh. You wiggle into the long grass and out again. Your man is standing back, pretending not to see. But you are stiff, Kurt, not like the man with the coat at all. You are awkward like a man. This man with the coat is as fluid and graceful as any woman.

Hoffmann lifts the flap. Dieter is no longer sitting still on his bed but shifting around the room, laughing out loud from time to time for no reason anyone can determine. Hoffmann tries to see the boy he used to know: the one who was always picking a quarrel, who would frequently come home from school with parts of him damaged like a tomcat back from a night on the roof tiles. 'What happened this time?' Hoffmann would say, shaking a leech out of a jar and enticing it on to the boy's black eye with a little milk. And the boy would shrug and smile so broadly that Hoffmann would smile and shrug too. Hoffmann closes the flap. The smile is still there, he realises, so infectious he finds himself once again smiling too. 'They looked at me,' Dieter would say eventually, 'so I gave them a clout.' Everything was quite simple as far as the boy was concerned.

'And this time,' Hoffmann would say later, smearing fat upon the angry impression of a row of teeth on the boy's leg, 'did the dog look at you too?'

And Dieter would nod and wince as Hoffmann bound up his wound with vinegar and a dressing of grease and paper.

'Why is he like this do you think, Doctor?' Dieter's mother would whisper. 'He steals sometimes as well, and once he set fire to a bag full of a classmate's books.'

Hoffmann never had any answers, and now, as he looks at this older Dieter, he realises he has no more answers now. 'Maybe he will grow out of it,' he had said. Obviously Dieter had not.

He had heard Dieter's voice as soon as he had got to the bottom of the stairs, and then all along the dark corridor he had felt him: a bang and then a few mutters, another bang and then a cry. He lifts the small flap on the door and again peers inside. Dieter is pacing the room, muttering something Hoffmann can't hear, then hitting either the door or the bars at the window when he reaches them. When Hoffmann carefully opens the door Dieter stops. 'He that is over-cautious accomplishes little,' he says, and begins to pace again. He reaches the bars of the window, stops and begins to hit them with the base of his fist.

'Antoni!' Hoffmann calls out of the door, then makes an attempt to grab hold of Dieter's hands. They are becoming bloodied now, the flesh bruised and ripped by irregularities on the frame. Each time Hoffmann catches one it is pulled away immediately.

'He . . . that . . . is . . .' Dieter says in time with his blows. 'He . . . that . . . is . . .'

The next blow misses. His hand strikes the stone sill and Dieter leaps back, sucking at his hands and laughing.

'He . . . that . . . is . . .' he says again, then, swooping to the floor, grabs hold of his night bucket and pours its contents over his head.

'Why was this not emptied?' Heinrich asks Antoni as he enters the room. Antoni grins. 'Well, looks like it is now, sir.'

They watch and then grimace as Dieter licks away the trickles of urine that run down his face.

'He . . . that . . . is . . . o . . . ver . . . cau . . . tious . . .' Now Dieter is swinging the bucket against the bars in time to his words.

'Antoni . . . if you please . . .'

They approach him together, carefully, arms outstretched, but just as they touch him he flies past them, swinging the bucket hard against Antoni and then the wall, the bed and lastly the door, running past it, hitting it so hard that the metal rings with different notes as it slams against the wall.

'I have often thought it strange, sir,' Antoni says, as Hoffmann helps him up, 'how the raving always seem to acquire a superior strength.'

'Lack of inhibition,' Hoffmann replies shortly. He reassures himself that Antoni is not severely hurt, then hurries out of the door after Dieter. Once he used to be fit enough to swim across part of the Main to an island in the middle. Now he believes that he would find it impossible to swim at all. His chest hurts and he can't seem to draw in quite enough air.

'What are we going to do, sir, when we catch him?' Antoni is more active, spends rather less time at a desk and rather more time doing jobs around the asylum.

'The straitjacket,' Hoffmann says shortly. 'The only answer.'

'The meek shall inherit the earth,' they hear faintly in the distance, 'they are too weak to refuse.' And this time the laugh seems to be meaningful and quite appropriate.

I am watching for the man with the coat. He is taking a walk before lunch. He seems to be able to take rather more walks than the rest of us, and is required to do rather less work. I think he is watching for me too. When I hang out the washing he is there, testing the clothes to see whether they're dry, holding them up to himself and asking me whether they are mine. A rather nice chemise, he says, do you mind if I try? And he unpegs it from the line and pulls it over his head. Do I not look splendid, he says, alluring, like a prince, and smiles when I nod. What is your name, I want to ask, but although the words form in my mouth I am afraid to let them out. It is better, I think, to drift away, to say nothing, but he catches hold of the shawl in my hand. He watches as my mouth opens and then closes again. He smiles. Fräulein? Do you wish to speak? I nod: it is a small motion but it takes all my will. Do so, then, he says. I am the most gentle creature, no one fears me. In fact no one regards me in any way at all. Then he motions at my mouth with his hand, as though he is drawing some-thing from there, and the words follow quietly in a whisper. He shuts his eyes and pulls harder with his hand. Your name? I say at last, and his hand falls, gripping the other end of the shawl, holding it up and stretching it out so that it covers half his face. Josef, he says, then, raising his voice an octave, quickly turns the word into Josephine, like Napoleon's bride, he says, beautiful just like her.

Letting go of one end, Josef throws the shawl over his shoulder and pulls it around, overlapping it in the front and tucking it tightly into his trousers. He hugs himself, gives Hannah a small, pleased grin and reaches up for a striped purple skirt.

'Let go of that, at once.' Angelika is at the door, her hands on her hips.

Josef gives a little hop, whoops as if he is afraid, then runs three paces to the wall. There he walks his bumblebee walk, hands on his hips to show off his wiggle, his head thrown back so his curls bounce on his face.

'I should like so much,' he says, pursing his lips, 'to wear a little silk tonight, peacock blue, soft and so . . . slippery next to my skin, and before that I would like to bathe in a bath full of rose petals . . . do you think that could be arranged, Angelika, my love?'

But Angelika says nothing. She just marches up to him and pulls the shawl away and then the chemise so roughly it rips. She stops, inspects the tear and looks with slitted eyes at Josef and then at Hannah.

'Oh, do not shout, my love, I hate to see you angry.'

Angelika turns her back on him and calls for Tobias. She checks each of the windows looking out on to the garden and then marches smartly over to Hannah and slaps her once across the cheek. 'This is your fault,' she says, thrusting the pieces of cloth into her face. 'My best chemise, ruined.' She picks up a basket of linen by the doorway and drops it at Hannah's feet.

'A present from the ravers' wing,' she says. 'I want these clean.'

But Hannah doesn't move.

'By midday, or there will be no special Jew's dinner for you, there will just be bacon, and I shall make sure you eat it with the rest of us.'

Angelika gives Hannah a small but vicious shove in her back and the girl moves.

I know it is always there. I know I can go back. But for now I don't. For now I stay. I bend. I see my arm stretch out. But I can do no more. I cannot pick them up. They are stiff with human waste. Every time I go near them I am repulsed, my stomach makes a short journey to my throat and I cannot swallow.

Dieter stamps through the asylum, sweeping away every-thing in front of him as he goes. He is a tall, well-built man, not as big as Tobias, no one is, but his strength, as Antoni has pointed out, is augmented by madness. He climbs the stairs two at a time, up to the men's floor, banging on each door as he passes, and is answered by screams and laughs. He throws a chair against the large door to the men's day room and then ascends more stairs to the series of women's rooms above. Most of these are empty; only the sickroom and rooms housing eight of the better class of patient are occupied, and these are locked. Their occupants are silent. He bangs at the door to the sickroom, aroused by the smell of camphor and brew of herbs. 'Dare to be wrong and dream,' he shouts, each word high pitched and precisely pronounced. 'Dare to be wrong and dream.' It is a chant now, his voice warbling up and down, as if he is following a catechist. 'Hate is protracted suicide. Opposition inflames the enthusiast, never converts him.'

Behind the door there is a loud whimper. He bangs on the door again and the whimper stops. From the bottom of the stairs comes a shout. He turns and thunders towards it, stumbling down the stairs, catching hold of the bannister and righting himself then continuing, his breath snorting from him like that of a bull about to charge. At the bottom of the stairs he pushes Antoni and Hoffmann aside with two short sweeps, stops to gasp in air then continues along the corridor to the kitchen. At the door he pauses again, then enters and sweeps everything from the surfaces. 'Dare to be wrong and dream.' His voice is a shout now, hoarse, the words indistinct. 'Hate is . . . suicide.' At the sight of an open door he roars and beats his way into the garden. In front of him are Angelika, Hannah and Josef, each one of them still, caught in a narrow beam of sunlight.

A roar. How can there be a roar? But there is. And before I look up, something big, strong, suffocating. A hand at my throat. Forcing, pushing. Down and down. Another hand. I do not see it. Just feel its force. Shoving down. And then screaming. From a distance. Not me. I am in my other place. Someone else screaming. Shaking the leaves.

Tobias and then Hugo, Antoni and Hoffmann come running and launch themselves at Dieter, but he throws them off as if they are straw-stuffed toys. Josef stands next to them and screams, his fingers in his ears. Dieter loops his arms around Hannah and pulls. When she doesn't move his large fists punch her: once in the chest, once on the side of her head. She folds, back and forth upon herself, the sound of air escaping from her like that from a bladder squashed flat. Where she drops she stays. Still, pale, completely silent.

I remember another time. It is easy to return. Another struggle but it ended soon. Another day, another year, and I am there now. This time I shall stay.

It is Josef's screaming that unnerves him. Dieter turns around to swat it out and he trips over Hannah's legs and falls to the ground. At once Tobias is on him, holding him down, while Antoni and Hugo tie up his arms and legs with pieces of washing line. Hoffmann turns and kneels beside Hannah. Except for where Dieter's fist has made a large weal upon her face she looks as if she is peacefully asleep. He checks her pulse and breathing and then levers her up. He is holding her in his arms as he once held Therese.

The Story of Cruel Frederick

Here is cruel Frederick, see!
A horrid wicked boy was he;
He caught the flies, poor little things,
And then tore off their tiny wings;
He kill'd the birds, and broke the chairs,
And threw the kitten down the stairs;
And Oh! far worse than all beside,
He whipp'd his Mary, till she cried.

The trough was full, and faithful Tray
Came out to drink one sultry day;
He wagg'd his tail, and wet his lip,

When cruel Fred snatch'd up a whip,
And whipp'd poor Tray till he was sore,
And kick'd and whipp'd him more and more;

At this, good Tray grew very red,
And growl'd and bit him till he bled;
Then you should only have been by,
To see how Fred did scream and cry!

So Frederick had to go to bed;
His leg was very sore and red!
The Doctor came and shook his head,
And made a very great to-do,
And gave him nasty physic too.

But good dog Tray is happy now;
He has no time to say 'bow-wow!'
He seats himself in Frederick's chair,
And laughs to see the nice things there:
The soup he swallows, sup by sup –
And eats the pies and puddings up.

CHAPTER 12

A Short History of our Existence in Frankfurt (notes, attributed to Ludwig Börne (1786–1837), presumably for his treatise of 1808, Freethinking Remarks)

PART 1 MASSACRES, FIRES AND THE JUDENORDNUNG

1241: First pogrom: Frankfurt Jews massacred – by their Christian neighbours.

1349: Plague year. Jews blamed – burned alive in their homes.

1452: Jews obliged to wear yellow rings on their chests.

1462: Jews (200 people) forced to settle in the Jewish ghetto of Judengasse (a gated street locked at night and on Christian holy days). Judenordnung established (regulations depriving Jews of rights).

1600: Population of Judengasse now 2,700 – crammed into the same area.

1616: Uprising against the Jews by jealous Christian guild members. Judengasse looted and Jews driven (temporarily) out of Frankfurt. New Judenordnung drawn up – but still no rights.

1711: Great fire destroyed entire Judengasse.

1728: Yellow ring on chest ruling officially repealed.

1796: Bombardment and destruction of northern end of Judengasse by Napoleon.

1808: New Judenordnung under French – little different from the decree of 1616. Continued repression, inequality and isolation.

The fight for emancipation goes on . . .

Hoffmann has to keep talking. He remembers the heaviness of her in his arms and he has to keep talking. 'The wounds on your face will soon heal,' he says, 'they are too shallow to scar.' He doesn't care whether she listens. 'Dieter will be taken for trial tomorrow. Until then we will keep him strait-jacketed and sedated.'

After the screams it doesn't hurt. In the quiet the leaves settle. A bird flies between branches. When it finds a place to settle it opens its beak. Its call is like the mewing of something very young.

I'M SORRY. The thought is screeching inside his head. It shouldn't have happened. And he drops his head, allows it to sink into his hands.

Kurt turns over in his sleep. The sun beats down. There are streaks of honey glistening on his shirt and flakes of comb around his mouth. The sweetest dreams, my love, I say, and pick up the pieces of wax with my tongue. In his sleep he smiles, then, with his eyes still shut, reaches out with his arm to draw me close.

'Who put this here?'

They stand in a circle, heads hung, mouths shut.

'I shall find out.' Hoffmann stamps out, carrying the paper between his finger and thumb.

When he is sure the doctor has gone Tobias looks down at everyone and grins.

'In Heidelberg, Hannah, I had a very good friend.' He turns the piece of paper over and over on his lap. They both watch the yellow ring appear and then disappear again. 'He was studying medicine too. His name was David Stein. As my father's freemason society supported me in my studies, so societies from his town supported his. We had little, but we often shared what we had. And we worked hard, Hannah, there was so much to learn, it was a rather dreary life of work and sleep, but we both knew it would be worth it in the end. Our fathers had both sacrificed much so that we could become professional men, men with a university education, something they were not, so we knew we had to work hard to repay them.

'But one day, a hot Sunday, towards the end of term, we found, to our amazement, that we had little to do. It was as if we had opened the day and discovered that it had been given to us as a present. We sat in my tiny attic room, we often met there even though it was a rather unpleasant place, too hot in summer and too cold in winter, but David was in lodgings with distant relatives, a rather noisy place, actually, although he did have a rather beautiful young cousin who I was hoping when she was old enough would show some interest in me, but she never did, which disappointed . . .'

Hannah shifts in her chair, scratches at the scab on her face. He is boring her.

'But you don't want to hear about all that. Anyway, this Sunday we decided to go up to the castle; we hadn't had time to go up there yet, even though we'd been in Heidelberg several months. It is quite a climb, and by the time we had reached the top and explored all the buildings and walls we were very thirsty. So when we came across a tavern on the way down I added up the change jangling in my pocket and decided that I probably had enough for two pitchers of beer. The tavern we found was a pleasant little place; the landlord had set out tables and sunshades in his yard, but there were few people sitting at them. It was still quite early in the day, I suppose. We were so thirsty we didn't sit down but went straight up to the bar and rang the bell on the desk there. The man who came out was a colourless fellow, with grey-blond hair and that blanched, creased skin of a person who enjoys rather too much drink. I ordered two beers and he blinked, brought out a jug and a glass, filled up the glass and held his hand out for my money. No, *two* beers, I said, smiling, indicating David, but the man just shook his head. I opened my mouth, I didn't understand, but David just touched my sleeve and started to walk back out past the tables and chairs. His face looked odd, it had an expression on it I had never seen before; resigned, disappointed, and sad, Hannah, so sad. When I asked him what had happened, why the man hadn't wanted to serve him, he just held up his hands so they framed his face. It's what I am, Heinrich, he said, it shows up as clearly on me as a label. I don't even need to wear a *kippa* for people to see it. And then I looked at David with the barman's eyes: his olive skin, his black curls, his prominent nose and hooded eyes. Of course, I knew already that he worshipped an older God, but it had never seemed to me that it should make any difference. I thought the word Jew applied only to the itinerant families of pedlars that sometimes come into town, and the brokers and moneylenders who live along the Judengasse. My reading of Goethe warned me to be wary of straying in there. I kept to my own kind. A Jew was something lowly, despicable, uncouth. But David was an Israelite, a man with my ideals, my education, a gentleman, as different from a wandering tinker as I was from my own humble ancestors. I thought people would judge him as I did, for who he was now, middle class, German, but I was wrong.'

He stops. He turns the paper over once more so that they can both see the gold ring, and then he tears it in half and then half again, smaller and smaller until the pieces are too small to be torn any more. Then he opens the door of the cold stove in the corner and throws them in.

'There,' he says, 'gone.' He rubs his hands together and sits at his desk again. 'Sometimes, Hannah, I think it is the little things we do to each other that hurt us the most. Words, gestures, expressions that ridicule or ostracise . . . these hurt more than a swipe across the leg. Your cuts will heal. You know that Dieter hit you not because of who you were but just because you were there. But those other things . . . they damage the mind and they leave their scars there. They hurt for ever, they are little sores that will not heal. From that day I looked at David differently, I changed towards him, I think, though of course he stayed exactly as he was. I realised that we were not as equal as I thought. He was more than me. I had wanted to rage at the barman for his ignorance. I had wanted to spit in his beer so he could sell it to no one else. But David had just shrugged and continued to walk down the hill. There will be other places selling beer, he'd said, maybe better ones. He could take these insults, Hannah, and not let them destroy him. I looked up to him, respected him too much for him to be such a close friend. We drew apart. Then when we left Heidelberg we lost contact altogether. I have always regretted it.'

He imagines he knows. He imagines he understands. But he cannot. He cannot see my mother walking quickly away from drunken chants in the street, squeezing my hand so tight that the bones rub together, or my father standing patiently in front of his shop and smiling as some woman spits as she passes. Inside he wipes it away. He uses a handkerchief and careful, delicate movements. Then he throws the cloth into the stove. We are all born knowing what we are, he says. Some of us fight, knowing that we have something given to us by God that we must defend with our lives. While some of us become apologetic and self-pitying. We are poor Jews, we say, persecuted for centuries, it has made us lesser men, but we will learn to improve if you let us. He pauses, looks at me with one of his black-brown eyes, a man once tall, shrunken by age, his back rounded by years spent leaning over his cloth. You, my daughter, must not be like that.

Now my father is standing at the living-room door waiting for my mother and me to join him. He still smells of the synagogue: I inhale it as he places his hands on my mother's head and then mine. May the Lord bless you and keep you. We stand waiting as his feet pad over the rug and then tap upon the tiles of the floor to the corner of the room. Water pours from the tap at the side of the cask into the bowl. Everything is special. Each Shabbat unique and mysterious. After my father has washed his hands and my mother hers my father gestures to me. Come. The water has been blessed with their hands, the cloth is heavy with my ancestor's stitches. On the table the bread and the salt lie waiting.

'From then on I noticed . . . I decided to make it my cause. When I spoke of revolution it is that I meant. All faiths should have equal rights . . . I petitioned the council, I set up a citizen association to help craftsmen and scholars find accommodation whatever their religion.'

Outside it is getting dark and the street is utterly quiet, even the birds have gone away. My mother lights the seven wicks she has braided this morning and placed in the seven-armed lamp. Everything is clean. Everything is ready. A moth flickers in, making big shadows on the walls. I sink into the comfort of the Shabbat; *nothing more has to be done; for a night and a day my parents will forget their bookmaking and orders.*

'I even left the freemasons because of it . . . when I discovered that they would not admit Jews . . . It is wrong, Hannah, I feel it so strongly. And this place . . . why should you be charged to have a place, when the other Frankfurt citizens are not . . . why do I have to not mention who you are, what you are, to the authorities? Your community pays their taxes, so you deserve the same treatment . . .'

The bread looks golden in the light of the flames. My father is singing the blessing. Blessed are you, oh Lord our God . . . my eyelids are creeping together . . . King of the Universe . . . I feel myself swaying in time with the words, waiting for the ending when he draws in his breath and stretches his voice to a higher, more joyful note . . . who brings forth . . . my mother smiles too . . . bread . . . 'Lechem,' *the word hangs there waiting . . . from the earth.*

He stops. He knows he has lost her. This was not meant to be one of their talking sessions anyway. He just wanted to apologise to her, to let her know that he knew and he was going to try to do something about it.

It must be getting late. He checks his watch. He should be going home. Frau Antoni has already lit one of the lamps on his desk and he notices that it is lighting Hannah's face. Just before he rises from his chair he pauses for a few seconds just to look at her. She has put on a little weight, her face has become slightly rounder and it suits her, very much, he decides, very much indeed.

As he had often done before,
The woolly-headed black-a-moor
One nice fine summer's day went out
To see the shops and walk about;
And as he found it hot, poor fellow,
He took with him his green umbrella.
Then Edward, little noisy wag,
Ran out and laugh'd, and waved his flag,
And William came in jacket trim,
And brought his wooden hoop with him;
And Caspar, too, snatch'd up his toys
And joined the other naughty boys;
So, one and all set up a roar,
And laugh'd and hooted more and more,
And kept on singing, – only think! –
'Oh! Blacky, you're as black as ink.'
Now tall Agrippa lived close by, –
So tall, he almost touched the sky;
He had a mighty inkstand too,
In which a great goose feather grew;

He call'd out in an angry tone:
'Boys, leave the black-a-moor alone!
For if he tries with all his might,
He cannot change from black to white.'
But ah! they did not mind a bit
What great Agrippa said of it;
But went on laughing, as before,
And hooting at the black-a-moor.
Then great Agrippa foams with rage:
Look at him on this very page!
He seizes Caspar, seizes Ned,
Takes William by his little head;
And they may scream, and kick, and call,
But into the ink he dips them all;
Into the inkstand, one, two, three,
Till they are black, as black can be;
Turn over now and you shall see.

See, there they are, and there they run!
The black-a-moor enjoys the fun.
They have been made as black as crows,
Quite black all over, eyes and nose,
And legs, and arms, and heads, and toes.
And trowsers, pinafores, and toys, –
The silly little inky boys!
Because they set up such a roar,
And teas'd the harmless black-a-moor.

CHAPTER 13

The London and District Diary, *20 June 1850*

We have to report that the so-called German revolution has apparently come to nothing. Two days ago the National Assembly, the Germans' attempt to establish a parliament for all of Germany, was officially dissolved in Stuttgart. The German revolutionary tricolour of red, black and gold is being torn down everywhere by the victorious reactionary forces of Prussia, Austria and Hesse. What an inauspicious end to something that started with such brouhaha in Frankfurt '48! But we can see now that the assembly was doomed from the start: after quickly excluding the tiresome democratic element the MPs rapidly succumbed to that German obsession of bureaucracy. It is reported that all of eight thousand petitions were presented for debate during the parliament's short lifetime!

The beginning of the end came just six months later with the bloody September uprisings in Frankfurt. The assembly had to appeal to the reactionary forces for assistance, and these forces have gradually gained the upper hand in a series of further uprisings throughout the Prussian and Austrian kingdoms. So that by the spring of last year King Frederick William IV could mockingly refuse the proffered crown of the German empire, declaring that he no longer recognised the parliament. Since then the assembly has been gradually dismantled. The whole episode has been quiet and subdued, the parliamentarians concerning themselves with petty matters of form to the end. The Germans after all are not a passionate race. They are like their close relatives the British: they have none of the volatility of their European neighbours . . . (cont. on page 9)

Carl Philipp is going away to school. It is decided. Hoffmann bangs the drawer of his cabinet shut. Decided by Therese. She had written the letter, informed the staff, her friends, even Carl Philipp himself . . . and then she had remembered to inform her husband. It's the only possibility, she'd said, when he had protested. At least he'll graduate from high school this way. No gymnasium in Frankfurt will have him; Fräulein Wolf, a neighbour who knew about these things, had made enquiries. And it's cheaper, Therese had said finally. As long as Carl Philipp is not here, the staff are quite happy to stay without the extra pay. And that, apparently, was that.

Hoffmann opens another drawer just to bang it shut again. You should have consulted me, he'd protested, but she had only given him her dry little laugh. You were too busy, Heinrich. But I'll miss him, he'd said, and she had laughed even more. Don't be silly, Heinrich, these days you never see the child. He tries to dismiss her words but he is afraid they are true. When was the last time he talked to Carl Philipp without telling him off? When did he last take him for his favourite walk? He frowns. They used to be so close; every evening the child would run to him as soon as he entered the house and demand a story or a song or a picture. Now when Hoffmann opens one of his children's books only Line and Eduard are interested. Even *Struwwelpeter* is ignored, and yet Carl Philipp was so fond of that book, so proud that it had been written for him and now the whole world was reading it. Hoffmann grabs a sheaf of papers from the drawer and holds them so tightly they crease. Things will change. Tonight he will endeavour to leave early, complete his doctor's rounds as quickly as he can and call Carl Philipp to his study for a chat. Maybe he can still persuade everyone to give the boy another chance.

He drops the day's cases on to the desk and riffles through them. Case after case is unchanged, with no sign of a cure. Grete Richter, for instance, the frail, beautiful monomaniac, her fascinating insanity expressed in just one way, an obsession with keeping herself uncontaminated. Perhaps just a part of her brain has gone bad, like an apple with a bruise. If there was a way of locating and cutting away the damaged matter then perhaps she could be cured. There are a couple of men who are similarly afflicted, their mania partial and localised: Wolfgang Brun and Ernst Volk with their persistent hypochondria, and that new patient, Josef Neumann, with his interesting case of delusion. Hoffmann suspects that all these cases are quite curable, but then there are the other cases which are certainly quite hopeless: the congenital idiots like Ingrid, most of them kept together and their useless lives managed as quietly as possible; the elderly demented, simply kept warm and clean so they can live the rest of their days with as much dignity as possible; the isolated epileptics whose insanity progresses with every fit and whose condition is thought to be contagious; the raving mad like Dieter, locked up in their rooms or occasionally strapped into a straitjacket or restraining chair; and, of course, the many cases of creeping general paralysis, an inexplicable modern phenomenon that affects mainly men but is also affecting the irrepressible Lise Schmidt. He makes a note to examine her as soon as he can. There is nothing much he can do even to slow down her inevitable deterioration, but at least he might be able to make her more comfortable. A wave of weariness causes Hoffmann to sit down heavily in his chair. Sometimes his role at this place seems so futile. He leafs through a few more papers and stops at Hannah's. He remembers her face in the lamplight and he is sure she has made some progress. But it is something quite intangible, maybe the way she doesn't seem to drift away quite so far. He will try again today, he is sure it is important to keep the sessions regular to prevent relapses. He feels a small thrill of pleasure at the thought of seeing her again. He turns to his diary and enters her name: the last session of the day as a treat to himself.

'I have always been a revolutionary,' he says.

He stops. Why does he not carry on? I see and hear him as if through the thickened glass of the base of a bottle. His voice is a sound almost as comforting as the wind in the trees. Why does he not carry on? I move to where the glass is thinner. I can see his face twitching slightly as if memories are flowing over it. Maybe he too has his own world. I wonder whether it is as comfortable as mine. I stretch out, peer through, will him to continue, and he does.

'I wanted change, Hannah, I could see so many things that were wrong, I suppose, being a doctor . . .' His voice changes, trails off. He sighs, rubs the area of skin that is not covered in whiskers. 'When I was very young I marched with my friend Körner in the street. He had the tricolour, you've seen it? Of course you've seen it. You know what they say, red for the socialists, black for the Catholics and gold for the Jews . . . of course, I was none of these things, but I supported all of them. Körner, later, he stormed the towers with the rest of the students.

My father thought I was involved somehow, even though

I was in Paris at the time . . .' He laughs: a spoken sound. 'Ha. How could I be? I just wished I was . . . that was long ago now, before you were born maybe . . . '33, were you born then?'

He looks at her, waits for her to nod, sighs when nothing comes. 'You were born then, I think, a young child, though, you can't possibly remember.

'Then later, at the music festival . . . I wrote songs, such dangerous, silly things, tales about a drunken giant rampaging across the land who was quite obviously the King of Prussia to anyone who listened. Oh, I was naive then, but I thought myself so clever and so immune to . . . anything, really. But then I met Therese Donner and it turned out I was just as vulnerable as the next man.'

He stops; the memories of the young Therese come flooding in so quickly he is distracted and cannot speak. His first impression of her had been that she was shy. She kept her head dipped when she talked to him, looked up through the decorations of her bonnet with large unblinking eyes. It was all just a pretence, of course. Therese Donner had never been very shy at all. He couldn't remember the first time he had actually seen her, she must have been part of his large circle of friends for some time before he had become aware of her: a small, delicate-looking girl with a short spoken laugh: ha-ha. After he had passed the salt to her at a restaurant he frequented with her brother, it seemed that she was always around: the dipped bonnet and the quiet ha-ha just within earshot. At last, towards the end of the celebrations for the first German singing competition, he had spoken to her. He had been part of the organising committee and it had been quite a success. Many of the participants had retired to the banks of the Main and had continued to eat and drink into the night. There had been many toasts, each one demanding, of course, that a little more wine be imbibed. He recalled now, with some embarrassment, that he had become sufficiently drunk to stand up and demand freedom for the press. The government, he had declared, as far as he could remember now, which was very dimly indeed, was muzzling the voices of the people and one day soon they would rise up and be heard. There had been wild clapping from some quarters and thereafter an expectancy of his support for their ideas of democracy, which he had had to disappoint. Therese, though, had been impressed; impressed, it turned out, with mostly everything he had done: the organisation, his song of freedom, and his toast, especially his toast. But she had still been quite young then, still in her teens; later her true revolutionary colours had appeared and these had turned out to be subdued, to say the least.

After that it was he who did the following: he nagged her for walks, visits to the theatre, and even persuaded her to attend some of his coffee club meetings. Eventually, in her brother's garden, he asked her to marry him.

Another pause. I want so much for him to go on, but the comforting sound of his voice has stopped. Instead I hear other things. Noises are creeping into my world behind my glass and I no longer feel safe: a roar that makes the floor shake, a scream that goes on and on, pauses for breath and then goes on again. I want to reach up to my ears, block it out, but the sounds are from within, and all I can do is pull myself away from them, strain to hear his voice, watch him where the glass is thinner and think about the parrot of a wife flying around him, squawking and beating her gaudy wings in his face, and imagine the touch of her feathers on my nose.

Hannah's sneeze brings him back to the present. He is supposed to be making her talk. 'Is there something you would like to say, Hannah?'

There is an almost imperceptible shake of her head, but Hoffmann knows it is there. He smiles, crosses his legs and sits back. 'Is there something you would like to know?'

Her mouth moves. He leans forward, listening intently, but there is nothing there.

'Again, Hannah, try again.' His voice is high pitched and loud.

She hunches her shoulders, draws her fists up to her cheeks, stares directly at him and, taking a long, shuddering breath, she tries again. This time he watches her lips rather than listens, then throws himself back with a laugh. 'My wife? You want to know about my wife?'

She nods. It is firmer and more obvious than the shake.

'Therese?' He laughs again. 'Well, let me see, what might interest you?' Still smiling, he pauses to draw his small scrap of beard into a point underneath his chin. He considers her face, withdrawn, but so young and vulnerable, and then remembers the opinion of Gustav Müller that young women are interested in only two things: love and marriage. It was their overwhelming preoccupation, he had once told Hoffmann, and just a brief mention of either topic guaranteed their undivided attention for a full ten minutes.

'My wife managed to ensnare me before she was even twenty-one. I was entranced by her, Hannah, totally powerless. I'm not sure what it was, perhaps her determination, her obstinacy – at the time it overwhelmed me, and before I knew what was happening I was in her brother's garden asking her to marry me. It turned out to be a rather clandestine affair; since she was so young marriage was impossible without the permission of her guardians, and her brother advised us that this was unlikely to be forthcoming since they were elderly and very particular in their ways. So we decided not to broadcast our engagement and try to keep it to ourselves.' He gives a quiet snort. 'But I couldn't keep a secret like that! In fact I was so excited at the prospect of acquiring a wife that I couldn't help but share my news with a few close friends, and of course they told their close friends and soon it was the worst-kept secret in Frankfurt.'

He slaps his legs and grins at her. He loves to talk and this is one of his favourite tales. 'The reaction was a little mixed, to say the least. The mother of one patient told me that she'd heard that I was going to marry "that stuck-up little piece Therese Donner" and that "the little bit" would not only expect her own salon but would see to my ruin with her extravagent indulgences. Can you imagine her face when the next month I turned up with Therese on my arm?'

He laughs again, stretches out his legs, and his smile slowly disappears. The woman had been right, of course. Therese might not have acquired her own salon but she seemed to have a big share in those of her friends. He sighs, puts his hands behind his head and continues, 'Now what else is there to tell? She is beautiful, of course, with big eyes and a small face. Intelligent, talks a great deal' – he gives a small snort – 'but not, as a rule, to me. Has borne me three children with great strength and fortitude. She loves fine clothes and is an advocate of health spas. What else?' He thinks for a few seconds. 'You know,' he says at last, 'I really can't think of anything.'

It will do. She is more canary than parrot. She flutters around him pecking and chirping, blinking her large eyes and preening her feathers – and yet he loves her still.

'And you, Hannah, is there someone that you love?'

Kurt, how would you describe me? Would you think of much to say? My Hannah, she is not quite beautiful. Would you say that? She has brown hair. She sews well and is well educated, especially for the daughter of a tailor. Oh Kurt, I am a little disappointed in you. Is that all you would say? Even though she is quite tall she folds up into something small in my arms. She is good at picking out the wax from the honey. And she is good at keeping accounts. Maybe you would say that.

'Well,' he says, 'Hannah?'

He will not let me stay silent this time. I form the word in my mouth and then, shutting my eyes, force it out. Kurt.

Hoffmann smiles. This, he thinks, is an important development. A small triumph, he is quite certain.

'And what does he look like, this Kurt?'

But she shakes her head. He waits, inspects her face, but nothing comes.

'Never mind,' he says at last, 'maybe later.' He leans forward, picks up a pen from his desk and turns it over in his hand. 'Perhaps you would like to hear some more about Therese. I have remembered something else. When it is her birthday I draw her a card with a picture of us all and insert golden ducats in them for the heads. She has quite a collection. You know all the different ducats we issued to celebrate the revolution? She has a complete set.'

I am swapping my world for his. The canary opens her card, her small beak trilling in delight. A golden ducat. It lies in the card, in place of the head of the man who adores her, and after she has prised it out there is just an empty space, but she doesn't notice. She places the ducat quickly in her purse and leaves the card on the table, where only he and I can see it: the round space, the careful drawing, the words he has spent so long composing. The canary hasn't noticed them. It is only the shiny things that attract her eyes, things she can hide away and keep for later.

Hoffmann shakes his head. He is finding it difficult to keep on talking today, it is most unlike him. His thoughts keep sliding in, interrupting him; distant memories that cause him to drift off and dream and sharper recollections of more recent events that demand his attention: Therese with her arms folded telling him about Carl Philipp's new school and how he will get there; her wave of dismissal when he had protested. The thought of Carl Philipp packing and going off to school upsets him. The house will seem so empty and quiet without him. He forces his mind away. He thinks of the ducats in the cards and the pleasure he had derived from devising the pictures. It seems so long ago now, but it isn't. It was just three or four years ago, a time even Hannah will remember clearly.

'Do you remember the first procession into the Paulskirche, Hannah?'

She nods.

'Were you there?'

Another nod.

'Tell me.'

It seems quite obvious to him she would like to speak. She sits up, the palms of her hands pressed upon her lap. She takes a deep breath, she opens her mouth, but the breath just slides out again noiselessly.

'Who were you with?'

My father. I say it before the words can settle in my mouth.

'I was with my father.' Her voice is only just audible. She pauses, swallows, looks at him without blinking. He smiles, raises his hand so it is near his mouth, and beckons out words. 'Tell me, Hannah, tell me what it was like.'

'It was hot. Even though it was still only March, it was hot.' She breathes in and then, with her next exhalation, forces out the rest. 'There were guards, flags, people waving, lots of noise, colour, military men . . .' She flops back in her chair.

'And through it all we came marching.' He does not want to leave a silence, and besides it seems important that she know. He has a ridiculous urge to impress her with his accomplishments and past glory. 'I had been voted in as part of the legislative body of Frankfurt in '46, and then part of the pre-parliament. Such an honour and such a splendid day. Of course, we were quite confident we would change everything then.'

'My father said it wouldn't.' Her words come quickly, a little louder than before.

He bats them back to her before she has time to think. 'Why not?'

She shrugs, then adds quietly, her voice fading, 'He just seemed to know. Too many people with different ideas and all of them obstinate.'

Hoffmann nods. 'And then lies, and cowardice.'

The same words as my father. I examine his face and he looks into mine. He has the same intensity, believes so much in what he says and does.

'I was so disappointed, Hannah. The democrats were expelled almost immediately, my friend Hecker shuffled back to Heidelberg to launch a putsch . . . and then there were the meetings. We had meetings about meetings. I realised very quickly I could not go on. I left, I joined a splinter group. I wanted to make the Prussian king an emperor over a united Germany, and all faiths and races to have equality, but I didn't believe in a democracy, Hannah. The right to vote should be earned. It is a privilege earned through good behaviour and citizenship.'

So in this world of his my father would have lived, would have had his say. He would have been able to justify himself, indicate his costs and ask for what he was owed. As things were he just looked away. He came home and said nothing.

'But even the splinter group became weak and divided further. There were factions too cowardly to listen. After a few months I could take it no longer. Everyone has their breaking point. I told them to go to hell and stamped out.' He smiles sadly. 'You see, Hannah, always the rebel.'

My father comes into the shop from where he has been taking down the garments that are hanging outside the window. They are covered in a fine white dust. He shakes them clean and at once the air is filled with the smell of smoke and ashes.

The city has changed overnight. The troops have been called in to quell the riots and the whole city smells of gunpowder. Streets are blocked at one end with barricades, and the main roads are choked with troops and horses. Everywhere there are booms and cries and shots and the sound of things falling. We do not want to go out but my father is owed money and the rent is due. You stay here, he says, but when I see that he has left his account book behind I know that he will need it so I follow him out on to the streets. I find him in a mob, his eyes wide. Around him there are people with sharpened sticks, long knives and stones tied on to rope. I call to him but he doesn't hear me. Between us is a man in an officer's uniform and a woman with a long black umbrella. He's the one, she screams, pointing to the soldier. Her voice is like a dog's in the dark. The rest answer her with bays. For a second I see the soldier's face and his hand reaching out, two white shapes, his eyes touching mine. Leave him, leave him! I call out, but my father has me in his arms. He is covering my mouth with his hand. It's too late now, he says, everything's lost. Then we walk home without words.

In the morning the world is white with ashes. They cover everything with the gentlest of snow. I call for my father, but he doesn't answer. There in front of our door are his footprints. They lead down to the river and do not come back.

The Story of the Man that Went Out Shooting

This is the Wild Huntsman that shoots the hares;
This is the coat he always wears:
With game-bag, powder-horn and gun,
He's going out to have some fun.

He finds it hard, without a pair
Of spectacles, to shoot the hare.

The hare sits snug in leaves and grass
And laughs to see the green man pass.

Now, as the sun grew very hot
And he a heavy gun had got,
He lay down underneath a tree
And went to sleep, as you may see.
And, while he slept like any top,
The little hare came, hop, hop, hop,
Took gun and spectacles, and then
Softly on tiptoe went off again.

The green man wakes, and sees her place
The spectacles upon her face;
And now she's trying all she can,
To shoot the sleepy, green-coat man.
He cries, and screams, and runs away:
The hare runs after him all day
And hears him call out everywhere:
'Help! Fire! Help! The Hare! The Hare!'
At last he stumbled at the well
Head over ears, and in he fell.
The hare stopp'd short, took aim, and hark!
Bang went the gun! – she miss'd her mark!

The poor man's wife was drinking up
Her coffee in her coffee-cup;
The gun shot cup and saucer through;
'O dear!' cried she, 'what shall I do?'
Hiding, close by the cottage there,
Was the hare's own child, the little hare;

When he heard the shot, he quickly arose,
And while he stood upon his toes,
The coffee fell and burn'd his nose;
'O dear,' she cried, with spoon in hand,
'Such fun I do not understand.'

CHAPTER 14

From Dr Hoffmann's case book, 14 April 1852

REPORT ON LISE SCHMIDT

Farm labourer, forty-two years of age, has a great-aunt who is insane. At the age of six she had psora. At fourteen the menses made their appearance spontaneously, and have since been regular. At nineteen she was married but the union has proved to be unproductive. Husband unfaithful and has passed on syphilis to her. This was subsequently cured with mercury. She is short, muscular, has chestnut-coloured hair, and until recent years has been very industrious. She is of a sanguine temperament and of a lively, passionate disposition. Four months ago, without any known cause, she conceived of a plan in which she exhibited most lewd behaviour and the patient was subsequently brought to the Institute for the Insane.

Embarrassments of walking and speech have led to a confident diagnosis of general paralysis of the insane. Nymphomania. At the expiration of fifteen days the embarrassment of the tongue increased and leeches were repeatedly employed to the head. The head is shaved to accommodate them. A seton was employed in the neck. On 11 April patient suffered a fit after which the paralysis was noticeably more advanced. She now moves with difficulty and her memory has deteriorated. The lower parts of her limbs prove themselves to be completely without sensation. She remains most of the time content but sometimes weeps without any apparent cause. Valerian is prescribed to prevent constipation.

Tobias has decided to transfer his attentions to Dagmar. She is, he has decided, more hungry than Angelika. Unfortunately she is also more vicious and mean spirited, but these attributes, he decides, he could turn to his advantage. Besides, he is desperate; the prostitute he used to engage has been taken over by another pimp and Tobias can no longer afford her services. He misses no opportunity to fawn on Dagmar. Every time he comes close he touches her in ways that are becoming less and less subtle and more and more intimate. His initial motivation was to irritate Angelika and, he hoped, make her jealous, but now the whole exercise has become a means to Dagmar herself. And Dagmar is loving it. She is a large woman with masculine features, square shoulders, a shadow on her upper lip and a rolling, awkward bearing. Her attempts at femininity, an especially frilly hat and blouse, and a pink-and-black-striped bodice and skirt, look incongruous, and serve only to draw attention to her awkwardness. Even though she is twenty-seven this is the first time she has received any masculine attention whatever.

'He put his arm right around me again today, and kept it there for such a very long time,' she complains happily to Angelika when they are alone together at night. The two women sleep in a small room in the loft of the epileptic wing. Like all the rooms here it has barred windows, and these are small and have very little view over anything except for the roof across the street. Apart from occasional visits home these women are as much inmates as the patients themselves. Their dreams of tomorrow are vague and usually involve unlikely encounters with wealthy young men in the street, rapid courtships and happy marriages. But now that Dagmar is preoccupied with Tobias they discuss this instead.

'And did his hands wander again?'

'A bit.' She doesn't want to say quite how much because she knows Angelika will just snort her contempt.

'I'd tell Herr Antoni, if I were you.' Angelika imagines complaining to Herr Antoni about Tobias herself. She would, she decides, break down before she had managed to describe very much and then Herr Antoni would comfort her. Angelika hugs herself in bed. Herr Antoni. Antoni Antoni. Only yesterday she had discovered that his first name was the same as his last. His arm would creep around her shoulder and he would hold her to him. She would feel the roughness of his day-old beard on her face and she would smell a faint whiff of his sweat. And then . . . She really can't imagine what would happen next. She closes her eyes. Just to know he cared enough to hold her would be sufficient.

'Angelika?'

But Angelika does not reply. She wants to relish this feeling of being . . . regarded. Not loved perhaps, but much liked. She shuts her eyes.

In the bed beside her Dagmar allows herself to think briefly of Tobias. She imagines that it is not Angelika lying beside her but the naked form of Tobias. She imagines how he would feel if she stretched out her hand. His skin would be smooth, she decides, perhaps slightly sweaty, and of course the bed would be very much sunken on his side. It would probably cause her to roll on top of him. She swallows a giggle. Perhaps she would be naked too and they would stick together on one side, trapped in the trough of the mattress. Like Angelika, she does not want to think about what happens next. The thought of any further movement makes her feel uneasy. Last night she woke from a dream gasping for breath, and a sensation that she was being suffocated. Tobias is so large and powerful. She turns over and falls asleep, thinking of a more happy entrapment.

Josef Neumann has his own room on the first floor, where the rest of the men are housed. He has asked for some of his own property to be brought in with him and the room is now decorated very much to his satisfaction. Every surface has its own embroidered cloth with lace trim, the wall is crowded with pictures, some of which he has painted himself (the particularly sentimental ones of dark-skinned women in lustrous fabrics holding various small animals); on a chest of drawers (his own, a particularly fine white and gold gilt specimen, the object that had been there removed, 'destroyed' were his precise instructions) lies a delicate jug and bowl, decorated in heavy rose-heads, while along a shelf at the back of the room is a series of 'souvenirs': a small tea service in Wedgwood, a statue of a shepherd holding a lamb, a matching well-dressed shepherdess, a large gilt hand mirror, a matching brush, then a small set of romantic novels set in the German countryside. Into a small space in the corner of the room he has squeezed a bureau and chair. It is here that he spends most of the day. Josef is from a wealthy family of lawyers and is therefore not expected to join the rest of the male patients making baskets in the day room. Instead he writes letters to friends and relatives in a flowery script, full of swirls and loops, as well as to journals: thoughts on fashion, furniture and art, in which fields he considers himself an expert. He writes under the name he considers to be his proper one: Josephine Champagne. As he removes his robe (it is one that he has been allowed to retain, although it is elaborately embroidered) and hangs it on the door, he looks down at his lace-trimmed nightshirt and the image of a face enters his mind and will not go away. He stops, wondering for a few seconds who she is, and then remembers. The girl with the washing. The girl that brute hit and knocked unconscious. He frowns and wonders how she is. She had such an endearing little face, and she had been so kind to pass him the clothes.

In the room above, Hannah lies awake. She sleeps little and has become used to waiting for the dawn. She has been lying as usual with her face towards the wall, but now she turns towards a sound and finds herself staring into Grete's pale eyes across the room. 'I think she has a pair of scissors,' Grete whispers, and points towards Lise's bed.

Something silver, reflecting the small fragment of moon shining through the gap in the curtains, disappears and then shines bright again. It catches my eye, makes me look. A fish surfacing and then plunging deep again, its underbelly glimmering suddenly and then the river water swirling over everything again, green, dark . . .

'Hannah! You'd better go to her. Hurry.'

A voice that knows my name. I see her as if through a shallow pool of water. Her mouth moving.

'Hannah! Quickly. I can't.'

There is something urgent in that voice that causes me to surface, my head bursting through the skin of the water into the air, across the room, one foot and then the other on to the floorboards, testing them for creaks. Nothing happens so I move again. There is a face in front of me, a round, flat face, looking down. I look to see what she sees. Her coverings thrown to one side. Her nightgown drawn up. A blade rising up and then diving down into the flesh of her leg.

'Stop, Lise!'
   But the flashing blade continues.
   'Just grab the scissors, Hannah.'

From somewhere in the darkness comes a command. A whispered order.

Who are you? The words form in my mouth and I spit them out at the voice in the dark.

'Grete, I am Grete. You have to stop her, Hannah. Listen. Do what I say. Take the scissors from her.'

I reach out. The darkness swirling round my hand like water. And then the moonlight: in stripes, touching my skin as rays of the sun once did through the river. My fingers stretch out, feel forward, grab and touch the smooth metal warmed by her hand, and something wet, warm too, and sticky.

'Do you have them?'

It is too dark. I go to the window and let in the moon. It shines on us all, making us grey. There in front of me is a grey-white leg with small black marks the size of a scissor blade. Above it the round face is looking at mine; a face that suddenly disappears and is replaced by a sob. The pair of scissors drops from my hand, disappears into the blackness of the floor. I stand quite still. There is nowhere to go, nowhere to hide. The pool, the river, the quiet place have moved to somewhere I cannot reach.

'Do you never speak?'

Hannah returns to her bed and watches the shadow of a cloud pass over the moon.

'Can you not even say your name?'

'Hannah.'

'Good. Now tell me where you're from and why you are here.'

There are sentences in my head. I try and make them appear in my mouth but nothing comes.

'No matter. A name will do. At least I know you can talk. And I know you can listen.'

Across the room come whispered secrets: a man she knows comes to the back gate of this place and just looks up at her window. A man called Cornelius who writes to her every day. The letter she is trying to write back to tell him that she doesn't love him. How she wouldn't mind if she just stayed in this place for ever if it meant she wouldn't have to see him again. But her parents want her to marry him because he has a business that would help theirs. They write letters too, but she doesn't read them. She just tears them up into small pieces and hides them in her apron. She stops. She looks across at me. Her face is thin, the cheeks below the ridges of her bones just hollows. What about you, she says, is there anyone who loves you? You're pretty enough.
    And then there are words in my mouth, escaping as fast as I can form them. Maybe it is the night that has loosened my tongue, or maybe it is because I can find nowhere to go. Kurt. I do not see his face. We will have loved each other for two years next March. He is a musician but his parents own a bank in the town. He came for lessons in a house in the rich end of the Judengasse and he happened to see me outside my mother's shop, hanging out the clothes we have for sale. He asked me to come with him and his sister for a walk by the river but the sister walked off. He has a head of brown curls and a mole by his lip. I try hard to see them in front of me but there is nothing there except the moonlight shining again on the jug and bowl beside my bed. Am I talking now or thinking? It is difficult to tell. He held my

hand. When he said goodbye he kissed me on the head but Elisabeth saw. The next time we went alone. We walked across the city until we saw his father's garden. At one end there are beehives and an old vine growing over a wall. One day we shall live there, Hannah, he said, and pointed to the grand old house in the distance. I laughed but he covered my mouth. Don't laugh, he said, we shall. Am I still talking? Maybe I am. The nightwatchman comes by the door and coughs. If we are quiet he will not come in.

Ingrid turns over in her bed, grunts, and begins a rhythmical high-pitched snore. There is little that disturbs her. In the next bed Lise gives a single snort. In the morning she will heave herself from her bed and stand inspecting her legs, touching the cuts with her fingers. For a few seconds she will have a final period of lucidity: 'I touch them but I cannot feel anything,' she will say to no one in particular. Her voice will have a certain wonderment to it, as if she is a child discovering a nest full of eggs. 'I did that?' she will ask Grete. And when Grete nods she will say, 'I thought I did.' Then Lise will tap her thigh and say, 'This does not belong to me, I wake every morning and wonder what this strange thing is in my bed. I try to push it out but then the rest of me comes too.' She will smile, then, just before the curtain over her mind is closed again, finally and for ever, she will ask whether it would be possible for someone to remove the leg with a pair of scissors because she has no use for it. And then her voice will fade. Her mouth will move but there will be no sound. She will stand swaying slightly for Angelika to fasten her bodice, and then step into the skirt and petticoats that Angelika lays out around her feet. When Angelika turns her around, Lise's eyes will be closed and her mouth will be smiling. 'Cloth,' she will say, 'soil, mistress.' And the

unwanted leg will fold beneath her and she will topple, as
if someone has chopped into her, on to the floor beside
her bed.

The Story of Little Suck-a-Thumb

One day, Mamma said, 'Conrad dear,
I must go out and leave you here.
But mind now, Conrad, what I say,
Don't suck your thumb while I'm away.
The great tall tailor always comes
To little boys that suck their thumbs.
And ere they dream what he's about
He takes his great sharp scissors
And cuts their thumbs clean off, – and then
You know, they never grow again.'

Mamma had scarcely turn'd her back,
The thumb was in, alack! alack!
The door flew open, in he ran,
The great, long, red-legg'd scissor-man.
Oh! children, see! the tailor's come
And caught our little Suck-a-Thumb.
Snip! Snap! Snip! the scissors go;

And Conrad cries out – Oh! Oh! Oh!
Snip! Snap! Snip! They go so fast;
That both his thumbs are off at last.

Mamma comes home; there Conrad stands
And looks quite sad, and shows his hands, –
'Ah!' said Mamma, 'I knew he'd come
To naughty little Suck-a-Thumb.'

CHAPTER 15

Institute for the Insane and Epileptic
Meisengasse
Frankfurt-am-Main
April 1852

My dear Cornelius,

How hard it is to write this! You have been so patient and understanding. Sometimes I wish that you were not. If you were less kind, less accommodating, then this letter would be so much easier. I do not love you. I have tried to tell you so many times, but you seem not to listen; neither do I think that I could ever grow to love you. That is a vain hope. Any union between us would eventually be so full of rancour I feel it would be quite beyond me to endure. It is not that I love another – I just do not love you. In spite of what you say I believe it would be important that I do. No one can have enough love for two! No! I do not believe it! Your life would be an unhappy one, forever yearning for something you will never have. It is far better for it to finish now.

I am mad, and not becoming any better. The old habits will not die away, in fact they become worse. The doctor can see no solution although he has tried every therapy that he knows. I am intractable, my dear friend, quite hopeless, it is far better that you understand that now and find another while you can. You are not yet old. Forty is no age for a man, and yet so quickly it can become forty-five and then fifty. Leave me now and find another. I am not worthy of you. You are a good man, Cornelius, and you deserve a woman who properly loves you.

Your most loyal friend,
Grete

Hugo is watching Tobias with disapproval. He has caught Dagmar on the stairs with some water and is blocking her passage down. As she moves one way so he moves too, and the woman, who is after all only a couple of years younger than Hugo himself, is laughing like a silly young schoolgirl. He frowns and settles into his place by the door. It is the duty he prefers. Tobias, he knows, becomes bored, even, on occasion, wandering off and leaving the door unguarded. Once one of the elderly patients with dementia actually managed to heave back the heavy bolt, open the door and wander a few paces down the street. That would never have happened if it had been Hugo's turn at the door. He is serious, dark, small, intense, his features are symmetrically and quite beautifully arranged about his face, and he has never been short of women who admire him from a distance. He is the opposite to Tobias in almost every conceivable way, except that he too hankers after Angelika. But Hugo is always guarded about his desires and never expressive. Many people find him cold, and this is why he is only ever admired from afar. Up close the perfect face appears stony. His eyes are never alight. His only laugh is a sardonic one, which makes the women retreat to observe him again at a distance. They find it much more satisfying to observe Hugo than to know him.

Eventually the two come downstairs with the bucket.

Tobias, in an uncharacteristic act of generosity, offers to carry it out into the yard. Dagmar smiles in what she imagines to be a shy and affectionate way and quickly demurs. Hugo looks at her and tuts. Dagmar, he thinks, has the innocence of a professional thief. The two of them go out together, her hand over his on the bucket; beside Tobias even Dagmar looks small if not dainty.

Dagmar returns to the women's work room with a slight flush at the corners of her face. She smooths down her skirt, fusses with her bonnet, and takes her place at the other end of the room from Frau Antoni. Frau Antoni, like everyone else at the Institute, has noticed her liaison with Tobias and has remarked upon it disapprovingly to her husband every night this week. Out of the fifteen female assistants who work at the asylum, Dagmar is probably her least favourite. She is sure the girl has a cruel nature, having once caught Dagmar watching an elderly patient crawl up the stairs unaided, until Frau Antoni had barked at her to help. The calm enjoyment on the girl's face as she had watched the old woman painfully reach up a step then fall back two had haunted Frau Antoni for several weeks, and she had suggested to her husband then that they let the girl go. But Antoni had shaken his head. It was so difficult to recruit staff to the asylum that it was essential they hung on to whomever they could.

Eventually the issue had faded away, but not before Frau Antoni had commented to her husband that he was storing up trouble, that Dagmar would, most likely, be a poor, even a dangerous, influence on the other, more impressionable assistants, and that if they were not careful the place would acquire an undesirable reputation.

When Antoni had heard about Dagmar's pairing with Tobias he had laughed. Surely a match made in heaven, he had said, I am certain they deserve each other. Now Frau Antoni watches as Dagmar walks around to where the new girl is sitting and reminds her sharply to work. The older woman has the distinct impression that if she had not been watching Dagmar would have added a little physical encouragement to her words, which were spoken with obvious menace. Evidently Tobias's attentions have not made the girl any more good natured towards her charges. Then, to her astonishment, the new girl talks back. It doesn't seem to be much and it is inaudible from where Frau Antoni is sitting, but at least the girl has spoken. She is evidently getting better. Frau Antoni grins and plans how she will break the news to her husband. He had decided that he would spend his guilder on another fishing line and a new bucket for his bait. It looks as if he might just have to stick with his old line after all.

Frau Antoni watches Dagmar bite her lip; she returns to her place then glares at Hannah across the room. What has the girl said? Frau Antoni is pleased at the response. Maybe she will try and smuggle a little cake on to the girl's dish before it is taken upstairs. Then she changes her mind. She is sure the cake contains no pig but she vaguely remembers there are other religious laws, something about cooking milk and meat separately. Maybe it is best to leave it after all.

I am trying to be there; searching for the place where you are, where I might see your face. But instead there is this: sky through the window which has the bright flat blueness of summer; a wood pigeon makes his throat throb with song; a sudden fragment of laughter; a scream from somewhere far away. In front of me is a great fold of cloth. In my hand a large strong needle. I rest them both on my lap and look around. I rub my eyes. Sometimes it feels that some of the lint from the cloth has floated into the air and come to lodge under my eyelids. Now there is someone in front. I cannot see the sky, cannot see the cloth, everything is dark, in shadow, as if a cloud has come. Then there is a voice. The voice of someone making threats that thump and bounce off my ears. I'm watching you, my little slut. I know exactly what you are. Be ready for me, my pretty one. I shall come to you later when we are alone.

A passage opens. It leads two ways. At the end of one is the outline of your face, indistinct, smiling. At the end of the other is a voice. You shall be well. I look up. Her upper lip curls upward as if something is keeping it there and around it are soft-looking black hairs, as thick as those of a boy who is becoming a man.

Pick up your needle, you little slut.

I shall tell the doctor what you say.

She opens her mouth again. The lip is still there: wet, pink, too large. A noise begins in her throat and stops. I gaze at her small eyes, a pale brown flecked with mustard, then deliberately drop my own again to my work. It is still too dark to see. But then the shadow shifts. Her eyes stay with me. I take up my needle and plunge it into the cloth. When I draw out the thread she is gone.

Grete is looking at Hannah with an open mouth. 'Why did you say that?'

Hannah shrugs.

Grete grins suddenly. 'No words at all for months, and then suddenly this.' She glances quickly over towards Dagmar and then down at her work again. 'What would you tell him?'

Hannah shrugs again.

'You have not been wise, Hannah, you have caused yourself much mischief here, I fear.'

I can choose what to see. I can retreat down a passage or I can look around me, really see, as if I am really here. A room full of women. In front of them mounds of hair or cloth. It is hot. Beside me the air has an extra pungency, strong and undiluted, the smell of an old woman who sleeps in her clothes. I do not turn my head. I keep my face pointed downward or in front. I know what is there: a small woman with a round face, with a shaved head and cuts where the leeches have been. She is only as old as my mother. She sits without moving, staring in front of her, from time to time saying a single word that makes no sense: cloth, cabbage, soil. Then her lips move silently as if they are praying. Does her God listen? Does mine? There is no sign. What is your name? I ask without turning my head, but the woman is at once mute. Around her neck are scarves. I catch their colours out of the corner of my eyes: bright only in the folds, otherwise dirty red, dirty blue, dirty green. I think of washing them and making them bright.

Frau Antoni sits and knits. She does not like her hands to be still. The clicking of the needles is loud among the rustles and creaks as the ticking is sewn and stuffed. Waves of smell are blown around the room by the open windows: horse, new cloth, smells she likes to draw in almost as much as those of her baking; then others, human sweat and dirt, which make her turn her head and long to be elsewhere. She sighs. Normally just now she would be baking. She has some new jam and some glossy green apples standing in her pantry. She looks forward to taking them out, removing the lid from the jam and peeling the apples and filling her kitchen with the smell of last year's autumn. But she will have to wait until the afternoon now. It is Angelika's day off and she has gone to see her sister, so for now Frau Antoni will sit here, waiting until one of the other assistants is free to relieve her.

To the other side of me is Grete. The voice in the night. Her hair is braided tightly and the braids pinned up. It is all sorts of colours: reds, browns, golds, and where the light catches it there are more colours again. My finest feature, she says, when she catches me looking, and smiles slightly. Her face makes new folds. It is as if the skin is too loose. It hangs from her cheek bones and sinks into the hollows below, and it is grey, dark as if it is unwarmed by blood. When we are given our food she doesn't eat. She moves her food up to her mouth and then down again, her lips scarcely touching it. She moves her mouth as though she chews and then swaps her full bowl for Lise's empty one. Even if she didn't reach past me I would notice. I notice because she checks her fingers, examines each one minutely before, during and after. She reaches past me without touching me.

Why? I force the word into and then out of my mouth.

She looks into my face. It's too difficult, Hannah, she says.

'It takes too long to eat, there is so much to do, so much to prepare. When the spoon reaches my mouth I am no longer hungry. And besides, when I walk now . . . I feel so light, when I am not tired . . . there is nothing of me here. It is as if I am disappearing and soon no one will be able to see me.' Her eyes are big, blue-green, light against the darkness of her skin. 'It makes me so happy, Hannah . . . I make no impression, I tread so softly no one notices . . . I am not here.'

Her hands flutter, one around the other, in the air and then down again. 'And Hannah, I have become a child again. I am no longer troubled by the monthly visitation. All that was womanly is gone. No one will love me like this, no one will want me. I shall be left alone.' The hands that check are trembling now. They fidget in her lap, rubbing one finger against the next.

Grete is the daughter of a small-time cloth merchant. It had been her duty to take the petty cash and check it against the books. But one day the figures and the coins had not added up and she became convinced that somehow some had gone astray. She had looked everywhere: on the floor, through all the drawers in her desk, through the hems of her clothes, but the coins had completely disappeared. From that day onward she had checked before she had started the books and checked when she had finished, and this checking had gradually taken longer and become more elaborate. Eventually she had been unable to do any work at all. Her checking had irritated everyone, and when she was inter-rupted in any way her efforts would start again, more fran-tically and more tearfully, until her father made her stop and sent her home. But then the checking started there as well. She knew that what she was doing was ridiculous and yet seemed unable to stop herself. Always it grew from some-thing small: sewing, knitting, spinning. At first she would work efficiently but then the checking would start: a stitch and then a row, and then the day's work and then the week's until she was unable to start anything else at all. Her parents remonstrated quietly and then loudly, and then they huddled together and discussed what was to be done in secretive tones. A doctor was summoned and then another but, apart from a little bleeding and a few purgatives, they could suggest nothing. She was sent away to live with an aunt on the other side of town, promising to improve, and at first she did. She would enter and leave rooms quite normally, she would sit at the table and eat or sew, but gradually the old habits began again, and gradually they became worse. Her aunt entreated her to stop but Grete explained through her tears that she could not.

Yet through all this Cornelius visited her. He was a thin, tall man with sharply shaped joints, a friend of Grete's aunt. His face was sallow and unhealthy looking, and every time Grete saw it resting motionless in one of her aunt's chairs she had wanted to pinch its cheeks just to prove to herself that blood flowed through them. After two weeks he had proposed to her and she had been speechless with shock. She had seen virtually no one since all the habits had started five years ago; moving from the house into the street had become such a perplexing ordeal that it had become simpler not to bother. She had lived the life of someone much richer, contributing nothing to the household and yet requiring to be fed and somehow entertained.

When her parents learnt of the proposal they were delighted. Not only would Grete be taken off their hands and maybe lead some semblance of a normal life, but Cornelius was in the textile business himself, in the complementary branch of retail, and together, her parents decided, they could be the main providers of coloured linen products in the city. They spent weeks at the table making plans, and while Cornelius and her father were each occupied with their work, Grete's mother was occupied with the wedding itself. Everyone forgot about Grete entirely, since she appeared to them to be quite happy in her own world, checking and rechecking, sitting, walking and checking again. Everything went well until it was time for Grete and Cornelius to visit the church to discuss the service. At first Grete thought that the reason she couldn't go into the building was her usual one; she might have picked up something from the outside that she would accidentally carry in. But when she began her checking she realised there was another reason as well. She finished running her fingers around her hem and looked up. She saw Cornelius's face white and patient in the dark entrance of the church and burst into tears. I can't, she said, just that, and would not explain more. When later that night she told her mother that she couldn't marry him because she didn't love him, her father began his first letter to the asylum. They had endured quite enough of Grete's silliness, he told his wife in bed. He was not prepared to allow her to ruin this one chance of happiness for them all. She had to be cured, and he had heard from a friend that the new doctor at the asylum was prepared to try most things.

You should eat, I tell her, but she shakes her head. I cannot.

CHAPTER 16

Inscription on a tombstone found in the Jewish Cemetery, Rat Beil Strasse, Frankfurt

Here lies the skilful tailor Mr Mosche Meyer
son of Mr Alexander Meyer
blessed be his memory who passed away 608
of the small calendar
23rd day of Elul
and was buried next day
In the prime of life
His soul
be bound
in the bundle of life of Abraham, Isaac and Jacob

Hoffmann looks out of the landing window on his way from the day rooms. There seems to be a woman among the men. He rubs the window clean and looks again. Josef. Of course. Hoffmann watches him walk. If he is just acting a role Hoffmann admires his tenacity. Somehow he has adapted the asylum clothes that he has been given into something extraordinary. His trousers have been bound with twine at the calves so they balloon out at the knee. His shirt has been exchanged for one several times too large. Again he seems to have done something with twine to this so it is drawn in at the waist and then flops over at the top. The front is undone almost to his midriff and the sleeves hang loose, with what appears to be a lace hand-kerchief tied to the ends, so that when he moves his arms they follow him slightly later. Hoffmann tuts with irritation. The man seems to be making no progress whatsoever. In fact, he has already admitted that he was quite happy with himself exactly as he was, saw no reason to change at all. It was just his relatives who seemed embarrassed. As far as Josef Neumann was concerned he was Josephine Champagne, commentator on the world of fashion, art and literature, prospective salon hostess. It had been his proposed salon that had finally caused Josef's family to make a proposal of their own: that he receive some treatment to cure him of what he was, this woman in a man's skin. Josef had had no choice but to comply – he had no real income of his own except for the paltry amounts he received for his articles – and so he had agreed to enter the asylum as an upper-class patient for just a few months, just to see what would happen. So far nothing much had, but at least, as far as his relatives were concerned, he was safely out of sight, a situation they hoped would continue for as long as he insisted on his bizarre behaviour.

Hoffmann watches as Josef takes delicate steps around the garden, as if his boots are still the silk slippers he used to wear. Whenever he meets another patient he makes a small but gracefully executed curtsy, then covers his mouth, presumably to mask a giggle, gives a quick shake of his untidily coiffured head and continues on his way. Hoffmann sniffs: not just a woman, but a very irritating woman. He is about to continue up the corridor to inspect the raving patients in the basement below when another figure catches his eye in the garden immediately beneath the window. Hannah. Whenever he sees her these days she seems to be on laundry duty. Josef sees her too and scurries quickly over to speak to her. He seems to be primarily interested in inspecting the washing that she is hanging on the line, and since it consists mainly of women's bloomers and pantaloons this seems to be causing him some amusement. Hoffmann leans forward. Is Hannah smiling too? Yes. It was fleeting but there: the top and bottom eyelids both curving upwards into crescents, a most appealing shape. A particularly large pair of pantaloons causes Josef to laugh out loud. Hoffmann smiles himself. They can only belong to old Frau Brun, one of their very well-fed upper-class patients. Josef snatches them from Hannah and holds them up to his chest. He has to hold his arms out wide in order to unfold them. Hoffmann opens the window. They are almost directly below him and he wants to know what they say.

'Both you and I could fit in there, I think, my dear sweet Fräulein.'

Her laugh. Hoffmann closes his eyes. If only all his work could yield such a reward. It is low, soft, rather like a brook in the mountains falling over stones. It causes his breath to catch in his chest. She is becoming well. There is no longer any doubt. He breathes out, slowly, but the tightness remains. He wonders at it, this feeling so close to pain which he doesn't want to stop.

'Allow me.' Josef hangs them on the line, carefully, three pegs along the waistband. 'And what else have you in there for me?'

Hannah bends over and pulls several brightly coloured items to the top, then holds up a square of crimson.

Josef claps his hands. 'Such an exquisite colour. And the texture's so smooth . . . Oh, Fräulein, Fräulein, it gives me such joy to see and feel such things.' He stoops down and picks up another square, this time in dark turquoise, then holds it up to the light. 'Oh, Fräulein . . .' he murmurs, squeezes the cloth together and then stretches it out again.

He sighs, holds the square to him and looks dreamily back at Hannah, his eyes half shut. 'Do you not think, Fräulein, that this is one of the most wondrous scraps of colour you have ever seen? Who is responsible for such a marvel? I wonder.'

Hannah pegs the red square on to the line. '. . . Lise's . . . She is . . . unwell.' Her voice is so quiet Hoffmann has to strain to hear. Every muscle in his body feels taut with the effort.

'Is that the poor woman who can no longer walk?'

Hannah nods.

'Well, she once had excellent taste. What sensational colours, so rich, so utterly decadent . . . I wonder . . . this silk, it will dry quite quickly, I feel . . . I think that maybe . . . if the poor woman is no longer interested in them . . .'

He holds one of the scarves against his face. 'What do you think, Fräulein, does it suit?'

Hannah nods and laughs again. At his window Hoffmann grips the sill. The sound makes him want to run down the stairs and demand that she laugh again just for him.

'Ah yes, ah yes, very much, I feel. I think, Fräulein, I shall be along this way again presently. I really cannot bear to continue my existence in these dismal colours now that I have seen these glorious alternatives. Of course, I shall ensure that the lady is fully compensated.'

Hoffmann closes the window again. He makes a note to ensure that Mr Neumann is kept fully occupied in his room until the washing is dry and brought in. Then he allows himself to remember the laugh. He hugs himself. The delight he feels stays with him all the way down the corridor, down the first flight of stairs and to the cell door of the first man in isolation. It is his reward as a doctor, he tells himself, nothing more. To hear a depressed patient laugh – what sound could be sweeter to a mad doctor's ears?

It is noon. For a short time the street outside the asylum will be baked in sunshine. Curtains and shutters are drawn against the glare. As she turns from the city streets bustling with shoppers, and businessmen taking a little air before lunch, to the road outside the asylum, Angelika is suddenly aware of the noise of her feet. Everything changes so completely so quickly. Her pace slows. She counts her last few steps of freedom until next month and a surge of hopelessness overwhelms her. Her younger sister has become engaged, her best friend has just been married, even the dog has had a litter of puppies, and nothing at all has happened to her. Her pace slows further, a sickening realisation hitting her in the stomach like a physical blow: that nothing ever will happen to her as long as she is trapped inside this hateful building with its dark airless rooms and thankless inmates. There will be no chance encounters on the street, no offers of love and happiness, no prospect of marriage and children, no natural and normal life at all. She has been incarcerated too, and everyone outside seems to have almost forgotten about her. She stops, holds on to the door jamb because she feels suddenly out of breath. They had given away Rosa's puppies before she had even had the chance to see them. The urge to run quickly back into town is almost irresistible but she holds on tightly. She hits the door once with her fist, as if she is drowning, and it opens unexpectedly quickly. There is Hugo: handsome but tedious, trapped just as much as she is herself.

He looks at her face. The sight of the desperate misery so clearly written there causes a reaction that is so much more instinctive than considered that afterwards he blushes when he thinks about it. He draws Angelika to him, presses her face into his chest, then, after she has soaked his shirt with tears, lifts her face to his and kisses it once, slowly and carefully on the lips.

It occurs to Hoffmann for a transient few seconds that there is something different about Angelika. He opens his mouth to say something but then realises that he can think of nothing appropriate: she looks well, reasonably happy, it is difficult to say what has changed but he just knows something has. Afterwards he will think of the word: disturbed. She enters the room quickly with none of her usual deliberation. 'Hannah, sir. I'll be along later when you ring.' And she dashes out again, leaving Hannah standing in the middle of the room, quite alert, he notices happily, and ready, perhaps, to talk.

I am a clockwork toy and he is the child. He picks me up, he turns the key in my back, he mutters quiet questions and then he puts me back upon the ground. We both watch me go.

'My father's footprints went one way that day,' Hannah says. 'They did not come back.'

   'I suppose that will happen to us all,' he says. 'Our footsteps will go one way and never come back.'

And for a few seconds we both see them in front of us.

'My father,' Hoffmann says, 'made footprints simply to his bed. He had been such a cheerful man when I was young, but he turned into someone quiet and taciturn. He seemed to be a different person. I felt so frustrated, I had learnt so much, and yet I knew of nothing I could do to help him. It was then that I first realised, I suppose, how little we doctors can do to cure. We know so little, we have explanations for disease but in truth I do not believe them. Symptoms appear and are assigned causes, but how do we know? It changes from year to year like the shape of women's dresses and the cut of our coats. What really causes cowpox to prevent smallpox? Where has cholera come from? What causes it to spread? No one knows anything. All I seemed to find was fever, fever, fever, and death following everything, inevitably and unrelentingly.' He stops. He has been talking too much again. He does not dare to look at her face. To find it closed again would be too much to bear.

But Hannah talks, as soon as he is silent she talks. The words come out quickly, one after the other, as if they had been caught somewhere and only now have been set free. 'I followed the footprints down to the river. I saw them climb on to the middle of the bridge and disappear, as if into nothing . . .'

Guns, cannon, shouts, the clash of wood, metal, flesh on flesh, dull thuds, groans, and there on the water: ash falling, ash and more ash, grey, brown, black, old bits of trees and branches, charred timber from houses, sacking, bones licked clean, pieces of clothing, old shoes, things that could have been bodies but were not . . .

She is looking ahead, staring, silent now, her mouth moving soundlessly.

'Go on, Hannah,' he says gently, but she says nothing.

A white box. The ash still falling. And still guns, still shouts, still men making war. How strange that on the pale wood the same ash now seems dark. On my hands it is still white. It makes patterns on the lid: continents, seas, islands. I watch them form and change. Why is there all this wailing? Why do they cry? He has gone to a better place, they say through their tears, praise the Lord.

Then afterwards. The empty rooms. Not enough voices. None the right pitch. Our meals without ceremony, and then, the books. So much unpaid. So much owing. We asked as he had asked, and like my father received no reply.

And then Hannah speaks again, as if her thoughts have suddenly become too loud. '"From now on," my mother said, in a hard and tight voice, "we take a deposit. A large one. And when they take the goods we wait until they pay. We are not going to be fooled again. We will have what is ours." So we gave up our first-floor rooms and made do with the three below: the shop, the living room which is also my mother's bedroom, and my own small room. The kitchen is in the hallway: a range and a sink. We looked around and said that will do. And we managed.'

'And is that how things are now?'

She nods.

My mother is watching me cook. She leans against the wall, looks up the stairs to make sure we are alone, then whispers. Her voice merges with the sound of the onions crackling as they hit the hot fat in my pan. All our problems will be over as soon as we find you a good husband, she says. The onions go yellow then brown and then black at the edges.

Remember Jakob, Elisabeth's brother? She says he would like to meet you. He needs a new mother for his two young sons.

But I don't like Elisabeth and I don't like Jakob. They go around picking fault with as many things as they can. I am surprised that I have survived their scrutiny.

He is doing well in his business now, my mother says.

But I shake my head. Jakob's business is butchery and I hate the smell of meat.

Elisabeth will be disappointed, she says, and walks back into her room.

CHAPTER 17

Fräulein Hannah Meyer: phrenological findings

OBSERVATION ON SIZE

Circumference of head at 21 inches is large, especially for a female from the Jewish race. Subject is of nervous temperament as expected. Incompatible with a bilious individual.

CLASSIFICATION OF ORGANS

(for brevity will consider only those of significant development or underdevelopment)

ORDER 1ST, GENUS 1ST, PROPENSITIES

Philoprogenitiveness. Extra Large. Excessive fondness for children; too indulgent.

Concentrativeness. Extra large. Great power of riveting attention. Tedious.

Adhesiveness. Large. Unalterable affection; enduring all things for love.

Destructiveness. Small. Extremely averse to action; lack of energy of character.

Secretiveness. Extra large. Crafty, deceitful, dissimulating, and given to intrigue.

Acquisitiveness. Extra large. Extremely miserly.

GENUS 2ND, INFERIOR SENTIMENTS

Self-esteem small. Apt to underrate herself. Too diffident.

GENUS 3RD, SUPERIOR SENTIMENTS

Conscientiousness. Small. Want of principle.
   Ideality. Small. Vulgarity and coarseness.

ORDER 2ND, GENUS 1ST, INTELLECTUAL FACULTIES WHICH PERCEIVE EXISTENCE AND PHYSICAL QUALITIES

Weight. Small. Absence of talent of discriminating weight.
   Locality. Extra large. Extraordinary love of travelling.

GENUS 2ND, REFLECTIVE FACULTIES

Comparison. Small. Superficial reasoning, no depth of thought or intelligence.
   Causality. Small. Deficiency in reasoning powers, and weakness of intellect.

Note: These results are exactly as expected from a member of the race of Abraham. Furthermore, in each case, the subject proves herself to be the complete opposite to the gentleman Herr Kurt Schröder. For example, where Fräulein Hannah Meyer's ideality organ is small and underdeveloped, Herr Schröder's is large, indicating that he is poetic and idealistic.

Bernhard Weber, professional phrenologist, Frankfurt-am-Main, 3 July 1851

Hoffmann paces about the room. Everything today has been frustrating. When he tried to help with Carl Philipp's packing he came so close to tears that he had to excuse himself and retire to his study. Carl Philipp himself seemed undisturbed, behaving much as he always did. Last night, for instance, Hoffmann had come across him wandering alone around the parlour hitting every surface he could find with a poker. After Hoffmann had prised the heavy metal rod from his grasp, with the usual protests and resistance from the boy, Carl Philipp had simply picked up a pair of tongs and resumed his activity. For a few minutes Hoffmann had stood silently, waiting for the boy to stop screaming his protest. The familiarity of the sound chilling him, he wondered whether Carl Philipp was becoming sick of mind; perhaps that was the cause of this change from docile child to intolerable youth. The cries subsided quickly and with them Hoffmann's fears.

'Why are you doing this, my son?' Hoffmann had asked at last, his voice breaking. 'Why can you not sit still like your brother and sister? Why do you always have to disturb everyone? Do you not want to be with us? Do you want to be sent away?' Hoffmann had sat down heavily on the chaise longue, burying his face in his hands. He had become aware of Carl Philipp standing before him only when the tongs hit him not too gently on the head. 'Why?' Hoffmann said again, rubbing his temple.

Carl Philipp had shrugged, thought for a few seconds then said, 'I suppose I just wanted to hear how it would sound.'

'Do you love us, Carl?'

Carl Philipp had shrugged.

'Surely you love your mamma?'

Carl Philipp had pursed his lips.

'Surely you enjoy the company of your sister, your little brother?'

Carl Philipp had said nothing.

'Surely just a little?'

Carl Philipp had shrugged again, turned, and walked towards the door. At the threshold he had stopped and looked back at his father. 'I suppose, sir, out of everyone, it is you I shall miss the most. But I dare say I shall think, even of you, very little. That is how things are. I have often seen it. Out of sight, out of mind, that is what they say, is it not, Papa?' And then he had shut the door behind him.

For half an hour Hoffmann had sat looking at the immobile door. It did not seem possible that the child who had thrown his arms around his father that Christmas eight years ago should now be so cold and distant. Hoffmann remembered his face, lit by the Christmas candles, utterly absorbed in the page before him, already beginning to mouth the words. As soon as his father had finished he had insisted that they begin again. He had admired the length of Struwwelpeter's hair; laughed at the dog eating Frederick's meal; sworn he would never play with matches; giggled at the hare with the gun; and then, when they had reached the tailor with the scissors, nervously taken his own thunb from his mouth and inspected it to make sure it was all there. Even the arrival of his mother and new baby sister in the room had failed to distract him, and at length Therese had insisted that he play with something else. He had obediently played with the new tin soldiers she had bought, but all the time his eyes had been flicking back to where his father's book lay on the chair. *Struwwelpeter* was still Carl Philipp's book, even though it had been translated, reprinted, the pictures changed and then changed back again. The book belonged to him, and Carl Philipp belonged with his family.

Later Hoffmann had gone to Therese and renewed his efforts to persuade her to abandon her plans, but she would not hear of it.

'I suppose I could just forbid it,' he had said at last.

But she had just laughed.

'Well then, I shall forbid it.'

But as usual she had persuaded him otherwise. After raging at him she had broken down into tears. 'Don't you see, Heinrich, he is making me ill? I wake every afternoon with a headache. I, none of us, can endure his malicious behaviour any longer.'

'I am sure he does not mean to be mal . . .'

She had stopped him with a wave of her hand, and then held a finger over his lips. 'Listen, Heinrich, it's the only solution. It might even do him some good.' She had pulled his head towards her and stroked his hair. 'Don't you see, my love, that he is quite impossible?'

And so, with his head resting on Therese's lap, he had agreed.

But now, back at the asylum, out of earshot of his wife's stupefying voice and away from her caressing hand, he feels duped. He feels an overpowering urge to hit something. He gives his filing cabinet a whack as he passes. The girl in the chair gasps.

'I'm sorry,' he says, looking round at her, 'it's just that everything about today has been so extremely vexing.' He sits again at his desk. 'Tell me, Hannah, is there anything you would like to talk about today?'

The girl shrugs.

'Births, marriages, deaths . . . maybe we should work backwards. We have dealt a little with death, maybe we should go on to marriage. Now your wedding day, Hannah, that should be the happiest day of your life, should it not?'

The girl nods, her face showing nothing.

'Well, Therese insisted that we were married in St Katherine's – do you know that church? The big Lutheran one near the Rossmarkt? It was rather grand, of course, a big ceremony, I *think* I enjoyed it. Of course, Therese was preparing for the event for weeks, she had very few relatives to help her, but somehow she managed to make it quite an occasion. Though in truth, Hannah, I think I would have preferred something smaller.'

In my room there are three things: a bed, a chest and a chair. There is room for nothing else, not even a mat on the floor. The rooms in the Judengasse are all so narrow, all so dark. The sun enters only in the summer, early in the morning. It is there only for an hour. The rest of the time the place is gloomy and smells of damp. But in this room I keep everything I own. The top three drawers of the chest are for my clothes, the next two for books and work, and in the bottom drawer I place all my most precious things: the veil that used to be my mother's, the tablecloth I started when I was twelve, and the dress I began two years afterwards. It is beautiful, my mother says when she sees it in the daylight. And for a time she is silent, turning it over, inspecting each side. I hadn't realised. In the lamplight it is so difficult to see. But the stitches are so fine, she says, the patterns so intricate, so many different blues, and the cloth another blue again. It would do for any sort of wedding, my mother says, looking up from the dress and into my face, liberal, conservative or Orthodox, whatever you choose. Or Gentile, I say to her, and she looks at me sorrowfully and shakes her head. As long as you are happy, Hannah. But remember your father, remember your faith. Remember where you belong.

Hoffmann pauses, considers how he can involve her in what is turning out to be yet another of his long reminiscences. 'What are Jewish weddings like, Hannah? I hear they are quite grand too.'

'There is a . . . *chuppah*, like a roof made of cloth, held over the bride with poles.'

'And then the bride goes to the synagogue?'

She nods. 'Sometimes. Sometimes in the open air.'

She closes her eyes. He opens his mouth to prompt her again but she continues. 'There is music: fiddlers and zithers marching in front of her. There are faces at every door, every window. And people in the street, lots of them . . . all shouting, waving . . . weddings are rare, you see, they are not allowed to happen too often.'

That is the wedding I have seen and this is another wedding I know. The bride is wearing blue; a simple design, but heavy with stitches, the work of almost a decade. Over her head is a veil, a little darker than the dress. She carries lilies: stiff white petals with an overwhelming perfume. At the front of this place is a holy man, white vestments covering black, and in front of him is a man with curly hair. As the bride reaches the altar, the groom turns around and smiles. Kurt. Of course it is you. I smile through my veil but you cannot see me. Words, words, words, I would swear away every part of me to be with you. You place the ring on the bride's finger. I look at it there. Another gold ring, but this time bringing such happiness. It is done. You lift the veil and smile at what you see. Beautiful, you say. I shake my head, again and again. Yes, you say, that is what you are, beautiful.

'Is that how you would be married, Hannah, with the zithers and the violins?'

She shakes her head. 'Kurt, he is a Gentile.'

'Ah.' He looks at her and waits.

'He said it wouldn't matter. It was a small thing. Nothing could come between us. He would see to that. He said that he would become a Jew too if that was the only answer. After that first walk of ours along the river he called for me every day. My mother said it was a nuisance, that I was getting behind with my work, but I didn't care. If Kurt was willing to do so much for me, surely I could sacrifice a pair of trousers for him. Sometimes we wandered the streets, once we went to his parents' house and hid in a summer-house in the garden. Once we saw his bees, but usually we walked by the river. One evening he took me by the hand with great excitement and said we were going to see something special, but I would not find out exactly what he meant until we arrived there.'

The River Main looks so calm in the sunshine. At the far side some children from Sachsenhausen are playing in its waters. I can hear rather than see them: cries and splashes among the overhanging trees. It is so hot, I wish I could join them. I suggest to Kurt that we go there instead, just walk in the shade among the trees there, instead of this after-noon sunshine, but he says that I shall find what he has to show me far more interesting. So we continue along the Mainkai, past all the grand big houses with their blank façades of evenly spaced windows, and watch the small ships anchored there and listen to their lines slapping against their masts in time with the small beats of the river. I slip my arm through Kurt's and he squeezes it there to keep it in place. When I look up at his face, he smiles back. Happy? he asks, and I nod. As if waves of warm fragrant water are washing over me: I could not be happier.

He stops by a set of steps, they are not quite grand, just enough room for one person at a time, but the door at the top opens on to a large and light entrance hall. There is grey-and-black marble on the floor, polished to a gloss, and around the wall large mirrors interspersed with wide wooden

doors. A footman bows at Kurt and nods to me. There is
nothing to take from us and it is quite obvious where we
have to go: one of the large doors is open and through it
we can hear the buzz of conversation.

A large room. Dark, heavy curtains at the side, billowing
in the breeze from the river through the open windows
behind. Dining chairs, about thirty of them, arranged in
rows facing the fireplace, where a man, almost completely
bald, stands, leaning on the back of a chair, a table by its
side.

Kurt, Kurt, sit down. Who've you brought? A man,
younger than Kurt, allows his bright, restless eyes to briefly
land on me and then alight again.

This is Hannah, Kurt says, nudging me towards an empty
chair towards the front. She is my friend, my very dearest
friend, Bastian, the one I was telling you about.

Oh, yes, he takes my hand, touches it with his lips, I'm
so pleased to meet you. Yes, please sit. Herr Weber will be
starting soon. You're just in time.

'When the man at the front began I learnt why we were
there. He was a phrenologist. He guaranteed a report at the
end of the session for anyone who wanted one.'

Phrenology, he said, can tell us all that we need to know
about ourselves and our neighbours. It is infallible, totally,
and will, he is in no doubt, be responsible for a moral regen-
eration among the members of our race. Our race. I look
down and then around me. All the heads are blond or brown;
their skin shades of peach and rose. Their race. Not mine.
Does Bastian know what I am? Is that why his eyes slid so
quickly from me? I shift in my chair. I want so much to
leap up, run to the door. But I do not move. I lay my hand
on Kurt's arm and he pats it once. Phrenology will allow

us to avoid evils, it will point out characters, dispositions and tempers of those we are about to employ. It will allow us to make the correct choices of profession and calling for our children. If we are about to marry it can predict whether the outcome will prove to be harmonious or otherwise . . . There is a short ripple of laughter around the room and Kurt looks at me, smiles, pats my hand, which is still resting on his arm, and looks away again. Phrenology is the science of determining character. From studying the bumps and lumps arranged about the skull we can determine the topology of the brain beneath, and since the development of our brain reflects the vagaries of our character, the expert phrenologist has a window to the temperament of the mind itself.

Herr Weber stops and feels his head, small pats from the back to the front. Unfortunately, he says, nature has ensured that my character is on show to all. Again the laughter is short. They want to see what comes next. When he calls for volunteers, Kurt is first at the front. He is seated at the chair while Herr Weber stands to his right. Since the young man is so enthusiastic I am sure he will not mind if I tell the audience what I see. At this Kurt looks a little uneasy but nods. For some time Herr Weber just looks at my love, shifting slightly to view him from all sides. Bilious, he says at last, and Bastian laughs. Strong mental energy, he says, and Bastian is quiet. A good space between the eyes, which suggests some aristic talent. Bastian smirks. Though not necessarily. Now Herr Weber stretches out his hands and drops them again. He sighs, shuts his eyes and opens them again, then he stretches his hands once more and gently, using his fingertips, feels along my beloved's forehead. Eventuality is undeveloped, he says, as is language. You see, young sir, you have no fullness of the lower lids. But your reflective organ, sir, is well developed. Kurt smiles. All true,

*he says. I am strong but reserved, and Bastian snorts. But
I sit forward with new attention: so far all that Herr Weber
has said is true. A tape and callipers are removed from his
bag for measurements. Herr Weber nods, notes and meas-
ures again in silence. Tell us what you've found, calls out
Bastian, is his head too large? No, sir, it is exactly as
expected. Now, young sir, I shall begin the examination
proper; starting at the domestic organs of the front.*

*Since the rest of the examination is performed in silence
the audience soon becomes restless. I am the only one who
watches. Herr Weber's hands pass slowly through Kurt's
curls, the fingertips rotating and shifting as he proceeds.
Every few seconds he pauses to add notes to his report. At
length he finishes. He holds up his hand. Well, says Bastian,
tell us what you have found. But Herr Weber shakes his
head. Not until I have discussed it with the subject. Bastian
boos. Well, do me next, he says at last, and walks up to
Kurt and pulls him from his seat.*

*When Kurt reads his report he laughs, and although I
plead with him to show it to me, he refuses. Not unless you
have one too, he says. So Herr Weber examines me too.
When he examines my face he frowns. Israelite? I have not
much experience, he says when I nod, but continues anyway.
His fingers work slowly through my hair, tangling it into
knots and then pulling them free. When he has finished he
hands his report not to me but to Kurt, who reaches out for
it. That's not fair, I tell him, but he takes no notice. He reads
it through quickly then turns to Herr Weber. Just tell us, sir,
are we compatible? But Herr Weber shakes his head. The
Christian and the Jew are never compatible, he says, and
shakes his head again as if he is sad. But Kurt just laughs,
a hard laugh that is without joy, and takes my arm. You
sound like my parents, he says. And they are wrong too.*

'Kurt said it was all rubbish and I nodded. I told him that I thought he ought to rip the reports into pieces and throw them into the Main but he would not. He stuffed them into his pocket and said he would burn them later, and soon I forgot all about it. It was summer, you see, every day was warm and fine, there was always something interesting to see or something amusing to do. Then one day he came to our house and said he had something serious to ask me. He picked me up, dropped me on to our counter and knelt in front of me. I laughed, asked him what he was doing. "I want you to marry me," he said, and I heard my mother gasp – she was listening, you see, she couldn't help it. The rooms in the Judengasse are so small, the walls thin, just a layer of wood. "Will you?" he asked, and I nodded. "Say it," he said. "Yes," I said, and I heard my mother burst into tears.'

There are certain moments I shall remember for ever. Every detail is clear. On the counter is some brown cloth, the sort that if you look very closely you can see is really many different colours one on top of the other. It is spread out where my mother has been showing a customer. By my right thigh there is some tailor's chalk, and next to that a large pair of shears. Someone is standing at the window, not facing in, examining the racks of clothes hanging outside. He is wearing a green jacket and hat. On the shelf next to me are three rolls of wool fabric, dark blue, grey and black. My mother is cooking a chicken in the kitchen, she has sprinkled it with rosemary, and I can smell its seasoned grease wafting into the shop. There is my mother with her face in her hands, dressed as she is always dressed, in black. And there is Kurt. Why can I not remember what he wears? All I see is his face, a reflection of mine. Joy.

Come, he says, grabbing my hand. I have found a place.

*I want you to see it. So I follow him out of the shop into
the bulk of Elisabeth. I apologise and she says that it is not
to her that I should be saying sorry. I follow her finger to
where my mother sits, her head in her hands, her shoulders
rising and falling. Mother? I call, but she does not look up.
Instead there is Kurt, grabbing my hand again, pulling.
Come, my little willow, he says, there is something you must
see. And we run past Elisabeth into the street.*

There is a knock at the door. Hoffmann rises at once; maybe
if he answers this quickly Hannah will carry on without
interruption. But before he reaches the door the knock comes
again. 'Dr Hoffmann, come quickly, sir, it's Grete. We can't
wake her up.'

Grete has not fallen far. Things are so cramped in the day
room that there is space only for her to sprawl across an adjacent chair and desk. Hoffmann checks her pulse – it is still
there, but weak and very slow – then feels the skin of her
throat; she is dry, very cold. He orders Angelika to move the
other patients away so he can inspect her more closely. She is
pale, great islands of freckles stand out on her skin. He catches
hold of her wrist. He rolls up her sleeve: the ulna and radius
bones of her forearm are clearly outlined; when he pinches
her skin there is just that – skin, no flesh at all. He motions
for Angelika to come close. 'Have you summoned Tobias?'

She nods. Again he notices her strangeness. Her cool
steadiness has been replaced by something frantic.

He opens the bottom of Grete's bodice to reveal the sharp-
ness of her rib cage beneath.

'The girl has starved herself, Angelika, how can this have
happened?'

'I don't know, sir. I check her dish every day. It always
comes back empty.'

'But is it she who has been eating its contents? I suppose we must also always check that.'

But it is he who should have noticed, he thinks, as Tobias lifts the girl up in his arms. He can blame no one else. If the girl dies . . . He clenches both hands into fists. It is his fault, completely, absolutely. He should have been paying her more attention. He has allowed his attention to wander. He has allowed his concerns at home to interfere with his work here; he has been too taken up with Carl Philipp when he should have left such domestic arrangements to his wife. But worse, he has been too besotted with his pet case, skipping over the rest simply in order to get to her. He has been neglectful of the others. He resolves to do better. Tomorrow he will end the experiment with Hannah. He will have to tell the girl first, of course, it would be wrong just to stop the sessions without warning. It seems a pity now that she has begun to show such improvement, but it is, he decides, the only possible course of action.

CHAPTER 18

A summary of the ideas of the revered alienist Carl Wigan Maximillian Jacobi, superintendent of the model institution for the insane at Siegberg as published in his book The Management of Insane Asylums

PART 4: DUTIES OF ATTENDANTS

1. Attendant must govern himself – never show irritation or anger. Always consider that the patient is unwillingly driven.
2. Treat patients as mildly as possible: if an attendant is found to blow or kick, withdraw food or steal any article from the patient, that attendant will be instantly dismissed.
3. Self-defence is permitted but should seldom be necessary if patients are treated with kindness and consideration.
4. No attendant should use rude or immoral language.
5. Patients should not be threatened, punished, provoked or teased.
6. An attendant will be dismissed if he is found repeatedly intoxicated or telling falsehoods.
7. Attendants are to be vigilant, keep patients in sight and observe everything they do so that the patients do not injure themselves or destroy clothes.
8. See that patients eat at the appointed hour.
9. Great attention is required for patients who continue to refuse food. Great skill and dexterity are required to overcome this obstinacy.

10. Any article of clothing dirtied or destroyed must be shown to the manager for replacement. Otherwise it must be replaced at the attendant's own expense.

11. After clothes are taken off in the evening, the attendant must examine the clothes to see whether instruments have been concealed.

12. Ensure that patients wash, aided if necessary.

13. Attendants must be vigilant in the sighting of vermin. If any are found the manager must be notified immediately.

14. If a patient is missed or attempts to escape the manager must be informed, taking care to keep the rest of the patients in sight.

15. Clothing must be dark, strong and respectable.

16. No attendant is allowed to quit his post without a ticket of absence.

Hoffmann leans on his desk and looks at them all: Angelika, Dagmar, Tobias and Hugo. He has decided to speak to four assistants at a time, since the office will not accommodate any greater number. He needs to remind them of their duties: Grete is still in the infirmary showing little improvement and he has still not found the 'artist' behind Hannah's gold ring. He looks around the room for a few seconds, keeping a deliberate silence in an attempt to unsettle them, but succeeds only in unsettling himself. Therese would call it an atmosphere. He examines each one of them in turn, trying to decide why there is this feeling of oddness. Angelika is withdrawn, her arms around her torso as if she is holding herself together, from time to time glancing across the room at Hugo and then glancing away again. Hugo is looking resolutely at the ground, while Tobias and Dagmar seem to be standing a little too close; in fact Hoffmann is beginning to suspect that Tobias may actually have his arm around

Dagmar's waist, although it is a little difficult to see from where he is.

'You are all aware of your duties as assistants, I believe.'

They say nothing.

'Do I need to go through them?'

Still nothing. He bangs the desk. Angelika gives a little cry and takes one step backward.

'ANSWER ME! I refuse to talk to myself. Each one of you has been at least a little neglectful of your duties!'

'We know our duties, sir.' Surprisingly, it is Hugo who speaks. 'It is just sometimes a little difficult to carry them out all at once, sir.'

There is a murmur of agreement.

'Nevertheless, it is important that you try your utmost to do so.'

Tobias gives one of his insolent grins. 'We'll try, sir.' He is clever enough to just cover his mocking tone with something a little more serious.

'I am, of course, referring mainly to the eighth rule. Can you remember what that one says, Angelika?'

The girl shakes her head. Hoffmann looks at her, but she doesn't return his gaze. Instead she gazes at the pointed toe of her shoe, her cheeks flushed a dark rose. He would never have described Angelika as shy or reticent and yet today she seems cowed and uncharacteristically nervous. He turns to the smugly grinning Dagmar.

'Well?'

'We should make sure they eat, I suppose, sir, as much as we can.' Dagmar folds her arms. Even with the 'sir' her reply sounds insolent. It is something in her tone, and the way she has her head tipped to one side, her lips pursed together in a pout.

Hoffmann decides to ignore it for now. 'Exactly, and report to me any difficulties. Is that clear?'

There is another murmur.

'Fräulein Richter is seriously ill' – he catches Angelika's eye and then Dagmar's – 'because of your negligence. At least in part . . .' He pauses, looks at Tobias and then Hugo, waiting until they look back. 'And now that other serious matter . . . I am sure you know the one I mean. No one yet has been honourable enough to admit to being the artist. I shall find out.' He tries to sound convinced. 'You may be assured of that.'

Tobias's smirk widens. Hoffmann is sure that he nudges Dagmar.

'Is there something amusing you, Herr Grün?' He glares up at the giant, aware of the incongruity of his trying to intimidate with a mere glare someone so much bigger and stronger and so insensitive.

'No, sir.' But the grin stays.

'Return to your charges, then.' There is nothing else to say.

Dagmar walks into the garden to test the dryness of the clothes. She reaches up to each garment, feeling along the thick edges of the waistbands. She takes her time, treads slowly; really this is a job for one of the patients, but a few minutes ago she saw Tobias sneak from his post by his door and edge carefully past the kitchen window. She had seen him trying to lower his back in an attempt to make himself look small and had smiled at the obvious futility. Now he thinks he is out of sight, but she can see his shoes protruding beyond the corner of the wall. The smell of his burning tobacco is a stain in the still air. It is sunny, very warm, and Tobias has given into his compulsion to rest. He lies, propped up on his elbows, head back, eyes shut, a monstrous lizard basking in the heat. She follows the clothes line with apparent innocence to the wall and then nudges his foot with one of her own. He opens one eye and smiles as if he has been expecting her.

Angelika is as aware of Hugo as she is aware of a small pimple on her neck. Both of them hurt when she touches them and yet she keeps touching them: the pimple with her fingertips, Hugo with her thoughts. The memory of that kiss both confuses and delights her and she comes back to it again and again. Sometimes it means nothing, sometimes it is a violation, and sometimes just an obvious expression of desire and love. She remembers the sudden warm touch of his lips, the way they forced her own apart, then she remembers the tip of his tongue, catching on her teeth then flicking on to hers, and then, to her shame, the way she had not resisted. Sometimes, in her memory, she pulls away, sometimes they just drop apart, but always she knows that here is something unfinished. She is careful not to seek him out and yet knows exactly where he is. When he is near her she stiffens, makes certain she does not look at him and yet is conscious of his face turned towards hers, his eyes following her movement. She feels they are pacing round each other, two caged animals, and sooner or later one of them must strike.

Hugo sits rigidly upright at his post by the door. He challenges himself to see how long he can keep absolutely still. He allows himself to blink. He counts the blinks. He allows his eyes to close slowly and open again. He remembers the softness of her pressed against his chest and the taste of salt on his tongue. He stands up, walks to the bottom of the stairs and looks up to the landing where she is now. He wonders what she is doing, whether she thinks of him even a little. She didn't draw back, he remembers, she subsided slightly against him, and when he kissed her her mouth opened slightly. He remembers that small movement, the way his tongue rushed in as if encouraged to enter. A door upstairs opens and he quickly walks away, listening all the time for the sound of her feet on the steps.

The kitchen is empty; Frau Antoni is out on her errands. Through the open door Hugo hears a sound that makes him approach and listen. A single peal of laughter; controlled, deliberate. Then from behind a wall Dagmar appears. The top of her blouse hangs loose, the neckline gaping open. She pulls quickly at the string that gathers in the neck, then smirks at something on the ground behind her. When she sees Hugo watching she closes her lips and wrinkles her nose at him, then, as she walks past, gives him a shove with her sharp elbow.

'Keep your nose out,' she says, and walks quickly up the stairs to the day room.

Josef straightens and looks at what he has removed from his drawer: a pair of trousers the colour of cow dung. He is sure that if he allows them to fall to the ground that is exactly how they will look, as if a cow has come into his room and allowed its semi-liquid effluent to fall upon his floorboards. He sighs and folds them back into his drawer. If only he had managed to acquire those scarves, but that doctor had deliberately engaged him in conversation in his room until they had all been brought indoors. Reluctantly he removes his satin robe and holds the stained-glass colours up to catch the weak daylight. It is the only thing of beauty that he has left. Underneath is a plain nightshirt. That, the doctor had said, was the only type of garment a man needed: something clean, tidy and serviceable. Josef sighs and quickly pulls the nightshirt off over his head. If he can't wear something of beauty maybe he will wear nothing at all. He looks at himself in his small hand mirror. He inspects his too-narrow hips and chest. Beneath his ribs his stomach swells in a small fleshy mound, the navel in the middle like the impression of a wooden spoon handle in some uncooked dough. Then, below this, a trail of thick black hairs leads to the offending organ. How ugly it is, the darkened skin hanging unimpressively from its nest of hair. How he wishes he could remove it, slice it away with a quick flick of a knife. Josef smiles grimly. They have taken away his knives. The thought of living with such an uncovered monstrosity depresses him so much he pulls out the pair of trousers again, shudders and quickly pulls them on. He takes the sash from his gown and ties it around his waist. He finds a white shirt and draws it over his head, too uninterested even to fasten the buttons. Why should he not wear exactly what he pleases? He has no desire for these drab men's clothes, he needs something to make him feel soft, vulnerable, someone who will be cared for with a loving hand. He sits at his desk and plunges a quill into his inkwell. An outrage, he decides, and smooths out a piece of paper on the desk in front of him. Outrage – a perfect word for the start of his letter. He will tell his brother that he will tolerate this imprisonment no longer. He must be allowed to come home. His brother has no right to keep him in here; his mind is perfectly sound and perfectly sane.

Now that Grete is in the infirmary everything is happening too quickly. It took no time at all this morning for Angelika to get the women washed, dressed and into the day room. Once there they sat immobile, Ingrid whimpering a little because she misses Grete's skirt; Lise staring straight ahead, her lips playing silently with words; and the other girl, Hannah, just keeping her head tipped down as if she is afraid to see. They were first in the day room and had to wait an age for Dagmar and the other assistants to bring in the remaining quiet, capable charges. There was too much time for Angelika to play with her pimple, too much time to make it swell into an angry-looking mark. Hugo had had no right, she had decided angrily, before breakfast was served. She distributed the food noisily, slamming down bowls and spoons so hard that even Dagmar looked up. After breakfast Angelika decided it was lust, and her movements became a little calmer. And just before lunch she decided it was love, and drifted around more slowly. By the afternoon she believes she might be in love too and imagines a daisy in front of her. She plucks out one petal and then another: love or hate, willing or unwilling.

After Dagmar's tryst with Tobias in the garden she too seems more soporific; her old vindictiveness is still there but tempered with a certain amount of lethargy. She looks carelessly around the room, snarling half-heartedly at any shortcomings. Even Ingrid's sudden laughter is ignored, continuing until it peters out on its own and the little woman becomes absorbed again in her cloth. Dagmar thinks about Tobias's hands, the sound of his hard, rough skin against the smoothness of her own. She tries to turn it into a story from a book; she stares in front of her and tries to imagine them both in a song. When the girl Hannah comes up to her to ask whether it would be possible to see Grete she simply shrugs and listens to the next line in her head. 'Go and ask Angelika,' she says at last, because the girl still hovers.

Then, because she has heard Hugo's distinctive footsteps passing along the corridor outside, Angelika decides to take the girl to the infirmary herself. It will be an opportunity to follow Hugo and observe him at a distance.

Hoffmann is examining Grete when they enter. He is absorbed, intent on checking every feature: the pulse, the results of his percussion and auscultation, and the condition of her skin, hair and breath. Everything is noted down. Grete is too weak to eat very much at all and so he has directed Beatrice, the new, young and very small assistant, to administer a broth and then a little beaten egg and milk by tube down her throat every hour. From time to time Grete's eyes open, languidly assess the scene around her and close again. She does not speak. Hoffmann has been with her since the early morning, leaving her only once to complete the rounds of his private practice.

In the morning, when her pulse was high and she seemed more frantic, he gave her a little digitalis mixed in with broth; in the afternoon, when she seemed a little congested, he rubbed in camphor dissolved in oil. The room still carries its distinctive piny scent. Tonight he will try six grains of opium to calm her enough that she might sleep. Even though she is weak and her eyes are closed she is obviously not at peace. From time to time spasms of agitation appear to overwhelm her; her hands become restless, one wringing the other, and her breath comes in starts. Beatrice, when she is not attending to the tube, sits patiently by the bed and strokes her hair.

'Hannah wanted to see her, sir.' Angelika looks around the room for Hugo but he is not there. He must be in the other ward next door. She walks to where she can see him through the open doorway. He is emptying the chamber pots and spittoons. She watches him stoop beside each bed. She notices that his movements are neat and nicely economical. She watches his trousers tighten and then slacken over his thighs, and she remembers the kiss: willing or unwilling?

Hoffmann beckons Hannah forward. She comes slowly, her eyes darting from his to the figure on the bed.

Pale, still, as if she is made from a speckled alabaster. Her hair, rose-gold, combed out from her head by the small, sweet girl who sits beside her. She must be dead. If I pick up her hand I am sure it will be quite cold. I cannot go closer. I cannot bear to see. I look beyond her into another place.

He watches her stop, grip the edge of the bed and stand still. What does she see? If only they were alone, if only he could ask her to speak.

I drift slowly to another time. There is no need for haste. But there is something here too, on the ground, something pink and lifeless, small, curled up beside me, as if she has been flung there. Again I stare past her. If I look away she won't be there. I tip my head until there is just the sky and the trees framing it. The scream returns. There are copper leaves among the orange ones, and the branches are not just brown but grey, blue, purple against the sky. All of them shaking.

Hannah is rigid, her eyes open but staring at nothing. Hoffmann touches her shoulder but she does not move. He calls softly into her ear but her hands grip the bed more tightly. Beneath her, Grete's eyes open but Hannah is still staring ahead at nothing. Then, as Grete drifts away again, Hannah's eyes abruptly overflow and her tears spatter the pillow below her.

'Angelika!'

The assistant comes slowly, pausing every few paces to look into the infirmary next door.

'Take her down to the office. I shall be along there shortly.'

And a smell, of something else beside the earth, the fungus, and the trees. Something heavy, sticky, sweet, like chestnut blossom, but it is too late for spring.

CHAPTER 19

Minutes of the Frankfurt Town Council, 1845

SECTION 56, SUBSECTION 78, PART 8:
MARRIAGES WITHIN THE ISRAELITE COMMUNITY

Henceforth marriage between Israelite citizens of the free city of Frankfurt is no longer restricted if the couple can show a joint income of fifty thousand guilders.

Previous requirements (viz.:–

(i) number of marriages restricted to fifteen a year, and

(ii) if potential spouse not a citizen of Frankfurt then that potential spouse must apply for citizenship)

are now to be waived.

Of course, if couple cannot show evidence of this capital sum then requirements still stand.

Furthermore, marriages between Israelite and Christian citizens are still unrecognised within the confines of the free city of Frankfurt.

By order of the Clerk of the Town Council, Wolfgang Weiss, 20 November 1845

'Just tell me, Hannah.'

But she shakes her head.

Hoffmann sits back. At least she is partly with him.

Leave me. I am safe here. Nothing will happen. The screams will stop and all will be at peace. But he will not leave me. He reaches into my place and takes my hand, as you once did. You led me to this place but he leads me out. Come, you said, and so does he.

'Tell me, Hannah.'

'Mushrooms, I can smell mushrooms.'

He leans forward, interested.

'Anything else?'

'No, just mushrooms.'

Hoffmann threads his fingers through his beard and strokes his chin. He has read many accounts of illusions of smell as well as sight and sound; many of the French alienists have remarked upon them. It signifies nothing.

'Do you often smell mushrooms?'

She does not answer. Her eyes drift, a sign, he thinks, that her mind too is drifting from him.

'Mushrooms thrive on the dead,' she says abruptly.

He waits but nothing further comes.

I see them as I turn away, beneath the wall, a small cluster of them, delicate, translucent stalks, too slender for the caps above. I stoop down, finger the frills that lie beneath the spores. They are soft like petals, but my fingers leave marks: just by touching them I have bruised them, and their grey-ness shines through the white like an accusation. Maybe they are poisonous, you say. Strange, isn't it, how they look the same, the poisonous and the edible? Maybe it is God, tempting us to take a chance. Should we eat them, Hannah? Should we see what happens? And I see us both, pale as the toadstools, still, cold, becoming them, lying together in each other's arms, and I feel entranced, bewitched by sorrow, and I gather up their pointed heads, divide them into two, and give the larger bunch to you. But we do not eat them then.

Hoffmann stands, walks around the room, tapping his thigh with his hand. He must tell her that it has to stop, he cannot go on devoting so much time to one patient, otherwise there might be other casualties like Grete. Grete: his hand squeezes itself so tightly his nails cut into his palms. He should have noticed. He blinks, makes another quick circuit of the room, struggling to control his face, then stops in front of Hannah. He had been hoping to tell her that since she was now so much better there was no need to continue, it was to have been his excuse for stopping the sessions, but now it is obvious that Grete's collapse has disturbed her so much she has become quite ill again. He looks at her small white face, her eyes moving, following some inner story. He fights an urge to stoop down before her, to reach out, cup that face in his hands, force her eyes to look into his . . . He beats his leg so severely that the flesh of his thigh stings through his trousers.

'Hannah!' he says. 'You must come back. You must listen.'

There is my name through the trees. Someone calling, but he doesn't know I'm here. What do you think, you say, isn't it perfect? Here is your seat, my love, and you point to a bough that is just the right height, just the right length to accommodate both of us.

'Hannah!'

This is ours, you say, your voice quiet, muffled by the trees. I found it yesterday. I wanted you to see. I sat here for hours and no one came near.

Then you sit beside me. I feel the warmth of you spreading from my side. Ours, Hannah. The bunches of toadstools are drooping in our hands. Their sad heads are downcast at what we are about to do. Your eyes watch mine. Your long fingers curl around the stems, gathering them up, squashing them in your fists, then you draw both hands up to your mouth. They come away empty, your hands dark with their juice, your mouth full. You chew, once, twice, and they are gone. You wait while I feed one and then another into my mouth, swallowing between each one. Then you draw me close. I am shivering but I am not cold. And we wait.

Hoffmann grabs her hands, shakes them in his. 'Hannah, come back . . . please. There is something I must tell you.'

Now we are one, you say. This is more than marriage, more than rites.

The moon has risen and there have been no pains, no sickness.

God has tested us and not found us wanting. In His eyes, Hannah, we are one. You kneel before me and take my hand. We are joined, you say. No one can drive us apart.

But something does. Something is calling through the trees and coming closer. Hannah, Hannah, Hannah. He holds my hand so tightly that it hurts.

'This must end, Hannah.' He speaks even though he knows that she does not listen. 'I am spending too much time on you. It isn't fair on my other . . .' He stops. Her eyes flicker then fasten on him.

'I was married,' she says, 'married in secret.'

'But you can't . . . you have no ring.'

'We didn't need one.'

He returns to his desk and sits. It is quite impossible for him to tell her that they must stop now.

'Where was this wedding, Hannah?'

She shrugs, says nothing.

'Who was it you married? Kurt?'

She nods.

I see you as I saw you last: scrubbed, your face shining. You are holding out your hand for me to take. You are wearing clothes I've never seen you in before: frock coat, black trousers, black hat. They look strange among the trees, among the long grass. Your cravat makes you look older, wiser, as if when you talk, people will listen.

'How could you marry Kurt? You have told me he is a Gentile. Did you convert, Hannah? Is all this effort we have gone to, with your food, your Sabbath and so on . . . all for nothing?'

You walk slowly. You know I am watching but you keep looking straight ahead.

'I wore a blue dress, the one I'd been working on since I was a child. I held lilies, white, like thick pieces of paper, curled into shape, their scent in my hair, their pollen staining my skin. We came upon some children; they cheered us when we passed. They sounded like cow bells, the sort you hear sometimes, on cattle that have come down from the hills. And then there were real bells. Singing so loudly for us I couldn't hear Kurt, couldn't hear what he said. I think he said . . .' Her voice fades away.

You are smiling. I didn't think that anyone could show so much joy. It is radiating from you like a light. Your eyes

are beaming in front of you; the dreaming eye and the seeing
eye. Both of them wide, settling on nothing. It is so raw,
so tender, it is too much to bear. I want to clutch me to
you so you are not hurt.

Hoffmann examines her hands, turns them over, inspects
the palm below the third finger of her left hand. There is
no slight yellowed callus, no suggestion that the flesh of her
finger has ever been held in by a band. Before he can drop
them she suddenly closes her fingers on his. 'Have you ever
seen joy?' she asks.

Her eyes are wide, dark, his face a reflection held by them.
He feels as if they are drawing him in, extinguishing his
breath, making him weak. 'No,' he says.

'Have you ever felt joy?'

Not until now. Her hands relax, but his do not.

Even at play the men and women are kept separate. After
the evening meal the plates are put away and the tables
stacked up. The men are kept occupied with a quiet game
of snooker or skittles, any dispute settled at once by one of
the assistants on duty. The women are entertained with
something less physical: knitting or a simple game of dominoes. There must be as little talk as possible. Everything is
bland, careful, unprovocative. The patients who are sentient
enough to be bored sigh. The rest spend their evening as
vacantly as they have spent their day. The assistants trade
and exchange periods of time off duty.

Dagmar is tired of this room, tired of this place.
Everywhere she looks there are people; even when she
escapes the mad there are the sane, and they irritate her
even more. She is conscious of her age, conscious of time
slipping by. Tobias seems to be her last and only chance of
happiness, and she is determined not to let him drift away.

Her brothers used to discuss their conquests together in their room next to hers. Because she was a silent, soft-footed girl they didn't ever hear her so had no idea that the walls were very thin and that every word they spoke carried almost as though there was no wall at all. They described their encounters with women in great detail. They assessed their every victory. Some girls were more eager for pleasure than they were themselves; they, she understood, were whores. Some girls had to be coaxed along, sometimes frustratingly, but both her brothers agreed they were worth the wait. The only girls they could not abide were the ones who teased. These girls apparently played along, eager and happy until the natural progression of things meant they were ready to be what her brothers termed bedded. It was the final and just reward for all their efforts. But these girls refused to cooperate. They demanded marriage. They claimed to have something that was precious, not to be given away without promises in front of witnesses. Invariably these liaisons ended in acrimony.

Dagmar considers her choices. Her brothers were adamant that it was quite possible for the girl's pleasure to be equal to their own. In fact they took pride in ensuring that it was so. At last she comes to a conclusion. Her preferred choice, of course, is marriage, but if necessary she will tend towards the whore rather than the tease. At least then she will experience some of what her brothers told each other in the night: the animal screams, the bites of pleasure, the nails tearing at clothes, and then, at last, that thing she had once heard, when one of them had eventually left home, leaving the remaining brother alone one night with his woman. For months afterwards she had tried to imagine herself in that room, on that bed with her own man, creating the noises she had heard through the wall that night: the two of them groaning and murmuring sighs of apparent delight, the panting and then that strange beating sound that grew faster and faster and ended with a single yelp of happiness, too high pitched to be a man's, and then the sudden quiet.

Dagmar thinks of that yelp now. The purest pleasure, one brother had once told the other.

'Imagine it, Augustus, night after night, that's what marriage must be: no tedious preliminaries, just the pleasure.'

'Then why are there so many miserable faces around us?' the other had asked. 'Everywhere you look there are husbands and wives scowling and grumbling; why aren't they smiling, why aren't they looking forward to the night with fevered anticipation?'

Dagmar dwells a little on this point too. She imagines being married to Tobias; would she always relish his home-coming or would it soon pall into something mundane or even unpleasant? She tries to push the thoughts away but they remain there faintly, making her uneasy. She looks around, pokes Lise and then Ingrid with little effect.

The door to the women's room opens and there is Tobias, searching until he sees her, making no secret of it. Dagmar notices him immediately, stiffens and pretends to look at the work on her lap. He smiles and his nose spreads across his face. He beckons with his hand but she shakes her head. Frau Antoni is watching with her mouth twisted. Stupid man, Dagmar thinks. If only he could learn a little subtlety. There is no chance she will be able to sneak away now. They need to work out a signal that he could use from the doorway without anyone else seeing. He continues to hover there, looking at her, unwilling to go, and she waves him away with her hand. Later, she mouths, later. His smile vanishes; instead his lower lip juts out to cover his top. It is the face of a little boy sulking, incongruous in such a large frame. Taking no notice of Frau Antoni's tuts, she walks over to him. She looks at Tobias, and as well as the small thrill that begins somewhere at the base of her stomach and spreads about the rest of her, she also feels a slight dread. Tobias is so large, and not at all gentle or tender when he mauls her during their snatched moments in the garden. 'She wants him,' one of her charges warbles at her elbow. 'She wants to roll around on the cellar floor with him. She wants to . . .' The woman's voice breaks into a laugh and Dagmar turns, her hand swinging out, but she remembers not to use it. 'Shut your mouth,' she says, her hand hovering.

The woman covers her mouth with her hands and attempts to stifle her voice. Tobias looks pleased. 'The cellar,' he whispers now she is close, 'a good idea. The middle one below the kitchen. Ten o'clock.' And without waiting for her to nod or say yes, he turns and closes the door.

Angelika noticed the door opening with interest but as soon as she saw it was Tobias she looked away. Hugo's kiss is still preoccupying her. She should have torn herself away, showed him that she wasn't interested, but she had not. When she was leaving the infirmary with Hannah he had turned around, and had looked straight at her, his eyes examining hers, as if he had been aware all the time that she had been looking at him and appraising him. He hadn't smiled. Instead he had raised his eyebrows, as if asking a question. What did that mean? She doesn't want to think about it. She sighs and looks at her selection of dominoes. 'Knock,' she says, automatically. She isn't concentrating. This is the first time she has joined the patients in one of their games and she isn't much enjoying it. It is proving to be less diverting than she thought. There is still plenty of time to think her uncomfortable thoughts; the way Hugo had looked at her so coldly just then, the way he hadn't spoken, not even said hello. She sighs. The patients, of course, play quite illogically. There seems to be little point in continuing but she stays where she is. Frau Antoni had looked so surprised

and pleased when she had sat with them she does not want
to disappoint her now by leaving them too quickly. She
glances around the room: except for Ingrid, who is, for some
reason, whimpering loudly and pulling at Hannah's dress,
the room is quiet. What is Hugo doing now? She tries to
remember whether he came down the stairs after them,
whether he stopped on the men's floor or continued to the
entrance hall. What does he think of her? She sighs again
and reinspects her blocks.

The child-woman is tugging at my dress. I think she wants
to rip it from me so she can inspect its threads. Maybe she
wants to unravel them as she does with every piece of cloth
she is given. I look down. Brown threads. I haven't seen
them before. I didn't choose them. I inspect the way they
lie, flat, each one of them the same colour, without interest,
without embellishment.

And now another dress. The threads all blues but with
different textures, different patterns. A rose, a spiral, a daisy
and then another, a chain of them encircling the bodice.
Then, in the skirt, bigger flowers. Great petals outlined and
filled in, stems twisting back in a chain of stitches, stamens
picked out in French knots. Beautiful, my father said, as he
patted my head, you will be beautiful, my child, and we
looked at the cloth together, inspected my work by the sput-
tering flame. Then my father looks into my face, smooths
my hair down with strong, short strokes. He will be a lucky
man, my father says, the one who beholds you in this dress,
the one who takes you from me and claims you for himself.

But now I look again and my father has gone. There is
just an aching space where he was and the smell of cinders.
I wrap the stitches away in fine paper, and the tissues whisper
as if they are telling me secrets.

They whisper now. They tell me that I should be waiting

longer. They tell me I am in too much of a hurry. I take no notice. They keep on whispering until the dress is over my head and its hem is brushing the floor. And then I reply. I tell them how much you love me. Then I walk, softly, satin slippers on my feet, down the stairs, through the kitchen and into the street. No one will see but you, my love. It is still night and the moon gives me a silvery sheen. A cat yowls at my passage. At a window a curtain twitches. Elisabeth. I hurry. I want to be there before you are. But you are first. Sitting with the lilies. Holding them out. Smiling. On our seat as the sun rises. Waiting.

CHAPTER 20

Report of the present condition of the Institute for the Insane and Epileptic at Frankfurt-am-Main, 1853 (First Draft)

PART C: SHORTCOMINGS OF THE PREMISES (NOTES)

There are splendid buildings in our city for many of the needy: the Hospital of the Holy Spirit is an example to all of Germany; the Senckenburg hospital, now that it has been extended, is a delightful place; as is the orphanage that lies opposite and the recently built hospital for sick children. Among all these shining examples the Institute for the Insane stands out as old fashioned and inadequate.

The insane asylum was, by tradition, abhorred. The mentally ill were handed over reluctantly and then forgotten. That time, praise God, is long past, but the distaste for the place remains. A better asylum would promote better understanding of the mentally ill, the ill would be brought in more quickly and this, in turn, would promote healing.

The situation of the Institute within the city. A mentally ill person has an urgent need to escape the city and feel the freedom and peace of God's own sky. It is essential to separate the patient from his former life in order to facilitate recovery; this has been shown time and time again by alienists such as Zeller. He has reported a cure rate of up to 66 per cent for patients brought into his asylum during the first year of their illness. Also, an institute within a city inevitably disturbs its neighbours: its inmates cry out, which can lead to erroneous assumptions among citizens about treatment and their care.

The inadequacy of the gardens. We have, at present, just two gardens separated by walls; several gardens are preferable for the different types of patients. Furthermore we do not possess a field. Horticultural work has been found to be of great benefit for mental recovery. At present our patients are able to work only indoors, which does not exhaust them physically, and so they do not sleep.

The washroom. We have, at present, a well in each of the two yards. One of the most important means of treatment for the mentally ill involves the use of water. Hot and cold baths, the shower bath, the falling of water, the chilled water bath have all been found of great benefit and require plentiful supplies of running water. We, of course, lack this most basic facility. An institute such as ours would be expected to have six baths. We have just one.

The separation of the sexes. It is usual for sexes to be kept separate in all such institutions. This is impossible to maintain in the Institute for the Insane since the women are housed directly above the men, and so often can both hear and see each other every day.

The separation of those who are recovering. The incurable and curable are obliged to live together in the Institute. This deprives the curables of hope of recovery and delays progress. Similarly, although we have been able to house the women epileptics separately, the men are obliged to witness attacks daily. Those suffering from senile dementia are also cared for with the rest which makes for a sad ending to a life, when all they desire is a peaceful, warm place by the stove. The only class of people that can afford isolation is the private patients, of which we, of course, attract few.

The cells for the raving are inappropriate. These cells have windows that open on to the men's garden, which is distracting for any calm patients taking exercise. They are also too small and generally inferior to any on offer elsewhere.

The use of the day rooms. These are too small and have to be used for both work and dining.

Other shortcomings. The kitchen is too small, necessitates that food is prepared and brought in from outside, and has access on to the men's exercise yard. The bathroom can be accessed only from the yard. We do not have a special infirmary for the very ill. We do not have a large meeting hall. There is no facility for wood storage. It is, at present, stored in the men's garden, which is dangerous. There is no secure grass field available for bleaching and drying laundry.

Dr H. Hoffmann. Superintendent of the Institute for the Insane and Epileptic

Hugo does not knock on many doors but he knocks on this one. He is quite certain that Josef is not in the least bit mad and treats him accordingly.

'The brown check this morning, I think, my man,' Josef says as soon as he enters. He is sitting up in his bed writing in a book, his inkwell and stand beside him on top of his dresser. 'Just for a change, you understand.'

Hugo goes to his drawer of clothes and grins. There is nothing but brown check there, no doubt one of the doctor's schemes to 'banish his unseemly vanity'.

Hugo pulls out the topmost pair of trousers and then searches in the next drawer down for a shirt. Although these seem simple affairs they are not. From somewhere Josef has acquired silk, and from somewhere else he has found bone buttons shaped like flowers.

'Fine, are they not? Quite exquisite, I thought.' He pats the bottom of his bed, inviting Hugo to be seated. 'I tiptoed up to the girlies' floor.'

Hugo opens his mouth, but Josef butts in. 'Don't say anything to anyone, promise.'

Hugo nods. 'But how did you . . . ?'

Josef taps the side of his nose. 'I have my ways, young man. I may be a little, shall we say, eccentric, but I am not stupid. Quite wily, in fact. Anyway I tippy-toed up there, and do you know, the place is just like ours, but smells a little better, and the ceilings are a little lower. It was very quiet. No one seemed to be saying anything. I had to pop my head around several doors before I found her.'

'Who?'

'That sweet girl. The one with the smile. You know, Hugo . . .' He gestures for the man to come close with a curling finger. 'I think that girl isn't at all mad either. She is just a little sad and a little shy.'

'But why did you go up there? God knows the fuss there'd be if someone found you. And how, for heaven's sake, did you open the doors? They're locked, all of them.'

'I know, I know. Josephine Champagne has her means, that's all I'm saying.'

'So did you talk to her, that girl you'd risked all this to see?'

'Oh yes, she had presents for me, just as I thought. The buttons, and look . . .' He steps gracefully from his bed, one foot reaching the floor and then the other foot joining it, then, pulling his nightshirt carefully down, walks delicately to his bureau.

'Her friend has no further use for them. The poor thing is quite gone, so I left her a guilder and took these with me. The girl – you know, the one with the sweet smile – was quite happy. I saw her washing them, you see. Though to be honest I think she was so distracted she'd have agreed to anything.' He giggles. 'Well, mostly anything. Anyway, I hid them on my person and put them in here.' He touches something at the back of one of the drawers and a lid opens. Inside are layers of colours. Using a finger and thumb, he carefully extracts something red. 'I thought I'd treat myself today. A red silk scarf, Hugo, what do you think? Ah, it is so soft, so fine . . . just this touch of colour, I thought, could make up for all the rest I have to endure.'

He pulls the scarf through the loop he makes with his finger and thumb, shivering at its touch, then lays it out on the bed with the trousers. Then he picks up his book, places it in his bureau and stretches.

'Why are you here, my lovely man? Do you have something for me?'

Hugo stirs; as usual Josef's den has intoxicated him. Each time Hugo enters another layer of exoticism has been added to the walls. Between the pictures there are now small pieces of animal fur and brightly coloured pieces of velvet. It's as if it is another world, he once told Herr Antoni, and Antoni had nodded. How does he do it? Money, Herr Antoni had told him, it can usually manage most things, and Josef Neumann still has access to quite large sums of the stuff.

Josef is standing over him, waiting. His hair has grown a little more and is now in long ringlets over his chest. 'I am such a lucky girl with my hair, am I not? My best feature, wouldn't you say, my dear one?'

Hugo reaches into his pocket. 'This came for you. Herr Antoni said I should bring it straight up.'

'Ah, a reply from Paris perhaps, or Vienna?' He turns the paper over, inspects the seal. 'Alas no, from somewhere less exotic. Frankfurt. How utterly, utterly boring. It is my brother's hand, I think, Hugo.' He rips open the seal, scans down the page then throws the letter on to the quilt beside Hugo. 'I had asked to be released but he has, instead, just promised me money.' He flops on the bed, causing Hugo to bounce, and then flings his arms around him. 'What am I supposed to do with money in here, my lovely man? I am not allowed to buy anything worth having, and anyway, where am I to wear it? What is the use of having a pretty frock if there is no one to admire it?'

Carl Philipp has gone. Hoffmann notices as soon as he opens the door to his house. The maid walks calmly up to him, smiles and takes his hat; the nanny calls out something in the room upstairs and Line laughs. In the parlour his wife is humming as she reads, and from the kitchen there is the sweet smell of honey and almonds toasting.

'There was an early carriage,' his wife says. 'I thought it best that he try to catch it. I expect he's at Obenstein by now.'

Saying nothing, Hoffmann sits heavily on the chair opposite her.

'Have you noticed how calm everyone is? Have you noticed the atmosphere? It's for the best, my love, you'll see.'

'But I didn't say goodbye!'

'Oh, Carl Philipp wouldn't have noticed. He was too busy poking the horses with his stick – until the driver took it from him. And then, after he had been persuaded into the carriage, he would not sit still. He was playing with the window, and then the back of the seat. I could see the other passengers had had quite enough of him before they had even started. Oh, it was such a relief to see him go, Heinrich, to know that for the next few months I shall not have to apologise for him or tell him to stop.'

'But Therese, it is never you that has to do these things. It is his nanny, the maid, whoever is with him, and that is hardly ever you.'

'But I am his mother, Heinrich.'

'Quite so.' And for a few seconds they glower at each other from either side of the fireplace.

'Perhaps, Therese, if you had seen rather more of him, he would not be as he is now.'

'You mean it is my fault?'

He says nothing in reply.

'Heinrich! I will not have it! Carl Philipp is wicked. He was born that way. The other children are like angels beside him. How can two of my children have turned out so well and the other have become such a . . . fiend? It cannot be my fault. It cannot be anyone's fault. That French man Roussmann . . .'

'Rousseau?'

'Yes, yes, Rousseau . . . He's quite wrong. Children are not born trailing clouds of glory.'

'That wasn't Rousseau, that was the Englishman, Wordsworth.'

'Well, he's wrong too. It is perfectly possible for a child to be born bad, and Carl Philipp was born a very bad child indeed.'

For a while he says nothing, her words stabbing at his head like tiny spears again and again. He looks at her closed mouth, her frown, and for a moment a wave of intense dislike overpowers him. He fights an urge to slap her, to inflict some sort of physical pain to match the hurt he is feeling inside his head. He rises quickly, holding his hands together behind his back.

'Heinrich?'

He takes no notice.

'Heinrich? I haven't finished.'

He slams first the parlour door and then the larger house door.

Even though it is late it is still quite light, the air is cool, and a light breeze ruffles his hair. Hoffmann rents their accommodation in the Hochstrasse from a Dr Pauli. Like all the other houses here, it is large, grand and new, its front dressed with pale coloured stone, with a wide entrance and many windows going up three storeys. It is a convenient place to live, just a ten-minute walk down the road to the Meissengasse and the asylum entrance. But tonight he walks in the opposite direction, east along the Hochstrasse until he comes to the medieval Eschenheim tower. As usual he stops to gaze up at its yellow stonework and grey slate roofs, each one sharpened like one of the English pencils. How Carl Philipp loved these towers; he was always begging his father to go up one of them, and Hoffmann always promised him later, later. Now there might never be a later. Hoffmann stiffens as a feeling of desolation grips him. It is too late now. When Carl Philipp comes back, he will no longer be interested in such things. He will be taller, broader and utterly changed, Hoffmann is sure of it. There will no longer be the child asking about long ago. There will be no stopping just to look and imagine the people pushing and shoving just to get through this very small gate to trade. The boy will be bored. He will demand to go on. He might pull his father away with surprising strength.

Hoffmann walks under the arch, listening to the echo of his steps bouncing off the ceiling. Just one pair of footsteps. This had always been the place they'd come when Carl Philipp had started being particularly difficult a couple of years ago. I'll take him for some air, he'd say, and they would come here. Carl Philipp seemed to like the place. It seemed to calm him. People as well as cattle had to pay just to enter, he'd told him once. And Carl Philipp had stopped running at the walls and come over to him. People had to pay just to come in? he'd asked, hopping from one foot to the other. And they had seen the ghosts of the Israelites together, herded like cattle and taxed like cattle, owned by princes and bought and sold to towns like provisions.

Some insomniac bird chirrups once from the top of the tower. Hoffmann stops and looks up. It is as if he'd heard Carl Philipp's voice, as it was a year ago, still with the high pitch of a young child. I thought people wanted to live in Frankfurt, the boy had said. I thought that was why it is so crowded. Then Hoffmann had given him a lecture about people's greed and intolerance, and Carl Philipp had become bored and continued with his running. But that word 'intolerance' seemed so very important now. Hoffmann had never thought this intolerance would be applied so early to his son. Boarding school for his son, ghetto for the Jews and the asylum for the insane. They were all places people were sent to be out of the way and forgotten. But he would never forget Carl Philipp, he thought, there would not be one day that went past when he wouldn't think of him. He walked on through a gateway into the Eschenheim Gardens. This was another of Carl Philipp's favourite places. There was space here for him to run and climb as much as he wanted. Hoffmann would never forget him. He would come here and remember, and, when Carl Philipp came back, he would bring him here as much as he liked. He would let him climb on these ancient fortifications. He might still like to climb. Hoffmann would tell him again about Napoleon bombarding them with his cannon and creating this patch of wilderness. And Carl Philipp would run and shout and no one would mind.

Hoffmann follows the gardens around the perimeter of the city eastward and then southward until he reaches the river. It is quite dark now and the river is lit in the distance by the lamps on small ships. The lapping of the water against the bank sounds like a hungry dog, that is what he would tell Carl Philipp if he were here. If he were here. He walks more quickly, passes the grand houses along the Schöne Aussicht, and then crosses the old bridge to Sachsenhausen. He cannot go home, not yet. He can't bear the silence of the house without Carl Philipp. He walks around the narrow dark streets until he is too tired to walk any longer, and then sinks on to a bench by a table and orders a jug of apple wine. Even though he doesn't much care for the stuff, he drinks jug after jug until the world seems a more distant place where nothing much matters. A child about the same age as Carl Philipp starts to sweep around the tables. Hoffmann watches until his eyes start to seep apple-wine tears. 'Keep an eye on him,' he tells the landlord hoarsely when he gets up to pay, 'they go if you don't keep watching them.' And after he has fallen against a bench, and picked himself up again, he walks slowly back to the Hochstrasse.

He wakes next morning in Carl Philipp's bed with a desperate thirst and no clear recollection of his journey the previous night at all.

Josef stops Hugo in the garden. Hugo is bringing in some firewood for the kitchen. 'I was wondering if you would appreciate a little change in duties,' he says. 'I would like to have my own personal assistant, and you are the prettiest specimen around here by far, apart from *moi*, of course.'

'You'd have to ask Herr Antoni about that, sir.'

Josef inspects Hugo's face, but it is, as usual inscrutable. 'But would you like it, my dear? I was thinking of that duty you have to perform' – Josef waves his hand in the direction of the house – 'at the door, waiting, doing nothing. It must get utterly, utterly tedious for an intelligent mind like yours.'

'I don't mind it, sir. But if you really want a full-time assistant, I'm sure that if you ask Herr Antoni he'll provide you with someone.'

'But I'd like you, my dearest one.'

'Well, let him know, sir.' Then, with the merest tip of his head, Hugo continues inside, small pieces of wood leaving a trail behind him.

Angelika is folding the clean linen for the press on the women's floor. After she has taken it up there she will just have time to have a little coffee in the kitchen, and then she will have to return to the work room to relieve Frau Antoni. She sits for a minute on a kitchen chair, stretching her legs out in front of her. It is a fine day, not too warm and with a pleasant fresh breeze. A silhouette appears at the doorway; a man with his arms full of wood. Hugo. She stays quite still. Maybe it is hotter than she thinks because the skin at the top of his cheeks is quite flushed.

'Hot?' she asks, and smiles. It is the first time they have spoken, the first time their eyes have met, since it happened.

'Not really.' His face remains exactly as it was. 'Have you seen Herr Antoni?'

'In the office with the doctor.'

He nods his thanks and continues past her. She stares after him, her eyes travelling down his body. He doesn't turn, doesn't smile. She remembers her mouth, the way she didn't clamp it shut. Not willing, she thinks dismally and desperately, not willing at all. She runs upstairs with the linen, unlocks the nearest door and throws herself on a bed.

Hoffmann looks at Grete's pale face. There is no improvement yet, but sometimes these things take time. She has developed a dry cough, and her hands and face have become oedematous. The swelling has, if anything, improved her appearance, and the young attendant Beatrice tells everyone who passes that Grete is improving, look, her flesh is filling out, all the soup and milk must be going in, although it doesn't really seem as if it is. But Grete's hair is suffering, and Beatrice has ceased her combing. Some has fallen out, and there are bare patches at her temples. She has produced little water in the past few days, but that which has passed quietly from her has been pus-laden and rank. It has caused them to change the bedding immediately. Hoffmann listens, feels and looks. Her lungs seem clear, her pulse, of course, is weak and rather fast, her skin cool and dry. He gives Beatrice a little smallpox ointment and some digitalis, to be administered if she is able to rouse Grete sufficiently to take the spoon.

It is as he leaves to attend a private patient that he remembers. Carl Philipp. What is the boy doing now? Is he missing him? He stumbles against a bed. The apple wine last night has left him with a head that feels like a dried-out gourd. When he moves quickly a drum that appears to be filled partly with liquid booms in his head.

'Are you all right, sir?' Beatrice calls from the bed. 'You don't look very well, sir, if you don't mind my saying so.'

Hoffmann smiles at her sweetness. 'I am quite well, Beatrice, do not concern yourself. Just see to the digitalis if you have an opportunity.'

As he passes the women's room he thinks he hears a voice. He stops. Hannah, he is sure it was Hannah. He listens but it doesn't come again. Speak, he thinks, laugh, talk to me.

Tobias is taking a rest. Altogether today he has eaten his breakfast, sat at the door for four hours (with short intervals for pieces of bread when the kitchen was empty), eaten lunch, resumed his post at the door for another hour, and then sneaked off to his room. If anyone asks, which they won't because nobody ever comes and nobody even ever walks past at this time of day, he will claim a sudden and chronic call of nature. This is very likely to become fact in the next hour, because from under his bed he has withdrawn a large bottle filled with a cloudy and potent liquid and, unable to recall exactly what it is, has consumed half of it in five minutes flat. Now his legs feel extraordinarily heavy, his head seems to have become part of his pillow and he is watching the patch on the ceiling, where a beer cork flew off and knocked away a little plaster, make strange little circular movements all on its own. He is, however, quite happy, and when there is a knock on his door his grunt is not really meant to indicate that he would welcome company. Dagmar comes in anyway.

For a second she just stands and sniffs. It is the smell of a man; the same smell as the one that lingered in her brothers' bedroom long after they were gone in the morning: a cloying smell of sweat and bad breath. She shuts her eyes, remembering: how she had to change her brothers' beds, empty their pots, sweep, clean, put fresh water in their jugs. It had taken her a full hour every day since she was ten, and all the time there would be this smell. How she hated her life then; she felt trapped, more than she feels trapped now. Her mother would watch her every move with undisguised disapproval from her cot in the corner. She had wanted, she said, a daughter as beautiful as herself, and all she'd got was Dagmar. The kitchen faced north and was surrounded by other houses so the sun hardly ever penetrated the corner where her mother half sat, half lay, but when it did, when a long narrow ray shone in and lit her bed, she would demand to see Dagmar and inspect her. 'No better,' her mother would say, shaking her head, and then would point out her latest aberration: the darkness of hairs above her upper lip, pimples in a rash across her forehead, vertical lines appearing above her nose. All these were noted and referred to frequently thereafter, a continual reminder that Dagmar was plain, unfit to be seen outside, unmarriageable. When her mother had died everyone had commiserated with the girl: where would she go, what would she do now one of her brothers had inherited the house and was proposing to move back in with his large and expanding family? But Dagmar didn't really care. Her eyes shone not with tears but with the thought of freedom. Live-in servants were in demand now that people were getting richer and she was

232

well trained. She would find somewhere interesting, somewhere she could be in charge. Then one day, in the market, she had heard Frau Antoni talking to another woman about their shortage of assistants at the asylum, and she had applied at once. She smiles. She expects her mother has found a cot somewhere in the afterlife and is looking down on her now with speechless indignation. She imagines her mother watching as Dagmar crosses the room to where Tobias lies, turns his massive head towards her with both hands and, ignoring the pungent fumes from his open mouth, shuts her eyes and covers his lips with hers.

Frau Antoni puts down her knitting. What is wrong with this place? First of all that Angelika, who has been behaving so strangely the last few days, all quiet and gentle in contrast to her normally bold and rather raucous self, entered the room, her face obviously swollen from crying, demanding to see Herr Antoni as soon as is conveniently possible. When Frau Antoni asked whether she could help instead the girl had shaken her head and declared that it had to be him, no one else would do, and then had sighed, almost as if she were in love with the man. Frau Antoni smiled tightly. Maybe her husband would be slightly flattered if that were the case, but apart from that the girl would be mightily disappointed. Herr Antoni's appetite for amour was irregular, as much dependent on the productivity of his fishing line as on the flash of a woman's breast or thigh, and anyway, after almost thirty years of relentless devotion to Frau Antoni, he was much too set in his ways to experiment now.

Then the second thing that happened, as soon as Angelika had settled herself with her sewing, was that the callous Dagmar had entered, her cheeks also flushed, her eyes also swollen, but Frau Antoni failed to believe that this particular woman was capable of shedding any tears. And anyway, Dagmar had looked angry rather than sad. She had immediately marched up and down the room, snarling at anyone who wasn't intensively working, which, it turned out, was most of them. The afternoon was turning out to be very hot, and the heat seemed to collect in this room, no matter how wide they opened the windows. Dagmar had snarled at little Ingrid so loudly that the woman had begun to scream and hit out with her fist. Frau Antoni had done nothing to assist, just sat there with her arms folded, waiting while Dagmar calmed the woman out of her tantrum herself.

Then the doctor comes in, looking rather as if he had spent the night with just a few bottles for company, marches over to Hannah and asks her rather urgently to come with him to his office. After they have gone Frau Antoni snorts; so much for his declaration to her last week that he was spending too much time with the girl and intended to finish her treatment at once. Moral therapy indeed. She is sure that he is a little sweet on her. She has seen the way he looks at her when he thinks no one is looking: much too often, and much too attentively. Herr Antoni hadn't believed her, but now she has fresh evidence. She folds her arms and looks forward to enlightening her husband over supper tonight.

The door opens again and the new assistant, Beatrice, enters.

'Aren't you supposed to be looking after Fräulein Richter?' Dagmar says over Ingrid's subsiding sobs. But the young girl says nothing. She looks quickly around the room and then runs across to Frau Antoni.

'What is it, child?' Frau Antoni asks, holding her weeping head away from her shoulder.

'It's Grete, I mean Fräulein Richter, she made a strange choking sound and now I can't feel her breath.'

Augustus was a chubby lad;
Fat ruddy cheeks Augustus had;
And everybody saw with joy
The plump and hearty healthy boy.
He ate and drank as he was told,
And never let his soup get cold.
But one day, one cold winter's day,
He scream'd out – 'Take the soup away!
O take the nasty soup away!
I won't have any soup to-day.'

Next day! now look, the picture shows
How lank and lean Augustus grows!
Yet, though he feels so weak and ill,
The naughty fellow cries out still
'Not any soup for me, I say:
O take the nasty soup away;
I won't have any soup to-day.'

The third day comes; O what a sin!
To make himself so pale and thin.

Yet, when the soup is put on table,
He screams, as loud as he is able, –
'Not any soup for me, I say:
O take the nasty soup away!
I won't have any soup to-day!'

Look at him, now the fourth day's come!
He scarce outweighs a sugar-plum;
He's like a little bit of thread;
And on the fifth day he was dead.

CHAPTER 21

Note pinned to the door of Haus Stein West, Judengasse, Frankfurt, 14 August 1851

To the filthy Jewess who lives here:

I have seen you and your sluttish ways. I know where you go and what you do. You are no better than a whore. You charge for your services with gifts and promises just as a prostitute would charge money. There is no difference. You are just as low, just as disgraced in God's eyes. Leave him. You know who I mean. He is not yours. Keep to your own dirty kind. I can bring shame on you and I shall.

A Member of Christ's Holy Army

He has hardly settled her when they come: Beatrice, Frau Antoni, Hugo.

'Come quickly, sir, something has happened.'

While the rest of them leave, Frau Antoni stays. 'Come with me, child. You can, I believe, drink coffee?'

It is perfectly obvious that Grete Richter is dead. Her chin is arched back, her mouth is open a little as if she is catching one last breath. Yet she does not look unhappy. Her eyes are closed and the rest of her face is quite calm.

'Tell her relatives that she died in her sleep,' he says to Antoni, who is in the room waiting for them when they enter. The man nods, sober and serious as usual. Telling Beatrice to cover the body with a sheet, Hoffmann notes the time of death on the pad beside the bed. He feels, he realises, nothing. As if it hasn't really happened, and yet he knows that Grete is dead. Knows it absolutely.

'You will be doing an autopsy, sir?'

Hoffmann nods.

'Shall I make the arrangements for the body, then, sir?'

Again he nods, and still he feels nothing. Grete Richter has died from starvation. He was indirectly to blame, and yet he feels nothing. All he thinks about is their house and the way it will seem so quiet and empty, even though it is full of voices and people. It is Carl Philipp's second day at school, and he dreads going home without him there.

Frau Antoni and her husband have just two small rooms, but they are sometimes willing to share them with a convalescing patient. It gives the inmate a taste of family life again, before they are released in stages back into the outside world. The manager's rooms are across the corridor from the office. One room is the bedroom, which has just enough space for a bed, a cupboard and a small chest, and the other is their living room, where they also eat. It is no larger than the bedroom. Into this they have crammed a table, four chairs, two lower, softer chairs and a sideboard. In front of the stove there is a rack with clothes drying. Every surface is piled high with objects – books, papers, pots, Herr Antoni's fishing tackle, Frau Antoni's knitting and sewing. When Hoffmann enters, Hannah is sitting on one of the low chairs and Frau Antoni on the other. The room is full of Frau Antoni's frantic chatter. When she sees Hoffmann she leaps up; since she is such a small, stout woman, her easy movement gives the impression she is filled with air.

'Well, sir?'

He nods. 'I'm afraid it's true.'

'Oh, I'm sorry, sir.'

Still he feels nothing. He turns to Hannah. 'Shall we resume?'

'You are asking her in now, sir?' Usually after a death it is the doctor's custom to confine himself to his office to write reports. He told Frau Antoni once that he found the clinical language comforting, reminding him that death is just a natural process, the inevitable outcome in his profession.

He tips his head slightly in reply, helps Hannah to her feet and leads her back into his office. 'I am afraid I have bad news: your friend, Grete Richter, is no longer with us.'

She looks calmly at him.

'You understand?'

She nods.

She will lie in a wooden box, her hair spread out around her like an aura. About her old women and men will weep and cry out their grief. Then there will be another: younger, thinner, his waiting over.

'Will you tell Cornelius?'

'Cornelius?' The name is vaguely familiar to him, but he can't quite place it.

'The man who loved her.' She tips her head, examines her fingers on her lap and her voice becomes lower and quieter.

He remembers now; the man who kept writing to Grete, letter after letter. The man she had been engaged to marry. Hoffmann had allowed her to receive his letters, thought that they might encourage her in her fight to become well.

'She said she saw him standing there, just looking up. He used to come to the asylum and spend hours just waiting to catch a glimpse of her. He loved her, you see, couldn't stop himself, just had to come and see if she could love him, never stopped hoping.'

She pauses, and when she continues her voice is softer still, and it is as if every object in the room is listening intently. 'How strange love is, nothing can make it happen. So many people love and are not loved back . . .'

Her words are as quiet as the watch that beats against his chest, but they are still quite clear and audible.

'Why did Kurt not love me?'

I hear my words. It is as if they are not mine but they are. They cannot be unsaid.

Hoffmann hears himself swallow, watches as a pigeon makes a clumsy flapping shadow across the window. The thumping in his head is confusing him. He tries to make sense of the words. Kurt didn't love her. Grete didn't love someone else. Grete is dead, but he still feels nothing. Who loves Carl Philipp? The thumping is louder, he tries to shake it away. Not you. Not you. He shakes his head, violently this time, so the swirling drums change tone. He starts again. Kurt didn't love her. Didn't love who? Hannah. Kurt didn't love Hannah. 'But there was a wedding,' he says at last. 'You wore that dress.' He listens to the room grow more silent.

I see you as I saw you last. Your face, smiling, scrubbed, red cheeked, smiling. Why did you not love me? You look around, you see me looking, your eyes, your dreaming eye and your seeing eye, drop downward, inspect the ground and then look up again. Your smile has gone. You see me but your smile has gone.

'But you wore your dress, you told me, that dress, the blue one you'd been working on for so long.'

My mother looks at me. So it's true, she says. Elisabeth has been telling me such tales. Where have you been? What have you done? Then she reaches forward and lifts up the hem and we look at it, green, brown, torn, bedraggled, the butter-gold pollen from the lilies spattered down the front, catching in the French knots and daisy chains. Ruined, she says. Then she turns me around and back again and looks at me with all the blood gone from her face, her mouth a line. I am married, I tell her, but she says nothing. Married in the eyes of God, I tell her, the trees and flowers our silent witnesses. Then she shakes me; my mother who has never before touched me in anger holds both my shoulders and shakes me.

'It meant nothing,' she says. 'A blackbird led the vows and a chaffinch the promises. Kurt said it was all that we needed but he was wrong.'

Hoffmann frowns, thinks back, sure there was something else, but it is all so difficult. What is delusion and what is fact?

'So there was no wedding at all?'

She looks down, examines her hands and then looks up again. 'There was a wedding, a real one, but it wasn't mine.' Her voice is flat, low, strained as she fights for it not to break. 'He married another. I went to see. Elisabeth told me but I didn't believe her so I went to see. I covered my head with my mother's veil, walked quietly in through the door, and inside it was dark and smeared with gold and reds just like a synagogue, there was no difference, except instead of a tabernacle there was a platform with a man being murdered on a cross.'

I am in the back, in shadow; a woman looks at me when I come in, I see her eyes travel down my clothes, they are not quite festive enough, since that day it is all I wear, black, grey, black, and now a dark veil over my head. When I sit down I am invisible. No one else notices. You do not see me, but I see you. You look just as you always looked, no thinner, no more sorrowful, smiling, as if you are happy.

'Elisabeth said . . .'
  'Elisabeth?'
  'A neighbour, a friend of my mother's, told me that he was marrying a widow, an influential woman, a friend of his family's, and then, of course, I knew. He didn't love her, he was being made to do it. I wrote to tell him I knew, but he didn't write back.'

When you see me this will stop, when you see my face come out of this dark place into the light you will come. You are married already. You will see me and you will come to me.

'So you had stopped the walks?'
  'After my wedding in the woods my mother wouldn't let me see him. She locked me in. I heard him knocking but she'd locked me in my room. I called to him from my window but he didn't hear. Then, after a month, when he'd stopped his knocking, I went to him.'

It is early and my mother has forgotten the lock on my door. Already it is autumn and a cold mist is loitering on the ground. It doesn't move for me, it cuts off my feet and makes me hover. It is still there when I reach your house. At the front door there is a young maid beating a mat. Even though it is still so early she is awake, dressed, beating the mat. Who are you, she says, when she sees me, but I don't tell her. I swallow. You don't look well, she says, looking at me, and I tell her that I have walked a long way and go and sit on the low wall that circles your garden at the side. My imprisonment has made me ill, I am not used to the streets, and whenever I run a sickness wells up and burns my throat. But I am not sick. I sit looking at the gutter but I am not sick. There is just the bitterness of bile and then the cloying taste of metal in my mouth. I look at the girl, who has finished with one mat and is starting on another, and consider asking her whether she knows where you sleep, but I know what she'd say, know what she'd do, so I look at the house and try to remember the things that you'd said, the clues that you'd given, but I can remember nothing. I sit until the sickness passes and then this is what I do. I have brought with me a note-book and a pencil and as I walk from your house to our glade in the trees I leave a note under every large stone, every fence post and every tree hollow. I tell you I love you. I tell you I'm waiting. I tell you to come soon but you don't.

'So then you went to the real wedding?'

You turn, you see me, your dreaming eye and then your seeing eye. The vows have been made to another but it doesn't matter. You were mine first.

'And did you speak to him? Did he see you?'
'It was afterwards, outside, he came out with her on his arm, and she was old, I could see it in the winter sunshine. He threw a cape around her, drew pale fur about her face, but still I could see – lines at her mouth and white hairs on her head catching the sun. Then he saw me.'
Her voice dies. Hoffmann waits. The feeling of numbness

has spread. He feels nothing at all, just an anxiety to hear the end of this tale.

'His smile dropped, as if it had fallen from his face, and as I moved forward so he stepped back, shaking and staring.'

Bigamy is sinful, I tell them, sinful in the eyes of God and in the eyes of Christ. Your guests look around. They look at me and then they look at you. Instead of human talk there is now just the chatter of the birds, our witnesses. He is already mine, I say, knowing the birds will agree, he swore himself to me, and I walk towards you with my hands held out, and you look at me with both eyes wide and still you back away and still I come forward, smiling, knowing that soon you will smile too and just waiting for the smile to come but it doesn't.

You stop because your back has reached the wall and you can go no farther. And then you laugh. I expected a smile. You point towards the wood and say do you mean that, that was nothing, that was just a piece of fun and I couldn't marry you not when you belong to another God not when you're dirty one of them not of us what we did was nothing meant nothing surely you couldn't think it meant anything God knows the birds and trees are not real witnesses surely I didn't really believe that I just did what I did because I could and because I fancied an easy girl and even though I know all of you are dirty I was willing to take the risk because you are a pretty little thing in spite of what you are.

'And when I reminded him about the woods he said he remembered it very well, and that we'd had a good time, as everyone could see, but that didn't mean anything. And then the old woman that he had married came up and took him by the arm and whispered to me that of course a young man must sow his seeds, it was only to be expected. And then they walked past me, the old woman giving me a shove with her elbow and pretending it was an accident, and I turned away and ran, after my trail of rain-sodden notes and decayed pieces of paper from so many months ago, back into the wood.'

She ends with a gasp and clutches her stomach with both hands.

'What is wrong, Hannah?'

'I am remembering.'

'Remembering what?'

'The pain.'

He fights an urge to hold her. Her pain reminds him of his own. He wishes he could curl up as she is curled up now, her body crouching over her arms, her arms in her lap, her knees drawn up. He is too old to hurt, too used to covering it up, pretending it is not there, but it is. It is. Carl Philipp. He feels as if a piece of him has been wrenched away and in its place there is a wound bleeding and burning.

'Enough, Hannah,' he says, reaching out, touching her on her shoulder. 'We'll start again tomorrow. I am, and you are, too tired now.'

CHAPTER 22

Frankfurt Fashion, Spring 1852: The Trends, the Style, the Colour

A REPORT BY JOSEPHINE CHAMPAGNE

It is such a joy to be a woman in Frankfurt now. At last the Paris fashions have reached our provincial banks and we are embracing it with much enthusiasm. The crin-o-line, for example, such a wonderful creation, it makes every woman such a sensual being; just the application of a little corseting and the fastening of hoops and it is quite possible for even the most stout of us to stir men's hearts with our wasp-like waists and our magnificent posteriors. Oh, it may be agonising to wear, and sometimes we may be a little short of breath or generate complaints that we are taking up more than our fair share of seat or pavement, but undeniably all these trials are vindicated by the result; just yesterday I was privileged to see from my window the most serene costume in peacock blue, the sleeves still quite large, but not unfashionably so, and set off by a rather magnificent shawl in crimson and green cashmere. This lady had taken care with every scrap of her attire, her bonnet matched her gown perfectly and her hair was dressed in the most exquisite fashion. I was stirred to having quite uncharitable thoughts concerning her tailor and her milliner.

But alongside all this I spare a thought for our men. What a sad prospect now for the less gentle sex. There is not a single creative outlet for them any longer; now that their gaily coloured waistcoats and complicated cravats are no longer de rigueur. It makes the world a much duller place, without excitement, without colour; I quite lose heart. How glad I am to be a woman, when there is so much more to occupy the mind: so many fine damasks, silks and luxurious velvets. How our menfolk must survey the wonderful land of our wardrobes and despair.

'What happened?' Angelika says, stretching out her toes.

'Nothing.' Dagmar turns over. She wishes she could pretend it never took place, but it did. She had got it wrong, terribly wrong.

'Is it Tobias?'

'That little piece of dirt.'

'Big piece of dirt!'

'He couldn't do anything, he was too drunk.'

She does not say the rest: the way she had thrown herself on top of him on the bed, the way she had squirmed and wriggled, hoping to initiate a reaction, and then the way he had batted her away, as if he didn't know who she was, muttering something about paying her later and pimps.

'All men are useless,' Angelika says sleepily, 'they're not worth bothering with.'

Hoffmann does not go home. Instead he goes straight from the asylum to the morgue, where he will spend the evening investigating the cadaver that had once been Grete Richter.

For a few minutes, before he makes the first stab, he allows memories of the living Grete Richter to drift through his mind. The feeling of numbness remains but distantly he remembers her. She had been such a gentle, interesting case, quite refined in her own way. He thought he had come to know her quite well, had spoken to her family several times, and yet he had never realised the importance of this Cornelius waiting for her outside. How being loved obsessively could be so very onerous if one didn't love back.

Grete, he was sure, had just spoken of him casually as if he were a friend. Maybe Hoffmann hadn't known her very well at all. Maybe if he had talked to Grete as he had talked to Hannah he could have helped, could have reassured her that it was not a sin to be loved and yet not to love back. He sighs and looks at the body again. It is a transformation he is used to performing in his mind. She is becoming just an object, a parcel of skin, bones, blood vessels and flesh: a machine he didn't know at all with parts that no longer work.

As usual he sections the entire torso in his hopeful search for the seat of her insanity. The stomach, he tells his assistant, who is eagerly taking notes at his side, is narrow, contracted in the middle, as expected in someone who has ingested so little for so long. The liver and kidneys are sound, but when he investigates the right lung he finds some tuberculosis, which he had not detected with his stethoscope, and also signs of more tuberculosis in the intestine. This he had not expected at all, but it did explain the cough of her latter days. The assistant mutters that perhaps this is the cause of her madness, but Hoffmann shakes his head.

'Tuberculosis,' he says, 'in its many forms, is rife. If tuberculosis really was responsible for madness, as some have actually suggested, then the world would be in chaos.' He waggles his scalpel in front of the young man's face. 'No, we will have to look for the cause of the Fräulein's compulsions elsewhere.'

Then he turns and begins the more strenuous task of opening the skull. The brain, it turns out, is normal. He tells his assistant to underline the word 'normal' in his notes. Although expected, this is also a little disappointing. Yet again he has failed to find a somatic cause of madness. This will add to the ammunition of the psychists and their moral causes, but will not alter the opinion of Hoffmann and his somaticist colleagues at all. Like Griesinger, he is becoming confident that madness is an organic disease of the brain; but it is such a complex organ, consisting of such intricate, opaque material, it is quite possible that they are just not able to see the full detail of its structure yet.

Autopsies always exhaust him. He thanks his assistant, a rather zealous student from the Senckenburg Insititute, for staying on so late and starts the short walk home. Now he is away from the stench of the morgue he allows thoughts of the living Grete Richter to intrude again. He remembers her anxiety to get better and her irritation when she failed; her condition was pernicious and quite beyond the efforts of either of them. A change of location subdued them for a while but gradually the symptoms would encroach again, simple checks leading inexorably to longer and more elaborate ones until her day was again dominated by her obsession. He had gone on to try every remedy, even balneotherapy; a taxing process owing to the precautions she had had to take before entering and leaving the water. He had talked to her, of course, but not to the extent he had talked to Hannah. If only he had, maybe she would still be alive in the asylum and becoming well. A yellow flame of lamplight touching a horse's mane summons up the memory of a sunny morning and the light catching Grete's hair as the new assistant combed it out. Maybe if he had talked to Grete as he had talked to Hannah he would have found out about Cornelius and her determination to deprive herself of food. He is sure now that the two were connected. He remembers Beatrice giving a quiet gasp as the hair she was combing fell out upon Grete's pillow. He wonders briefly whether Grete had been aware of her baldness and decides that she had not. She had always seemed so lonely; her obsession had had the effect of isolating her completely. Monomania, he decides, is a more cruel fate than a full mania. The monomaniac is partly sane and fully aware of their madness; and yet quite unable to do anything about it. The full maniac, however, lives in happy ignorance of his degraded state.

At his front door he catches himself giving his customary glance up to the window of Carl Philipp's room to see whether a light is still showing. It is, of course, quite dark. He curses himself for his stupidity, and then a thought he has been trying to ignore for the last few days bursts into his head so violently that he winces: perhaps Carl Philipp has some form of monomania too. Even though he tries to force it away the thought continues to nag at him as he walks quickly up the stairs and into Carl Philipp's room. Maybe his son's recent behaviour has been the result of some lesion of the brain. Hoffmann hangs his jacket over a chair and pours himself some water from the jug on the stand in the dark. Maybe if Therese had thought of the boy as ill rather than naughty she would have let him stay, but then again it might merely have increased her desperation to let him go. She might even have insisted that Hoffmann find a place for him in his asylum so that he could be properly cared for. He lights a lamp, then loosens his cravat and peels off his tight trousers. He shakes his head. Carl Philipp was not mad, it is a ridiculous concept. He had no obsession, no mania, he was just wilful and disobedient and intent on receiving some attention. Carl Philipp had wanted love and yet his mother had been quite determined that he should go, and just at this moment Hoffmann feels that he will never be able to forgive her. Things have changed, he thinks dismally, and they can never be changed back again. He should have stood up to her, he should have insisted that the child stay. He lies on the bed in his shirt, looking at the blackness of the ceiling; sure that this feeling of guilt and bitterness will haunt him for ever.

Beatrice looks in the mirror as she combs out her hair. The daylight is weak but there is just enough to see. Each strand, she notices, is exactly the same as the next, a dark cocoa brown. She remembers combing Grete's and the strands, all of them, suddenly coming away with the brush. She had stopped and stupidly tried to pat them back. Now it seems that all she was doing was futilely trying to stop Grete's life from escaping. It was as if it were seeping from her and she was trying to spoon it back. Like a bucket with leaks, she thinks, angrily giving her hair a pull; she had no hope at all but no one ever told her that. They must have heard her jabbering away about how Grete was at last putting on weight again and laughed. It was all just water, Frau Antoni had told her when she had mentioned it last night, that's all it was, a sign that Grete's heart was failing; the plumpness a sign of impending death. Beatrice pinches her cheeks. She looks so tired this morning, her skin is sagging like Grete's did before the swelling. She wonders whether she should stay in this place, whether she can bear the frequent deaths and the general feelings of hopelessness. She had heard that sometimes people were cured, that they were allowed to return to the outside world, but she has seen very little evidence of anyone becoming better in the month or so she has been here. She hadn't expected it to feel quite so desolate. She had expected the mad to be interesting, even funny, but they were not. Mostly they were miserable, mostly they cried or wailed, mostly they looked as if their madness was holding them captive and all they wanted to do was to break free. She wondered whether it was infectious; whether it was true that witnessing a fit could be dangerous and induce one in the well. Even if she escaped madness she would probably not escape bitterness. If she were to stay, she would become like the two assistants in the room next door; old although they are young, hopeless although their lives stretch before them. She twists her hair into a braid and then fastens it on the back of her head before tying on her cap. Her mother had said the cap suited her, made her look sweet. She frowns. She certainly doesn't feel sweet now, she feels as sour as an apple plucked too soon from the tree. She creeps down the stairs past the women's epileptic rooms, which today are strangely quiet. What is in store for her, she wonders, now that Grete has gone? Grete. She pauses a minute to think of her. It seems wrong not to miss her, to just go on as if she has never been.

Dagmar looks at herself in the mirror and decides it didn't happen. Probably Tobias won't even remember anyway. She will carry on exactly as if yesterday had never been, but from now on she will be a little less easy. He will have to fight to have her. Men like to achieve victory, she thinks, remembering her brothers' tales of triumph exchanged behind the thin wall. The chase was sometimes almost as good as the catch, one of them had said, and the other had murmured agreement. She decides she will feign reluctance to meet him, may even refuse once or twice to meet him at all; maybe she will claim headaches and dizzy spells and other feminine infirmities. She will promise and then keep him waiting. He will be like a dog waiting for his bone, and an image of Tobias comes to her, squatting on his haunches, a very large, fat tongue lolling from his mouth. She smiles: in the end he will be so hungry for her he will not be able to bear it and will pull her to his room right in front of Frau Antoni's nose.

When she is close to the bottom of the stairs she sees him on his seat by the door, staring ahead. For a few seconds she stands quite still, inspecting him, remembering how he was yesterday when his head seemed full of some other woman. She remembers a name called out, and then, soon afterwards, a promise of money. A shudder of revulsion passes through her and she tries futilely to force it away: that nose, the forehead ridged like that picture of an African monkey she once saw in a schoolbook, but most of all that shockingly stupid expression, just as if his head holds nothing at all. She shifts and he sees her. He leers and winks so knowingly that it is obvious he has at least vague memories of yesterday afternoon. 'You can have me tonight if I'm not too busy,' he says, loudly, careless of anyone hearing. 'But be careful with me, Fräulein, I'm quite a delicate little flower, you know.'

She lowers her head and dives quickly into Frau Antoni's kitchen.

'A bad business, yesterday,' Frau Antoni says as soon as she sees her.

For a few seconds Dagmar stares, wondering how she knows. She imagines Tobias telling Hugo and Hugo telling Herr Antoni and then the whole household knowing and laughing.

'Poor Grete, such a lovely girl, such a shame.'

'Oh, I thought . . .'

'What?'

'That . . . that she would live.'

'Oh, I knew that death was ready for her. When you've been here as long as I have, you can see him waiting at the shoulder. But it makes you think, doesn't it, Dagmar?'

'Think what?'

'Think about your life, and what is to come, how your actions in this life determine what comes next . . .'

Dagmar looks at the older woman, her eyes narrowing. 'I believe, Frau Antoni, that I have nothing to fear.'

'Oh . . . well . . . I'm sure you examine your soul, my dear.'

A death changes everything. Even the women who seem to live completely in their own world are unsettled, edgy. After chapel they return to the day room and their normal Sunday afternoon activities are ignored; the books are left unread, the dominoes remain in their cupboard, and there are none of the familiar sounds of ball hitting ball or ball hitting skittle from the men's room below. Ingrid rocks on her chair, her knees drawn up to her chest, rhythmically groaning and crying; Lise sits motionlessly, continually mouthing words; and Hannah periodically lays down her work, glances towards Grete's seat and just stares. All around hoots, cries and the occasional laugh are immediately silenced. The assistants sit passively at the sides, doing little, watching silently, occasionally swooping up to help a woman to the door.

Frau Antoni tells her husband later that when she entered the day room that afternoon a feeling of depressed listlessness hit her, like a door in the face, and then, shortly afterwards, she had the bizarre feeling that something was about to happen, which of course it did.

Josef spreads his silk gown upon his bed and smooths it with his hand. At his desk there is an unfinished letter, and on an easel, which is a recent addition to the room, a half-finished painting of a cat. It is a distorted and less lifelike copy of a picture pinned to the bookshelf in front of him. The room smells strongly of turpentine.

'I would just like your answer, Herr Antoni, yes or no.' Josef's voice quivers.

'Well, sir, I think the answer must be no for now. We have not enough staff, you see, so Hugo cannot be spared. Maybe your brother could find someone for you.'

'But I should like to have Hugo, Herr Antoni, I'm afraid no one else would do.'

'I'm sorry, sir, but Hugo cannot be spared.'

'Very well.' He returns to his easel ands eases a perfectly clean smock in crimson calico over his head. 'I had a cat like this one, you know. He disappeared, no one ever found out where he went. He was a tom, of course, a nasty little thing really, sprayed all over the curtains. My brother's wife loathed him, loathed him with a passion.' He stops, picks up a brush, dips it into a puddle of red on his palette and dabs it on the cat's side. 'Do you think, Herr Antoni, that the gentler sex are in fact the less gentle? Do you think, for instance, that they could take an innocent creature and wring its pretty little neck?'

'I am sure that some of them could do that, sir.'

'Yes, Herr Antoni, that is my view also.'

'I'm afraid I shall have to go now, sir. Is there anything else?'

'Just one more thing. You discussed my proposition with Hugo perhaps?'

'He'd told me you'd asked him, sir.'

'And what was his view? Did he make himself clear?'

'Well, you know Hugo, sir, I am sure he couldn't care one way or the other.'

Josef's brush hits the canvas again and again, leaving small spots among the lines of dappled brown and ginger fur.

CHAPTER 23

Observations on the protection and fastenings of windows in the lunatic asylum (précis)

From the outside the windows of a lunatic asylum should look like the windows of any other comfortable establishment. They should not remind the patient that they are imprisoned.

However, it is also essential that the windows are safe. It is essential to ensure that (i) the patient cannot open them, thereby escaping or causing injury, and (ii) the patient cannot break the window and injure himself or others with the fragments.

The other requirement of a window is, of course, that it should be an adequate defence against weather of all extremes.

While point (ii) above can be adequately prevented by using an internal wire mesh, (i) is more problematic. The usual solution is to use a latticework in which only small areas may be opened. There are various designs: diamond shapes work better than squares, and in Brussels I have seen frameworks in wood in different mathematical shapes which are both efficient and appealing to the eye.

Heinrich Hoffmann, 1857

When Hugo passes Angelika on the stairs he touches her on the shoulder once. She stops, rests one hand on her hip and asks him what he wants.

'Just to tell you I'm sorry.'

She starts to smile. She has been practising what to say.

'About Grete. It must be hard on you, knowing you might have done something.'

The smile disappears. She opens her mouth but her words are never heard.

From the bottom of the stairs Herr Antoni calls: 'Hugo, quickly, come with me. Angelika, fetch the doctor. It's Josef, he's on the roof.'

Josef has tied all Lise's scarves to the sleeves of his asylum jacket, two to each arm, attached by two corners so they are stretched out and catch the wind. On his head he has tied another scarf from which his ringlets hang out below, loose like a savage's, and around his neck he has attached his silk paisley dressing gown so it falls like a cape.

'I am going to fly,' he says, and he spreads out his arms. 'How beautiful I am, like a bird, just like a bird.'

Antoni and Hugo are at the window of his room while Hoffmann and Angelika stare upward from below. 'In God's name, Angelika, how has he managed to get out there?'

'Herr Antoni said he didn't know, sir.'

Hoffmann squints at the window; the fastenings look secure, only a small part of the window open, he could not have got through that. Then he looks around the building. There on the women's floor is another window, one he has never noticed before, different from the rest. 'What's that?' he asks Angelika. Although the window is not large it is bigger than a man's head and it is fully open.

'I think it's a window in the laundry store, sir, but it's kept locked all the time, I don't see how he could have got in there. We always lock it, sir, we make sure of it.'

'Well, it looks like he has.' He raises his voice. 'Herr

Neumann, climb back into the building and come down, at once.'

'Why? What is there to come down for? I have nothing left, nothing. Everything I love is denied me. There is no beauty anywhere. Everything is grey, dull. There is nothing left, nothing to live for.'

He walks along the narrow ledge just in front of the guttering. From the ground it looks as if there is no space in which to walk at all, but Josef walks, his arms outstretched, tipping from side to side as he maintains balance.

'Herr Neumann, you must come down. Taking your own life is a crime against God.'

Josef begins to laugh. His hands flap. 'What is God? Who is God?' He swings around, stumbles, falls against the sloping roof and then leans against it. He shouts hoarsely at the sky. 'If You are there, if You truly exist, then You are the most cruel joker. Why did You make me? What was the purpose? I am no use. Everyone tells me so. I am just a decoration with no function at all. And now I am not even allowed to be beautiful.' He stands again, stretches out his arms. 'I shall have one last outing, one moment of fantastic flight. I shall be beautiful beyond measure and you will all remember me as I was meant to be: Josephine Champagne, striking, splendid, an inspiration.' He steps back, lifts his arms up high so the wind catches the scarves again: four brilliantly coloured flags.

Angelika gasps, grips Hoffmann's coat sleeve with both hands.

'Josef?' A voice calls from high in the building.

Josef stops, tips his head to one side. 'Is that you?'

'Yes, it's me.'

'O object of desire, o thing of great beauty, let me see you.'

Hugo appears at the open window and pokes out his head, then his shoulders, and eventually squeezes through entirely.

'O such joy, for this to be the last thing I see.'

'Come in, Josef. Herr Antoni has agreed that he can spare me, if you still want me.'

'Is that true? Antoni, tell me, is that true?'

'Yes, sir, that is the truth.' Antoni's voice is immediately below him. Josef starts, looks down, giggles. 'Well, if that is the case then maybe I shall live a little longer after all. Hugo, promise me that it's true.'

'It's true, sir, you have my word. Would you come in now, sir? Would you like some help? I think I could . . .' Hugo is on the roof now. He stands up, takes one hesitant step forward, tips to the side, falls violently back against the roof.

'Hugo! No!' Angelika pulls on Hoffmann's coat. 'Please tell him, sir.'

'Herr Jung, I think what you are about to attempt is most inadvisable,' Hoffmann yells up hoarsely.

'And there is absolutely no need, o most divine one. I am coming.'

And the splendid human bird trips lightly along the roof to follow Hugo back in through the window.

Hoffmann walks back inside the building then watches as Angelika rushes past him and runs up the stairs. Following more slowly behind her, he arrives on the men's landing just in time to see her rush up to Hugo, throw her arms around him and bury her head in his chest. For a second, just a second, Hoffmann sees Hugo's face change; it softens, his mouth opens slightly and an expression of naked tenderness passes fleetingly across it, and then it drops.

'Where is Herr Neumann, Herr Jung?'

'In his room, sir, with Herr Antoni.'

Hoffmann passes, puts his hand on Neumann's door then looks back. He has forgotten something, something he should have said. 'Thank you, Herr Jung. That was most commendable. An act of courage, sir, and insight. I am most grateful.'

'Sir.'

Hoffmann watches as Hugo detaches the young woman and holds her from him. Then Hoffmann looks away, not wanting to see what might come next, and opens the door into Josef Neumann's cavern.

The commotion outside has brought everyone who can walk in the day room to the window. In the Meissengasse, the small crowd of people that had gathered to stare up at the roof is slowly moving away. Frau Antoni ushers the women in the day room back to their seats. The crisis has passed, no one fell, there were no cries or screams, just a murmur once, of a crowd enjoying a spectacle. The doctor is right, the Meissengasse is the wrong place for an asylum. They need somewhere more tranquil, somewhere farther away from eyes hungry for sensation.

Strangely the incident has improved the atmosphere in the day room. Frau Antoni looks around; it is noisier, the women who can talk are doing so, and for a while she allows the assistants to just let the chatter continue. After the twitchy silence of earlier it is a relief. A step has been taken beyond Grete's death; from now on things will settle.

I know now. There are two different places, two different lives: the life I lived before and the life I live now. I cannot remember one becoming the other but it has. They used to be indistinct, merged, cream mixed in with the butter-

milk. But one by one the memories are gathering themselves together, floating to the surface, and I gaze at them and wonder: now or then; this life or the other? For instance, there is this: the man with the scarves. I woke and he was there: half dream, half real. I had seen him before, somewhere the birds chattered. Can I have these, he asked me, holding up some scarves. They were not mine, I remember that, I had washed them for someone else, but when I'd looked around the room where I was then, where I am now, all I could see were people with empty eyes. So I said yes to this man, please take them, because how can anyone with a vacant mind own anything at all? Then he smiled and I reached up to feel whether he was really there and this wasn't a dream because sometimes it is difficult to tell. I touched just once but took my hand away quickly because I had never felt a man with skin so smooth, not a single brush of a bristle on his cheek. And I asked him who he was, what he was, and he said Josephine, you remember, I told you before. They are talking about him now. They say he has gone on to the roof and threatened to jump but he didn't and I want to know why, why did he want to jump, and tell him that he is not alone, that I would like to jump too, if only I could, if only I could reach the roof, if only I had more will than I do.

Hoffmann retreats to his office, holding Josef's keys in his hand. Josef will not say how he got them, where he found them, but Antoni says they must be the master set, which belongs in his office in a cupboard he hasn't opened for weeks, and when he goes to check he sees that they have gone.

'Perhaps,' Hoffmann had told the trembling Josef, 'we have allowed you rather too much liberty.'

The man had said nothing in reply, merely demanded again to see Hugo. When Hoffmann had explained that this would not be possible, Josef had crumpled into a corner of his room, his scarves and cape folding beneath him, muttering that yet again he had been deceived, and that the world was indeed just as spiteful and abhorrent as he had always thought. Hoffmann had nodded to Antoni, and together they had begun to empty the man's room. In Hoffmann's experience the inventiveness of a man determined to take his own life knew no bounds and the safest procedure was to leave him with virtually nothing at all. Even his clothes would have to be replaced with small items; nothing that could be torn up to make a noose.

'Here is Hannah again, sir.'

She sits in the chair. He can't remember what she said last, can't remember how to start. For a few seconds he sits, floundering, then glances at his notes. Pain. She was talking about pain. At once he remembers and feels it too: the pain of Hannah and his pain of Carl Philipp's departure. His breath is drawn in so sharply it is almost a gasp. She glances quickly at him.

'You were talking about pain,' he says. 'Do you remember?'

She nods.

'What was this pain? Was it real?'

She nods again. 'Here.' She touches her stomach.

'And does it still trouble you?'

She shakes her head. 'After the baby came it went away.'

When the rain comes tumbling down
In the country or the town,
All good little girls and boys
Stay at home and mind their toys.
Robert thought, – 'No, when it pours,
It is better out of doors.'
Rain it did, and in a minute
Bob was in it.
Here you see him, silly fellow,
Underneath his red umbrella.

What a wind! Oh! how it whistles
Through the trees and flow'rs and thistles.
It has caught his red umbrella;
Now look at him, silly fellow,
Up he flies
To the skies.
No one heard his screams and cries,
Through the clouds the rude wind bore him,
And his hat flew on before him.

Soon they got to such height,
They were nearly out of sight!

And the hat went up so high,
That it almost touch'd the sky.
No one ever yet could tell
Where they stopp'd, or where they fell;
Only this one thing is plain,
Rob was never seen again!

CHAPTER 24

The Dangerous Times in the Life of a Woman (An anonymous 1851 reworking of Laycock's ideas of 1840)

A perfect maiden in the bloom of youth is indeed like the most exotic flower. But she is in thrall to the vagaries of her uterus rather than her brain and needs constant careful attention.

The woman's brain, of course, is 10 per cent smaller than a man's and, more importantly, is lacking in frontal development. This causes her to be less capable of dealing in the abstract, in fields such as philosophy and science, but causes her to excel in the dealings of the heart. Education is undesirable and even dangerous in a woman, especially those in the lower social orders, and can lead to obscene language and conduct. But most problems arise from irregularities of her nervous system and reproductive organs, and there are times in a woman's life when she is particularly vulnerable.

The onset of puberty can be particularly problematic. If menstruation is not established successfully and at once, she can become artful, hysterical and monomaniacal and particularly subject to, for example, the influences of the unscrupulous mesmerist.

In pregnancy, obstruction of the menstrual flow, especially in those who are young and unmarried, may cause longings, for example a hankering after raw meat, which may sometimes only be satiated by killing. In these cases controlled haemorrhaging by scalpel or leech may be the only recourse.

At other times ovarian irritation may burst forth without warning. A beloved member of a household may become irreligious, self-willed, drawn most unsuitably to members of the opposite sex. She may lose self-control, become over-stimulated and seek gratification. This moral insanity will lead inexorably to nymphomania unless treated: galvanism, medication and moral and hygienic therapy have all been used with success.

But the most dangerous age for a woman is undoubtedly the approach of the critical period. The celibate woman in middle life has a great void of nature unfilled. The age of pleasing is past though the desire is still there. It is then that in desperation she may make a match with an unequal companion; someone younger and of lower class. Otherwise she will concentrate her love on a particular animal, for example a parrot, a cat or a poodle.

With the shrinking of the ovaries the woman becomes lean, angular and wrinkled. Her hair loses its colour and her skin loses its lustre and transparency. She is a virago, offensive to men and women, intrusive, mischief-making and jealous. This can be treated with strong cordials to allay nervous tension.

A heaviness, a heaviness growing, something I have felt before but it wasn't like this. This time it grips me, squeezes once, hard, and harder still until I cry out. I stop, lean over, make it go, a tightness and then a blessed relief, and then I go on again: beyond the wall to where the street becomes track, where fence becomes hedge and there are no lamps or houses or people, just the trees and the birds, my witnesses.

I am both heavier and thinner now. Thin arms, fat waist, thin legs, breasts swollen, veined, my skin dark: a snake that has opened its jaw and swallowed an egg. But I have swallowed nothing. The thing that has infected me came inside me when I slept and grew. Sometimes I think about what it must be: perhaps a toad or bird. Sometimes I feel it fluttering.

My mother sees only my arms, only my face, makes me soup from the scraps of the chicken of another meal and watches me eat it, and all the time there is the taste of iron in my mouth, all the time there is a feeling that there is something else sharing my body, blowing bubbles in my stomach, shifting and stretching out, making me sick. I hide it all with my clothes: my thick skirt with just one petticoat, the belt let out two notches, then over this my apron and over this my shawl. Are you cold, my mother asks, and stokes up the fire, are you ill, you look so pale, so tired, and she feeds me more soup, the fat resting on the top in glistening puddles.

Don't pine, my mother says, it does no good to pine, it won't bring him back. And I look at her, I let her see my eyes throw out sparks and say nothing. She knows who it was who sent him away, locked me in my room. She knows why I am as I am. I have no hope, no joy. All I had is gone. I shut my eyes but there is just blackness there. Even that part of him is gone. Eat, my mother says, when she sees my face. Talk, she says when I am silent. I sit below the lamp, let my needle rest, just for a second, lean back and I am gone. Into that place where everything is forgotten. When I wake my mother is there. Looking at me, her eyes narrowed. I am losing everything, she says. You are all I have left and I am losing you too.

But Elisabeth knows about the bird. I see her looking at where it flutters. I see her eyes watching when my shawl slips, noting how my apron strings strain when I stretch up outside the shop to rearrange the clothes. So you are soiled, she says. My brother will not be interested now. He would want something pure and untouched. And I press my hands over where the bird pecks.

And Elisabeth knows about Kurt. She knows when he marries and she knows where. Then she comes to me with a smile and tells me because she likes to see me hurt. Does he know, she asks, and stares at where the bird is sleeping.

In the night I watch it move. I lay on my bed with a candle and see it stretch its wings, shift and stretch my skin. My belly is patterned with its claws, red lines dividing where the flesh has torn beneath. I hold my breath and hope it will die. But it doesn't die; now as I run again into the wood I feel it somersault. You have a baby in there, Elisabeth said, but I shook my head. I am ill, I told her. Something has crawled inside me and is making me sick. Then she tipped her head in the way she does, made crescents of her eyes and smiled so I could see her teeth all pointed and small. Is that what you think? And then she turned away and laughed.

I reach the trees. I hang on to the nearest slender trunk and wait for it to pass. A heaviness is punching at my lungs, forcing out cries. The trees shake. The birds start from them, with cries of their own. When it is finished there is a silence as soft as moss. I go on, deeper and deeper, find the place with the bent trunk, the bower of trees, the flattened grass, the memory of clover and dandelions, but there is nothing there now. Just ghosts of more screams. Just the feeling of being pushed down and the grasses snapping beneath us. Just your hands unfastening my dress and my hands helping you. A blackbird cries out twice and you have the dress in your arms. We don't need this, you say, and gather it up, all my stitches, all my work, but I don't mind. It is crumpled but I don't care. I watch it make a small loop through the air on to the branch beside me. It hangs there like a piece of sky, blue, an entrance to His heaven. I watch it tremble, fall, stay. Now we are married, you say. In God's eyes. He sees us through His blue gateway in the trees. My God and yours. The God of all things. The one that the birds know. But my God knows I have not bathed in the woman's bath and I wonder whether I shall be punished. The mikwe *lies unused in the Judengasse, its waters empty. Beside it my mother wails. And you look at me. We have no bridal belt of jewels and gold to encircle us, so I trail a stem of creeper around us. It has tiny white flowers, each one a diamond, each one a star. May our descendants be as many as the stars in the heaven, I say, and you laugh. We have no wine to drink but the canopy of the trees can be our* chuppah. *It is too late to braid my hair, too late for my mother's veil. I look at you without modesty and I know my God is watching and I wonder at what He will do. Underneath my dress there is nothing at all, no chemise, no petticoat, just the map of my body on my skin, the tender mountains and gentle valleys, and you trace a route with your finger. My love, you say, and you continue your journey with your tongue. My wife, you murmur, and you are lying on me, your skin on my skin, joining, coming apart, joining again. I love you, you say, and the deepest part of me divides and softens.*

Is that when the bird entered? Sometimes I think it was. Something flew into me then and you covered my mouth with your hands.

I cry out again. The new cries fit into the imprint of the old. The same branches shake but now their leaves are curled up and new, waiting to burst forth. The leaves that shook before are withered, crackle where I lie, brown, orange, a bright red and a purple. I watch them through every new wave of pain but they do not change. On one there is a network of veins picked out in red, and on another there is a piece taken out like a bite. I sit up, wait for the pain to come again and it does. I look at the leaf; at the edges there is a little brownness, a little decay, and underneath there is the red and white brilliance of a toadstool. I reach forward, wait and the pain comes again. The leaf falls away. There is the toadstool, the spots painted on, each one perfectly round, perfectly formed. The spots form the outline of stars and then circles. I follow them until the pain fades, but then it immediately comes again. And this time something is coming with it, the promise of an end; the certainty that if I were to push it will stop and I shall be rid of it. So I wait. I breathe in. I watch a leaf twist from a branch and fall. I reach out to the toadstool and touch its surface. And then it comes: a splitting, burning sear, something I have to push away although it hurts even more, and then push again, downward, harder and harder until my breath runs out. And then it ends. There is nothing left. The toadstool is crushed in my hands and by it is the bird. Flung out from its nest. Pink, raw, covered in yolk and sticky albumen, with arms instead of wings and hair instead of feathers.

'What happened to the baby, Hannah?' Hoffmann says abruptly, anxious to continue. She seems to him to be ready, alert, the pain of yesterday evening subdued. Hannah holds her hand out flat in front of her, palm upward, and looks at it. 'She was so small, hardly bigger than my hand. And so warm. I didn't expect a baby would be so warm, and when I held her, when I picked her up, she was heavier than I thought, so small and yet so heavy. But she didn't move. Her eyes were shut as if someone had sealed them up, and from her stomach a worm, moving on its own, joined to what came next, from me, slithering out to join her between my legs.' She allows her hand to drop upon her lap, watches while the fingers of her other hand creep up to hold it.

She glances up at him. She seems so sad, so isolated. He reaches over, takes both her hands in his and squeezes them tightly once. 'It's all right,' he says. 'You're here with me now. Tell me what happened next.' He kneels before her, dimly conscious of his knees upon the ground, and looks up into her face. 'Tell me, Hannah.'

'Already she was becoming cold, so I held her to me, but she became colder still. I licked her face and all at once she mewed, weakly like a cat caught in some distant place, and so I opened my blouse and held her to me again, felt her mouth close around me, her tongue flick out and then stop.' She pauses, swallows.

'Go on. It's all right. Go on.' He drops her hands, rises a little, puts his arm around her shoulder and pats her gently. She looks down at her hands and her voice begins again, quiet, and then becoming quieter still. 'I shook her slightly, stroked her head, told her she must suckle, but she did not. She grew colder still. I drew my skirt around her to cover her but still she grew cold. The great blue-and-purple worm stopped its throbbing and grew cold too. And then I just sat. I sat until the sky darkened to indigo, until a sliver of moon appeared among the branches and a bat began its swooping search overhead.'

She looks at him again. Her voice has faded to nothing. He crouches beside her, one arm around her, the other holding her hands on her lap. He can smell her: the spice from her last meal on her breath and the faint odour of coal tar on her clothes. And he can feel her warmth, even through the layers of cloth he can feel her warmth. He moves slightly closer. Silently her eyelids press downward and then rise up again. She seems to be asking him a question, one he doesn't want to hear: why? There is no answer, he thinks, no answer to anything. So many children come painfully into the world only to very quickly depart it again, sometimes without a murmur. There seems to be no reason, no sense. He swallows. Carl Philipp had been such a healthy baby. The wet nurse had joked that he regularly sucked her dry. It seemed to everyone that he smiled early, walked so steadily and chattered easily. He remembers how Carl Philipp used to wait for him at the top of the stairs, *Struwwelpeter* clutched to his chest. Then, as soon as Hoffmann opened the door, there was that infant voice, a duck-like quack: 'Papa! Can I have "Cruel Frederick" tonight, Papa? Please, Papa?' The nanny used to try to hush him, but Hoffmann always waved her away, and he would run up the stairs, sweep the child and the book into the nursery, and they would read together until Carl Philipp fell asleep. He sighs, unconsciously squeezes Hannah against him so her head rests on his chest. She shudders. He raises his hand, lifts her chin with his forefinger. Her lips are parted; the tip of her tongue darts out, sweeps the corner of her mouth and disappears again. How close she is. Her breath touches his face, mingles with his own. He watches as her lips close and then part again with the sound of a kiss. His longing to feel their warmth is sudden, urgent and intense.

He swallows, shakes this nonsense from his head. He has slept so little that his mind is playing tricks on him, allowing ridiculous ideas to take hold and blossom. He allows her chin to drop. Her story is not finished. She must tell the end.

'And where is the baby now, Hannah?' he asks gently.

Her hands twist in her lap, one around the other. For a while her mouth just moves soundlessly.

'Hannah?'

'I . . . made a hole . . . a nest . . . in the leaves. I put her there. She looked . . . happy . . .' She looks up at him. 'Like your baby in the box. She looked happy. Not smiling. But happy.'

'And then you left her?'

She nods.

The baby is asleep. I close her eyes. Around her I lay all her possessions, all the things she knew, the piece of flesh that followed her, the length of blue rope that twitched at her stomach and now lies there quite still. I touch her, remembering her, wishing I had known her. She is not mine. She is just something that appeared and then went, and now that she is gone I wish I knew more of her. I take a handful of leaves and hold them over her. The brown-gold rain flutters down and soon only small scraps of her remain. I stand. My legs feel weak but I can walk. I flatten down my skirt and it sticks wet and cold to my legs. I hitch up my shawl, draw it up over my head because I feel cold. I reach the edge of the wood where there is a wall. I bend. My legs are shaking so much I have to lean against it while I gather my stones. The shaking travels from legs to hips to stomach to arms and head. My jaw rattles, but still I gather my stones. The pockets of my apron are full. I move heavily, slowly, even though the bird has gone. When I reach the river the moon seems fuller, brighter. Its crescent shines over the water and is broken into pieces. There are still lights on some of the boats, still the smell of meat cooking and a faint whiff of gunpowder. Near by a woman cries out and a man laughs. I am close to the bridge. I walk along the river until I see the place where the bottom of the river rises gradually towards me to form a bank. The sand is soft under my feet. The heavy stones in my pockets make me go deeper. It is so much effort to pull out one foot and then the next. But soon there is water at my ankles, at my waist, at my chest, cold, numbing, smothering, and through the water a shaft of light, the moon making rays, a white dust making footprints. I follow, I follow, water in my ears, in my throat, in my eyes; all I have to do is keep them open and I shall see.

The silence is smashed. Around me lights, people, an oar

waggling at my face. Grab this, for God's sake grab this. There is not enough air, not enough time to say for the love of God let me be, for the love of God . . . But He doesn't listen.

CHAPTER 25

*Uses and Problems Arising from Leech Therapy:
A summary*

(FROM THE *SCOTTISH JOURNAL OF MEDICAL
PRACTICE*, EDINBURGH, 1832)

The medicinal leech is a common enough organism found throughout
Europe, the Americas and the Indian subcontinent. It is of use almost
universally, applied directly where needed. For instance, Dr Vaidy
reports that thirty leeches applied to the chest will cure chronic
pleurisy, and twelve leeches applied to the jaw will cure a toothache.
In cases of fever Dr Beddoes recommends that relays of dozens of
leeches are used in order to accomplish sufficient letting of the blood.
Leeches are of particular value in the treatment of nervous diseases,
for instance leeches applied to the temples of children will bring immediate relief to those suffering a fit, and Dr Esquirol reports the success
of leeches in the womb to re-establish the lochia. This is essential in
order to bring about the recovery of a woman suffering from melancholia after childbirth; and also at the anal opening in order to imitate
haemorrhoids, since the healing of these is often associated with
various types of madness.

Although these treatments usually take place without incident there
are occasional problems associated with their use. The main problem
occurs when the leech is removed, and due to active attraction of
blood from the surrounding tissue towards the leech's puncture the
wound bleeds excessively. In this case the best course of action is to
apply gum arabic or pressure or sponges coated in liquid pitch to the

wound. Another problem occurs when the leech strays from where it is needed or is inadvertently ingested into the throat or stomach. In this case the use of vinegar or mustard is advised. It is not recommended that leeches be used where a patient is of a general gangrenous condition or that leeches ever be applied directly to ulcers or inflammation.

Hoffmann drums his fingers on the desk. According to Esquirol premature cessation of the lochia is a frequent cause of melancholia. Esquirol's idea was that the system had become blocked and this blockage caused an imbalance; remove the blockage and the system restores itself. Esquirol has claimed some success: his case book is filled with his examples. Hoffmann looks at Hannah; how can he bear to do what Esquirol recommends? It seems so primitive. This whole idea of blockages and balance is already beginning to look a little old fashioned. Even though medicine is gradually becoming more scientific, everyone continues with what they have done for centuries – bleeding, purging and applying blisters – because this is what is expected and this is what they know how to do. And because he is determined to complete the cure there is no alternative but to follow Esquirol. He calls Herr Antoni and asks him to find some morphine. It will be better if she is relaxed.

Have I drowned? Did I drown? I remember gasping at the air. But was it too late? I remember coughing, and with the coughs came great mouthfuls of river water and vomit, but maybe it was too late and everything that follows is a dream. It seems like a dream now. There is a light. An oil lamp held in front of my eyes so I see nothing but its flame. I keep looking at it. It flickers only when they talk.

The infirmary has a high table convenient for such operations. Not that it is really an operation, of course; the only cuts will be minuscule and leave little scarring. He calls for Beatrice and Hugo, and after they have arranged Hannah on the table he dismisses the man with a small flick of his hand. Beatrice can stay. He checks Hannah's pulse, listens to her lungs, feels her skin. Every measurement and sensation is noted.

I cannot move, even though no one is holding me down I cannot move. They remove my clothes, ease them from me, one after the other, and each time my flesh is made bare it is replaced with a sheet. Always there is the flame. I watch it sway and then move back again.

Beatrice passes the jar to him. He inspects the contents, considers their dimensions in the newly fashionable French system: about two centimetres long, and there are about twenty altogether. Hoffmann likes to see the leeches swimming. He thinks that they move quite beautifully; their black bodies flatten into ribbons and they ripple in the water until they find some sort of anchorage, when they convert again into the folded-up form, small and inconspicuous, awaiting prey. But this leech jar is only a little moist and the leeches are stuck quite firmly to the sides. He has to shake then prod them to make them fall on to a sheet of paper. Here they at once anchor themselves firmly at one end and begin to search with the other. Usually he has little time to watch but today he does. As they stretch they thin out and it is quite possible to observe the head. It is the slightly thicker segment at the end. He also observes something he has never seen before: the leeches are not, as he thought, completely black. If he looks closely he can see that there is a subtle and rather attractive mottling along both sides of the central black strip, and underneath they are not black at all but a pale green, and on top there are fine yellow bands. Hoffmann stands, watching the leeches stretch, detach their back ends and move quickly along the paper. Beside him Beatrice shifts uneasily. 'Don't you like them?' he asks.

She shakes her head. 'Once, when I was a child, I fell into a pond, and when I came out there were lots of them stuck to my legs, I couldn't get them off, and when I did at last they just stuck on again and again.'

'But if you look at them closely, Beatrice, you will see that they are quite admirable. God has designed them so well; they are so perfectly suited to what they have to do.'

She looks more closely, shudders and then looks away. 'I think they are rather like small, moving sacks of tar,' she says, 'the way they can go so thin and then so fat. What are you going to do with them?'

Hoffmann pauses. He does not like even the thought of what he is about to do; he wants even less to say it.

'Fräulein Meyer needs to bleed in a very specific place,' he says at last. 'It will, I believe, make her feel much better if she does. Sometimes, Beatrice, nature needs a little helping hand.'

He takes a breath and lifts the sheet to reveal the length of Hannah's legs and the base of her stomach. Although she is sedated her head shifts and she breathes more quickly. He shifts her legs, divides them, and bends each one at the knee.

'In there, sir?' Beatrice's voice is small, a little incredulous.

'Yes, *ad labia*.' The Latin gives an immediate and welcome clinical edge. She is no longer Hannah Meyer but Patient H.

Someone there, someone opening me, as if I am a flower coming out of bud. As if something is warming me, making me open. Like the spring sun. Like a flame. I watch it move

*with his words. This will not hurt. Something I heard before,
the same voice saying the same thing. He opens me a little
more, shifts the flame so it is farther away. Then his touch,
unexpected, a shock. I know I should recoil, cry out, but I
do not. All is well, and there is something in his voice that
soothes me. Something that makes me watch the flame, just
that, watch it disappear then rise up again.*

'Those, Beatrice, are the labia and that the perineum. As
you see, it has been a little torn. Ah, if I had delivered this
woman of her child, I would have seen to that . . . as it was
she was all alone. It is too late now, of course. You need
to wash just here, firstly with a little warm water and a very
little soap, and then with just water alone.'

The girl nods.

*Now he is at my head. Smoothing my hair. If I could just
move my eyes from the flame I would see him. But the flame
captivates me. They are attending to the place that burnt.
Perhaps they are trying to soothe the hurt away but I think
they cannot. It will not go.*

'And now, Beatrice, the leech. It will not take long.' Wearing
a pair of kid gloves, Hoffmann tries to transfers a leech to
the washed dark flesh with a pair of forceps. At first it
dangles from the metal, then he encourages it to detach with
a wooden spatula. 'You see, Beatrice, we must be sure not
to damage the creature.'

At last it drops. It is quite silent. It anchors itself quickly
into place and starts to fill.

*I look for the trees but they are not there. What has made
them disappear? There is no sky, no moon, just the flame
and the sound of murmuring voices. Everything else has*

gone. Something cold replaces the burning. One thing drops, holds on, and then another.

'I think four will do, Beatrice. We must keep a close watch. As soon as any one shows a sign of moving we must make sure we return him to the pot.'

The small black curls widen, become rounder, less black, more red.

I look for you but you are not there. I look for you in the flame and inside the lids of my eyes but nothing of you appears. I have lost you but I do not feel empty. Kurt. There is only your name left. There is nothing else, no love, no desire, no longing. Just the knowledge that you are gone. I do not feel empty, merely clean. I do not feel finished. I am just waiting to start.

The first leech rolls away and Hoffmann swoops forward with his forceps. Where it has been a bubble of blood appears and quickly becomes larger.

It happened. I know that now. It happened and now it is finished. I loved you. I would have always loved you. I would have given up my world for you, I would have waited for ever. But you did not. You did not wait. You settled for less. You gave in. I did not.

The two fleshy petals are bleeding copiously now. Hoffmann nods his approval. He feels the pulse in her neck and looks at her face. The morphine is wearing off. Her eyes drift slowly towards him. 'I would like Beatrice to help you dress now, Hannah. You will bleed for a while but that will help you. I shall see you again tomorrow.'

She nods and then, as Hoffmann watches, a slight smile

appears then disappears again. He feels his breath catch. No longer Patient H. His heart beats more quickly. He remembers the flick of her tongue at the corner of her lips. She is calm, quiet. Hoffmann clenches his fist and allows himself to feel a little happiness. He has cured her. He is sure he has cured her.

CHAPTER 26

Come, Take the Waters at Wiesbaden!

Twenty-six springs, renowned since Roman times, will rejuvenate you and cure you of all ills. Our fine hotels will pamper you and see to your every whim.

Our fine clear air will clear out the stench of the city and allow you to breathe deeply again.

Then, when you have emerged from our warm waters so rich in health-restoring minerals, you will be spoilt by the richness of the Wiesbaden night . . .

Music! Casino halls! The seat of the Duchy of Hesse-Nassau! Socialise in Style and Opulence in our modern buildings and wide avenues. Everything is presented in the most exquisite taste for your complete satisfaction and comfort.

Come to Wiesbaden once and you will want to return – again and again.

H. Knopf, Pension, Roeder Strasse, Wiesbaden

Hoffmann considers his notes on Hannah. 'Indications that lochia interrupted by shock. This was re-established using leeches.' Such inadequate words. He looks at the empty chair. He remembers her face gazing up, her lips and that flicking point of tongue. He tries to force this image from his mind, tries instead to summon up a picture of Therese, but the one that appears before him is frowning, disapproving, her tuts rattling in time with his tapping on his desk. He gives up on this too, and glances at his notes again. Maybe he could publish her story: 'The case of H – A Cure Using Moral Therapy?' He would have to argue that all this talking had simply led to information about the somatic cause of her affliction. In the end he had not achieved any moral therapy at all. Her soul was just as corrupt or as good as it ever had been. Hannah was not ill because of her own wrongdoing but as the result of everyone else's. That was his opinion. No doubt Heinroth's view would have been very different. The girl was ill, he would have said, because she had allowed her primitive will to take control. She would be cured when she fought to resist these temptations and led a more virtuous life. Heinroth did not allow for love. Whereas Hoffmann would show that talking had served merely to give a clue to the physical cause of the disease, and that by treating this aberration of the body he had succeeded in healing the mind: hence the lochia, and hence the leeches. It was a textbook case; Esquirol would have approved wholeheartedly.

Hoffmann smiles, sits back, relaxes, but at once it is there; the thought he has been endeavouring to keep away: Carl Philipp. He allows himself to dwell on him a little, to finger the edges where it doesn't quite hurt. Then another thought occurs to him that causes him to slam his case book shut and pick up his bag. Maybe Carl Philipp has written, he would just have had enough time. He calls goodbye to Herr Antoni and without waiting for a reply nods at Tobias at the door and walks into the finest drizzle of rain.

But Carl Philipp has not written. Without a word the maid hands him just two letters, which are both from addresses in Frankfurt. He suspects that Therese has been telling the servants that the master of the house is in a very bad temper and to leave him alone as much as possible. At the top of the stairs two small faces appear and then, squealing, disappear again.

'Line? Eduard?' He holds out his arms. 'Come to your papa.'

'No, no, we're afraid.'

He roars and they squeal again.

'I'm coming to get you!'

Eduard is laughing so much he has given himself hiccups. Hoffmann runs up the stairs roaring and laughing, his arms stretched out, and at the top collides with Therese.

'I am sure, Heinrich, that their nanny will not appreciate their being excited quite so much before supper.'

He stops. It is the face he saw earlier, the same frown. Then she turns and marches to her room while he marches to Carl Philipp's and sits on his bed.

The room still has the boy's presence, mostly his destructive one: a handle is missing from one of the drawers and is hanging by a thread from his curtain pole, his cupboard has a large chip removed from one side and a long scrape on the other. His mirror is scratched, the jug in the bowl is chipped in two places and the surface it is standing on is curiously pitted all over with small dents like the surface of an orange: obviously the work of several hours. Carl Philipp was always busy in his own way.

There is a rustling at the doorway. He looks around.

'I was wondering, Heinrich, if you were honouring us with your presence at dinner tonight. We have guests, in case you've forgotten.'

He had forgotten. The thought of talking, and, worse still, keeping up a front that everything between them is well, exhausts him. He sags down on the bed.

'Well, are you going to be there?'

He could sneak out, grab his coat and bag and just leave.

Everyone would assume he had received an urgent call from a patient: one of the advantages of his profession.

'I'll see.'

She snorts and turns away. He lies back on his son's bed, listening to the sound of his wife's footsteps fading away down their small landing. It was always so easy to tell Therese's mood from her footsteps. Fast meant angry or impatient, slower meant her mood had improved. Usually, these days, her footsteps beat about the house in a manic staccato. He shuts his eyes. It hadn't always been like this; once, he was sure, she had been quite happy to see him. He had been a young doctor then, busy, a glamorous, slightly rebellious air about him. He smiles; that was what someone told him she'd said. Although in reality his life wasn't ever very glamorous at all. He had always been desperately short of money. Of course, Therese hadn't know that. She'd probably been under the impression that he was quite affluent: his two rented rooms in the Meissengasse for his practice, his visit to Holland as the private doctor for a travelling Russian officer and his wife, his work at the charity hospital, all of which paid very little, of course. It must all have sounded quite promising to a young girl so short of relatives but so full of social aspiration.

'Are you going to get ready, Heinrich?' Her voice, strident, and impatient, calls from their room.

Groaning loudly enough for her to hear, he raises himself slowly from Carl Philipp's bed. The sound of it creaking reminds him of the many times he has rushed in demanding that Carl Philipp desist from his jumping at once for fear of the bed breaking. Therese is Carl Philipp's mother, he reminds himself. There is a little of her in Carl Philipp too. He will remind her later. The thought gives him some satisfaction as he whistles the tune that she hates and enters their bedroom.

Therese has decided to invite their single friends: Fräulein Wolf, who proved to be so useful in ascertaining that there was not a single school in Frankfurt willing to take the boy, the Fräulein's older sister, also a spinster, and Frau Weiss, a youngish widow of about thirty-eight. Therese has also invited Gustav Müller, partly as a sop to her husband but mostly as a possible suitor for Frau Weiss. But Gustav Müller is irritating his friend. Often, after he has drunk his way through an entire bottle of wine on his own, Herr Cabbage becomes too garrulous even for Hoffmann's normally tolerant tastes.

'Ah, and the women there . . .' he is saying.

'Where, Herr Müller?'

'At Wiesbaden, of course . . . that's what I've been talking about to Fräulein Wolf for the last half an hour . . . their décolletage!' He raises his eyes to the ceiling. 'Apparently it's all the rage in Paris this summer to let the necklines sink as low as is decently possible, which according to some good ladies in Wiesbaden is very low indeed, and a damned good . . .'

'Herr Müller!'

Herr Cabbage takes no notice, simply raises his voice to add emphasis. 'And a DAMNED fine idea it is, too. When will it catch on in Frankfurt? I wonder.'

'Not too soon I hope,' says Frau Weiss, glancing down at her unimpressive bosom.

'Ah, never mind, my dear young lady, I am sure you have other highly desirable qualities.'

Frau Weiss looks slightly flustered, the dilemma of both wanting and not wanting to show that she is flattered by his labelling her 'young' and his faith in her other attributes confuses her.

There is a short pause which lasts just long enough for Therese to jump in. 'We are hoping to visit Wiesbaden ourselves, are we not, Dr Hoffmann?'

Hoffmann mumbles something he hopes is non-committal into his soup.

'We have heard such wonderful things about the properties of the water there. I understand there have been scientific analyses of the water and they have been found to have quite wondrous concentrations of health-giving minerals.'

Hoffmann snorts.

'Indeed so.' The younger Fräulein Wolf joins in enthusiastically. 'They have found that it is just as the Romans claimed so long ago: warm waters with amazing natural powers of healing. I have heard tales of cripples being lowered into the water unable to walk more than one pace, climbing out themselves after a couple of hours and walking completely unaided.'

This time Hoffmann's snort is louder.

'Did you say something, my love?'

'Rubbish, that is what I meant to say, absolute humbug.'

Herr Müller laughs.

'Dr Hoffmann, that is a little rude!'

'I am sorry, but propagating such deceits I believe to be quite wrong, quite dangerous.'

'You do not believe such accounts, then?'

'No! Neither do I believe in all the poppycock that is circulated in such places: mud baths, mesmerism, phrenological readings, galvanism.'

'Galvanism? But Heinrich, you have practised that yourself.'

'Scientifically, as an experiment. I do not advocate using it to treat the perfectly well. And anyway, I am sorry to report it didn't work. Neither do a lot of other things.'

He is abruptly quiet. His fingers clench around his spoon. If he carries on in this vein he will go on to talk about the hopeless lot of the modern doctor, who is in the hapless position of knowing that most of the things he carries in his black case and most of his treatments have no point at all, except perhaps as placebo or comfort. 'And of course it is all extraordinarily expensive,' he finishes, knowing that he has again annoyed Therese, this time with his vulgar mention of money.

In the distance there is an insistent knocking at a door.

'Not for us, I'm sure,' Therese remarks, passing around some bread, but a few minutes later the maid enters, almost at a run. She bows slightly in the general direction of the table and then rushes up to Hoffmann. 'If you please, sir, you're to come quickly. There is a man called Pichler here and he says his wife needs your urgent attention.'

Feigning regret, Hoffmann dabs at his mouth with his napkin and rises immediately from the table.

As he passes the stairway on the way to the front door he hears it creak, once. He turns, expecting it to be Carl Philipp – it was one of his favourite games when they had dinner guests, to sneak out of bed and stand listening at the door – but of course there is no one there. Line and Eduard are too young or too wise or too cowardly to play such a game; they are probably lying asleep in bed, their cherubic faces as good and as characterless as those of angels.

CHAPTER 27

The Establishment of the Eichberg Asylum, 1849

We, the governing body of the Duchy of Nassau, are pleased to announce the opening of our new modern asylum built on the same principles as Dr Maximillian Jacobi's model asylum at Siegberg. This large Eichberg asylum will supersede the smaller Eberbach asylum. Henceforth the insane will be held in a completely separate establishment from the confirmed criminals. Furthermore the patients will be subdivided following Dr Jacobi's system into the curable, who will be treated in a mental hospital, and the incurable, who will simply be comfortably detained.

Published by order this day 24 August 1849

In the entrance hall there is a young man with a wiry black beard pacing the short breadth from the bottom of the stairs to the door and back again. When he sees Hoffmann he rushes up to him and grabs him by the arm. 'Dr Hoffmann? Please come, come at once.' Then he is at the door, fumbling at the catches, while Hoffmann holds out his hand for the maid to bring him his hat and bag.

'My dear young man, I am afraid you are going to have to walk a little more slowly,' Hoffmann says as the man sets off at a swift trot down the road.

'I'm sorry, sir, but it's my wife. You must see her. I think she's . . .' He stops where he is and sobs. 'I do believe, sir . . .' He grabs Hoffmann and pulls him by the arm. 'It's just this way, sir, please hurry.'

The young man hurries off again. He is slight, not much bigger than Hoffmann, and tidily dressed, with a professional rather than wealthy air about him.

'Sir, please, this way.'

He hurries up the stairs to a house very much like Hoffmann's own in a street just off the Hochstrasse. In the hall there is a collection of inner doors each leading to separate apartments. Pichler unlocks one to the left. 'In here.'

His wife is lying on the floor, in their bedroom, both hands clutching at her throat. Her eyes are half shut and she is panting. From time to time a weak groan escapes from her and one of the two maids who are kneeling beside her reaches forward to fan her face. When they see the doctor the girls, both quite young, stand and back away.

'I found her like this, Doctor, she won't tell me what is wrong.'

Hoffmann kneels beside her while the girls curtsy and start to walk quickly from the room. He calls them back. 'A moment, please.'

They stop, look at each other and then at Hoffmann as he begins to examine his patient. She groans and shudders when he touches her neck. Her pulse is weak. When he tries to remove her hands from her throat her fingers tighten.

'No, leave me be.' Her voice begins and ends with a gurgle.

There is something wrong with her mouth. Her lips are too red and a trickle of saliva is seeping steadily from a corner. 'Could she have . . .' It is hard to find an appropriate term. 'Taken something that could perhaps have been poisonous?'

Pichler opens his mouth, covers it with his hand. 'I don't know, perhaps, no . . . I don't know.'

Hoffmann looks at the girls. They are quite pale now.

The younger one has mimicked Pichler and holds her hands over her mouth. She removes them slowly, her eyes wide. 'I was looking for the washing soda a little while back, sir. I couldn't find it, I . . .'

Hoffmann holds up his hand and the girl stops. He inspects Frau Pichler's hands, wipes a little white dust from a palm, tastes it on the tip of his tongue and nods.

'Can you get me some vinegar?'

The girl nods and runs from the room. Hoffmann turns to the other girl. 'Go with her, you understand? We also need some water, and some cooking oil or some eggs.' She also nods silently and follows her companion out of the room.

An hour later Hoffmann and Pichler are sharing a little brandy in the couple's dining room. Hoffmann looks around him over his glass. 'You're a designer?' he asks, noting the plans that litter every surface.

'Architect.' Pichler takes another sip of brandy and then looks quickly at Hoffmann. 'My Rosa, she will be all right now?'

'The poison has been neutralised, yes, but as for your wife's well-being, Herr Pichler . . . Was there any sign she would attempt such a thing?'

'We have been unhappy, sir, since the death of our child. I . . . well, I have had my work, sir, but Rosa, she has no one, will see no one. She spends all day in this place alone, refuses to leave, and will not talk.'

Hoffmann nods, regards the young man over his glass, and waits for him to continue.

'Do you think I need to do something, sir? I hear you work in the asylum, surely I don't need to send her there? I couldn't, sir, the thought of her in that horrible place, full of people screaming and crying. Not my Rosa.' He puts his glass on the table beside him, covers his face with one hand. 'She wouldn't be able to stand it, sir, I'm sure.'

Hoffmann crosses over to him, puts a hand on his shoulder. 'Your wife needs to be safe, Pichler, needs to be taken away from all that troubles her here so that her mind can heal. She is ill but she will become well again, you have my assurance. And it really isn't that bad, you know, there are people in there . . .' He stops. He thinks of Carl Philipp lying in one of the beds, working alongside the other men weaving baskets. He thinks of Hannah sitting surrounded by screaming, laughing women but still quite alone in her world. 'But I am afraid we are a little short of room,' he says, 'certainly for the more sensitive class of patient. I know Dr Roller, the superintendent of the big new asylum in Illenau, it is very modern, is well equipped. Maybe you can take your wife there. You can tell her that she is going for a cure. I shall make enquiries tomorrow.'

Pichler looks up, smiles briefly. 'You are most kind, sir.'

Hoffmann waves the thanks away and sits back. 'If it is acceptable to you and your wife, I should like to accompany you both. I would appreciate an excuse to see my friend Dr Roller again and also a chance to inspect his new asylum and his methods.' He smiles. This young man is intense but pleasant company, and the prospect of leaving Frankfurt for the day fills him with so much pleasure that he forgets Therese and the inmates of the asylum. For a few seconds he even forgets Hannah and Carl Philipp.

Frau Antoni settles into bed beside her husband. The bed makes its usual sighs and creaks and once again Frau Antoni complains that the mattress is really becoming far too uncomfortable and that she will order another one just as soon as an opportunity arises. Herr Antoni just grins at this and turns over because his wife has been saying exactly the same thing most nights for the last ten years.

'I shall,' she says, as though she can hear him smiling in the dark. Then, after a few minutes, she adds, 'Well, this has been a dismal couple of days, even for this place.'

Her husband does not reply. The bed in darkness has always been one of Frau Antoni's favourite places for talking, and if encouraged she will lie there gossiping and going over her various concerns and worries for the next hour. Herr Antoni is tired and anxious to get up early in the morning to catch a fish or two before he has to start work.

'First Fräulein Richter, then that poor Neumann on the roof as well as all that business with the assistants . . . Has the doctor found out who drew that golden ring?'

Herr Antoni grunts a no.

'My money would be on Tobias. Or maybe Dagmar . . . no, Tobias, he's stupid enough. You know, I think those two have had some sort of tiff.'

Herr Antoni gives an obviously manufactured snore. She nudges him gently with her elbow and turns over. She imagines Josef on the roof and then Grete lying pale and still on the mortician's slab, then, because neither of these two images is conducive to sleep, she forces herself to remember the smaller images of the day: a glimpse of the backs of Angelika and Hugo as they walked through the gate from one garden into the next; the sound of Tobias's high, wheedling voice calling after Dagmar and then Dagmar immediately appearing in the kitchen, her forehead crumpled in a frown. Then little Beatrice coming in with a giggle, saying that Tobias had asked her to rearrange her day off so they could go out for a walk together over the river. And Dagmar trying to ask her quite casually whether she will go, but the tension quite clear in her voice, and the innocent Beatrice smiling and saying of course not, he was far too old, and ugly in looks as well as character, and she could well imagine her mother's face if she appeared at the door with that monster on her arm. And then a tense sort of quiet, interrupted only by Dagmar rattling the pans more loudly than usual. Then, later, Frau Antoni remembers seeing Hannah Meyer. It is this memory which finally sends the woman to sleep: Hannah and Angelika walking side by side like friends. Hannah's face flushed, a little swollen around the eyes, as if she had been crying, but smiling now, following Angelika's words intently and adding a few of her own, and Angelika looking happy too, her arms moving as she talks, and then, as they disappear into the work room, Frau Antoni hears a laugh. A real laugh, a sound of happiness rather than the sound of mania, so unfamiliar that Frau Antoni has to wonder to which one of them it belonged. And then the door is shut and the laughing stops and Frau Antoni stands there, still wondering and waiting, before the smell of burning draws her back down into her kitchen.

In the room on the top floor the three remaining occupants are asleep. Today was Lise's last day of sitting upright. Tomorrow, when she wakes, she will find herself unable to move. This is something she will be aware of only dimly. She will struggle and twitch and then give up. Every part of her is gradually seizing up. In contrast with her bladder, which has been left permanently open, her digestive system has been shut down. Food and waste lie within her slowly decomposing; and tomorrow she will be transferred to a small room of her own where she can be treated with frequent enemas, changes of sheets and washes. The real Lise, the one that used to inhabit this body, is mostly gone. She had a last moment of lucidity some weeks ago when she realised that she no longer owned her legs, and from then on this vital essence of her gradually disappeared. She has died slowly, unremarkably, and completely unaware.

Hannah sleeps. It is something simple and yet extraordinary. For the first time since she came to this place she has slipped into unconsciousness easily and rapidly. She will wake astonished.

For now Ingrid will continue exactly as she is, exactly as she has been for the last fifty years of her life. Most of the time she is content. That is what she would say if she knew the word: content. Nothing more, nothing less. If her stomach is full, if she has a piece of cloth in her hands which she can examine and then pull apart thread by thread, she will be content. As long as she has that her day is marred only by her occasional wants. They come upon her without warning: a seat in the sun; an extra piece of bread; another piece of cloth; her next-door neighbour's skirt. Her desire is absolute and, because she cannot express it with words, she cries urgently with gestures. If Angelika is in a good mood she will understand immediately. If she is not she won't. Ingrid's contentment depends directly on Angelika's, and today Angelika has been most content. Ingrid's sleeping smile is a reflection of Angelika's in another room not far away.

But Angelika is awake. There are so many thoughts leaping and diving inside her that she cannot keep still. She lies on her back, curls up on one side and then the other. Hugo loves her. He said so. Even though his face did not change, even though it was as still as it ever was, he said those words and she believed him. He has loved her for some time from a distance but was afraid to come close in case she turned him down. Dreams are better than nothing at all, he'd said. Now he wants them both to leave this place and start somewhere else. He has other dreams too, he says, and if this Angelika dream has come true then so might all the rest. He thinks they would be happier. Would she come? Angelika squeezes herself tight. She will tell no one, not yet.

Beside her Dagmar grumbles softly. She is dreaming. In her dreams she is bigger and heavier than Tobias, has leapt upon him and is slowly and very happily squeezing every morsel of air from him.

Josef closes his eyes. The room is bright with moonlight, even the curtains have gone. They have left him with nothing. There are just bare walls, a bed with grey blankets and his desk. Even that has been emptied. Just a handful of quills that can do no damage and a small pot of ink. Not even enough ink to drink. A tear collects at the corner of his eye and rolls down on to his pillow. And they deceived him. He has seen not one sign of the beautiful Hugo since it happened. Antoni said he was busy, but the old man's eyes had rolled away from Josef's face when he'd said it.

Josef opens his eyes, looks around the room again: wall, bed, desk. Nothing beautiful, nothing even interesting. They have taken everything. But then he looks at the desk again and remembers. He gets up, walks over to it and presses on the back. The flap opens. Hugo didn't tell anyone. He kept his promise. The scarves are gone, but there is something left, something very useful. Josef decides to wait a little longer, until the birds have started to announce the dawn.

CHAPTER 28

Frankfurt Asylum Statistics 1851–9 (classification inspired by Griesinger)

Melancholy: 22 men, 29 women, 51 total; 52 per cent cured, 9.8 per cent died.

Mania: 29 men, 36 women, 65 total; 40 per cent cured, 21 per cent died.

Partial insanity (or monomania): 8 men, 15 women, 23 total; 13 per cent cured, 7.2 per cent died.

General confusion: 7 men, 2 women, 9 total; 22.2 per cent cured, 0 per cent died.

Terminal dementia: 14 men, 13 women, 27 total; 15.3 per cent cured, 37.5 per cent died.

Symptomatic dementia: 7 men, 7 women, 14 total; 7.1 per cent cured, 88.2 per cent died.

Inborn dementia (or idiocy): 9 men, 6 women, 15 total; 6.6 per cent improved enough for discharge, 26.6 per cent died.

Hoffmann wakes and at once wonders where he is. Carl Philipp's room. For a few minutes half-formed thoughts tumble with scraps of dreams: a white face, still as death, a missing child, a smile that is not his to kiss, a woman crumpled on the floor and someone falling from somewhere high above him. He takes a breath, sorts the images into order. Carl Philipp is not dead, merely sent away. It is the only thought that gives him comfort, the only one he can bear to touch in any way at all, but even this still hurts. Why hasn't the boy written? Surely someone could have helped the boy to write. Gradually he remembers the rest: he had come in late smelling of brandy and Therese had not been impressed. She had made it quite obvious that she hadn't believed much of his tale and had stamped upstairs to her room and slammed the door behind her. He lies there for a few minutes looking around Carl Philipp's room. It is quite clear from the light that it is still irritatingly early and yet he is wide awake. Gradually he remembers what he is to do today and once again the thought of riding through the Rhine vineyards cheers him a little. How he needs to escape from Frankfurt, just for a few hours. He doesn't think he could bear another day in the place. He rises from his bed, rings for one of the girls and she comes, untidily dressed, her hair not completely in her bonnet. He tells her that he will be requiring an early breakfast and she skulks away with only a rudimentary curtsy. Since the servants always seem to take up Therese's mood and amplify it, it is quite clear that his breakfast this morning will be served with a certain sullenness and little grace.

Josef opens his eyes; in spite of everything he has been asleep. For a few seconds he just looks around the room. It is quite as dismal as it was yesterday, except the dawn light seems to add an extra blue-greyness to the walls. He turns over, slowly stretches out his legs and levers himself on to the floor. He has the slow movements of an old man, as if every part of him hurts. He shudders once then straightens. He starts to step across the room but at the sound of a quiet creak he stops and listens. Nothing else happens. He reaches into his bureau and withdraws a keyring from his secret drawer. There were two sets of spare keys. Antoni had only remembered about one. Holding them tightly so that they do not jangle, he unlocks his door and glances into the corridor. He is still in his nightshirt, his feet are quite bare and silent, and his movements are slow and careful. Every few minutes he stops and listens. There are plenty of sounds, plenty of moans, calls, the occasional scream or laugh, but nothing close. He continues, clutching the keys to his chest.

Hoffmann sighs, rustles yesterday's paper, rattles his cup in its saucer. The maid comes over but asks him whether he will be requiring more coffee with such vehemence that he meekly says no before he has even had time to think about it. He folds his paper. There is nothing left to do but stand and retire to his bedroom to dress; it is still only six in the morning.

Josef reaches the wood-lined corridor on the ground floor. The ceilings are higher here; everything is grander and more ornate than on the floor above. It is the public part of the asylum, the part on show for visitors, but they are few. From close by there is the sound of Herr Antoni coughing and then clearing his throat. Josef stops, listens. Silence. He continues on his way again. He has never been into the garden this way before. There is a door at the end of the corridor leading to the women's garden. Usually he goes through the kitchen to the men's. There is a catch and a lock. He turns the key but the door doesn't open. He removes it, inserts and turns it again and again, but still nothing happens. On the third attempt he jangles the keys, and they ring like tiny chimes up the corridor. He stays very still and listens. In the Antonis' room there are voices and then all is quiet again. Josef tries the latch, twists it one way then the next. It clicks. The door opens inward and the keys fall back into his hand. He stops at the threshold. His night-shirt is made from cloth so fine that it is translucent in the morning light. He spreads his arms out, and for a moment the sunlight catches him there: his long curls hanging loosely down his back, his body clearly visible through the cloth, and for that moment, if anyone were to see him, they would say he is what he so desires to be – a young girl stepping out into an early summer morning. Josef breathes in deeply once, then again, throws the keys as far away as he can, then follows them on to the wet grass in his naked feet.

Hoffmann dresses carefully. He will need his coat, just a light one in case the day turns cooler, and he will need some food and drink. He thinks about asking the cook to make up a basket but decides against it; it will be much easier just to buy something on the way. He glances at his watch. He expects Carl Philipp will still be asleep in bed, wherever that bed is, or perhaps he has been lying awake. Perhaps he has been lying awake night after night, wretchedly crying into his pillow. Hoffmann forces the thought away and replaces it with another: Antoni will be getting up soon. He will just have time to see him before calling on the Pichlers to start the journey.

The women's garden is different from the men's. The men's consists of grass under the washing line, a few bushes and small fruit trees, but mostly vegetable patches interlaced with paths. The women's garden is more decorative; there are small flowering bushes, flowers and, at the back, a couple of large trees with twisted trunks. Josef stands beneath one and looks up, then at the object he has in his hand: a coil of washing line he found hanging on the wall between the women's garden and the men's garden next door.

The Hochstrasse is surprisingly full: Hoffmann had no idea there were quite so many people with so much to do this early in the morning. There are women delivering bread in large baskets, men cleaning the street of yesterday's manure, quiet conversations being conducted below stairs, a girl standing aimlessly with churns of milk by her side, horses stamping on the ground, their breath steaming from their nostrils and adding to the mist on the street. Everything is quiet; it is as if the world is smothered in a thick cloth which muffles all sound. Hoffmann is careful with his feet, but even so he hears them, sharp and loud on the pavement. Then beside them he hears another set of feet, smaller and louder. Carl Philipp's. He remembers they cannot be his before he turns to look. It is just a boy, about the same age as his elder son, delivering newspapers.

Josef pauses. He is not much used to climbing. In fact he cannot remember ever climbing a tree before. It is an activity he overlooked in his childhood, and now that he has started so late in life he is finding it a little more difficult than he anticipated. His nightshirt keeps catching on branches, and the rough bark hurts his feet. Even though the air is still quite cool he is becoming hot.

When Hoffmann turns off the Hochstrasse on to the Meissengasse there is deepening quiet and shade. He feels as if he is sinking into something, maybe a lagoon or a deep cave.

Josef sits on one of the branches, swinging his legs. This will do. He looks around him. If he keeps his eyes down it is easy to imagine he is somewhere quite ordinary, not this dreadful dreary prison. He has been tricked, he thinks, tricked so many times: his brother, his brother's wife, their doctor, this doctor, even that old man Antoni has tricked him – he has seen that exquisite creature Hugo only once, in the distance, since he was enticed from the roof. He shudders. Hugo had had his arm around one of the plain female assistants, not the grotesque one, that was true, but one still plain enough to contaminate Josef's image of him for ever. He would never now be able to see one without also seeing the ghost of the presence of the other. Josef kicks out his legs and wonders how such a beautiful being could contemplate taking up with a girl so ordinary. He breathes in deeply. The air is full of perfumes he has never noticed before: grass, the faint scent of rose. Even this tree has a smell: slightly peppery, a little like soap. He stands up. Above him a blackbird twitters noisily and angrily flies into the next tree. He takes the end of his washing line and ties it carefully into a noose. Then he tests it, making sure it will tighten, and places it around his neck. He swings the other end over the branch above him and fastens it tight. Then, smiling admiringly at the sight of his ankle protruding delicately from beneath his long white shirt, he slips off the tree.

There is no one at the door. Hoffmann glances at his watch. It is nearly seven o'clock; there should be someone at the door. He bangs loudly and waits again. He fancies he hears shouts and then footsteps running but still the door is not opened. Sighing, he walks to the epileptics' wing and lets himself in using his key.

I open my eyes and I know: everything has changed. You have gone. The day lies waiting.

CHAPTER 29

Mainquai 45,
Frankfurt-am-Main,
21 April 1852

My dear brother-in-law,

Please take heart, the doctor says that you are making some progress, I am sure things cannot be as dreadful as you say. I know it may seem hard to be deprived of everything that interests you but I am sure we must trust in the opinions of the doctor and be compliant with all his wishes. He is held in such high esteem in Frankfurt, and I hear his reputation is growing throughout Germany. He wrote a book, did you know that? It is that brightly coloured children's book everyone greeted with such enthusiasm a few years ago. I believe that every educated household in Prussia as well as Frankfurt has a copy. Even the Kaiser is an admirer. I hear the doctor is also quite a prolific writer of pamphlets and various satirical works, so you really have much in common with him. I am sure that if you were to mention that you too have an interest in the written word he might be able to provide some useful advice and even introductions. Everyone here is most anxious that you become well and take your rightful place among us, but unless you give up this bizarre and wilful insistence of yours, until the doctor is convinced that you are cured, we cannot even contemplate entertaining any prospect of your discharge.

You are always in our thoughts, dear Josef, your sweet little nephews are always asking after you and demanding that we visit. We are, of course, awaiting the doctor's advice in anticipation of that most joyful day. I hope it is soon, for your sake.

Please do your best, dear man.

Your affectionate,
Julianne

I see now, everything is clear, the edges distinct. When I reach out my hand touches and I know it is there. The dawn light is making everything sharp. The things I already know are new, clear, fresh: the stitches on my blanket, the face of Ingrid, the face of Lise, the arrangement of trees through the window. I watch and it changes. Something falls. It hangs and swings. I breathe in and the breath stays there. Someone in a nightshirt with his head dipped down. I scream and bang that part of the window I can reach. No one comes.

And then, later, I have Ingrid close beside me. Her too-warm body leans heavily against me. I steady myself, stop myself falling. Then I see them come running out. The big one first, his head reaching the branch, stretching out, holding the head of the man with the broken neck and then letting go. I hear his shout, something loud without words, and then the others, the one with the unmoving face, a few I haven't seen before, and the older man who walks slowly. They all stand around the swinging man. They all touch. The big one reaches up with a knife at last and cuts the line. And then the doctor comes. He lowers the man with the snapped neck and kneels over him. He touches him and listens to his body as he listens to mine. Then he walks away, his head down, his shoulders hunched. He comes under the window and I

*strain to see: an old old man, much older than yesterday. He
does not look up.*

Hoffmann calls another meeting in his office. Just the men
this time. He crams in as many as he can and climbs slowly
on to his desk so they can see him. He has no energy. He
tries to shout but he does not have the resolve.

'Who left the door open?' he asks at last. No one replies.
He looks slowly around the room. 'Well, someone must
have left it open,' he says, 'he didn't break it down.'

'Perhaps the mechanism was faulty, sir,' one of the more
mature men says. 'We've all been having trouble with it.'

'Did you know, Herr Antoni?'

Herr Antoni sorrowfully shakes his head.

'Well, it's too late now.' His quiet voice has more effect
than his louder one. All the small sounds in the room stop
as the men strain to listen. 'I know the situation here is not
ideal, but we have to do what we can.' He pauses, sways a
little; all the men watch intently as if they think he is about
to fall.

'It is a tragedy, gentlemen, a most appalling tragedy. One
for which we must all take some blame.' He feels decidedly
ill, a little faint. 'We must examine what we do, each one
of us, and see if we can do better.' The floor is spinning,
the colours in the carpet by the desk merging into brown.

He lets the men go, drops to his knees then allows himself
to fall off the desk.

'Are you quite well, sir?' It is Antoni, of course. 'It's just
that you look a little pale. Frau Antoni has been remarking
on it for a couple of days now.' He helps him to his seat.
'You know, sir, this place, it is quite a strain. Dr
Varrentrapp always made sure he got a break, at least once
a month.'

'Ah yes, Antoni, I was . . .' He remembers the Pichlers.

He looks at his watch. It is time he was with them, but he can't go now, not after this. 'Antoni, perhaps you would do me a favour. If one of the assistants could be spared, perhaps they could take this message for me.'

Even though she knows Tobias is safely confined in the office with Antoni, Dagmar opens his door cautiously and sniffs. Up until now the job at the asylum has been satisfactory. She had had no large expectations when she applied and so she had not been disappointed. She had rather enjoyed the patients; erratic people with no voice to whom she could mete out the same punishments that had once been dealt to her. But this business with Tobias had changed everything. Never before had she been made to feel so foolish; ugly and unnecessary certainly, but never foolish. She looks around his room. She doesn't know why she is here. She has some vague idea of revenge, but even this is not fully formed. The room seems more like a depot than a place where someone would sleep or live. Under the bed is an assortment of bottles, some full, most empty, and his pot, thankfully also empty and rinsed out. Beside the bed a chest has all its drawers open, the contents spilling out – shirts, jumpers, trousers, all jumbled together, some of them clean, some of them clearly not. She resists her compulsion to tidy and sort and instead opens a cupboard at the other end of the bed. She stops, puts her hands over her mouth and gasps. Tobias has a secret hobby. On a shelf is a stack of thick paper and above it small jars of paint and brushes. Then, pinned to the backs, sides and the inside of the doors, the results of his handicraft: lewd pictures of women; men and women doing things to each other she cannot believe; and then, on smaller bits of paper, pigs and people, figures representing Jews with tall hats and long beards, sucking at the udders of sows, eating the pigs' excrement; and then, on smaller pieces still, yellow rings.

Dagmar closes the doors and backs away. Behind her Tobias enters. His mouth changes from an O to a horizontal line.

'Still hungry, then?'

With the palm of one massive hand, he pushes her on to the bed and allows himself to fall after her.

He is sitting at his desk waiting for me. It is as if every part of him is pressed down. Ah, Hannah, he says, and tells me to sit. For a while he just looks at me, his head resting in the cup of his hands, and then he says, you look a little different, you know, I am not sure how, but it is as if you . . . And I want to tell him about how things are and how things were, about the place with the leaves that has gone for ever, and the thought of you, Kurt, how you were there too, but how now you've gone, and when I think of your face now I remember how it really was, about how your dreaming eye would sometimes stray so far away from me, how you were always looking, looking, as if you were looking for someone else, and I can see now how things really were. But I can say none of these things. I remember the pain. Not the pain of the child or the fluttering bird, but the pain of knowing you, the real you, the one who said he loved me but never did. I remember it engulfing me: not just my body, but my soul, my heart, my mind. How it took my mind. I could think of nothing else. It hurt me and yet I searched it out for it to hurt me more. I look at him and I say none of these things. I look at him and wait for him to speak because in his face I see the same pain. I saw Josef, I tell him, I saw him in the tree. And his head sinks. And there was Grete too, I think, but I do not say that.

He moans. I cannot see his face any more, just the top

of his head, the hair a little thin. The moan does not stop.
I stand. I reach over. I stroke his head, smooth down the
hair, and he looks up. And I see such longing in his eyes.

CHAPTER 30

From the popular magazine Frankfurt Life, *August 1844*

What a danger these new phosphorus matches are! Every day one hears yet another story of an accident or a near-conflagration. They ignite too readily or sometimes not at all, are thrown away and then they burst into flame. Of course, they are a particular hazard in the hands of children and should be kept well out of reach of little fingers at all times.

With memories of the scenes of the devastating fire in the Hanseatic city of Hamburg still quite fresh, it is no surprise that any slight whiff of smoke in an unexpected place, or the sight of a curtain catching light, is enough to send the whole neighbourhood into a state of hysteria. Like many old cities, part of Frankfurt is a veritable tinderbox, and the dictate that each household must keep ready a volume of water in case of fire is of little reassurance. We have learnt little from the fires that devastated areas like the Judengasse time and time again. We need to ensure that our ability to prevent and fight fires is improved with the acquisition and organisation of proper equipment, and does not consist, as it does at present, of merely making a lot of noise and fuss at the first trace of smoke.

'I have lost everything.' Hoffmann grabs Hannah's hand, pulls her towards him. 'You are the only one who will listen, the only one who . . .' He stops. He looks at his hand holding her arm and lets it go. He takes a breath. 'But it is you who is ill, not me.' He passes his hand through his hair and looks at her. 'It's just that I thought with Josef, I could cure him. If I just trained his mind he would see things differently. God made him a man. God makes each one of us what we are. It is something we have to accept. Something we can do nothing about . . .' He pauses, stares at her intently. 'Antoni says that one of the assistants thinks Josef wasn't ill at all. He says he didn't need to be cured, that he just needed to be left alone. Do you think he's right, Hannah? Is all I'm doing here wrong? Are there, really, any mad people at all?'

'I don't know about madness, sir, but I am sure there are people who are so sad that they cannot bear it.'

He tips his head. He notices that her hands are quite still in her lap and her face has an alertness he hasn't seen there before. 'As you were?'

She nods. 'As I was . . .'

He smiles tightly. 'So I am allowed one success?'

'I am sure you have other successes besides me, sir.'

He shakes his head. 'Sometimes it feels that all I do is fail. There is so little I can really do, about Josef, about Grete, about anyone. All I can do is watch as the people I am trying to save perish before my eyes.'

'But there is me, sir, I have not perished, I am well.'

He waves her words away. 'Once I thought I could make a difference, Hannah. I entered this profession with such enthusiasm. It took just one young woman . . .' He stops, looks at her. '. . . very similar to you, in fact, to make me realise the pathetic limits of my power. For a time afterwards . . . I felt I couldn't continue. Everything seemed so futile. But somehow I have to keep on trying. There is nothing else to do.' He drops his head again so that his face is hidden by his hands. She watches as his fingers knead his scalp. 'She was such a brave young woman. I thought there was surely something I could do. In spite of her great pain she seemed so . . . vital. It didn't seem possible that she could fade away, but she did, just like everyone else.'

Hannah reaches over to him again. Her fingertips lightly touch the hands on his head. 'Perhaps,' she says, 'you should tell me.'

He looks at her again. 'Perhaps I should. Even though I can't see a reason . . .'

'I should like to know.'

Her voice is different now, he thinks, assured. He grins. 'As if you are the doctor and I am the patient.'

She grins back and nods.

'It happened fairly soon after I started at Frankfurt as a doctor, before I met Therese. I rented rooms, I think I've told you, on this street for my practice, and of course I practised at the charity hospital . . .'

He takes me into his world. I see what he sees: a servant girl still dressed in the charred remains of her uniform, her friends around her wailing and crying, but her mouth still. Even though they carry her as carefully as they can, even though they do not jolt her, she cries out. She gasps, she cannot help herself. He strips her clothes from her, one fragment at a time, taking care, but each piece pulls away a little of her skin. He gives her what he can to dull the pain but there is not much he can do. He stays with her day and night, talking to her, just talking. She tells him of her life, how she came to be where she was and little by little she entrances him.

'She had eyes like yours, Hannah, why did I not remember before? Like your eyes are now, moving, taking everything in. And her voice, it was like a reed singing in the wind. I could have listened to it for hours. She had come from a large family and had gone into service early. She had started as a scullery maid but had gradually worked her way up to a more senior position. She was still a maid, but she looked after the mistress of the house and was in charge of two others. On the day of the fire she had risen early as usual and gone into her mistress's bedroom to make sure she was still asleep. Then she went into her master's bedroom. He said he was in love with her, you see, Hannah, and every morning they would meet in his dressing room before breakfast. She was most devoted. She believed him when he said that he hated his wife and wanted her instead. She thought that what she had to say that morning would make a difference. She thought that if he knew he'd run away with her.'

'But he didn't.'

'No, he didn't. She told me quite calmly. He said that he had five perfectly acceptable children already and what could he possibly want with another? Then she said that she realised there was something in the back of her head, like a voice, that had told her he never would, that she had known all along that when . . . anyway, he wouldn't.'

He stops. Hannah's mouth has opened, as if she is going to speak. When nothing comes he continues. 'You see, it is not just race that separates us but just about anything else you can name, anything that divides one part of humanity from another: race, wealth, language, age . . . anything at all.'

'And he wouldn't cross it?'

'Exactly.'

Hannah looks down, inspects her fingers on her lap, then looks up again. 'So what happened next, why was there a fire?'

'She was making up the fire in the parlour when it happened. Her master had given her one of the new small phosphorus sticks and warned her to take care. She had heard how dangerous they were, how the sparks can fly off and light up anything. But she struck it anyway. When a piece of the phosphorus flew from the stick, she watched it land. It was like a seed landing on the curtain, and where it landed a shoot sprang out and quickly climbed up to the curtain pole. She just watched, without moving, without trying to make it stop.'

Hannah stares at his face. Somehow this story belongs to her as well. When he pauses she continues. 'She watched because there was nothing she could do. She knew that. She was powerless. Everything just happened around her and there was nothing whatever she could do about anything. She was like a doll without will.'

As soon as her voice fades his begins again. It is important to continue. Important not to stop.

'She watched the fire burst into bloom, watched it throw out fresh seeds, and soon the room was ablaze with flowers, all of them burning, all of them spreading pollen like smoke.'

'And still she did nothing. She was like me. She did nothing. She let it happen.' Hannah sits rigidly upright in her chair, her eyes fixed on his.

'And soon the smoke was inside her, its minute particles of ash making her choke.'

'And still she did nothing.'

'And so they found her, put wet rags over their mouths and dragged her out.'

'But she didn't really want to come, did she?'

'She died and there was nothing I could do. She hurt and all I could do was give her morphine. Her eyes lost their life and there was nothing . . . nothing at all I could do. Just like Grete, and Josef, and that child in the box . . . and afterwards, it always seemed to me that there must have been something, if only I could think of it, if only I'd been there. I should have been there for the child in the box, I should have noticed that Grete wasn't eating . . . and Josef . . . I should have given him a little of what he wanted to make him happy.'

'But you did what you could.'

'I could have done more.'

'How?'

'I don't know. All I seem to do is lose the people I come to love. My mother, my father, my son . . .' He shakes with a single sob.

Hannah rises from her seat and holds each of his shoulders. 'But you have done what you could. You fought.'

'Not enough.'

'Enough. Listen to me. Enough.'

They look at each other. Their faces are close, level. For a few seconds they hold each other's gaze, then Hoffmann holds her chin and draws her face closer still.

'Hannah, I . . .'

She draws away.

Kurt. In this room. How can you haunt me still? I see you in his eyes, your hunger, your intention. But you do not love me. You want to take just a part of me and you call that love. But it is not love and you shall not have it.

Angelika has discovered a place in the garden that is hidden from the house. It is behind the wall that Tobias knows so well, and if she were to inspect the ground carefully she would notice the faintest outline of his gigantic form upon the grass: it is slightly less green, the merest amount flattened. When she pulls Hugo there he shows no interest, he just looks ahead unsmiling, so that she almost loses heart. 'If you don't want to come with me, you don't have to,' she says at last, and in reply Hugo merely kisses her jutting lip.

It is a warm April day. They sit against a wall that has been soaking up the sun all morning long and is now allowing the heat to seep out into their backs.

'I can't tell with you, Hugo, what you want, what you feel.'

He says nothing in reply, just takes her hand and holds it to his lips.

'Why don't you show . . . anything?'

He shrugs and kisses each knuckle in turn with small pecks.

'Stop it, there's something I want to tell you.'

He stops, at once, his tongue protruding from his mouth: the expression of a dog waiting for his mistress to throw a stick. She laughs and pinches his cheeks.

'Listen, will you, this is important.'

He folds his arms and his face assumes its normal lack of expression.

'Better. It's something bad, Hugo. Something you need to know about me. You know that ring? The drawing that the doctor found? The one on Hannah's dish?'

He nods.

'Well . . .' She takes a breath, spits out the words. 'It was me. I told Tobias . . . about the Jews . . . about how they . . . don't let you in . . . how underneath, in spite of what they say, they think they really think they are God's chosen people.'

His face shows nothing.

She looks over to where the trees sway by the wall. She remembers a time when she knew no trees, just houses and more houses: houses back to back and side by side, no space for anything except that which was absolutely necessary. She didn't mind. When she had finished her chores she had been allowed to run where she liked; from one side of the Judengasse to the other; from where the

Judenmauer had once stood with its privies to where the other wall had stood on the other side. She used to peep into the rooms and count the people there, and no one minded; everyone was used to living in such close proximity that an unexpected child was usually a welcome visitor. So many people living in such little space, she realises now: on the ground floor of the easternmost house the Jacobs with their six children, maid and grandmother, then the Wertheimers with four children, and their maid, and above these, in the same wooden house, three more families. Then there had been a small back yard and another house, again packed with people: on the ground floor a family of assorted nephews and nieces, about seven of them altogether, and the Linheimers with their five children, including their daughter Rebekka, who was her best friend. Then there was the Judengasse, and on the other side two more houses back to back, but already she had lost count, too many people, and too many coming and going to keep track. But a child loves what she is used to, and she had been happy there, making up games with Rebekka on the pavement or quietly talking on the stairs leading to their rooms above. But then one day something happened; people would become strangely quiet whenever she came close. People would look at her when she walked down the street, she could feel their eyes, and when she turned these eyes would drop away and pretend to be looking somewhere else. When she called for Rebekka she wouldn't come out. Doors were shut to her and she could no longer play her game of counting. It had been something to do with her hair, which had been blonde then, the fact that she looked and was different. You're not ours, Rebekka's mother had said at last after she had nagged for a reason, you're not what we thought you were. Angelika's father had said little, except that the truth was out, and soon afterwards they had packed their bags and moved quickly to where there was more space but less to do. He had told her later that they were not Jewish, that he'd given them the impression that they were. He'd wanted a job and it was the only place he could find one. After that they were poorer and sometimes hungry.

Angelika kicks a stone in front of her feet and looks at Hugo. 'You hate me now, don't you?'

Hugo says nothing. For a few minutes he sits leaning against the wall, his eyes shut, perfectly still. Then he rises quickly, reaches down and grabs her arm.

'Come,' he says, 'with me, quickly now.'

He walks rapidly so she has to take two quick steps to keep up with him. They do not speak. She wants to tell him about the Judengasse, why she had to go, how she wonders, even now, about her friend Rebekka and whether they'd recognise each other if they met in a street. But she can say nothing. She is supposed to be in the day room with the other assistants, and if she doesn't go back very soon she will be missed, but there is no time to breathe, no time to protest, no time to explain. Hugo walks ahead of her, pulling her, through the kitchen, into the oak-lined hall and up the stairs to the men's floor. He flings open the door to Josef's almost empty room. He swings her on to his bed while he takes two strides to the desk. He punches the back so the small cupboard opens and then turns to look at her. 'That's where he kept them, Angelika,' he cries out, 'and I knew, I let him.'

'Kept what?' Angelika wants more than anything to cry, to break down inconsolably just so he can try to comfort her and tell her that nothing matters.

'The keys. I knew he had them. He had two sets. They found only one. But I knew about the others. You see, Angelika, I thought I knew everything. I thought I knew the difference between a mad man and a sane one. And there isn't. We are, all of us, mad . . . and all of us sane.'

He sits beside her, and to her astonishment buries his face in his hands and sobs.

The Dreadful Story about Harriet and the Matches

It almost makes me cry to tell
What foolish Harriet befell.
Mamma and Nurse went out one day,
And left her all alone at play;
Now on the table close at hand,
A box of matches chanc'd to stand;
And kind Mamma and Nurse had told her,
That if she touched them they would scold her.
But Harriet said, 'O, what a pity!
For, when they burn, it is so pretty;
They crackle so, and spit, and flame;
Mamma, too, often does the same.'

The pussy-cats heard this,
And they began to hiss,
And stretch their claws
And raise their paws;

'Meow!!' they said, 'me-ow, me-o!
You'll burn to death, if you do so.'

But Harriet would not take advice,
    She lit a match, it was so nice!
It crackled so, it burned so clear, –
    Exactly like the picture here.
She jump'd for joy and ran about,
And was too pleas'd to put it out.

        The pussy-cats saw this,
And said: 'Oh, naughty, naughty Miss!'
        And stretch'd their claws
        And rais'd their paws:
' 'Tis very, very wrong, you know;
    Me-ow, me-o, me-ow, me-o!
You will be burnt if you do so.'

And see! Oh! what a dreadful thing!
The fire has caught her apron-string;
Her apron burns, her arms, her hair;
    She burns all over, everywhere.

Then how the pussy-cats did mew
What else, poor pussies, could they do?
They screamed for help, 'twas all in vain,
So then, they said, 'We'll scream again.
Make haste, make haste! me-ow! me-o!
She'll burn to death, – we told her so.'

So she was burnt with all her clothes,
And arms and hands, and eyes and nose;
    Till she had nothing more to lose
    Except her little scarlet shoes;

And nothing else but these was found
Among her ashes on the ground.

And when the good cats sat beside
The smoking ashes, how they cried!
'Me-ow, me-o!! Me-ow, me-oo!!
What will Mamma and Nursy do?'
Their tears ran down their cheeks so fast.
They made a little pond at last.

CHAPTER 31

Recommendations for the building of a new asylum in the Free City of Frankfurt, 1853 (draft)

I have already outlined, thoroughly and at length, the reasons why a new asylum at Frankfurt is essential. I now need to recommend what is built in its place. Fortunately this can be summarised in a few words: a building, outside the city, built following the models of asylums which have been built over the last few decades, for approximately 150 patients, with living quarters for the superintendent and staff in a convenient area with enough space for approximately twelve to fifteen gardens or fields.

Dr Heinrich Hoffmann

At first Frau Antoni doesn't recognise her. She thinks that maybe it is one of the patients escaped somehow from one of the rooms upstairs, not one of the passive ones either, but one of the wild, uncontrollable women she doesn't know. It is only when she stoops down to look into her face and help her to her feet that she realises: Dagmar.

She is near the steps to the cellar, sitting on the ground, making herself as small as a woman her size can make herself, and she is shaking, violently, her hair loose over her face.

'What is wrong, woman? What has happened to you?'

But Dagmar shakes her head. She allows Frau Antoni

to help her up and then starts for the stairs to the day room.

'Dagmar, you can't go in there like that!'

Frau Antoni trots after her, pulls her from the stairs and then into their private living room. There is a little more light there and Frau Antoni can see that her normally neat clothes are torn, there is a little blood on her blouse and her face is scratched and bruised.

'Who did this to you? One of the patients? Has one of them escaped? Shall I tell the doctor, or Herr Antoni?'

Dagmar shakes her head. 'No, nothing like that. I fell, down the steps to the cellar. That's all it was.'

Frau Antoni looks at her doubtfully. 'That's not what's happened. I'll get you some water, and while I'm gone you'd better think up something else that I might believe.'

Angelika thinks that she has learnt to read a little of Hugo's face. Its signals are more subtle than most but they are still there: happiness is indicated by a slight upturning of the corners of his lips; anger when a line appears by his left eye pointing upwards; sadness by his blinking quickly once; embarrassment by the touch of pink on the centre of each cheek just below the eyes . . . and guilt by his dropping his face in his hands and sobbing loudly without restraint.

'Hugo?'

He shakes his head. She allows her arm to dart out, wrap itself around his shoulders and draw him close.

'You weren't to know.'

'No, no, I should have told the doctor. I just thought they were being so . . . cruel. He had nothing left, nothing at all.'

'It's not your fault.'

'It is.' He looks up.

Angelika starts back. She has never before seen so much misery written so clearly on a man's face. His eyes and nose are dripping tears, his mouth is downturned, open, a silent cry for comfort. She draws him to her again and smooths his hair. For a while he rests there, his head on the softness of her chest, her chin catching his head and holding him close.

'Why did you come here?' he asks her. 'To this corner of hell?'

She draws breath. It is her chance to explain, but she cuts it short, saving it for some other time. 'Because I was alone, I suppose, with nowhere else to go.'

And at last he draws her closer to him, at last he lets her in.

A curtain has been drawn away and I can see. This man before me looks with your eyes. I can tell what he wants.

'Hannah?'

She does not look up.

'What is wrong?'

She does not reply. He reaches forward, lifts her chin with his fingertips, but this time she resists, shakes his hands away.

'What is it?'

She stands up. 'I think I should be discharged now.'

Still he looks. Still he pleads: the desperation I have seen before.

'But why? Is this place so bad?'

'There are things wrong that can be put right. If only you could see.'

'What things, Hannah?' His voice is quiet, shocked.

'There is not enough space, not enough room, the water

supply . . . Then there are the little things. The way some get better food, better clothes, the way the doors are not locked. The assistants are cruel, callous. They play games with us . . .'

I remember a slap, a pinch, a bruise spreading on my arm. I remember another world intruding. It tries to creep forward again but I force it away. This is something I can do. I can make things go; all the things that should not be there, I can make them go. I will not be like the girl in the fire. I will not let things just happen. The fire will burn because I want it to burn.

She stops, looks at him, her eyes narrowed. 'Is this how things are everywhere?'

He shakes his head. 'In some places, the superintendent lives in. In Siegburg, Jacobi considers himself to be a father figure, a model, someone the patients and assistants can turn to . . . he says it works well. There is more discipline among the staff, more order, the superintendent is always there, you see, watching. Of course, for a man with a family it would mean having a suite of rooms . . .' He breaks off, laughs dryly, then adds, 'Therese would never allow it.' He glances at her and she looks back at him in silence. 'I suppose I could insist,' he says uncertainly, then his voice gathers strength. 'I could explain what it means to me, perhaps she would listen. I could even suggest that she involve herself in the place as well. She could follow the example of Frau Antoni, give the patients tea, engage them in conversation.' He pauses. 'No, she would never agree.'

'Perhaps, if you gave her a chance?'

He shakes his head. 'Well, I suppose I could try.' He leans forward, takes her hands. 'It is what I most want to do,

Hannah, to cure, to make a difference.'

'Well, do so, then, sir. Make plans, act, ensure that things happen. It is what we all must do, I think, sir, we all must have a reason for being, otherwise we shall die purposelessly – like the girl in the fire.'

'And do you have a reason, Hannah?'

'Not yet, sir, but I shall find one.' She drops his hands and walks to the door.

After a few seconds he follows her. 'It can be a long search.'

'I would like to start now.'

For a full minute he regards her face.

'Now, sir?'

He quickly draws her to him and kisses her briefly on her forehead. Then, opening the door, he stands aside to let her pass.

Beatrice can see a light beneath the door. She knocks and then quickly enters. The doctor is still there. She expected him to be gone. She expected the lamp to be burning without purpose, but it is lighting a large picture book and some papers on his desk. He motions her over and together they look at the book as he turns the pages.

'I made this for my son, Carl Philipp,' he says. 'He is away at school, and I am not sure that I want him to be there.'

'Then you should tell him to come home, sir.'

'Perhaps, or perhaps I should leave him where he is.' He turns another page. 'Pretty pictures, and merry rhymes,' he says, 'except my wife thinks that it could be improved, she says that a professional artist would do a better job . . . and yet I like my pictures as they are.' He sighs and closes the book. 'Do you think that it is possible to tell a life in so few pages?'

'Perhaps, sir, if the life is not yet finished.'

He looks at her, his hand combing his beard, then he replaces the book on the shelf and turns back to his desk, smoothing out the large piece of paper that lies there.

'Pichler's,' he says. 'His wife was admitted to an asylum in Illenau yesterday because we didn't have the facilities to treat her here. He came to me today, indignant that a rich city like Frankfurt is so ill equipped to deal with some of its most wretched patients. He has ideas, Beatrice, like mine, plans, he is an architect, you see . . .'

'And is this what you intend to do next, sir?'

'Yes, Beatrice, I think it is.'

Frau Antoni lies beside her husband and listens to his snores. How annoying the man is, always falling asleep so quickly and so loudly. She wonders whether what she thought she saw was real when she came down the stairs just now: the hem of Angelika's dress and then Hugo's fingers reaching for the bolt and closing the front door after them.

Dagmar lies upon her bed. She wonders why Angelika is so late. She has so much to tell her: it was not how she thought it would be at all. She rubs her bruises and fingers the cuts on her face. This must be how it is on the other side of the wall. She hadn't known it would hurt. She hadn't expected that it would be quite so fast, quite so violent. But she had groaned and then cried out. Surely that was enough. She looks at the wall behind her bed. It is quite blank, perfectly silent and stretches out in a cold colourless nothingness until it becomes ceiling.

Struwwelpeter

or

Pretty Stories

and

Funny Pictures

When the children have been good,
That is, be it understood,
Good at meal-times, good at play,
Good all night and good all day, –
They shall have the pretty things
Merry Christmas always brings,
Naughty romping girls and boys
Tear their clothes and make a noise,
Spoil their pinafores and frocks,
And deserve no Christmas-box,
Such as these will never look
At this pretty picture-book.

My dear Marky,

I have to report that your pa has failed once again in his attempts to get your Stroovelpeter book appended with a signature. The author is proving himself to be quite elusive. You see, the folks here in the town of Frankfort are a very busy lot, scurrying and rushing about all the day with no time for anything, and added to that they do not of course speak English, which as you can imagine is a mighty big problem when you are a man like your pa who has very little leaning towards foreign tongues at all, as you know.

The other day, I thought I had gotten quite close. There was a woman who overheard me shouting at a bookseller in the hope that he might understand me better if I talked a little louder.

Dr Hoffmann? she asked. What a mighty fine thing it is that at least the man's name is the same in German as it is in English.

Stroovelpeter? I replied.

But she frowned, did not appear to know the word, but it turned out in the end she did, because when I showed her your bedraggled tongue-eared book, its pages worn so much they are almost falling out, she smiled and said a word like

Stroovelpeter *but which wasn't that at all. Anyway, she then said something else, quite a lot else in fact, and of course I couldn't understand a word of it.*

I think I must have looked a little dejected. You see, my Marky, it was my last day and therefore my last chance in the place, we really have to finalise matters tomorrow, and she got out a scrap of paper for me and wrote his name and then some other words below.

Here, she said, which means the same thing in German and English, and pointed to the words below which I guessed must be the man's address. So I thanked her and took the paper out into the street, and proceeded to stop one busy person after another, showing them the piece of paper, and they pointed and smiled, and I followed their fingers until I was quite a way out of town, almost into the countryside. Well, at first I thought they were all tricking me, this could not be the right place at all, but in the end I kept going because everyone I showed the paper to grinned and nodded and all pointed in the same direction.

Anyway, at last, after about an hour's walk in baking hot sunshine, though not quite as baking as our hot sunshine, I came across a big driveway and trees and in the distance a monstrous building, with a wildly fanciful front, and towers and everything, and I thought our author must be a very, very rich man to live in such a place, and I vowed once again to take up the pen as soon as I get home to you, Marky, because I always think I have more tales in me than business sense.

But do you know, Marky, this place which looked a little bit like a castle turned out not to be a private residence at all but some sort of institution. Once I stepped inside the door I could see at once that something was wrong. The fellow who greeted me, for one thing. He was a mighty enormous fellow, white haired, bearded, like the proverbial ogre, and when he stood he seemed a little unsteady on his feet, and he couldn't seem to manage many words either, even German ones. I showed him the paper but he grinned at me like he was an idiot, which he may well have been, and eventually he led me into a most amazing hall, very large, enough to house a hundred-odd people, enough for a grand ball, in fact. And as he led me across this hall, I could see he had a strange walk, dragged his feet as if he was a little too fond of the old grape or grain or whatever liquor they drink over here, but no one else seemed to notice. Anyway, eventually he stopped this stony-faced old woman with a moustache as thick and dark as many a man's, and I thought, are all the people over here in this place so plain they would curdle milk? Well, it turned out these two were the ones in charge. The stony-faced woman gave the man the dirtiest look you could imagine, but he didn't seem to notice and just turned tail and staggered back to his door. Then the woman turned to me, looking not at all pleased, but at least seemed to know what she was doing. She gestured to me to follow her when I said Dr Hoffmann, then took me to another large room with lots of chairs and said I would have to wait. Well, I think that's what she said. I showed her your book, Marky, but she didn't seem interested. Vartenzie is what she said, which I think means wait. Anyway, she was such a confoundedly bossy woman I didn't dare argue. I sat down on one of the chairs there and did what I was told.

It wasn't long before some other people came in. At first I stood as each one entered, expecting it to be him, but it wasn't. After about five I gave up and just stared at everyone who came in, which seemed to be the custom. First there was an elderly woman, then a young girl, then a young man and a middle-aged one, then a rather handsome middle-aged Jewish woman who came to sit by me and smiled. And then it seemed that half of Frankfort was joining me in that room, which soon didn't seem quite so large after all.

Vas ist *this?* I asked the pleasant-looking woman sitting next to me, and she smiled and asked me whether I spoke English. Ah, such a relief, Marky, to find someone that at last understands me and is willing to practise her English in this place. And she was willing to listen. Unlike other Frankfort citizens this woman seemed to have all the time in the world. She explained to me that this was the Frankfort asylum for the insane, the mad house, Marky, which explained the doorman, I suppose, and that I was in the middle of a tour for the chief fund-raisers. She herself represented the Jewish women's group, and they had managed to raise quite a large sum, in fact were nearly the biggest supporters of the asylum. We are going to be presented to the superintendent, she said, a most esteemed gentleman, so we were very fortunate.

So we continued chatting as we waited. I showed her that picture of you and your ma that I have and she showed me a picture of her two boys and her husband, although she explained that they weren't really hers at all, but step-children, and I commented that I had thought that they did seem too old to be her boys, which seemed to please her quite considerably. Then she said that she was unable to have children herself although she had once had a child when she had been quite young, but it came too early and she had to bury it in the wood, which seemed to me to be a rather strange thing to confide to a stranger, but you know how it is sometimes, Marky, people feel compelled to tell a stranger their innermost secrets, maybe because they know they will never meet them again, and I explained to her that tomorrow I was about to embark on my passage back across the Atlantic.

Well, then, of course, we got on to the subject of business

and it turned out she was in the same line as me, or at least her husband was, Jakob his name was, he had been a butcher but had turned his hand to textiles to please her because she couldn't stand the smell of dead meat, and she had helped him and now they were doing quite nicely. This was how she could speak such good English, she had set her mind to learn it so she could deal with her husband's imports and exports. So after that, of course, we exchanged addresses, and I said that if she ever found herself in our new world she should be sure to come and pay us a visit. And she said she would in the way that people do when they know that they never will. I was just about to ask her about the Hoffmann fellow when the door opened and in came this little old man dressed in mourning. Everyone stood up and I asked the woman about the man's clothes and she said it was on account of his son, who had died quite recently. And of course I felt sorry for the old man then because it is a sad thing to lose a son, and I thought of you, of course, Marky, and suddenly I missed you so much, and I can tell you that now because by the time you read this I shall probably be home as well looking over your shoulder at my own letter.

Anyway, it looked like this superintendent of the mad house was very well regarded by all the people there, and though he seemed a little too full of himself to me, the woman next to me bowed and simpered when she saw him, then said her name out loud, Hannah Goldstein, as if he should know her. I suppose she thought that he might since she was such an important fund-raiser. But at first there wasn't a flicker in the old man's eyes. And it was only after she looked away that I saw the old man regard her again, a thoughtful kind of frown on his brow. He opened his mouth, and I swear he was going to say something, but then he must have changed his mind because he just closed it *again. But the woman saw nothing of this. She just dropped back and looked so disappointed that I felt I ought to console her, but I couldn't think how, and anyway a man has to be so careful where a lady is concerned. So I thought I'd better not. So after we had all bowed and said our names the old man led us on a great tour around his establishment. Even though he was old he walked quite fast. I must say he was inordinately proud of the place, though I couldn't see for the life of me why. The people looked so unhappy, so bored, all of them cooped in or if not cooped in working like navvies in the fields. It seemed to me to be just a prison for the mad, but everyone else was most impressed and seemed to hang on his every word, although of course I couldn't tell what those words were.*

Eventually the whole sordid tour finished and we were free to leave, past the demented porter and down the steps on to the rather grand driveway where I found Mrs Goldstein again in front of me. She asked me whether I had enjoyed the tour and was I glad that I'd come. It was then that I confessed to being a little bemused. I had wanted to meet the author of the book Stroovelpeter, I said, not join a tour of the mad house. Mad people didn't interest me at all and my son Marky was most anxious for me to meet the author of his favourite book. She looked puzzled so I brought out your book. Then she laughed. You've just missed him, she said. That little old man, that was the author, you should have given him your book, he would have been delighted to sign it.

I looked back. I wasn't sure I could bear going in that place again but I thought of your disappointed little face and turned. Why didn't he say? I asked the woman. He doesn't think it's important, she replied. It's this asylum that he's proud of, it's his life's work, that is just a silly little children's book.

Silly little children's book! If only you had heard. I assured her that it was my son's most treasured possession as it had been mine before him. I think you would have been proud of me, Marky, I put her straight immediately, if only you could have heard me. This book, I told her, is important, it is known the world over. Everyone loves it, everyone. This asylum is just a place, a dreadful jail for poor mad people, it will be demolished one day and no one will remember it, but this book, it is a work of art, it will live for ever, it speaks to millions.

And with that I bade her good day and walked back up the drive, but that strange doorman ignored me and would not let me in.

But I shall try again tomorrow. There is just time before the train leaves. I shall knock and knock until they let me in. Don't you worry, Marky, your pa will succeed in the end.

I shall see you soon now, counting the days,

Your loving pa

AUTHOR'S NOTE

In 1861 Hoffmann's new mental asylum was opened on a large site outside Frankfurt. It was modelled on Esquirol's, each patient housed according to class, sex and stage of madness, each section having its own garden and access to the kitchen. He considered it to be his lifetime's work, and it was the result of years of research and campaigning. Together with the architect Pichler, Hoffmann had made an extensive tour of the asylums of western Europe to ascertain the best asylum design and best practice. His account of his visits are amusing, dwelling on the hospitality that he received in each place rather than his opinions on the quality of care.

In 1864 the Hoffmann family took up residence at the asylum in specially designed quarters adjacent to the calmer patients. Following the ideas current then and now, the patients had access to the open air and were expected to undertake hard physical labour in the farms and gardens and thereby banish morbid preoccupations and thoughts. There were also facilities for taking advantage of the gentler bath therapies that were widely reported to be beneficial.

The move was against Therese's wishes; when first told of his plan to live there she had been incredulous, but eventually she came to follow the example of Frau Antoni, hosting tea parties for those patients who were almost ready for discharge and reacquainting them with polite conversation.

In 1865 Line was married in the asylum's chapel; Eduard,

much to Hoffmann's satisfaction, became an important civil servant, while at his boarding school Carl Philipp learnt to speak English like an Englishman and eventually became a businessman. However, he continued to lead a troubled life, eventually ending up in Lima, Peru, where he died of yellow fever in 1868 aged twenty-seven.

Hoffmann continued to write books for children and various satirical works, but not one came close to achieving the popularity of *Struwwelpeter*. In 1888 he retired with his wife to an apartment in Frankfurt and spent his remaining years writing his memoirs. By the time he died in 1894, *Struwwelpeter* had conquered the world. As he noted in his memoirs, it was a peaceful conquest without bloodshed. Mark Twain had translated it loosely for his daughters in 1891 and it had been fêted by the Prussian Kaiser Wilhelm I. After his death Therese oversaw the publication of the *Beautiful Struwwelpeter*, a prettified edition of the book which completely missed the charm and point of the original stories. The original book has been constantly in print ever since and frequently used as the basis of parody, notably of Wilhelm II during the First World War; in England 'Swollen Headed Peter' and another similar work appeared twenty-five years later, this time parodying one Adolf Hitler.

But Hoffmann's reason for being, the most important aspect of his working life, was his care of the insane. His asylum came to be well regarded and he advised on the building of other asylums in Germany and Switzerland. With Hoffmann's encouragement the Jewish population of Frankfurt contributed to the cost of building the new asylum, and so were entitled to the same rights and care as the rest of the Frankfurt citizens. Jewish people had not been admitted to the old town asylum for many years, and certainly not during Hoffmann's time, so the case of Hannah is entirely fictitious. I have, however, used Hoffmann's case notes on his treatment of a young woman suffering from a similar disorder as my partial guide. He describes using all the techniques depicted here with the exception of galvanism, although this was widely used at the time, and certainly by Jacobi, who was one of Hoffmann's mentors in the care of the insane.

The extracts, letters and notes, etc, which head the chapters are invented, although some of them rely quite heavily on contemporaneously published works and are intended to summarise the ideas and views widely held at this time in western Europe.

BIBLIOGRAPHY

I am indebted to the authors of the following books:

Ackerknecht, Erwin, *A Short History of Psychiatry*

Basse, J. H., *Catechism of Health*

Berg, Manfred, and Geoffrey Cocks, *Medicine and Modernity: Public Health and Medical Care in 19th and 20th Century Germany*

Berrios German, E., and Roy Porter, *A History of Clinical Psychiatry*

Bienville, J. D. T. de, *Nymphomania*

Blockey, Peter J., *Asylum Days*

Bonner, Thomas, *Becoming a Physician 1750–1945*

Braun, Dagmar, *Vom Tollhause zum Kastenhospital*

Broman, Thomas H., *The Transformation of German Academic Medicine*

Browne Taylor, Jenny, and Sally Shuttleworth, *Embodied Selves*

Bynum, W. F., *Science and the Practice of Medicine in the Nineteenth Century*

Cox, Joseph, *Practical Observations on Insanity*

Doerner, Klaus, *Madmen and Bourgeoisie*

Drummer, Heike et al., *Museum Judengasse*

Efron, John M., *Medicine and the German Jews. A history*

Ende, Aurel, *Battering and Neglect: Children in Germany 1860–1978*

Esquirol, Jean E. D., *Mental Maladies*

Evans, Richard John, *The German Family*

Finzsch, Norbert, and Robert Jütte, *Institutions of Confinement*

Gay, Ruth, *The Jews of Germany. A historical portrait*

Geller, Jeffrey L., and Maxine Harris, *Women of the Asylum*

Giebel, Wieland, *Insight Guide Frankfurt*

Goldberg, Ann, *Sex, Religion and the Making of Modern Madness*

Goodman, Robert, and Stephen Scott, *Child Psychiatry*

Grell, Ole, et al., *Health Care and Poor Relief in 18th and 19th Century Northern Europe*

Griesinger, Wilhelm, *Mental Pathology and Therapeutics*

Harrington, Anne, *Medicine, Mind and the Double Brain*

Heinrich Hoffmann Museum, *Der Struwwelpeter Entstehung eines berühmten deutsches Kinderbuchs*

Herzog, G. H., and Marion Herzog-Hoinkis, *Heinrich Hoffmann*

Herzog, G. H., et al., *Struwwelpeter – Hoffmann Gestern und Heute*

Heuberger, Georg, *Ludwig Börne – A Frankfurt Jew Who Fought for Freedom*

Heuberger, Georg, et al., *Jewish Museum Frankfurt am Main*

Heuberger, Rachel, and Helga Krohn, *Hinaus aus dem Ghetto*

Hils-Brockhoff, Evelyn, and Sabine Hock, *The Paulskirche*

Hoffmann, Heinrich, *Struwwelpeter*

Hoffmann, Heinrich, *Lebenserrinnerungen*

Hoffmann, Heinrich, *Schriften zur Psychiatrie*

Jacobi, C. W. M., *On the Construction and Management of Hospitals for the Insane*

Kitchen, Martin, *Germany (Cambridge Illustrated History)*

Klötzer, Wolfgang, *Studien zur Frankfurter Geschichte*

Korn, Salomon, *The Synagogue at Frankfurt's Börneplatz*

Lenarz, Michael, *The Old Jewish Cemetery in Frankfurt am Main*

Lundy, Allan, *Diagnosing and Treating Mental Illness*

Neuburger, Max, *British and German Psychiatry in the Second Half of the Eighteenth and Early Nineteenth Century*

Pfeiffer, Carl, *The Art and Practice of Western Medicine in the Early Nineteenth Century*

Porter, Roy, *Medicine (Cambridge Illustrated History)*

Porter, Roy, et al., *The Anatomy of Madness*

Richarz, Monica, *Jewish Life in Germany. Memoirs from three centuries*

Sacks, Oliver, *The Man Who Mistook His Wife for a Hat*

Sorkin, David, *The Transformation of German Jewry 1780–1840*

Stafford, Ezra, *Medicine, Surgery and Hygiene in the Nineteenth Century*

Stone, Michael H., *Healing the Mind*

Thiersch, H. W. J., *Christian Family Life*

Tildes, D., *Report of an Examination of Certain European Institutions for the Insane 1857*

Tuchman, Arleen Marcia, *Science, Medicine and the State in Germany 1815–1971*

Walsher Smith, Helmut, *Protestants, Catholics and Jews in Germany 1800–1914*

Wiedmann, Ulrich, and Beate Zekorn-von Bebenburg, *Struwwelpeter wird Revolutionär*

Wyhe, John von, *The History of Phrenology on the Web*

ACKNOWLEDGEMENTS

This is a work of fiction and any mistakes are, of course, my own, but I am most grateful to the following people who helped me in the writing of this book:

Kevin Hancock, consultant plastic surgeon, and Marina Jennick, keeper of the leeches (not her official title) at Whiston Hospital, Merseyside; David Thomas, curator at the Science Museum, London; Helga Krohn of the Jewish Museum, Frankfurt; Beate Zekorn-von Bebenburg of the Heinrich Hoffmann Museum, Frankfurt; Marion Herzog-Hoinkis of the Struwwelpeter Museum, Frankfurt; the staff of the Wellcome Library and the British Library, London, and the Library of the University of Frankfurt; the staff of the fascinating Old Operating Theatre, London; my brother David R. Jenkins for his medical advice; my former creative writing tutor, Gladys Mary Coles; my editor Carole Welch, assistant Amber Burlinson, publicist Jocasta Brownlee, and agent Rupert Heath; my friends in Chester: Chester Writers, Words and Biscuits, the reading group and Ali's aerobics group, including Irene, Pat, Jan, Ravi, Ros, Sheila, Dilys, Elizabeth, Gill, Annie, Jane, Maureen, Adrian, Liz, the two Mikes, Simon, Yvonne, Lindsey, Lynne, Denise, Sian, Claire, Linda, Maria, Kay, Ali herself, Sandra, Helen, Raynor, Anne . . . thank you all especially.

Thank you to the Heinrich Hoffmann Museum in Frankfurt for providing the source of the images for the illustrations in this book – Dr Heinrich Hoffmann's book of cautionary tales for children, *Struwwelpeter*.

But most of all I would like to thank my family: my mother, father, Huw, Yasmin, MD, Kay, my long-suffering sons Tom and Jack and my husband Chris. Thank you for enduring yet another of my obsessions.

C. J. D.

FOR MORE CLARE DUDMAN, LOOK FOR THE

One Day the Ice Will Reveal All Its Dead

In this unforgettable debut novel Clare Dudman has imaginatively re-created the life of the German scientist Alfred Wegener, whose theory of continental drift—derided by his contemporaries—would eventually revolutionize our perception of the world. Wegener's irresistible urge to discover the unknown takes him from the horrors of World War I's trenches to several lengthy expeditions across the unexplored ice of Greenland, an extraordinary quest that—with the support of a remarkable woman—gives birth to a powerful idea worth fighting for. Distinguished by its evocation of the unforgiving beauty of the Arctic, this stunningly written tale of obsession and courage will thrill readers of scientific history and the best adventure writing.

ISBN 0-14-303473-1

FOR THE BEST IN PAPERBACKS, LOOK FOR THE

In every corner of the world, on every subject under the sun, Penguin represents quality and variety—the very best in publishing today.

For complete information about books available from Penguin—including Penguin Classics, Penguin Compass, and Puffins—and how to order them, write to us at the appropriate address below. Please note that for copyright reasons the selection of books varies from country to country.

In the United States: Please write to *Penguin Group (USA), P.O. Box 12289 Dept. B, Newark, New Jersey 07101-5289* or call *1-800-788-6262*.

In the United Kingdom: Please write to *Dept. EP, Penguin Books Ltd, Bath Road, Harmondsworth, West Drayton, Middlesex UB7 0DA.*

In Canada: Please write to *Penguin Books Canada Ltd, 90 Eglinton Avenue East, Suite 700, Toronto, Ontario M4P 2Y3.*

In Australia: Please write to *Penguin Books Australia Ltd, P.O. Box 257, Ringwood, Victoria 3134.*

In New Zealand: Please write to *Penguin Books (NZ) Ltd, Private Bag 102902, North Shore Mail Centre, Auckland 10.*

In India: Please write to *Penguin Books India Pvt Ltd, 11 Panchsheel Shopping Centre, Panchsheel Park, New Delhi 110 017.*

In the Netherlands: Please write to *Penguin Books Netherlands bv, Postbus 3507, NL-1001 AH Amsterdam.*

In Germany: Please write to *Penguin Books Deutschland GmbH, Metzlerstrasse 26, 60594 Frankfurt am Main.*

In Spain: Please write to *Penguin Books S. A., Bravo Murillo 19, 1° B, 28015 Madrid.*

In Italy: Please write to *Penguin Italia s.r.l., Via Benedetto Croce 2, 20094 Corsico, Milano.*

In France: Please write to *Penguin France, Le Carré Wilson, 62 rue Benjamin Baillaud, 31500 Toulouse.*

In Japan: Please write to *Penguin Books Japan Ltd, Kaneko Building, 2-3-25 Koraku, Bunkyo-Ku, Tokyo 112.*

In South Africa: Please write to *Penguin Books South Africa (Pty) Ltd, Private Bag X14, Parkview, 2122 Johannesburg.*